CLEVER

CONTENT & TRIGGER WARNINGS:

Animal Cruelty

Cancer/Illness

Grief/Loss

Trauma

CLEVER

DARCI COLE

Ember Rose Entertainment

CLEVER
Book Three of The Unbroken Tales

Cover art by Anna McEwan, Typography by Jerah Moss
Cat icons from Freepik, Cat eyes design by Elizabeth Kaneda
Continental map by Dewi Hargreaves, www.dewihargreaves.com
Regional map by Cody James King, @dungeonmastersdiary ig/tt
City tower map by Chloe Bolland, www.chloethecartographer.com
Formatting by S.D. Simper

An Ember Rose Entertainment Book
Published by Ember Rose Entertainment LLC
Mesa, Arizona

www.darcicole.com

ISBN 978-1-955145-09-1 (paperback)
ISBN 978-1-955145-08-4 (hardcover)
First Edition: November 2024
Printed in the United States
0 9 8 7 6 5 4 3 2 1

To my kids, J, P, K, C.

Thank you for understanding your mom needs to write.

May you always stand true to who you are

—whoever you choose to be—

and remember that I love you

more than any words on any page.

TABLE OF CONTENTS

N
THE
UNBROKEN
LANDS
Ignatia
KIWAN
Kiwa Peak
Teao Mountains
River Tardus
GALANIS
Regania
Arontas Mountains
Cliffs of Antos
Fugera
Vei Lake
River Veiro
ISILLE
REINOS
Nosar River
Tiero Mountains
Medelios
The Hollow Desert
Shano River
TAEJA
Somnuria
Avir River
Avir Lake
Calidar
ENSET
Avirmi River
Rico Peak
Perdonio
CASIR
By Deni Hagans, Cartographer
Property of the Royal Rezanian Library

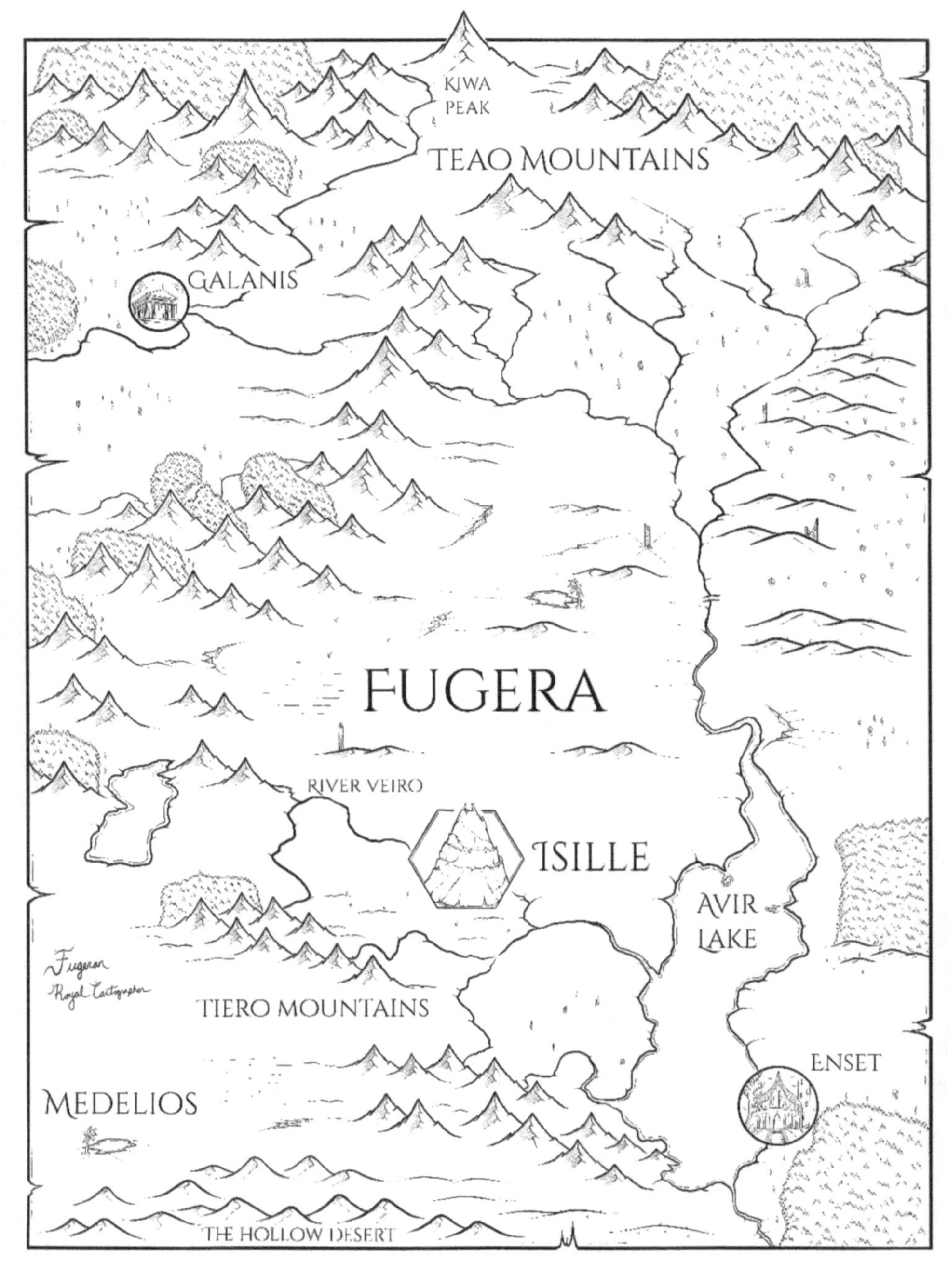

KIWA PEAK
TEAO MOUNTAINS
GALANIS
FUGERA
RIVER VEIRO
ISILLE
AVIR LAKE
TIERO MOUNTAINS
ENSET
MEDELIOS
THE HOLLOW DESERT
Fugeron
Royal Cartographer

The City of Isille
RUINS
LEVEL NINE
DANGEROUS
LEVEL EIGHT
LEVEL SEVEN
LEVEL SIX
LEVEL FIVE
DUSTY DRAGON
LEVEL FOUR
LEVEL THREE
MARKETPLACE
PALACE
LEVEL TWO
LEVEL ONE
MERCHANT DISTRICT
MEDICINE SHOP
UNDERGROUND
MESS HALL
MILITARY TRAINING
PALACE LEVEL ONE
SERVANTS QUARTERS
KITCHENS
PALACE LEVEL TWO
THRONE ROOM
PALACE LEVEL THREE
ROYAL QUARTERS
QUEEN
PRINCE
PALACE LEVEL FOUR
ROYAL COUNCIL
Chloe Bolland - Figeran Royal Cartographer

Previously in the
Unbroken Lands

Year: 700 AP
BOOK ONE: TARGET

Prince Alexander "Lex" Galani, crown prince of Regania, ran away from home to find his true love, quickly realizing what a terrible choice that was. On his travels however, he was semi-captured by a group of outlaws led by a girl named Robyn who had built a system of trade and distribution that cared for the lowly classes of Regania—people Lex thought were fine, but were actually suffering under greedy lords. Through getting to know these outlaws, Lex learned of a plot by one of the Reganian High Lords—Maximus Valio—to assassinate his parents and take the throne—a plot that the outlaws were trying to stop.

Carina Valio made the best of her life, despite her abusive father. But when she learned of his plans to steal the Reganian throne by murder and intrigue, she knew she had to do something to fight against him. Helping from the inside, she joined forces with Robyn's band and did what she could to sabotage her father's efforts, putting herself at risk each time.

Together with the outlaws, and through a series of rough days, Lex and Robyn gathered forces loyal to the prince and marched toward the capital to stop the assassination, but on the way learned they were too late. Lex's parents were dead, and Maximus Valio had manipulated his way to the throne.

Lex was heartbroken, but—with the support of Robyn and their friends—determined to continue their march and retake his crown. The battle was quick and ugly, with cherished lives lost, and Lex was captured by Valio's forces. Robyn took what help she could and stealthily entered the palace, shooting an arrow into the eye of Maximus Valio and allowing Lex to take his rightful place on the throne.

Lex asked Robyn to stay in the capital and run her organization from there, with the proper funds and support of the crown. And, to stay with him. She accepted.

Year: 702 AP
BOOK TWO: SUMMON

When Carina Valio helped Lex and Robyn to defeat her father, she learned her life was worth saving. And so, keeping her title but renouncing her land, Carina left Regania and made her way to her mother's homeland of Medelios.

After two years of wandering, wondering, and not finding what she was looking for, Carina learned that the old king—childless and widowed—was holding a tournament to choose his heir. Then, at the end of a long day of travel, she found herself being attacked by a wildcat. In the impulse of searching for a weapon, she drew a pristine sword from a stone in the middle of the desert and slew the beast.

With this sword in hand, Carina continued to think of the king's tournament, and whether she would be a good fit. Then, a young man with magic and charm crossed her path and claimed to be connected to the sword she'd found—Merlin, here to help her win the tournament. Through deep consideration, and learning the poor state of the lower classes of Medelios, Carina chose to make her way to the capital city of Reinos and enter.

Through multiple events, straining her both physically and emotionally, Carina began to succeed in the tournament while also working through her own trauma and pain that her father left behind in her. With Merlin's help—and soon, his love and care—Carina began to make allies. One in particular, Ahnri, a servant of Carina's rival who scoured the city for information, and used it to help Carina progress.

When Carina's rivals find out Ahnri is helping her, they capture and torture him, trying to learn what makes Carina so special. Ahnri is rescued by a friend, healed by Merlin, and continues to help where he can.

Upon the final duel of the tournament, Carina learned her opponent was using magic to strengthen herself and deftly cut off the ear that held the magic token, leveling the playing field. When victorious, Carina addressed the crowd gathered in Reinos, promising that if they accept her as their queen, she will do all she can to serve and protect them for the remainder of her days.

Merlin, bound to the sword and the strange magic therein, knows he will not be able to remain forever, but has no way of knowing when he'll be shunted away. Carina asks him for a single night with her, and they agree that he will take Excalibur and go, leaving Carina with a proper goodbye, but never to know how much time they could've had together.

Part One

Prepare

I

AHNRI

Sticks was a game you had to play to understand. It involved throwing five flat sticks—each marked on one side—onto the ground. Each that landed mark-up was worth one point, and you could collect as many of those each throw as you wished, then throw your remaining sticks to try for more points. The key was knowing when to stop while you were ahead—because if at any point you threw no marks, you lost all points accrued that turn. Not everyone had the instinct for it.

Not like Ahnri.

Ahnri pulled one of the mark-up sticks from his toss, and added two more silver onto the wager. They'd gathered quite an audience, the pile of coins growing beside them.

"You play dirty," the other man said.

Ahnri smirked, looking up through pale waves of hair that fell across his eyes. "How do you mean?"

"No one leaves marks on the table," the man said.

"I do," Ahnri said.

A memory floated across his mind, of Damond—his late surrogate father—being accused of cheating with the same tactic. But there weren't any rules that said you *must* pick up *all* marks. Damond was the reason Ahnri won so often at this game.

"Your go," Ahnri said, leaving three of his five sticks on the ground.

The man grunted, glaring as he tossed all five of his sticks.

Four out of five face-up.

Impressive luck.

That put him at twenty points, the numBer to end the game unless Ahnri matched or beat it. Which meant that if Ahnri got nothing on his next toss, he'd lose. But if he got these last three face up, he could keep going.

The man smirked, picking up all five to end his turn, rather than risk throwing only one, and gestured for Ahnri to go.

With steady motions, Ahnri picked up his final three. While some carried fancier sets, his were simple and smoothed by years of use. And on one side of each, a burned triangle with a diagonal line through it.

He ran a thumb over the mark of one. He had a good chance, with three left. He readied to throw, when a quiet mewl sounded from behind the other man. A cat, short-haired and gold-eyed with stripes in shades of grey and white, wound its way between them.

Ahnri met the cat's eyes and smiled. He'd always loved animals, from the birds he'd fed as a child to the horses he rode in his travels. Most small cats were too skittish for him to get close to, but this one seemed curious, eager.

"Stupid scavenger," the other player grunted, shoving the cat away. "Are you gonna throw or fold, boy?"

The cat rolled, popping up unscathed as cats do. Ahnri took a breath, then tossed his sticks to the ground.

The crowd around them leaned in. Two of three. Ahnri swore to himself. That put him at eighteen. Unfortunately, with the other man at twenty, Ahnri had no choice but to continue, and pray the gods had pity on him.

Four in one hand and his final stick in the other, he let it fall. Time seemed to slow as it hit the cobbled stone on one end, then the other, rolling a little, before it stopped.

Face-up.

"No!" The big man shouted.

Ahnri grinned. Nineteen. He picked it up, and tossed all five at once to continue his turn, and got three more face-up, which put him at twenty-two total. He'd won.

"Great playing, friend," Ahnri said, hurriedly scooping the coins into his money pouch. "It's been a long time since I came so close to los—"

A fist collided with his jaw, sending him skidding across the stones as the crowd scattered.

"You cheated," the man said, rising to his full height. "No one cheats me."

"I didn't cheat, you idiot, I—"

A kick to his stomach. It knocked the breath from his lungs. He struggled, trying to pull in enough air, when he was grabbed by the front of his cloak and yanked to his feet, the bearded face of his opponent before him.

"I'm gonna make you wish you'd never met me, you puny little—AAARRGGH!"

The cat leaped onto his face, clawing and hissing as the man tried to bat it away.

Ahnri ducked away, scooped up his sticks, and ran.

Over cobbled streets and between buildings of sun-baked mud and clay, he kept moving. Shouts rose behind him, calling to stop him, but by the time anyone heard he had already passed.

The outer city of Isille, capital of Fugera, was a maze of structures both permanent and temporary. Ahnri glanced behind him once to be sure he had a lead. To his surprise, the cat bounded close behind him.

Ahnri wouldn't be able to run forever though. It took a bit more searching before he reached an alley where two buildings stood only about six feet apart. Without pause, he ran toward the back of the alley where a wall stood ten feet high. Two steps up the vertical surface, then with a grunt he pushed off, aiming for the left building, then pushed off again toward the other.

A few feet at a time, gripping with the tips of his fingers, Ahnri made his way up the sides of the buildings, and pulled himself over the ledge of the roof, lying flat on his back in the full heat of the desert sun, mere moments before his pursuers turned into the alley.

"Where did he go?" one man shouted. "He came this way, I saw him!"

"He was fast," another said. "Maybe he hopped that wall?"

They continued arguing, going so far as to boost one of them up to look over the ten-foot wall. But there was only a small storage space there for the blacksmith who worked on the other side. Full of scrap metal and tools, he'd have made a racket getting through there.

Ahnri waited, listening

"*Mrrr…*"

Ahnri turned at the soft sound. The cat had hopped up onto the roof from another side, holding one of Ahnri's sticks in its mouth.

"Sshh," he said, waving the cat toward him.

The animal padded closer, and dropped the stick into Ahnri's hand. He hadn't had time to realize he'd missed one.

Below, the men had given up. There were no ladders, no ropes or clothesline, no handholds… surely, he must have turned somewhere else, they said. They left the alley empty save for a few crates and pieces of trash.

"*Mrrrowww.*" The cat gave a low, growl-like sound. Stalking, it made its way to the street-side edge of the roof, and its gaze followed the men back the way they'd come.

Catching his breath, Ahnri looked up at the heart of Isille: the tower. A huge mountain of stone, hundreds of feet high, into which their ancestors had carved rooms, tunnels, and bridges that made up the central heart of the city. The levels of the city were numbered from lowest to highest, the lower levels being wider and made up of businesses and larger homes, while the upper levels held mostly small apartments.

The palace—where Ahnri would head first—made up the core of the structure from levels one through four. Though for security purposes, there were no roads leading directly from the exterior to the palace until level three. Any invading force would have to climb, or walk the outer road that spiraled its way up the structure, which gave the defenders ample opportunities to rain stones or arrows on them.

Ahnri caught his breath while examining the tower, planning his path up so that he could avoid the crowds and traffic. Windows in the stone city loomed above, but he doubted anyone up there cared to notice one street kid resting on a random rooftop. And if they did, they needed to find something more useful to do with their time.

"Mrrow?"

Ahnri straightened to greet his new feline friend. "Hello there."

The cat paused, then sat straight, cocking its head to the side, eyes narrowed.

"What is it? Do you need food?"

In a rather un-cat-like motion, the animal rolled its eyes.

Ahnri blinked. He spoke to animals often; an eye roll was…not normal cat behavior.

He frowned at the cat. "What are you, then?"

The cat licked its paw, seeming to ignore the question.

Ahnri glanced at the sticks in his hand, all five. "Listen," he said, "thank you for bringing this to me. My father helped me make them." He paused, then pulled out a small pouch where he'd tucked a few pieces of smoked chicken he'd not finished the day before, and tossed one to the cat.

In a few snaps of teeth, it was gone.

Ahnri reached forward, scratching at the cat's ears and neck. It leaned into the touch with deep purring before rolling onto the dusty rooftop to begin batting at Ahnri's hand.

"I'm very grateful for your help back there," Ahnri said. "But I've got somewhere I need to go quickly, and I don't think you'll be able to follow."

The cat stood.

Ahnri watched it.

The cat watched back.

"You want to come?"

"Mrrow."

Ahnri glanced back up at the tower city, then back to the cat. "All right. See if you can keep up then." Then, on a hunch, he added, "I don't know if you can fully understand me, but if you lose me, can you make it to the market on the east side of level three?"

The cat *nodded.*

Ahnri grinned, excitement rising in his chest. "I'll see you there, then."

With a running start, he leaped from the rooftop to the one across the alley he'd escaped. He didn't watch for the cat, he simply ran. From that roof, he crossed to another, and another, until he reached the stone of the city tower.

The outer wall's rough, natural stone might've scraped at his hands if not for the callouses he'd built up over his nineteen years doing this. Unlike the polished smooth surfaces found throughout the interior of the structure, here he could find hand- and footholds with ease as he made his way up.

One hand after the other, leaping from one thin edge to the next, he made a distance in a few minutes that would take an hour on the roads that wound up and through the city. When he reached the outer road on level three, he had to pause at the railing there and wait for carts and horses to pass before he hurried across and through the nearest archway, into the structure itself.

He entered a market, as busy and bustling as any he'd ever been in, except that it filled a wide, high-ceilinged cavern. The arching entrance lit the space nearby, and farther in were lanterns hung on merchant stands, or chunks of lumenite—a stone native to Fugera that absorbed sunlight and gave a soft orange glow.

Ahnri pulled his hood up, moving slower now, and stepped quietly behind the closest stand—sugared fruit and nuts—before moving on to the next—distilled oils from Somnuria—and the next, and next. Light glinted off of gems in the styled hair of market-goers; the jingling of anklets and bracelets mingled with unrestrained laughter in the morning air.

He kept his head down, kept moving. He hardly caught a glance from the merchants as he passed, they were far too busy trying to sell to actual buyers on the street to notice someone moving with purpose behind them.

Scraps of conversation drifted to him as he passed.

"—beautiful sunrise today."

"Do you have more? I need double if—"

"—can't be serious. He's such a—"

Relief washed over him with such trivial conversations. At least the queen's schemes—whatever they were—hadn't alerted the general populace yet.

The market cavern ended in a huge archway that intersected another street, this one lined with many bright lanterns. It circled the core of the city—the palace—and wound up and up to level five, where it broke off into smaller passageways through the upper half of the city. But up was not where Ahnri wanted to go. Not yet.

He stepped off to one side of the archway. The queen's private balcony drew the eye on this section, and the thought of the woman made Ahnri's blood heat in his veins. Five months ago, Damond had overheard information he shouldn't have. Within two days the queen had him killed, and Ahnri arrested for consorting with "a traitor." Then she'd sent Ahnri on a pity mission that had nearly killed him. Luckily, thanks to magic and some actual decent people, Ahnri had begun to hope again.

As far as he knew though, the official word had been that Damond died "in service to the crown."

Only Ahnri and Queen Elya knew the truth.

For a moment, a box in his mind shuddered—where he kept the memories and emotions surrounding Damond's death. He took a breath, forcing those back. He couldn't let his want for revenge drive him right now, though there would be a time for it.

But the prince…

There.

The window. A little to the right and above the main balcony. Draped with purple velvet curtains and framed with a gilding of gold. Prince Remi's window.

It led to an office of sorts that connected to the prince's private suite. But Ahnri knew that room, and he knew that with a careful check of where the guards stood and when they changed, it wasn't too difficult to get to—not for Ahnri, anyway.

A twinge of fear slipped into his mind in that moment, however. Ahnri had sent a message via his carrier hawk before coming, but Remi hadn't replied. The queen might have told him Ahnri was dead—that possibility left a sour taste in Ahnri's throat. Would his presence be welcome? Ahnri didn't want to intrude. Maybe after sundown…maybe then he could get a note in through the window.

Something pressed against his leg and Ahnri looked down. The striped cat stood beside him once more, where it mewed at him.

"I'm very impressed," he said. Then a thought struck him. He knelt, meeting the cat's eyes. "Could you do me a favor?"

"*Mrrow.*"

"Worth a shot." Opening his pack, he pulled out a bit of paper and a charcoal pencil, and wrote:

Wait for me?

Words he hadn't written in months, yet they sent a rush of joy through his body. It wasn't a code, just a thing they said. But to him and Remi it had become something special. Both a request, and a promise.

Ahnri hoped the prince hadn't stopped waiting.

He folded the paper, and held it out to the cat. "See that window? That's Prince Remi's office. I need you to take this to him, but you can't be seen. Think you can do that?"

The cat tilted its head, but this time it was less curious and more exasperated. It took the note carefully between sharp teeth, and bounded across the street, winding between every set of legs and wheels, and Ahnri watched in amazement as it seemed to find footholds in the column that even he hadn't seen. In less than a minute, the last flicker of a tail had disappeared between dark, heavy curtains.

Ahnri waited. Tucked into the corner of the archway, out of sight and hidden in shadows. But his eyes were on the window.

The curtains parted, and a young man peered out. Coppery brown skin, pale hair pulled back into a tail with curling pieces falling from his temples, and—Ahnri knew without being close enough to see them—eyes of a pale amethyst that he could've stared at forever.

He wouldn't see Ahnri, but the message had been received. The cat slipped past the prince, back down the column. And Remi's eyes followed it—shock and wonder clear in his expression, even at this distance—until it made its way back.

For the first time in five months, Ahnri felt that gaze rest on him. And, for the first time in five months, finally felt like he'd come home.

2

AHNRI

Ahnri moved like a ghost through the city, staring every so often at the note Remi had sent back with the cat.

Come through the halls at sunset, I'll let you in.

His heart raced at the sight of it. The handwriting so familiar. The sight of the prince. Memories of incense and late nights and soft smiles…
Sunset.
After the dozenth time, he tucked the paper into a pocket and the thoughts back into a corner of his mind. He had to focus for now.
Today was for scouting. Ahnri bought food for himself—and the cat, who followed along without prompting. But it wasn't long before Ahnri grew tired of referring to the cat as an

"it" and, while making a pass through level four, pulled aside into an alcove of one of the major corridors to address it.

"You," he said, "are not a normal cat."

The cat stared at him.

"I'm not even sure how to address you. Do I call you Cat?"

For the second time that day, the cat rolled its eyes.

"You don't speak, how am I supposed to know?" Ahnri thought for a moment. "Do you have a name?"

The cat blinked.

"Any ideas how you can tell it to me?"

Then the cat sighed. It turned toward the base of the wall and scratched at the stone floor, leaving light lines behind. A moment later it stepped back. Carved into the stone, and not at all practiced, was the letter P, and what looked like either a lowercase E or perhaps I, followed by what could've been R or N.

"Per? Pin?"

The cat seemed to shrug.

"I'll go with Pin, then," Ahnri said. "And I'm not sure how else to ask this, but I feel it would be rude to *check*…are you a he or a she? Or do you care?"

The cat stepped forward, tapping its paw on Ahnri's arm.

"Don't know what that means. All right," he held out his hands, palms up. "If you're a 'he,' tap my left hand. If you're a she, tap my right. If you prefer something else, come sit at my feet."

The cat tapped Ahnri's left hand.

"He. Got it," Ahnri said, satisfied. Then he held for a moment, and tried to read the cat the way he would a human suspect. Ahnri prided himself on a fairly strong instinct for when someone could be trusted—it's what made him ally with Carina and Merlin back in Medelios in the first place. And here, now, he leaned into it.

This cat could very well be acting the helper in order to spy on Ahnri, and if that were the case, Ahnri needed to lose him, get him to stay away. But...

Pin took a step forward and placed a paw on the back of Ahnri's hand. At the contact, something inside told him to trust.

Ahnri shook his head. Thinking back to his interactions with Merlin—being healed from burns all over his body, and seeing assassins die at a touch—he'd seen some unusual things...he could accept this one. He scratched at the cat's ears.

Pin purred, seeming grateful, and they continued on their rounds. As they did, Ahnri found he rather enjoyed having someone to talk to, even if Pin didn't reply in more than expressions.

Over the coming days, Ahnri needed to confirm the queen's movements and any variations in them, and hopefully learn the windows of opportunity to get into her private offices and gather what information he could. He could potentially try the city records, but it wasn't official documents he sought. He needed proof of what Damond had overheard all those months ago. Proof of what had gotten him killed. The queen had mentioned gathering Viruses—channelers of Death magic—to form an *elite force*. Whatever her plans, she did not want it known.

Ahnri made a point to watch the palace windows, and by the end of the day he'd managed to spot the queen a few times, noting her location and actions. A good start, and he would continue each day until he felt he had a good chance at getting in unseen.

Just before sunset, with most of the city focused on their meals and socializing, Ahnri made his way down to the palace's lowest level where the royal kitchens and servants' entrances were located.

Servants here unloaded a cart of wine barrels, overseen by a very focused guard. The man was tall and thin, with black hair and a full beard—unusual coloring for Fugera, but not unheard of.

Ahnri frowned. At his feet, the cat meowed. He glanced to Pin, then gestured toward the guard. "Think you can distract that one?"

Pin nodded.

"Go on, then. Follow behind me if you can."

Without a sound, Pin slipped around the corner behind which they hid, and made his way past the cart, to the feet of the guard.

"Look at you," the guard muttered. He knelt down, petting the cat, and a moment later picked him up. Pin nuzzled against the guard's chin. "Well, aren't you just purrrr-fect?"

While the guard chuckled at his own joke, Ahnri straightened, stepping out and following confidently behind a servant to lift a barrel.

"Martin?" another guard called. "Where's you find that cat?"

Ahnri used the barrel to block his face and made his way inside—easy enough.

He entered the royal kitchens, warm and bright with flames roaring in huge ovens and brick fireplaces. The scent of sweetbreads made his head spin a little. Other servants passed them, going back out to get more of the shipment, and Ahnri stayed behind the servant in front of him and delivered the cask where the rest had been laid. Taking a quick glance to remain unseen he ducked into a side passage, snatched one of the spare servant smocks that hung from the wall, and left the kitchens.

In moments he had removed his cloak, tucking it into his bag, and pulled on the smock, buttoning it as he reached the end of that service hallway. The simple unadorned passage met up with one of the main corridors of the palace complex, displaying an extravagantly tiled floor, lit by sconces embedded in the walls. He stopped here, checking up and down the corridor.

A soft meow sounded. Pin lean against his leg.

"Glad you could make it," Ahnri said. "Next, unless they've rearranged, is getting past the Vessels in the library."

A paw tapped Ahnri's leg.

"We can't use you as a distraction every time, someone'll catch on."

"*Mrrow*." He sounded rather annoyed.

"Stay close."

Ahnri turned back into the servants' passage and backtracked until he found an offshoot. He took it, passing curtain-covered doorways and taking in the familiar sounds and smells he'd missed while he'd been in Medelios. Glass goblets clinking, sandalwood bathing oils, the tinkling of anklets, citrus pastries on platters, slippered footsteps too precious to allow outside the palace....

The corridor ended in another gilded hallway. Across from Ahnri's exit stood a wide arched entryway, the stone carved and painted with intricate designs of the gods—a swirling wave for Amplia's Life, a seed and sprout for Crescere's Growth, a stone and crystals for Sileo's Stability, and a hooded skull of smoke for Fina's Death. The patterns wove in and out of each other all across the archway, and beyond stood dozens of bookshelves. Lanterns bobbed between them, servants carrying light for every Vessel whose arms were laden with books.

There didn't seem to be anyone nearby...

Ahnri bowed his head and moved to cross, but the cat clawed at the hem of his trousers, scratching at Ahnri's ankle and causing him to flinch back.

"What the—"

Footsteps. Ahnri pulled back into the shadows as two female Vessels came down the corridor, their soft motions and voices so low he could hardly hear them as they passed right beside him. They were immediately followed by a male servant carrying a stack of books—spectacles hanging precariously from the tip of his nose.

One of the women called back, "Grant? Are you all right with those?"

"Fine, mistress!" the man said, scurrying onward.

Ahnri waited until they were out of earshot before speaking to the cat.

"Thanks."

Pin didn't respond, focused on the hallway before them.

"Let me know when it's clear."

Pin poked his nose out, paused, then moved forward. They exited the servants' hallway and made their way down another corridor, up two flights of stairs, and past two sets of guards who stood before the queen's chambers.

Ahnri didn't make a move toward it, so they ignored him, but something in the back of his mind noted the oddity of there being four guards to that door rather than the standard two.

Down the hall, around one more corner, and Ahnri pulled into another alcove—this one housing a statue—staying in the shadows. Here—a hundred paces from him—stood the double doors to the prince's quarters. Except two guards flanked those doors. Which, while not unusual, was unexpected. In the past, when Remi knew Ahnri was on his way, he would send the guards on short errands. Now, Ahnri frowned. Had he misread Remi's expression earlier? It was nearly sundown, so he had the time right...

He knelt beside Pin and whispered. "Can you get into the prince's rooms again? Let him know I'm here?"

Pin licked his paw, then stared, seemingly into nothing. A moment later, he bounded off, back where they'd come from.

Well, that wasn't much of an answer, but he'd give the cat a few minutes. So long as Ahnri wasn't spotted, he could wait.

The guards muttered softly in the distance. Ahnri couldn't make out their words. Then, after a minute or so, a low *thunk* sounded and the doors opened.

"Highness?" one of the guards said.

"Yes, good evening gentlemen. I need one of you to send for my dinner, and the other to deliver this message to Councilor Lita. Thank you."

The two guards paused, one staring at the sealed paper.

"What are you waiting for?"

"We're supposed to always have someone here, sire. Queen's orders."

Ahnri could practically hear Remi's eye roll. "And as everyone knows, my mother is extremely overprotective lately. We all know I'm not leaving these rooms for the remainder of the evening, and there's no way anyone could get in or out without me unlocking these doors, which I will not do. I'll deal with my mother if necessary, you will suffer no punishments, you have my word."

Reluctantly, the two men turned away from the doors and down the corridor toward Ahnri's hiding place. He stayed frozen behind the statue, hardly breathing until they'd passed. And he noted, Remi hadn't yet closed the doors.

When the guards were around the next corner, Ahnri stepped from the darkness and hurried down the hall.

Remi held the door. Ahnri slipped inside. A heartbeat later the lock clicked, and the boy Ahnri had missed more than anyone turned and threw his arms around him.

"You're truly alive," Remi said, breathless, his body trembling in the embrace. "Thank the gods. It was all I could do not to leap from my window this morning."

Ahnri embraced the prince, his heart hammering inside his chest at being this near to him. The wavy white-blonde hair tickled Ahnri's cheeks. He buried his face in the crook of Remi's shoulder, his nose brushing the skin of the prince's neck, and breathing in the soft scents of lavender and sage. The tension of the past months began to wash away.

"Ahnri," Remi said, pulling away slightly, then frowned. "What happened to your hair?"

"Ah," Ahnri said, running a hand through the short locks. "It got burned. Not by choice."

"Burned? What?"

"I was in a house fire," Ahnri said, waving a hand. "It was months ago, but I've kept it short since. I'm fine now."

"You cannot simply say you're fine after that," Remi said, stepping back and looking him over more carefully. Then he spotted one of the scars.

A line on Ahnri's collarbone where Rosaline had pressed hot metal against his skin, trying to get him to talk. One of the wounds that had…what had Merlin called it? Cauterized…closed itself up, before he could heal it to avoid scarring.

Remi reached forward, running a finger over the jagged scar.

Ahnri forced himself to remain still at the touch.

"Five months," Remi whispered, lowering his hand. He met Ahnri's eyes. "My mother, she—"

"Thinks I'm dead?"

"Yes."

"Hm." Ahnri turned away toward a small side table and poured two glasses of wine.

"How?" Remi said. "I thought..."

"Skill. Helpful friends. And a lot of luck."

Remi stared, his lavender eyes wide and bright, and a gentle warmth grew in Ahnri's chest.

"I just..." Remi said, "I can't believe you're here."

Ahnri handed him one of the glasses of wine. "I arrived in the city this morning. I admit to getting some breakfast and gambling a bit upon arrival, but you think I'd visit anyone else first?"

Remi nodded, then blinked and turned away, stepping toward his desk on the far side of the room.

"Rem?" Ahnri asked. "Is something wrong?"

The prince set his glass on the desk, leaning forward as though bracing himself. "I thought you were dead."

"Remi…"

"I got your note, and I didn't reply because I feared it was fake." Remi closed his eyes tight. "These days, everything that doesn't come through official channels is considered suspect. I didn't tell anyone though, I…I hoped it was real."

Ahnri waited, not speaking yet.

"Even this morning," Remi said, opening his eyes and shaking his head, "I told myself I could be dreaming, imagining you. I've wondered so many times what it would feel like to see you again. I hoped that maybe you'd lived, maybe the reports had been wrong…"

"Rem…" Ahnri said softly. "I'm here."

Remi's shoulders loosened at those words.

Ahnri took a step forward and set down his own glass. He waited, giving the prince time. After a few breaths, Remi straightened. Ahnri wasted no time taking Remi's hands in his.

"I missed you, my prince."

Remi's hands tightened around Ahnri's, and he wanted nothing more than to lean forward and kiss him. Except…even standing here, staring into Remi's eyes, Ahnri wasn't sure whether it would be welcome at this moment, after so long apart.

He'd tried not to think of this while he'd been away—the warmth, the safety, of simply being with Remi. He'd managed to keep it boxed up in that far corner of his mind where he always promised himself he'd think about it later.

But here, now, that box lay wide open and its contents strewn about the floor of his mind, memories flashing one after another of their time together. Something about the prince had always made Ahnri feel as though anything were possible. Remi saw him more than anyone ever had.

As children they'd been brought together in an effort by Remi's father to expose his son to the common folk. A nursery of sorts where children of palace staff were able to meet and play with the prince himself. That was where Ahnri and Remi had become close friends, along with Natalia, who had completed their trio. They'd grown up together, shared secrets and experiences. Until, of course, Remi's father had passed, and the queen put an end to those excursions.

From childhood friends to courting in secret—because the queen would never approve of her son being entangled with a lowly son of a palace guard—Ahnri recalled so many secret moments with this boy who now stood before him.

Remi's lips parted. "Ahnri, I—"

A *thunk* came from behind them, a knock at the door.

Ahnri leaped away, turning toward the next chamber and dove under the bed.

He hid in the darkness, watching the prince's feet—a chain of coins jingling on his right ankle—as he went to the door and opened it.

"Mother," Remi said.

Ahnri tensed. Staring out from beneath the bed, he saw slippered feet framed by deep red robes enter the room.

She was *right there*.

He'd told himself repeatedly that he had no desire for revenge, but knowing she was so close, knowing that he could very likely remove her from this life before she could call her guards...the temptation burned in his chest.

"Did you get my message?" Remi said.

Immediately, Ahnri's mind snapped back to reality. Elya might be close, but Remi was also here. Ahnri couldn't do anything to her that wouldn't also hurt the prince. As much as Ahnri wished that a swift dagger strike would solve all his problems, the situation was far more complicated than that.

"That's why I'm here," Queen Elya said, her voice low and serious. "You said to stop posting guards at your door. You do realize you're the crown prince, yes? It's normal for royalty to be guarded at all hours of—"

"I sent them on errands," Remi said, sounding bored. "They'll be right back. Honestly, you're too paranoid lately. Look. I'm fine."

"This time," Elya rumbled.

Ahnri held as still as possible, watching as Elya moved farther into the room. The anger inside him threatened to boil up again. He clenched his jaw, shoving it down.

Now. Was not. The time.

"Every time, Mother," Remi said. "I'm fine. I'm in no danger."

"That's the comfort they want you in," Elya said, "before they strike."

Remi paused. "Who strikes?"

"Our enemies," the queen said.

"Mother, really. We—"

"Enough!"

Ahnri closed his eyes. *That's* the tone he remembered.

"You are my heir," she snapped. "And you have a responsibility to *live*, do I make myself clear?"

A beat of silence passed, before Remi replied. "Yes, Mother."

Ahnri stayed perfectly still.

Elya moved to go, then paused near Remi's desk. "What is this?"

"Wine," Remi said.

"Why would you," Elya said, "an individual, pour yourself two glasses of wine?"

A string of curses wound themselves through Ahnri's mind.

"Well, I've been curious lately," Remi said, leaning sideways against the wall, "whether wine tastes different after it's been sitting out for a while. I was about to test these. One is fresh, the other has been out for an hour. Would you like to try?"

Elya didn't move for a moment, and Ahnri could feel the tension in the room. Then, she seemed to relax. "Insolent child. Lock this behind me. And stop sending your guards away. If I hear of it again, there will be consequences."

The doors shut, Remi latched them.

Ahnri stayed still. He watched as Pin made his way over to the doors as well, ears perked high. A few moments later, Remi unlocked the doors once more, peering out into the corridor.

"She's gone," he said, relocking the doors.

Ahnri slid out from under the bed.

"You know," Remi said, "I've grown closer to my mother in the time you've been gone. She's much less abrasive these days."

Ahnri raised a brow at that, choosing not to address it, while he patted dust off himself. "Your staff haven't cleaned under your bed in a while."

Remi smirked. "There's been little need. It's not like I had a lot of company hiding there while you were gone."

"So, you're saying the dust reminded you of me?"

"Well, it's certainly as irritating sometimes."

Ahnri smiled.

And Remi smiled back.

A heartbeat passed. Ahnri grew unsure what to do with his hands, unsure where to look. He wanted to look at Remi, to reach out to him, for the rest of the night—or longer.

Ahnri cleared his throat. "I'm sorry I stayed away for so long."

Remi's eyes softened.

"There are…so many reasons," Ahnri said, reaching out for the prince's hands. "And I want to tell you everything. But I don't want to get you in trouble."

"Such is the life of a spy. Don't worry, I won't tell my mother you're here—or alive—unless you say it's safe to."

Ahnri squeezed their hands. "Thank you."

"Mrrow!"

They both turned at the sound. Pin stood near the doors, and patted a paw against them.

"I think that means you have company again," Ahnri said, moving toward the window. "I'll see myself out."

He'd stepped on the ledge when Remi called out, "Wait!"

Ahnri turned back, and Remi seemed to steel himself. He took hold of Ahnri's cloak, and in a heartbeat, the prince's lips brushed against Ahnri's—softness, a contact that stopped his lungs from functioning, and brought a lump of nerves and hope to the base of his throat—and then it was gone.

"Can we meet at the ruins?"

Ahnri blinked, coming back to reality.

"The ruins," Remi said. "Up on level ten remember?"

"Tomorrow?"

Remi grimaced. "I can't tomorrow, I've got dinner with Mother. The next day?"

"At sunset?"

"Yes, please."

"Two days from now, at the ruins," Ahnri said. "I'll be there."

He leaned in and stole another kiss as he heard the doors *thunk* open once more, and ducked through the curtains.

3

NATALIA

Natalia Aimar sat straight, her quill scratching softly as she took notes on the dramatics of the men and women surrounding her. At seventeen years, she was the youngest person sitting on the royal council, and only because Councilor Mari—her mother—had fallen ill. Nat was *not* a council member, she merely took notes for Mama and voted in her place. But with Mama so ill, Nat did more than any of these people realized. All in the effort of keeping Mama alive.

"I still don't understand why the outer city needs more funding," Councilor Erre said in his gravelly voice. "The entire sector is temporary. They're nomads, coming in and out. All they need is a spot to pitch their tents for a few days. That funding should be spent to rebuild the upper levels."

"Have you ever traveled with them?" Councilor Lita snapped back. "Have you ever even visited the sector? No one lives in the upper levels anymore, but thousands call the outer city home. There are most definitely needs."

The Fugeran Royal Council was comprised of a number of elected representatives from various sectors of the city. The council served as a balance to the court and monarch, and could even, if necessary, vote to dethrone a ruler—though that hadn't happened in over a century. These days they focused on administrative duties and managing city needs.

Exhilarating, of course.

Natalia glanced from Councilor Lita to the head of the table, where Prince Remi sat reading over the proposal. As the councilors debated, Remi glanced up, eyes scanning the room until he met Nat's eyes. He gave an expression that plainly said, *"This is exhausting."*

Nat pressed her lips together to keep from laughing.

"Councilor Erre," Lita contiNued. "I have reviewed these points multiple times in these meetings, but it seems as though some of you have not paid attention. I'd be happy to go over them again if you'd like."

"That won't be necessary, Councilor Lita," Prince Remi said. "Anyone who has read through your request can see you care greatly for the nomadic population. This line here, for example: 'If Isille is the beating heart of Fugera, the nomads are the flowing blood. They are as much citizens as those who live here year-round.' It's truth, that can't be argued."

Nat watched with pride. Prince Remi had sharp mind, and a smile that could weaken the knees of anyone if he met their eyes—she would know. Watching him guide these meetings, being the leader she'd seen him raised to be by his late father, was a highlight of a very complicated situation.

While Natalia sat on the council, Mama lay bedridden in their apartment one level below. An interior set of rooms—no windows, no sunlight. They'd always had interior rooms, ever since Nat and her little brother Tomaz were young. It hadn't been an issue then. They'd spent most of the day working and walking the city enough to get the fresh air they needed. Now, it had been weeks since Mama had seen the sky, her health declining at a rapid pace, and Nat's worry grew each day.

She already had no idea whether her father still lived, and her brother had been gone for months…she couldn't lose Mama too.

"Forgive me, Highness," Councilor Erre said, "I did not mean to imply they were not Fugeran citizens. I simply don't see what more they need in those sectors that they don't already have."

"Plenty," Counselor Lita replied. "I listed them in the proposal. Security, waste management, clean water—"

"But they *have* those things," Erre said.

"Barely!" Lita snapped.

Nat noted each time one of them spoke against another. Their desires were a mix and sometimes two who were opposed on one issue were allied on another. So, they managed things, one slow meeting at a time.

She checked the timepiece on the wall—if they talked much longer she'd miss her appointments.

"Your Highness," another councilor Nat couldn't remember the name of stood abruptly. "I must side with Erre on this, I'm afraid. We do provide these things to the outer sector, and we haven't had any complaints—"

Councilor Lita scoffed. "Then you haven't been listening."

The prince stood then, signaling for the others to be seated. "Because we have reached the end of the day, I'm going to make an executive call. Lady Fira," he said, turning to the head of the Royal treasury, "Councilor Lita and her committee are requesting a twenty percent rise in their funding, please see that they receive an eight percent increase moving forward, and Councilor Lita, you may begin making improvements with those funds immediately.

"We can debate the rest tomorrow and for the remainder of this week if you all wish, but I would encourage all of you," he eyed Councilor Erre and the other one Nat couldn't remember, "to *thoroughly* review the proposal before our next meeting. I personally believe the added support would help, and we should be able to make it fit within the royal budget. However, I won't sign off on more without the council's approval. Meeting adjourned."

As everyone stood and gathered their things, Remi made his way to Natalia. She made sure to curtsey, letting him be a *little* taller than her for a moment.

"Your Highness."

He waved a hand as he always did, to show she didn't have to do that with him. "How is your mother?"

Nat's smile fell. "The same, mostly. We're getting by."

"Are you sure?" Remi said. "If you need anything—"

"Your Majesty!"

Remi turned, and Nat's gaze followed, to where the double doors of the council chamber opened wider to reveal Queen Elya herself, followed by a contingent of four guards.

"Mother!" Remi said, hurrying to her side. "What a pleasant surprise. We just ended for the day."

"Hello dear," the queen said "Please return to your seats, everyone."

Remi gestured to his seat at the head of the room, and the queen took it. She glanced over the council with calm, shrewd eyes. A soft scent of jasmine drifted from her as her robes settled. Queen Elya had taken over ruling Fugera when King Alain had passed only three years ago, and hadn't made many changes, except that she'd put her son entirely in charge of running the city while she handled more important affairs. What those were, Nat didn't know, but the queen constantly insisted the council could function well without her.

Therefore, seeing her here now left everyone unsure what to do.

The room went entirely silent; hairs on Nat's arms tingled with nerves as Queen Elya scanned each council member one at a time. When her gaze fell on Natalia, the queen's head tilted to one side, and Nat quickly bowed her head in respect. By the time she looked up, the queen had moved on.

Nat glanced to Remi, whose eyes were on his mother.

"I know I rarely attend these sessions," Queen Elya said. "I wanted to come today to express my gratitude to all of you,"

Queen Elya went on. "You continue to manage the city with grace and consistency under the direction of my son. The gods surely are pleased, as am I. The work we do in these days will bring glory to Fugera for generations to come. Thank you for your efforts, your support, for all you do for our lovely kingdom."

"I wanted to inform you all personally that the Fugeran military is recruiting for a special new division. I encourage you to send anyone interested to General Saunier's offices in the military level underground. Again, I thank you for your consistent support. If there is ever anything you need, the prince and I are here to serve. Enjoy the rest of your day."

And with that, the queen stood and made her way out. Prince Remi nodded to the room, catching Nat's eye with a look of surprise, then followed his mother.

The council members seemed unsettled by the visit, and Nat didn't blame them. She'd been filling in for Mama for nearly a month now, and she'd never been in the same room as the queen before today. Surely most of the others had, but not in some time. That such a visit would occur so randomly left her confused.

Nat hurriedly gathered her things and made her way from the chamber. Unfortunately, not fast enough. Councilor Lita cut her off just outside the doors. "Miss Natalia," Lita said, a smile on her face that Nat could tell was forced. "I've been meaning to ask you a few things. May I walk with you?"

Nat widened her eyes to their most innocent and naive appearance. "Oh, of course, I'd be honored."

Lita's grin sharpened as they made their way down the corridor. "You know, your mother and I have always been close. I do hope you'll pass on my best wishes to her?"

"Of course, Councilor."

"And we can count on your vote for the outer sector budget proposal, of course?"

No subtlety at all, Nat thought. "Oh, I think so. I'll have to speak with Mother about it tonight and make sure I understand. You said there needs to be more guards?"

Lita gave a hesitant laugh. "Well, yes, among other things, child. The budget would help many people."

"Oh, I know," Nat said. "I'm so excited. Though, I do understand Councilor Erre's argument too, that money could go toward many things…"

"Yes, but we should consider the most important things, which are—"

"Oh!" Nat tripped then—on purpose—spilling her book and a few loose papers. "Oh, silly me. I'll clean this up. Thank you for your time, Councilor! I'll see you tomorrow!"

As Lita walked away, Nat got the feeling the woman was glad for the excuse. Natalia pressed her lips together and gathered her things once more, making her way quickly to a servants' hallway nearby.

She *would* most likely vote with Lita for the budget raise tomorrow; Mama would agree with it. However, she didn't want the other councilors able to depend on her for anything. This position wasn't something Nat wanted. She simply had to do it while Mama remained ill. If she didn't, the council would simply replace Mama, and then they wouldn't get paid…they already didn't have enough.

A member of the royal council earned a handsome stipend, usually enough for a nice apartment and plenty of comforts. Except, as the newest council member—and therefor the lowest in seniority—Mama also received the lowest payment. A generous amount that usually covered their needs, but in the last month nearly every coin they'd normally use for food had gone toward extremely expensive medicine.

Nat had however found a way to earn a little extra money on the side, to supplement their needs. While Mama hadn't improved *yet*, she at least remained stable. And Nat was determined to keep her that way.

Making her way through the palace, she entered a servants' washroom. There, she took a moment to tie her mane of pale curly hair back into a bun and cover it with a kerchief, then changed into plainer clothing, and tossed on her hooded cloak. She flipped her satchel inside-out, making sure to place her council notes in a hidden pocket to keep them safe.

When she left the washroom, *Miss Natalia* had become the Rat Girl.

She had three appointments to get to before sundown, which gave her only an hour. The first and closest was on level three—a well-off family who reported a single large rat that made itself at home in the pantry. Nat kept her gaze low, her shoulders stooped, as she spoke to the parents.

"How long is this going to take?" the fAther asked.

Nat kept her eyes down. "It depends. It could take a few minutes or an hour, however long it takes to draw the creature out."

The mother sighed, rolling her eyes. "Very well. Do what you must."

"You have a bag?"

They held out a small bundle, which Natalia examined. A drawstring bag that had lost its string. It would do.

"Thank you," she said. "Please do not enter until I come out. It's very important we don't let it escape accidentally."

"Understood," the father said. The two parents and three children made their way out, closing the front door behind them.

Nat took a deep breath, taking in the scent of leather and dust coming off the shoes just inside. In the kitchen, she opened the pantry door a bit, then carefully lowered herself to the floor near the table and chairs. From her bag she drew a small pouch containing some seeds and dried angfruit—which, even when dried, had a strong sweet scent that carried far. This she poured into a small pile in front of her, then she sat very still beside the little bait pile, and rested her hand on her knee, mere inches from the food.

A deep breath. Exhale. Reach for the shadows with trembling hands.

Despite wishing she couldn't, Nat pulled Power from the darkness. For a moment, the section of shadow beneath the chair beside her simply…vanished. She couldn't explain it, and no priest had ever been able to either. They accepted this phenomenon as fact, but it bothered Natalia. The shadow vanished, and a few moments later, repaired itself like fabric re-woven on its own.

The same way water did when Cures drew Life from it, or a plant would when a Shifter drew Growth, or how stone and dirt would when a Clarity called forth Stability.

Natalia wasn't like them—she was a Virus.

Energy flowed into her from that shadow. It felt odd to describe it that way, the Power of Death itself, but it was an energy nonetheless. It hummed inside her, discontent, eager…angry.

Nat held it, contained it as she always did, though holding it like this made her heart race, her hands shake. It wasn't illegal to be a Virus, but the ability she held frightened her. What if she got distracted? Let it go accidentally? She held the potential for hurting someone at her fingertips. She had to be careful.

She only drew in a small amount, enough to take care of a rat, no more. Then, she waited. Still and silent. For the poor rodent to make its appearance.

Minutes passed, and Nat, as usual, was left with only her thoughts for company—not good while holding Death magic inside her. For the first few years of her life, she hadn't known what she could do. Then, at the age of five, she'd visited a temple with Mama where she'd learned of the gods, their relationships, the Four Powers. And finally, they told her what she'd been blessed with.

Or cursed.

She'd lost count of the number of pests she'd disposed of now…it had to be over a hundred. She'd started doing it a few years ago to earn a little extra money, but recently, with Mama falling ill, it had become more necessary. She'd never used her powers on another person—thank the gods—but insects, rodents, even a stray dog once. She hadn't meant to. She'd cried for days afterward.

Finally, while seated as still as a statue on the floor of this family's kitchen after she'd counted to one hundred twice, a tiny pink nose peeked out from the open pantry door. Natalia's bones seemed to hum inside her, the Power—small amount though it was—begging to be set free, to hurt, to destroy.

Her teeth clenched together, she kept herself still as the rat skittered out, coming nearer to the pile of food. She held. The magic wouldn't work from a distance, she needed to touch it. Finally, the pest drew up to the food.

Nat reached out and grabbed it—a flash of purple light.

The rat was dead.

Quick. Painless. Simple.

Natalia swallowed a lump in her throat as she dropped the rat's body—now limp. She gathered the food back up—it could be used again today. The rat's body she placed gently in the bag the family had given her. That little pink nose and the thin whiskers had been so cute…now they weren't moving at all.

She opened the door to find the family bundled together across the hall.

The father stepped forward. "Well?"

Nat held up the bag. "Got it."

The mother let out a sigh of relief. "Thank you."

"Mama," one of the children said, "How do we know she got it, and didn't just pile food in a sack to steal from us?"

Suppressing a sigh, Nat opened the bag, and let the child glance inside.

"Ugh," they cringed.

"Enough," the father said. He held out a small pouch. "Five silver. And you have our gratitude."

Nat took the coins offered, and quickly went on her way.

One down for the day, three more to go.

Then, to the medicine stall.

4

AHNRI

Ahnri found a room to rent on level six, which suited him perfectly. It even came with its own moderately-sized lumenite crystal for light, to avoid use of oil in the early evenings.

A fraction of the size of the lower levels, and in spite of the ratio of people to space being similar, level six simply felt less crowded. And his room had a window to the outside, which would be useful if he needed to get in or out without using the interior tunnels.

He woke on his second day in the city to the sound of hissing. Kahn—his carrier hawk—perched at the window, while Pin had crept into a corner, his back arched and stance defensive.

"He's a friend," Ahnri said, still half asleep. "Calm yourself."

Pin gave a low growl.

Rubbing the sleep from his eyes, Ahnri went to Kahn and ran a hand over the hawk's head and back, scratching at a spot on his back. Kahn let out a chirp, and tapped his beak against Ahnri's chest.

"Thank you, friend," Ahnri said. "You're staying out of sight, yes? Elya might recognize you, so do not go inside the tower." Kahn clicked his beak—about as much response as Ahnri expected. Then he opened the small cylinder attached to the bird's leg to remove a tiny, tightly-rolled paper.

A note from Carina.

Her Royal Majesty Carina Valio had recently been crowned the new ruler of Medelios, a kingdom to the south of Fugera. She was also Ahnri's new boss. Through a series of events that had led to Ahnri being presumed dead, Carina—along with an annoyingly smart mage named Merlin—had helped Ahnri survive a number of incidents. Ahnri, in turn, helped Carina secure her place as heir to the Medelian throne, and had sworn himself to her service in gratitude for her—and Merlin's—help in saving his life.

He'd come back to Fugera under her direction. Though admittedly, he had pushed for the chance to do it.

Ahnri frowned as he read through the coded message. "Asking for a report as soon as I arrive. She says she has a squad ready to travel if necessary, in case I want backup." He considered this. They'd both agreed he should come alone, so to receive this the day after arriving told him she was worried...

He didn't blame her. Ahnri was very good at his job, but even he could admit he might be a little too close to the situation to keep a clear head about him. He pulled a piece of venison from his pack for Kahn, and tossed one to Pin as well, before going to the hawk and scratching his neck, rereading Carina'S message.

While it had taken Ahnri ten days to travel from Reinos to Isille—by use of ferries and horses—it took Kahn three to four days, depending on the weather, and how easily he could find food on his path. Not to mention Ahnri and Carina agreed they should allow Kahn at least one day to rest between such long trips. If Ahnri sent him back to Medelios now, Kahn wouldn't return with a message from Carina for at least six days, likely more.

No, he needed to wait until he had more information before sending Kahn away. He re-rolled the paper, then held it over the flame of his lamp. When the flame caught, he dropped it onto the stone floor and let it smolder out.

His entire purpose here was to find proof of what they already knew—what Damond had overheard, and had lost his life for: that Elya was gathering Viruses to build an elite force.

The repercussions of Damond's death had kept Ahnri away from Isille for five months. Now—under Carina's direction— he would learn what exactly Elya had planned, and stop her before she hurt anyone else.

"Today we do more scouting," he said, watching the last of the paper burn before him. "I need to know where the queen will be at every hour of the day, and preferably learn this from outside the palace. So, if you have any ideas, I'm open to them."

Pin managed to meow through a mouthful of food, and Ahnri had to laugh.

"Don't rush yourself," he said. "We have time. Eat."

While Pin settled down and made quick work of the food, Ahnri triple checked his pack. Notebook, pencils, water, food, his Sticks set, a few vials of poison, some rope, his small daggers—one of which he slipped into his boot. He took out a day-old half-loaf of bread for himself then, and sat on the floor to eat, watching the cat and the bird, letting his mind wander. And, as often happened these days, he thought of Remi.

It seemed that Remi wasn't directly involved in whatever the queen had planned, though he could easily be drawn in. Ahnri chewed and considered. It would be wonderful to have Remi on his side, but he couldn't risk giving Remi the whole truth unless he knew it wouldn't get back to Elya.

If he didn't tell Remi *anything*, and Ahnri worked against the queen, that could mean working against Remi…he wasn't sure he could do that. These thoughts had been eating at him for days on his journey here.

First, he had to get to the queen's private records. Not city or kingdom related, but her personal notes and letters. He'd learn what he needed there, he was certain. And if he was wrong, well, he'd deal with that if it came to it.

He stood, shouldering his pack, strapping it tight against his body. Kahn would know to stay here until Ahnri sent him back, so he looked to the cat.

"Coming?"

Pin responded by going to stand at the door. Ahnri followed, opening and locking it behind them.

They spent the next six hours making rounds. Once with his hood up, once with it down, once with a hunch, and once carrying his pack swaddled in his cloak like an infant. The palace took up the central portion of the tower from level one up to level five, all around which Ahnri noted where guards were posted, and when they changed.

The ground level of the palace was made up of servants' quarters, kitchens, storage, and everything else it took to run a palace that royalty didn't want to see. Teeming with workers and motion, and no one looked twice at an extra body.

Along with his ability to disguise himself, Ahnri's skill in not being noticed lay mainly in knowing how to move in a given environment. If he stayed in well-traveled areas he could move freely. But when he went into less-populated spaces, he had to walk with more purpose. He'd found he could get by posing as a servant in most parts of the palace interior, and in the city, he could hide in the crowds so long as there *were* crowds to hide in.

Level two required more subtlety; he had to watch from the road below, or find windows in the tunnels across the main thoroughfare. This level held the throne room in the very center, surrounded by conference rooms and guest suites for visiting dignitaries. Here, he spotted the queen the first time. He couldn't be sure if this was a regular visit or not, but he'd check again tomorrow. He managed to catch her again on level three through the windows of her private suite, and later through the drapes of Remi's office window.

Each time, it seemed only luck that he'd caught a glimpse of her, because as soon as he did, a guard stepped between her and the exposed window or exit. After the second sighting, Ahnri made a mental note to try to count how many guards she had. On the third, he saw at least three, but assumed there would be a fourth. Guards in Fugera preferred to work in pairs, so as to always have backup.

Level three, along with housing the royal family, also held rooms for their closest staff and higher-ranking members of the Isille city council, those who didn't live out in the main portion of the tower city. At that thought, Ahnri remembered an old friend who was probably still in the city—Natalia. Her mother was on the council, maybe she'd know more about the queen's new project.

He didn't make as many rounds of level four which, despite being official palace property, was largely ignored by the queen herself. This held apartments for the rest of the court, the directors who worked for the council and were responsible for communicating with the people of Fugera, making sure every city outside the capital had food and supplies, as well as bringing in wrongdoers to be judged by the council.

Pin kept up much better than Ahnri would've expected, and in fact managed to help Ahnri stay unseen a few times. Ahnri prided himself on having extremely good senses, but Pin's help made a significant difference. Together they made their way through and around the palace, pausing here and there to let servants or officials pass. Pin often bounded ahead to check the next corridor and would hurry back, though he disappeared a few times only to show up again later. At one point later in the afternoon Ahnri noticed the cat return again and knelt to meet him.

"You know, we should probably talk."

Pin meowed defensively.

"I want to know why you're so smart," Ahnri said, keeping his volume low. "I've been around a lot of animals and you're the first who seems to genuinely understand me."

Pin paused, watching Ahnri for a moment, before shaking his head.

No answer then. "How about…of all the people in this city, why did you choose to follow *me*?"

Pin cocked his head, and Ahnri suddenly felt silly for asking a cat such detailed questions. "I wish you could mucking *talk*," he muttered.

By mid-afternoon Ahnri's time had been well spent. He now had a tentative schedule for where the queen had been throughout the day, where the variations were, and a solid idea of her activities. Except for one stretch of a few hours, when he hadn't been able to find her anywhere either yesterday or today. For her to have vanished at the same stretch of time two days in a row felt ominous.

Disguised as a palace servant now, he made another note as he watched her enter the council meeting chamber, which seemed an odd move for her. She tended to let Remi handle the council, from what Ahnri remembered. And sure enough, he heard Remi speak, "Mother! What a pleasant surprise. We just ended for the day."

"Hello dear," Elya said. "Please return to your seats, everyone."

The doors closed behind her, leaving two guards outside. Ahnri kept his head down and knelt to the floor to begin scrubbing. The guards paid him no mind, but—as he'd hoped—they soon began talking.

"One more hour," the one on the left muttered. He stood tall and broad, and wore a thick mustache. "I'm sick of this."

"Agreed," the right guard said. Though rounder of body, this one carried himself like a practiced swordsman. "I'd much rather be out in the city than in here. It's so…repetitive."

"Not to mention dangerous."

"Right? I couldn't believe—"

"Shh," the mustached guard cut him off.

Ahnri kept his eyes averted, sure they'd noticed him. He increased the volume of his scrubbing.

"Right, right," the round-faced guard said.

"We do our jobs. Protect the queen, then go home."

"Right. Protect the queen." A pause. Then a whisper, "What did he do though?"

"The official word is she accused him of being a foreign spy. Passing information."

"She have proof of it?"

"Not that I've heard. Though maybe she wanted to keep it quiet. Either way, one minute a squad leader, the next—"

Ahnri glanced up to catch the man running a thumb across his neck, then checked down the corridor.

Elya had executed one of her own guards? For *suspected* treason? And without a trial, it sounded like…

"He was a good man," the round-faced man said, clearly shaken.

"He was," the mustached man said. "But don't let the queen hear you say anything about it. You'll meet the same end."

The guards went silent. Ahnri considered as he scrubbed the floor…if this kind of whisper network were going on among the palace guards, what else might they know?

The council chamber doors opened then, and Queen Elya floated out followed by her adviser and guards, the two at the door taking up the rear.

Ahnri continued scrubbing, eyes on the floor, as he listened to Remi and the rest of the council exit. Once left alone in the hallway, he hurried to follow where the queen went, dropping the bucket and brush in a servant's station on the way.

So…Elya had executed a guard suspected of spying on her. Whereas five months ago, she'd had Damond killed for *overhearing* sensitive information. The circumstances were eerily similar, and something in Ahnri felt the need to protect these guards from her wrath. She'd never admitted what she'd done to Damond, but Ahnri knew the truth. A week later however, she'd granted Ahnri the chance to serve her rather than be executed. A mercy, certainly. But only to further her own ends.

Now, she simply ordered executions? No secret assassination, no offer of service, no trial, just…death?

Ahnri's heart grew cold in his chest at the thought. He caught up enough to see they were heaDing for Elya's rooms—the exact place he wanted to go. Turning, he spotted Pin a few paces behind him and had an idea.

Kneeling to meet the cat, he said, "I need keys to the queen's rooms, but not from the guards. I don't want them getting in trouble. Any ideas?"

Pin narrowed his eyes as though in thought, then looked up and nodded, one paw lifted as though waiting to be told to go.

Not incredibly confident in this, Ahnri still thought it worth trying. "Right. Off with you, then. Meet me in the market."

He made his way out of the palace—always easier than getting in—and went to the archway intersection that gave him a view of Remi's window and the queen's balcony. Remi had said he'd be at dinner with the queen tonight, so maybe—if Ahnri had the keys—tonight may be his first solid shot at getting into her rooms unseen. He'd still do surveillance to see what he could learn, but if he *knew* she'd be out…it might be worth a try.

The market behind him still bustled, telling him it likely wasn't quite sundown yet. Ahnri looked around, watching the citizens and merchants nearby, the carts and horses and camels making their way up and down the interior road. He hadn't been truly alone since meeting Pin, but his mind felt cluttered with the cat gone.

He took the time to think through his next steps. If he *could* get into the queen's study, he'd have to find some proof—specifics. Something to tell him what exactly she was up to. If he knew her plans, he could stop them. Stop her from hurting anyone else the way she'd hurt him.

The Damond box in his mind trembled. He pushed it back.

He didn't need revenge. He didn't need Elya's life. He simply wanted to see her stopped.

But first, he needed information. He stared at the palace walls, light from street lanterns reflecting in the polished stone. Half an hour passed before Pin bounded across the street, something dangling from his mouth. The cat stopped in front of Ahnri, and dropped it to the ground. It hit with a small jingle.

A set of unmarked keys with a tag on the ring labeled, "Masters." If they wanted to avoid trouble, he'd have to have Pin return these to wherever he took them. Which, if he'd gotten them so easily, shouldn't be a problem.

"Are you certain one of these goes to the queen's rooms?"

Pin turned away, looking offended.

Ahnri shook his head. "I don't know where you came from, but I am very grateful for your help."

Pin licked his paw then rubbed his ear, as though intentionally ignoring Ahnri's amazement made him even more impressive.

5

AHNRI

The lanterns of Isille made sneaking around very easy. As long as you stayed out of the light, you were basically invisible. Ahnri and Pin made their way to the same servants' entrance they'd used to get into Remi's rooms, and—with the benefit of a different guard to distract—Pin got them through again without issue. Ahnri let out a breath of relief as he made it into the kitchens. That wasn't going to work every time.

It had been easier before, when Damond was alive and a younger Ahnri had been a frequent sight around the palace. He'd been able to go in and out of the place as he pleased—though not always to Remi's rooms. Now, it seemed he knew no one. Faces were unfamiliar, though he kept an eye out for any who might remember him. At this point he didn't *want* to be recognized unless he trusted the person could hold their silence.

Now it was near dinnertime, and the queen would be in the largest meeting room on level two, taking dinner with Remi and a few council members. Which would leave her study on level three empty and, hopefully, unguarded. Ahnri made his way through the kitchens then paused, putting his back to the wall to wait for Pin. A moment later, the cat rounded the corner.

"Ready?"

Pin nodded, leading the way with his keen senses. Ahnri followed, his heart pounding in his chest.

Together they made their way through the palace, pausing here and there to let servants or officials pass. Pin bounded ahead to check the next corridor, and hurried forward. Two staircases and a few hallways later, the doors to the queen's rooms stood before them—unguarded, but locked.

Ahnri tried keys in the door while Pin kept watch. Luckily, the third one worked. The two of them slipped through, and Ahnri relocked it behind them.

He'd never been in these rooms before, and something in him recoiled at his mere entering. A pungent floral incense burned nearby, attacking his senses; his eyes watered and acid rose in his throat. That scent—jasmine and a hint of lemon—took him back…his knees scraping on rough stone, the maddening drip of water somewhere down the line of prison cells…

He paused, closing his eyes tightly for a moment to clear his head of the unpleasant memories, then glanced around at a sitting room: sofas, silk pillows, and fur rugs. Across from him hung heavy curtains, which he knew led to her private balcony.

Through an archway to the left stood a magnificent four-poster bed with heavy purple hangings, a delicate gauzy material of pale gold falling between them.

And to his right: the queen's personal study.

He made his way into the dimly lit space and nearly tripped on a thick rug.

Ahnri scoffed at the plushness of it. "Excessive," he muttered.

Bookshelves lined three walls of this room, while the fourth—the exterior wall—held two windows framing a wide, white granite fireplace. Above the fireplace hung a gold-framed painting of the Arontas mountain range at sunset, shades of pinks and oranges fading into purples and blues. Seeing this, annoyance poked at Ahnri. Elya didn't deserve to have this beauty in her rooms…he doubted she ever looked at it.

In the center of the room sat a heavy wooden desk of deep brown, the edges carved in intricate designs of the sun and moon, and gilded with silver, matching the silver studs on the velvet-upholstered high-backed chair that sat behind the desk.

With a deep breath and mentally reviewing his training, Ahnri first glanced over the papers on top of the desk, without touching. There were ledgers listing kingdom finances, spending plans, and something about the prince's upcoming birthday celebration. On a loose sheet he spotted a note, which appeared to be only a list of letters and numbers. Beside that, a schedule. Useful, and essentially confirmed what Ahnri had already gathered from his scouting, including a single word in the place where he'd had a hole in his:

Lab.

He thought back to what Damond had told him…*gathering Viruses…an elite force…attempt to take over the Unbroken Lands…*

So she had a space somewhere that he hadn't seen yet. It made sense. Of *course,* she would work on her secrets somewhere inconspicuous. But could he find it?

Briefly, he checked to see where Pin had gone and spotted the cat in the archway of the study, watching the entrance they'd come through.

In that moment he recognized how much trust he'd already come to put in this cat. Animals always held a special place in his heart, but one who could actively help him work more effectively? Even better.

He should've probably been more suspicious, but over the past two days Pin had consistently proven to make each task easier. If the cat betrayed him, Ahnri would have only himself to blame.

"Pin," he said. "You'll let me know if you hear anything?"

"*Mrrrow.*"

Ahnri took that as confirmation, and moved on. He pulled out his notebook and began to copy down the information he'd already found. He could crack the code later.

Then, he let his instincts take over. Like a soft breeze, he opened drawers, checked through shelves, pulled out stacks of paper, read everything he could find and placed it back as carefully as he could. Everything Damond had taught him about being precise and intentional came back to him now, as he made his way through Elya's study—present, but so gentle, so slight, the details would never be noticed.

A few minutes had passed when he noticed a small knot in the wood under the lip of one of the bookshelves. It seemed to shift slightly when he touched it, so, curious, he pressed.

With a deep *thud*, the entire shelf shifted, dust falling down from the ceiling where it parted. The shelves moved backward into a space, then shifted to the left to reveal an opening.

Ahnri's mouth hung open. He turned to Pin.

Pin shook his head.

Ahnri picked up a lantern from the wall and stepped inside. It was…nothing more than an empty room. And absolutely *covered* in dust.

Pin trotted over, sniffing at the floor of the hidden space, and sneezed.

"Right," Ahnri said, "if Elya is aware she has an emergency escape, it seems like she hasn't used it in decades. No one has."

He turned to examine the walls more closely. At the back of the space, Ahnri noticed holes in the wall, where pockets of earth had been cut out.

He raised a brow, impressed. As someone who instinctually looked for ways to climb around, Ahnri knew handholds when he saw them. He held the lantern high to see a tunnel shaft, winding up through the city. Perhaps only one level or two, but since it began in the royal chambers, he felt confident there had to be an exit at the other end.

"All right," he said, coming back into the study. "That's our way out."

He left the space open, returned the lantern to its place, and continued searching the room. Nice though it was to find a secret entrance to the queen's suite, he'd rather find information. Worry began to wear on him that there wouldn't be anything else, when finally, in a lower drawer of the desk he noticed an inconsistency in the build. He had to laugh.

"First a secret tunnel, now a mucking hidden drawer."

Pin approached immediately, sniffing the spot. Ahnri carEfully reached to the back of the drawer, feeling around, until—

Click.

The false bottom of the drawer popped open, revealing a small space containing a few papers. On the top lay a small note, on parchment, lying as though it had been rolled and then spread flat so many times that only the corners turned up now.

Queen Elya,

We have asked multiple times and received no response from you. Medelios has reached agreeable new contracts with every other kingdom, yet you refuse to even consider an arrangement that differs from the one you've had for half a century.

Change is inevitable. If we do not welcome it, surely it will overcome us. Do not underestimate Medelios; we are more powerful now than we have ever been.

It was signed, *Queen Carina Valio*, and held the royal seal.

Except…Ahnri knew Carina's seal, and this was not it. More importantly, he knew *Carina*, and she would not make a threat like this.

As far as he knew, Carina had reached out to Queen Elya precisely once, and he'd read and offered critique on that communication. It had been a simple extension of greeting, an introduction of Carina as the new Medelian ruler. Certainly not a threat.

He looked closer. The slant of that M felt off… and the tail of the Q curled around a little too much…

"This is a forgery," he whispered.

What would that mean?

He'd come here on a reconnaissance mission. Information-gathering only, so that an actual plan could be made between himself and Carina using the resources at her disposal to stop Elya from following through on the plan Damond had overheard all those months ago. But if Elya was being tricked, or lied to, that could make her reckless. Pushing the timeline forward.

Or, perhaps Elya herself had created these letters? Using them to push her agenda and create urgency where none existed? She was already killing her own guards for little more than suspicion, what would she do with "proof" of an impending war? And what might she cover up in the process?

Ahnri swore under his breath. Did Remi know about this? He copied the text into his notebook, then skimmed through the other few papers there. Two more were letters from other rulers—the Somnurian king, and the High Councilor of

Calidar—also asking Elya to enter agreements with them. They weren't outright threats, but the insinuation was there.

Last, he found a list of names with the word, "Enlist" at the top. He stared for a moment, something familiar about them. Following his instincts, he stood and cross-checked the first few with the note from the desktop: all matches. The letters were initials of these people, but he still didn't know what the numbers meant.

Ahnri copied them all down. Were these people Viruses? If Elya feared a threat to Fugera, would she use these Viruses as captains in her army? Solo assassins? Would she have them imbue weapons with Death magic? He needed more information…

At the side of the list, disconnected from the rest and in a different handwriting, he recognized a name: *Natalia Aimar?*

"Natalia?"

He, Remi and Nat had been inseparable as children, though he hadn't seen Nat since Damond's death. Ahnri frowned at her name, unnerved. Cross-checking with the list of initials, she was not included there. Was her name here for a different purpose? He should find her. Maybe he could learn why she was on this list. He included that in his notes.

The final paper showed a dig plan—an architectural layout for a small room below the palace, to be built near the military training areas. He'd been in those subterranean caverns before, and recognized exactly where this new room would've been built.

Ahnri stared at it, dumbfounded for a moment. Then copied it down, like he had for all the documents here. He needed to be able to examine these again, all of it. And whatever that room was, he had a feeling it held answers.

He'd visit there next.

He'd barely finished copying the map when, from the archway, Pin let out a hiss, then bounded toward the secret entrance.

Ahnri hurried to stuff the papers back and close the hidden compartment and the drawer itself. Then he swore again. He hadn't cleaned the dust, nor had he tested how to *close* this thing.

He quickly ran a foot over the line of dust, scattering it as best he could. Then, praying whoever built it did so with the same thought process in mind, Ahnri pressed on the knot once more.

The shelf began to shift back into place.

"Thank the gods," Ahnri muttered, hurrying to join Pin as the doorway sealed with another *thunk*, followed by a small *click*.

He stood in darkness for a moment, knowing Pin was close by, and listened. The musty air felt suffocating, but he waited. As his eyes adjusted, however, he noticed a soft orange glow coming from the stone around him.

Veins of lumenite snaked through the rock here, lighting the space—at least, as far as he'd held the lantern. He breathed a little easier, grateful not be in total darkness for the moment. Beyond his hiding spot, a farther door clicked and creaked open, and a conversation carried through the wood of the bookshelf.

"—why they're refusing. Certainly, they know of one," the queen said, anger clear in her tone. Her footsteps made their way into the study, another set following behind.

"They are religious fools, obviously," a second voice said. Feminine, but one Ahnri didn't recognize. "They're going to need more encouragement."

"Or," the queen said, "we follow our last lead. I think we're out of options."

"It will have to be handled with care."

"It will be." A sigh, then a creaking sound Ahnri imagined to be a chair. "Reports from the general?"

"Recruitment is slow," the second voice said. "Without a cause to fight for, people aren't likely to become soldiers."

Elya let out a string of curses on the general and captains of her army. "I need something," she muttered. "Some way to motivate them. Threats are not useful when I'm trying to grow my military. I need them to *want* to be there..."

"Or," the second voice said, "at least *believe* they want to be there."

"Exactly," Elya said. "Once they're in the army, they're mine. They don't need to know what we're doing. No one does."

A beat of silence. "Perhaps you could offer some incentive for joining? Or raising the benefits, like pay or privileges?"

"Yes," Elya said. "Money can make people do amazing things...write that down." The creaking sound again, and footsteps. "I need a sleeping draught, and a masseuse."

"I'll see to it, Your Majesty."

A pause. "What is this?"

"Dust?" the second voice said, also closer now.

Ahnri mentally kicked himself.

"Perhaps the staff missed this section."

"Someone has been in here," the queen said, a shudder to her voice.

"Unlikely, Your Ma—"

"Someone is after me. They've gotten too close this time."

"Your Majesty—"

"I can't stay here tonight. Prepare the spare rooms, Brielle. Immediately. I need to—"

"Now, now," the other voice—Brielle—said calmly. "Even if someone was in here, why would they leave a trail of *dust*? This is nothing. Easily tidied up."

"But they got *in*, don't you see? If they got in, they—"

"They entered a room completely empty of life and unguarded," Brielle said firmly. "Of course they got in. It's all right. I want you to check your personal records, your desk, your books, any sensitive information, and I'll order for more guards."

"Yes," the queen said. "More…more guards."

"At the interior entrance and the balcony tonight."

"Yes. Yes, thank you."

Ahnri's heart raced in his chest. He'd never heard the queen like this before…worry and fear coloring her voice, paranoia making her jump to the worst conclusions. She wasn't *wrong*, however. He *had* gotten in. But he hadn't gotten in to hurt her.

Not tonight, anyway.

"I want someone to come test my wine as well," Elya called. "And clean up this dust. I don't want to see it anymore."

Her footsteps made a rapid pace out of the room as Brielle replied, "Right away, Your Majesty."

Her footsteps followed, and Ahnri tried to recall what he knew of Brielle…he recognized that name. The queen's adviser. Damond had mentioned her as well, hadn't he? She'd been pArt of the conversation…

Their voices carried from the far rooms, but he couldn't make out words. His heart racing, he turned away from the shelves and knelt to find Pin.

"Well, I suppose there's only one way to go from here," he whispered.

Placing the cat on his shoulders, Ahnri went to the handholds at the back of the space and began to climb. The lumenite's light grew dimmer the farther he went from where he'd held the lantern, and after about twenty feet he left it behind entirely, climbing through darkness.

The tunnel went straight up at least one level, then turned horizontal for a length, before hitting a dead end. So used to the outside and jumping from rooftop to rooftop, this space had grown oppressive to him. Especially as he had no light, and had to work completely by touch.

In an effort to make his mind think he'd chosen this, he closed his eyes to the darkness and felt around. Searching for any kind of latch or button similar to the one he'd found on the bookshelf.

It took a minute, but he found it, and pressed.

The stone before him shifted, and torchlight cascaded over them. He and Pin quickly exited, covered in dust. After letting his eyes adjust to the light, Ahnri reached in and pressed the button again to close the mechanism. He leaned back against the wall, forcing himself to take deep breaths of fresh air.

"Level four," he said, noting a particular well spring farther down the hall. "I recognize it. This is one of the apartment complex wings."

"*Mrrow?*"

"No, nowhere else tonight," Ahnri said. "Too much I need to remember. Let's head back to my rooms. I've got a report to write."

6

NATALIA

Natalia rubbed at her eyes, brushing curls back from her face as she started a fire in the stove and put a pot of water on to make rice for breakfast. Then she went into Mama's room to check on her.

"My heart," Mama said, raising a hand.

Nat gently took hold, sitting on the edge of the small cot. "How are you feeling?"

"I'm all right," Mama said. "I love sleep, but I am stiff."

"A warm meal should help then."

"Do we have any pear syrup?"

Nat's brow raised. "Sweet rice today?"

"Mmmm," Mama closed her eyes, smiling.

"I think we do," Nat said. "Let me check."

Nat drizzled the warm rice with cactus pear syrup and a pinch of salt, then brought it back to the bed, blowing on a spoonful before feeding it to Mama. They enjoyed a comfortable silence while she ate. When the bowl of rice was nearly gone, Mama sank deeper into her bed.

"Let's apply the medicine while you're relaxed," Nat said, reaching under the bed.

She lifted a box meant to appear heavy and full, but instead revealed a hidden cut-out where three items sat—a dark brown glass jar with a metal lid of deep purple, a tiny red cloth pouch, and a blue glass bottle corked at the top.

Callidian medicine. Her rat-catching money—and a significant part of their stipend—went toward this, lately. This medicine was the reason Nat couldn't rest longer than absolutely necessary. Because keeping Mama alive was more important than rest.

Nat removed all three containers, quickly setting the jar on the nightstand—despite it being the magic she herself wielded, holding it sent bumps across her skin.

"Natalia," Mama said softly. "You could try—"

"Mama, please don't ask me to," Nat said.

"It would be so much more powerful."

"And it could kill you as easily as I kill those rats," Nat snapped. "I can't risk that."

Mama closed her eyes, letting the subject drop.

Nat took a breath, centering herself. "I can't lose you."

Mama's hand found Natalia's knee, and squeezed. "I understand. I'll stop asking."

Nat turned away. She knew Mama didn't mean to lie, but this was the third time in a week she'd said she would stop asking. The illness wasn't in her mind, but it made her exhausted. That caused her to forget things...

Nat refocused on the medicines. There was an order to these, so said the Callidian medics she'd spoken to when Mama first fell ill. The blue bottle contained a liquid infused with Life magic. The jar held a salve infused with Death magic. And in the red pouch, a powder infused with Stability.

Having done this every morning, midday, and evening for three weeks, she worked quickly and efficiently, and Mama followed along. Gently lifting Mama's left arm, Nat pulled the loose tunic up slightly to reveal the spot under Mama's armpit where the lump grew. It appeared as a dark spot on the skin, slightly bulging and unnatural. Nat slipped on a pair of gloves, and began.

First, a pinch of the Stability powder on the tongue to clear Mama's mind while the other medicines worked.

Then, a spoonful of the Life liquid for her to swallow, and Mama would get a boost of healing and energy that should last long enough to protect her from the final piece. But if they weren't fast enough, the Life syrup would also assist the thing growing inside her—so the salve was next, to try to kill the thing. They had to be done as close together as possible, so the Life could fortify Mama, while the Death could wear away at the illness Mama couldn't fight on her own.

When she'd finished, and hid the expensive medicines back in their box, Nat threw the gloves in their sink to be washed for later. She let out a breath, loosening her shoulders as she sat again on the edge of Mama's bed.

"Thank you," Mama said.

"Of course," Nat said. "We need to get you better. The council needs you back."

"You're handling that very well, you know. I'm proud of you, my Natalia."

Nat scoffed quietly. "I feel like I'm barely hanging on. You're much better at politics than I am."

"You're better at it than you think."

"As long as I have you to guide me, I think I'll be all right. Then when you're better, you can take over again."

Mama's eyes grew sad, then. "My heart…"

"You should rest," Nat said, hastily standing. She knew what Mama had been about to say, and she did not want to hear it. "I don't have any jobs tonight, so I can stop by the market for more angfruit and still be home early." She placed a kiss on Mama's forehead, and turned to go.

"Natalia?"

She looked back. "Yes?"

"I love you, my heart."

"I love you too, Mama."

Nat exited Mama's room, dimming the lamp and closing the door to the bedroom. She stood near that doorway for some time, listening, waiting, until Mama's breathing had settled into a slow rhythm.

Taking care of Mama was getting more and more difficult each day. But she did it. Because Mama needed to live. And Nat would do anything to keep her.

Including, unfortunately, sit on the royal council and take notes like her own life depended on it.

Nat gathered her things quietly, using a two-pronged pin to twist back her hair, so it wouldn't draw too much attention. Notebooks and coin in her bag, she slung it across her torso and opened the door.

As she turned to lock her door, an older man turned the far corner, hobbling in her direction, a grey cat trotting along beside him. He had a curved back, his hood low, his face a mass of wrinkles. As he drew near, he gave her a slight bow. "Good morning," he said, voice like the creak of a door.

"Morning," she said, moving past him.

"Mrrow!" The cat approached Natalia, putting both paws up against her leg.

"Hello there," she said, crouching to pet it.

"Ah," the old man said. "You like cats?"

"The nice ones," Nat said.

The man chuckled, and Nat looked up to see him straighten his back. She watched with wide eyes as his face relaxed, and he lowered his hood to reveal the warm smile of a friend she hadn't seen in months.

"Ahnri?"

"The one and only." He grinned.

Nat flew forward and threw her arms around him, squeezing tightly. Ahnri had a way of disguising himself far too well, and had their entire lives. The number of times she and Remi had thought they were speaking to a stranger but it was really him—his appearance brought all those playful memories back to her in a rush.

"Where have you—" She pulled back, staring up at him. "I mean Remi said you'd left the city but he never told me why—some kind of royal secrets—you don't have to tell me where. But stars, it's been too long!"

Ahnri laughed, hugging her back. "It has been too long. Ah, let me introduce you to Pin—" Ahnri said, gesturing to the cat. "He's been following me since I returned to the city."

"Hello, Pin," Nat said, scratching the cat's ears. "Would you like some milk?"

"Mrrow!"

Nat re-entered her apartment and gathered a small bowl, pouring a bit of milk and setting it in the hallway for the cat.

"That's very kind of you," Ahnri said. "Tell me, how are you?"

Nat's joy faded slightly, being reminded of Mama, and Nat's own responsibilities. She wound her arm through Ahnri's and tugged him down the tunnel corridor, making her way toward the stairs up to the council room.

"What is it?" Ahnri said.

"I'm…fine," Nat said. "My mother came down with an illness, something the Cures can't seem to heal. Every time they try, it makes the thing worse."

"That's terrible," Ahnri said. "I'm sorry."

"I appreciate your sympathy," Nat said. "Unfortunately, Mama being ill means I've been asked to sit on the royal council to take notes for her."

Ahnri's eyes widened. "You're sitting on the council?"

"Temporarily," Nat clarified. "Until…"

"Until…she improves?" Ahnri said.

Nat opened her mouth to speak the lie she'd been saying for weeks. That of course Mama would improve, that she would be fine…but it wouldn't come.

They'd reached a wide staircase leading up to the next floor and the council room. As she stared up that hallway, she stopped walking, and spoke the truth.

"She's very sick," she said. "I'm doing all I can, but I'm worried it won't be enough."

"What all are you doing?" Ahnri asked. "If Life doesn't help…"

"Surprisingly," Nat said, "there is a Callidian Death medicine that is helping. But it requires precision, and regular applications, and…it seems to be maintaining Mama's health, but not improving it."

Ahnri frowned. "*Death* medicine?"

"Yes. In Calidar they infuse foods—sometimes even the ground—with the Powers, and something about the process keeps it contained until it can be ingested. It's rather incredible, though I've never seen it done."

Ahnri's face went from wide-eyed impressed to brows-crinkled curious in a flash. "Do you know anyone who can channel Death magic?"

Nat froze. Despite knowing and being close to Ahnri and Remi since age three, she'd managed to keep her abilities a secret, even from them. But then again, neither of them had never asked so directly before.

"I…" What was the question precisely? *Do I know anyone?* "I've known some," she managed.

"In Calidar?"

"There and here," she said. "But mostly I deal with the medics. They have a shop in the market on level two."

"That is fascinating."

"It's been…life changing. Quite literally."

Ahnri paused, and Nat shifted under his gaze. "You're worried. About your mother."

Nat gave a wry smile. "You read me too well."

"Can I help?" Ahnri asked.

Nat met his eyes, taking in a breath, then hugged him. He held her for a moment, and the familiarity of it gave Nat a boost of confidence. She often wished she could hug Remi the same way, but, well, there were rules surrounding royalty.

And truly, Remi had offered to help as well, but Nat felt…wrong, accepting help from the prince because of their friendship. Especially since the greatest help they could have at the moment would be more coin, in order to pay for more medicine.

"There's really nothing more to be done," she said, pulling away. "Nor anything I could ask you to do for me…a hug is enough."

"Well, I'm back in the city," Ahnri said. "But also…I'm *not* in the city, understand?"

Nat nodded her understanding. Ahnri had trained with Fugeran Intelligence; she'd been fairly certain his long absence had been related to that, and this was confirmation for her.

"I have a lot to do," Ahnri said, "but I'll try to keep an eye out for you, come see if you need another hug."

"Thank you. It's good to know you're here. And good luck."

Ahnri pulled up his hood with a bow of his head, and turned back the way they'd come—the grey striped cat following behind.

Nat took a moment to collect herself. She liked who she was around Ahnri—he made her more herself. Smiling, she continued toward the council room, slightly worried that she might now be late. As she rounded the last turn, however, she came face to face with the queen herself exiting the council room.

She stepped to the edge of the corridor and dropped into a curtsey. "Your Majesty."

Queen Elya approached, her gait elegant and her expression demure. "Good morning, Miss Natalia."

"Good morning, Your Majesty," Nat said, curtseying.

The queen stopped before Natalia, and Nat couldn't help a flush of nerves flooding her cheeks.

"Rise, child."

Nat slowly glanced up, straightening from her curtsey. She stood taller than the queen at her full height, though she attempted to curl in on herself a little, to appear smaller. Only now did she notice the attendants surrounding the queen—six guards, the adviser from the day before, and three young girls carrying trays of food.

"You are filling in for your mother, I believe?"

"Yes, Your Majesty," Nat said.

"Councilor Mari?"

"That's right, Your Majesty."

"Hmm…I see her in your features. Though of course—" The queen reached out to run a finger along a loose curl of Natalia's thick, coarse hair. "—some features come from your father's side, correct?"

"Yes…yes, ma'am." Nat fought the urge to flinch or bat her hand away. Her hair, despite being the same pale blonde of most Fugerans, drew an uncomfortable amount of attention with its shape and texture—which she got from her father. People unfamiliar with it often tried to touch it, and Natalia had grown used to slapping their hands away. However…this was the *queen*.

"Hmm," the queen said. "Your father is foreign. Do you know where he is?"

The words were like a punch to Nat's chest. She forced herself to take in a breath. "N-no, Your Majesty. He left to find his fortune…to support us. He hasn't come back yet."

"Hm." The queen pursed her lips. "Is your loyalty to Fugera true?"

"It is, Your Majesty," Nat said truthfully. Though she couldn't imagine replying any other way in this circumstance.

"You seem very dedicated to the task of filling in on the council. How is your mother?"

"Um…the same, ma'am."

"Does she require a great deal of care?"

"She does, ma'am."

"And you provide that, yes?"

"Yes, Your Majesty."

Behind the queen and her entourage, the council chamber doors were closing. Nat caught the eye of Remi inside, with a frown of confusion on his face.

"Miss Natalia," the queen said, "I have a task I believe you could help me with. I'd like to meet with you privately, soon, to discuss it. Would you be amenable?"

Nat's eyes widened. "I…yes, Your Majesty. Of course."

"In exchange for meeting with me, I will see that the two of you—you and your mother—have what you need. And if you agree to help me, you will be handsomely compensated."

Nat's chest filled with hope. "I would be beyond grateful, ma'am."

Queen Elya smiled softly. "I'll send word soon. Be on your way, child."

Nat bowed low as the queen and her associates continued on, leaving her behind. She glanced up in time to see the queen's adviser glancing back, and caught a glint of curiosity on the woman's face as they left.

Nat had refused to accept help from Remi on multiple occasions now, but finally she had an opportunity to *earn* it. Nat had no idea what help the queen needed or what or assistance she would bring, but the simple promise of possibility meant everything to her.

Feeling as though she were walking on clouds, Natalia took the final few steps toward the council chamber. As she reached for the door handle, however, her own pain attacked her.

A sharp pinch in her back, on the lower spine, taking her to her knees. Nat curled in on herself, her hand tightening around her satchel for comfort. The thing inside her attacked, squeezing her insides as easily as a press juicing berries for wine. And like the berries, she crumpled beneath the pressure.

Through the pain, Natalia reached for the shadows. Focusing, aiming…inside.

Carefully directing the magic, she sent it to the source of the pain. No purple light flashed this time—thankfully, her being in a public hallway—as the effect targeted a thing within her body. In a moment, the pain had subsided, but the magic lingered, as did a particular soreness that came after the pain. Together, it left her drained and nauseous.

She didn't know why she didn't kill herself every time she did this, but however it worked, it *was* working. Forcing slow, deep breaths, the memory of the pain like a stone holding her down, she dragged herself to her feet and pasted on a smile as she entered the royal council meeting.

It happened every few days, that she needed to fight off the thing growing inside her. But it always came back. The thing killing her mother had begun to slowly kill her.

7

AHNRI

Ahnri's chat with Natalia stuck with him. She'd seemed nervous when he'd asked about Viruses, but that wasn't unusual. The topic of Death magic—understandably—made most people nervous. Not to mention she'd already been upset from discussing her mother's circumstances. Though glad to have found her, he had no idea why her name would've been on a list of people in the queen's hidden drawer.

He spent the entire following day watching Elya again, verifying her locations and noting where her movements differed from the day before. But as the sun drew nearer to the horizon, his focus faltered in favor of his next meeting with the prince.

He made his way up the tower, taking his time rather than hurrying up the outside like he might normally. Level ten was very high, and Ahnri had come a little too close to dying recently. The higher he went, the more empty the tower corridors became. So much of the population had spread out from the ground level that the bulk of business, trade, and socializing took place down there. That left these higher levels basically empty save for a handful of people trying not to be found by the law, and maybe some rats.

Ahnri made his way to the western wing of level ten, where the stone had begun to crumble a few years back. Deemed unsafe for habitation, no one lived there anymore. That made it a perfect spot for friends to meet—particularly when they didn't want anyone to listen in on their conversation.

He approached the spot slowly, nostalgia welling in his throat as he recognized specific sections of the space. There, he'd once dared Remi to swallow a lizard. And over here, they'd stayed up far too late discussing the intricacies of fried sael bread. Remi had been under house arrest for a week for that one night, but it had been worth it.

Five months didn't sound like much, but it could be so long...

As he neared their spot, he looked up and froze. Two armed royal guards stood before him. Fear flared in his chest and he moved to run.

"Wait!" one of them said. "It's all right, we're expecting you."

Ahnri halted, waiting for more information.

"He told us you'd probably try to run. He's back there." The other gestured out the crumbled doorway.

Ahnri came forward, caution ringing in his mind. They nodded as he passed, then made their way farther down the hall toward the only entrance to this section of the ruins.

Ahnri rounded a final corner, coming into the light of the sunset and a warm breeze carrying the scent of ivy and desert rain, to find the prince waiting, sitting on a fallen wall they'd always treated like a bench.

"Did you tell them who I am?" Ahnri asked.

Remi stood, turning to face him. "No…I told them I'm meeting with an informant."

"How much time do we have?"

"Only ten minutes," Remi said. "But we won't be interrupted."

"Good. That's…perfect." For a moment, he took in the view. A stunning sight of pinks and oranges as the sun fell beyond the distant Arontas mountain range. Then his eyes sought the prince. The way the waning light colored his skin, and pinks and golds reflected in his pale hair.

Remi noticed him watching. "What?"

Ahnri smiled. "Enjoying the view."

Remi rolled his eyes, but there was a slight flush to his cheeks.

Ahnri opened his mouth to speak, but cut off as Pin rounded the corner and jumped up onto his shoulders.

"Ah, I believe you've met Pin?"

"I did." Remi reached out to pet the cat. "Thank you, little messenger. He's adorable."

"He's been following me since I got back to Isille."

Remi scratched at Pin's back, and the cat leaned into his arms to snuggle his head under Remi's chin. "Oh, he is darling," Remi said, laughing. "You, sir cat, are welcome to visit me anytime."

"Does that invitation extend to me?" Ahnri asked.

Remi met Ahnri's eyes for a moment before turning away, some kind of sadness in his eyes that Ahnri couldn't parse.

Ahnri took half a step back. "I know it used to, but…"

Remi set Pin down, moving to the ledge where he leaned against the broken wall, looking out over the city and the distant dunes.

"I'd like it to," Remi said. "I…first I thought you were dead, and then you were back and I couldn't help fearing maybe…maybe you'd stayed away because someone else had caught your eye…"

"Rem." Ahnri laughed softly. He stayed a few steps back in case he was reading this wrong. "My 'eye' doesn't get caught on anyone but you. And you have my heart—that's not going to change."

Remi wrapped one arm around himself, gripping the opposite shoulder as though for security. "It's silly, I know. But I haven't had anyone I could be as close to since you left. I see Natalia nearly every day but we never get to spend time together as friends. It's been…well, I've been very lonely."

Ahnri moved to the prince's side. He slid his hand into Remi's, interlocking their fingers slowly so that if Remi wanted to pull away, he could. And even then, Ahnri asked, "Is this all right?"

"It is," Remi said, though a tear rolled down his cheek.

Ahnri reached up to brush it away. "Tell me how to help?" Ahnri said. "Please. I want to, but I don't want to get it wrong."

"Kiss me," Remi said.

Ahnri did not hesitate. He stepped closer and wrapped his hand behind Remi's neck to draw him in. Their lips met, and the familiarity of it took Ahnri's breath away. Remi was soft, pampered, all smooth skin and gentle touches. Ahnri was the hard angles and callouses; every ounce of strength he reserved for climbing came to call as he held on, and remembered what it felt like to kiss his prince.

His heartbeat reverberated in his head. One kiss turned into two, then five, then a dozen. Remi tugged at Ahnri's tunic so desperately it pulled loose from his belt.

How he'd missed this. He'd been gone so long…

Ahnri gripped the prince by his hip with one hand, pulling him closer, the other hand buried in his hair. Tugging gently, Ahnri angled Remi's head back, giving himself access to kiss the perfect skin of the prince's jaw, and neck, and collarbone…

"Ahnri…"

That voice. Ahnri wanted to listen to it forever. And yet…that voice was at risk.

Danger…secrets…lies…

Remi's mother was keeping things from him. From the army, from everyone. Remi could be hurt…

Ahnri couldn't stop himself. Remi hummed softly as Ahnri's hand moved to press against his lower back. Remi held tight, fingers digging into to Ahnri's shoulders as though he were a lifeline.

Danger…

The forged letters, the potential to frighten Elya into rash action—the threat pressed like a knife to all their throats. Ahnri had to tell him…couldn't lose him…Remi had a right to know…

Ahnri dragged himself away. His hands trembled. His mind reeled. His heart beat a frantic pace. The prince's voice reminded him exactly why he was here, why he'd come back—to protect what he loved. Stop Elya from hurting anyone the way she'd hurt him.

He braced himself. "Rem, there's something—"

"Why did you stop?" Remi said.

Ahnri refocused. Remi stood before him, disheveled and disoriented, cheeks and neck flushed, his bright eyes wide and glinting in the sunset like amethyst. The prince stared at him expectantly, and Ahnri wasn't sure he could give what Remi wanted. Ahnri shook his head. He couldn't think of that right now.

"There's something I need to tell you," Ahnri said. "Before we go any farther."

"What else could possibly need to be said?" Remi snapped.

"It's about your mother, she's being lied to. She has fake letters—"

"You—" Remi waved his hands, cutting Ahnri off. "You came to a clandestine sunset meeting and kissed me like *that* to tell me about my *mother?*"

"Remi, I would love nothing more than to spend every minute of all my days kissing you."

"Then *why aren't* we?"

"Your mother is making decisions based on forged documents! You've got to listen—"

"No, *you* listen!" Remi's already flushed face grew angry. "You have been gone for. Five. Months. The last three of which I thought you were *dead.*"

Ahnri felt his heart crack at the prince's words.

"I prayed," Remi said, "night after night that you were alive, and then you reappear and sweep into my life again and I wish it could be the same but it's not. I'm working with Mother much more closely now, and it's a *good thing.*"

"I'm worried," Ahnri said firmly. "About your mother, and about you. Do you have any idea what she's actually doing?"

"I can't listen to this." Remi waved his hands as though he could make it all disappear. "Do you know how this makes me feel? Like you're only seeing me to use me for information on my mother."

"That's not true."

"Then what *is* this?"

Ahnri fought for words, but they weren't coming easily. "I—I don't want you to get hurt."

"I'm *fine!*" Remi shouted. "My mother *trusts* me now, and I her." He stepped back, forcing himself to take a breath. "I hear you. You say she's working off of forged documents? Fine, I'll speak to her and find out. Maybe then you'll stop pulling on my heart only to let it *snap* back at me like some barbed whip."

Ahnri froze. Desert wind lifted his hair from a sweaty brow for a moment before it settled. All he wanted was to tell Remi everything, but…if Elya knew he'd discovered even this much, she'd come for him. The risk was too great. He couldn't say more.

"Remi, I—"

"I need time," Remi said. His breathing had grown ragged again.

Ahnri's heart broke knowing he'd caused it.

"All I wanted was to see you," Remi said. "To know you're real, and here, and alive and you still…care for me. But obviously you have other priorities right now."

"Remi."

"I'll put the ribbon out when I'm ready to talk again."

"Remi, please—"

"*Goodnight*, Ahnri."

Then he was gone.

Ahnri stood there, listening as Remi and the guards left; the sound of their footsteps drifted back to him until they were out of earshot. Ahnri's heart pounded inside his chest, and his jaw clenched, trying to hold himself together.

The touch, the feel of him…the kiss…the refusal to listen… the disbelief…or was it distrust?

It was no use. Ahnri went to the edge of the broken exterior wall, and looked down. Then, swallowing the hurt rising in him, he leaped.

The upper sections of the tower city were smoother than those below, weathered from time and the elements. Ahnri set his feet and let himself slide, faster and faster, past level nine, eight, seven, six, until the angle of the tower shifted slightly and he managed to slow himself before catching a window ledge. Then, he began to make his way around the structure.

From one handhold to the next, letting his feet find grip through his boots, he didn't stop. He leaped and gripped in the fading light of dusk as sweat beaded on his skin and short strands of pale hair fell across his vision. He went down past level five, four, then back up toward level six, then seven once more but this time on the northern section.

Remi leaving angry had caused emotions to rise in Ahnri's heart that he wasn't sure how to handle. And so, he wasn't handling them. He would give his heart something else to focus on—not dying—in order to keep the emotions at bay. Put them in boxes. Shove them to the back of his mind. Hidden away.

Level eight. Level nine. The tower's smoother surface here meant fewer handholds, and he had to hold occasionally to locate his grips. Which meant the emotions were catching up to him.

Pain. Grief. Loss.

Damond…

Watching Remi walk away…the thought of losing him struck like a knife to Ahnri's chest. The only time he could remember feeling more pain was when he learned of Damond's death.

Reluctantly, Ahnri found a window that led into a deserted hallway on level six, where he could at least walk back to his room. Out of breath and aching, he slumped to the floor, closing his eyes.

As far as Ahnri knew, the mucking queen hadn't bothered to give Damond a proper funeral. Ahnri didn't even know where he was buried. Or *if* he'd been buried. It was possible Elya had simply burned the body and scattered the ashes to the desert wind.

He took comfort in knowing Damond would've found a certain poeTry to that.

Ahnri bowed his head. His hand formed a fist. When he'd learned what happened, the agony of loss had quickly morphed into anger, and then to determination—to escape the queen at all costs. To never give her the satisfaction of his service again. And then he'd met Carina, and Merlin, and it seemed as though he might have a chance at something greater…

And yet, here he was again. Back in this city, slumped in a corner, that same agony raking over his heart like a thunderbird's talons.

How was he supposed to stop Elya if Remi didn't believe him? Was he supposed to just work *against* the boy he loved?

He put his face in his hands. He'd known it would be a possibility, but he'd hoped…

"*Mrrrow?*" Nearby, Pin had rounded the corner, his gold eyes staring, worried.

Ahnri sighed. "Sorry for leaving you behind."

Pin blinked. Then approached and nuzzled his head under Ahnri's hand.

Scratching the cat's ears gave a sense of comfort, somehow. As though that simple act would make everything right. It wouldn't, he knew. But for a moment, he let himself believe it might.

"What do I do?" he asked out loud. He didn't know if he was asking the cat, or simply voicing his concern to the nothingness around him, but the question remained.

Pin's eyes grew wide and sad, but—as always—he couldn't really respond.

Then, Ahnri wished he could ask Damond for advice. For the most part, Ahnri was capable of taking care of himself. He was strong, smart, trained—he knew this, and he used it…but there would always be these things he couldn't parse. Damond used to help him with those.

"*You're thinking too much*," Damond would say. Or, "*Now you're not thinking quite enough*." It always depended on a context Ahnri had never been able to grasp.

The sun continued to set while he sat there. There was so much to do, to consider, that he sat frozen. Unable to commit to any one thing, knowing the first would affect the second and so on.

Pin snuggled against Ahnri's leg.

"I don't know," Ahnri said. "I can't let Elya go through with what she's planning, I know that. Even a small force of soldiers wielding Death magic would be devastating. But I hate lying to Remi."

Pin mewed quietly.

Fugeran tradition said that when a person saved one's life, one owed their life to them. Elya had tried to manipulate this to force Ahnri into a blood debt to her—tried to make it out that her sparing him was her *saving* him—but Ahnri hadn't seen it that way. However, when Merlin brought Ahnri back from the brink of death, Ahnri *did* honor that. But Merlin had left, and asked Ahnri to serve Carina in his place.

His loyalty was to *her* now. But that meant keeping secrets from the one person he'd always told everything…

"I need someone to talk to. I need advice. But I don't know who, I don't have anyone—"

Then, in an instant, an idea formed in his mind.

"Come on," he said to Pin. "I need to send a message."

8

MERLIN

Merlin woke to the pain of something sharp slicing his fingertip.

"Ow!" He flailed, swatting at whatever had done it.

Kahn bounded away, letting out an offended screech.

I was only trying to wake you, Kahn said, through a series of clicks and gestures.

Most people couldn't understand birds, but Merlin had spent enough time around them to learn the language.

Merlin sighed, shaking the finger. "Right. We need to come up with a better way of doing that." Even as he spoke, however, his body drew from whatever magic it was he had in him, and closed the bite marks.

He straightened, stretching as he gazed out at the Fugeran desert and the moon rising on the horizon. He lay at the highest level of the city of Isille, in a room with hardly any walls left and a ceiling that seemed about to fall in.

A pristine sword lay sheathed and wrapped in fabric, propped in a corner as far from him as possible; Merlin could always feel its presence.

You'll be glad I woke you.

"Is that right?" Merlin muttered, reaching for the tie on Kahn's leg.

I don't have to show you their messages, you know.

Merlin eyed the bird. "I know. And I'm grateful. I don't mean to be rude, but being woken up only an hour after I've gone to sleep—especially by a cut on my finger—tends to make me grumpy."

He unrolled the letter carefully, doing his best to not crease the paper in any odd way. At least he knew this one would be in Ahnri's hand, not Carina's. Seeing her handwriting always hit him like a lightning bolt to the chest.

Every time, he reminded himself that he could disappear from this world at any moment, and if he were there it would leave her heartbroken. He refused to put her through that. He'd left because they'd both agreed it was for the best…that didn't make it not hurt.

Carina was doing wonderfully, however, and she did not need him pining over her. Being a young person again—particularly after being old for so long—was a wonderful experience indeed, but it came with downsides.

Namely, hormones.

Could he age himself up and get rid of them? Certainly. Did he want to? No. He wanted to hurt a little, because this pain was the kind that the magic couldn't heal. And if he was being honest, he savored it just a little. It made him feel like maybe everything he'd been doing for the past thousand-some-odd years had mattered.

Just a little.

Merlin read the note, then blinked, rubbing his eyes, and read it again. Ahnri's notes were usually coded, but this one was…most definitely not.

Merlin-

I hope you're close, I can't spare Kahn for too long. I know it's been months, but I could use some advice if you're near Isille. Can you meet me? If not, at least let me know you received this. I can send more details coded.

-Ahnri

"Well hell."

Kahn laughed.

"Did *you* tell him I'm here?"

He can't understand me, Kahn said. *Even if he could, I wouldn't have told him. You said you wanted to remain hidden.*

"That doesn't seem to have helped."

He really could use someone to talk to. All he has right now is a stupid cat—I think it wants to eat me.

Without answering, Merlin pulled a freshly killed rat from nearby, and set it on the floor in front of the hawk.

Thank you.

"No, thank you," Merlin said. "I know you don't have to do this, but it means a lot to me to keep an eye on them."

I know.

For a moment, Kahn stood there, staring, and Merlin's ability to read him stalled. "What?"

You're a good person, Merlin.

Merlin scoffed. "How would you know."

I watch, Kahn said. *People come in all varieties, like the rodents of the desert. Some are sturdy and durable, others soft and easy pickings. You're one of the sturdy ones. You stick around.*

"Right. Like how I stayed with Carina?"

That's different. She asked you to go.

"I offered," Merlin said. "To save her pain. They're not the same thing."

Kahn remained still, but Merlin's emotions were getting to him again. He took a breath, letting his eyes scan over the eastern dunes of Fugera. If he looked hard enough, he thought he could see Avir Lake barely visible on the horizon.

Kahn clicked his beak to get Merlin's attention again. *Why don't you go back?*

"What?"

To Carina, Kahn said. *If you miss her, and you're still here after all this time...why not go back?*

Merlin turned away, staring at the blankets below him. "I made a promise. I don't know why the stupid sword's magic works the way it does, I only know that I *don't* know when it's going to shunt me somewhere new. And after everything she'd been through, I can't just disappear on Carina."

So you keep an eye?

"So I keep an eye," Merlin said. "At least until I'm whisked away."

They sat in silence for a moment, and Merlin's mind wandered back to what Ahnri had told him all those months ago. His father had overheard some top-secret information and been killed for it, then Ahnri had been sent away on the mission to Medelios. And now he'd come back to Isille—Merlin assumed—to try and learn more about what had killed his father. Ahnri moved with purpose and direction; he knew what he wanted and would see it through.

Meanwhile, in a stunning example of—well, *not that*—Merlin had come to Isille more or less by accident, simply to wait out his time until Excalibur took him to its next future-monarch. He hated wandering aimlessly like this, especially knowing he could be spending the time with Carina—he shook himself. No. They'd agreed. He'd promised.

Nearby, Kahn clicked his beak, breaking Merlin's train of thought. *So…do you have anything to reply to Ahnri?*

"I don't know." Merlin slumped back onto his bedroll. "Despite what you and he might think, I can't just snap my fingers and fix all his problems. The magic around me guarantees the success of *one* thing, and that's already done this round."

I don't think he needs magic, Kahn said, his clicking and chirps softer. *I think he needs a friend.*

That caused Merlin to waver. How long had it been since someone had asked to talk to him as a friend? With no other motive? Ahnri would probably ask for help, but if all he truly needed was a listening ear and maybe some words of wisdom…Merlin could do that.

He's worried about the prince, Kahn said.

Merlin frowned. "The prince?"

Ahnri loves him, Kahn said. *Though I don't know if he's ever said it out loud.*

"Aaahhh." Understanding clicked in Merlin's mind. "Ahnri loves the prince, the prince is an innocent bystander, but working against the queen means possibly hurting the prince by proxy."

I…think so.

Merlin thought for a moment. He'd grown close to Ahnri while helping Carina, and if he *could* help, he gladly would. Going to his pack, he pulled out ink and paper and wrote.

Ahnri–
You're damn lucky. I'm happy to talk. Meet me at the Dusty Dragon on level five in an hour.
–Merlin

He rolled it up and moved to Kahn, slipping it into the small cylinder on the hawk's leg.

You're staying here, then?

"I was already planning that," Merlin said. "If Ahnri needs someone to talk to, I can certainly listen." He met the bird's eyes, "I know he's important to you. He's important to Carina too, and to me. I'll do my best to help him."

Thank you.

With that, Kahn flew off into the darkness. Merlin watched as he circled a few times, before diving into a window a few levels below.

Lying back on his bedroll, Merlin stared up into the night sky, watching the stars peek out one by one. He'd finally asked Kahn the other day how he and Ahnri had become friends, and the story was a simple one. Kahn had been bought by Damond, Ahnri's surrogate father. Kahn joined their family only a few years ago, purchased from a traveling salesman in the Fugeran market. In a matter of weeks, Damond had trained Kahn to carry messages. The bird was incredibly intelligent, even if most humans couldn't understand him.

It didn't take long before Merlin grew restless, and began to gather his things. This included the stupid sword, and trying to ignore the ache in his chest whenever he thought about the person it technically belonged to at the moment. Everything neatly packed, he made his way down into the tower city of Isille to wreak some havoc, and find the spy boy.

9

AHNRI

Seeing Merlin's reply, relief washed over Ahnri like the arrival of a thunderstorm. He hurried to the Dusty Dragon, a slightly lower-class tavern on the inner sector of level four. He hadn't stopped for a drink since arriving. A shame, as Isille had some of the best spirits in the continent—or so he'd been told by many a traveler. Ahnri saw them less as noteworthy and more like nostalgia.

Dim light filled the space, with a ceiling so low he could reach up and touch it. A dozen or so circular tables were scattered throughout, with most occupied this time of night, and the bar at the back of the room spanned the entire wall looking well-kept, if a little worn on the edges. Ahnri approached a tall woman behind the bar whose hair fell in a thick braid down her back.

"Evening," she said as he drew near. "What would you like?"

"Something strong," Ahnri said, taking a seat. "And an ale to wash it down."

"I've got just the thing." She reached under the counter and pulled out a clear glass bottle with a pale pink liquid inside, labeled with a black and white sketch of a basket of sunsetberries. She poured him a healthy measure, and passed it over. "That'll be two silver."

Something bumped against his leg. It was Pin, tapping him with a paw.

"Right," he said. He offered the barwoman three silver, and said, "Do you have any scraps of meat from dinner, for my cat? And maybe some sael bread for me?"

The woman leaned over the bar to look down at Pin, and beamed. "Adorable. I'm sure we can find something. Give me a moment."

She disappeared through a swinging door. While waiting, Ahnri leaned against the bar and took a moment to close his eyes. Then…listened. Something he hadn't yet done since arriving back in Isille, and he really should've been.

To his left, a table of men let out boisterous laughs.

"—make me climb all those stairs and ramps only to get to this place."

"Quit complaining. You know it's better than the ground-level bars."

"You could use the exercise anyway!"

Meanwhile, a table to Ahnri's right sounded much more subdued.

"—heard about that sinkhole north of the city?"

"Two camels lost. I feel for them."

"At least his goods made it past. Did you know—"

Ahnri heard the door to the kitchens open and opened his eyes in time to see the bartender set a plate of trimmings in front of him, along with a second plate of freshly fried sael bread, dusted with sugar.

"There you are, love. Enjoy."

"Thank you," Ahnri said, then went to find an empty table out of the way of foot traffic. He set the plate on the floor beside him, and Pin helped himself.

Finally seated, Ahnri took a sip of his drink, savoring the mixture of sweet and tart, as well as the kick to the back of his throat at the end. Maybe this could help clear his head. He watched around the bar, noting the men he'd heard speaking before. He hadn't heard anyone discussing the army recruitment or any suspicions about the queen, so maybe the general public wasn't worried…hopefully that was a good thing.

Ahnri finished the stronger drink and took a few gulps of his ale and bites of his bread before a pale, dark-haired man entered. Ahnri watched him go to the bar and order wine, before coming to join him.

Merlin had grown a bit of a beard since the last time Ahnri had seen him. He raised his glass in greeting. "It's very good to see you."

"Likewise," Merlin said, raising his glass in turn. "You look rough though."

"I've only been back in Isille for three days," Ahnri said. "And I've got a lot on my mind."

"Well, before we start, I want to show off." He dug in his pocket and pulled out a pouch, which he opened and dumped onto the table.

A set of Sticks made of a wood so dark it appeared black in this light, with marks painted in white and lines decorating the ends.

Ahnri picked one up, admiring the craftsmanship. "These are beautiful."

"You got me hooked," Merlin said. "I have three sets now, and it's all your fault."

"Well, you still can't beat me with any of them."

Merlin scooped up his set and put it away. "Maddening how this one game eludes me. All right, I can't promise I have all the answers, but," he tapped at his temple, "young as I look, I still have centuries of wisdom in here, and I've been told I'm an excellent listener. So. Lay it on me."

Ahnri didn't recognize the saying, but it got the point across. He looked around to be certain they weren't overheard. "Carina sent me here to gain intelligence on what the queen is planning. Based on what my father heard that got him executed—Damond, you remember?"

"I'm following, go on."

"I found," he leaned in, lowering his voice further. "I found multiple letters from other kingdoms asking Fugera to enter into negotiations. A series of them, leading to threats of attack if Isille doesn't agree to terms."

"Which kingdoms?"

"Somnuria, Calidar, and Medelios. Except—" he cut off another question from Merlin, "—they're fakes. Forgeries. The one from Medelios was signed in Carina's name, but it was *not* her handwriting or her seal."

"So you're saying—" Merlin started.

"Either someone is maniPulating Elya into believing she's being threatened, or Elya herself had these made to convince others of that. Either way, she's working on something down in a secret room below the city with a hidden entrance, and I'm certain it has to do with forming some kind of elite squad of Viruses."

Merlin sat back in his chair, crossing his arms. "Is she only *gathering* them, or also training them to use their abilities in a certain way?"

"I don't know," Ahnri said.

"Hmm…" Merlin leaned back in his chair, crossing his arms. "I don't like that this puts Carina in danger."

"There's something else," Ahnri said, staring at his hands. "I've been…close friends with the prince for most of our lives, and—"

Merlin sipped his wine loudly. Ahnri looked up to see Merlin eyeing him over the lip of the cup with one brow cocked in interest.

"Why do you have to make that face?"

"Why do *you* have to pretend that 'close friends' is a sufficient description for possibly the most important relationship in your life?"

Those words were a punch to Ahnri's chest. "How did you know—"

"Kahn told me."

Ahnri turned away, staring at a burn spot on the table's surface. He spoke softly, hesitantly. "I tried telling him his mother is planning something dangerous, but he wouldn't listen to me. And then he left angry."

"And your inclination is to explain everything to fix the problem so that Remi won't be mad at you anymore."

Ahnri grimaced. "Why do you have to be so…accurate."

"I think it comes from *literal lifetimes* of observation."

Ahnri sighed. Yes, he hated knowing he'd upset Remi. Hated knowing he couldn't simply spend time being close to the prince without betraying him…

Or betraying himself?

Ahnri's loyalty to Carina centered on a life debt, his knowledge that she was a genuinely good person strengthened that bond. He trusted her, and did not take that lightly. While he hadn't known Carina for long, he did feel he knew her deeply. She now ruled Medelios with compassion—and it was working. The kingdom had grown stronger by far than it had been five months before. *That* deserved his loyalty.

On the other hand, Fugera was his home. His comfort place, the most familiar thing in his life. Remi represented that in many ways. In their youth they'd been nearly inseparable.

They'd grown up together, gotten into trouble together, told each other secrets, and kept each other safe. He *knew* Remi.

But Ahnri also knew Elya. A more or less absent parent who had left the childrearing to Remi's father, or to governesses, nursemaids, and babysitters. Ahnri could count on one hand the number of times he'd seen Elya approach Remi in their youth…which, now he thought of it, made her appearance in his room a couple of days ago extremely odd. But Remi had said she'd changed in the months Ahnri had been gone…

Changed how, though?

Hadn't he just witnessed her instability the previous night? A bit of dirt had led her to nearly sleep in a separate suite entirely because she worried someone would come for her. Elya had always ruled with a heavy hand. The fact that she'd given Ahnri a chance to serve her had been a surprise, but also not. Because she'd used tradition to try to get him to obey. It hadn't been murderous, but it *had* been manipulative.

Remi *was* his heart, his home. Everything he'd known and loved for most of his life. He didn't want to work against that. But Remi was connected to Elya, who had dangerous plans. Her path would result in death.

Was it loyalty to Fugera to support that, or loyalty to stop it?

"Last time I saw someone think this hard, he had mathematical calculations floating around his head."

Ahnri blinked himself back to the present. Merlin watched him intently.

"I got you a refill," Merlin said.

Ahnri took a drink.

"This is really weighing on you, isn't it?"

"It is."

"Sounds like you have a choice to make, my friend."

"But what's the right choice?"

"I can't tell you that, unfortunately."

Ahnri grunted, putting his face in his hands.

"Listen," Merlin said. "I'm here in the city if you need to talk. Or if you need healing or any other magic I can offer, I'm happy to do it. But I cannot make life-altering decisions *for* you. You're the only one who can do that."

"Right," Ahnri said. "I suppose I understand that."

"Whatever you choose," Merlin said, "my advice is this: stay true to yourself, and accept that not everyone will see the same truth you do. You have a moral compass inside you, Ahnri, and it is dependable. Part of life is learning how to hold your ground, or, learning how to adjust. If you've learned something that has genuinely changed what you believe, don't be afraid to change it. But if you're simply sitting here asking me to say you don't have to do a difficult thing because it'll mean standing up against someone you love and respect—whether that's Remi or Carina—I'm sorry. I can't do that."

Ahnri let out a breath. The memory of Remi stepping away from him, disappointed and hurt, replayed across his mind.

"Sometimes people grow apart," Merlin said quietly. "That's not bad or wrong, that's life. If losing someone means betraying yourself, it's not worth fighting to keep them around."

Ahnri closed his eyes. He'd already lost his parents—he hardly remembered them, and that alone hurt to think about—and then he'd lost Damond…Remi was all he had.

But Remi refused to listen. This had become bigger than their relationship. If Elya's plans succeeded, she would hurt more people than she would help—and that included Remi. That alone was reason to stop her.

"There it is."

Ahnri blinked. "There what is?"

"That look." Merlin grinned. "You've decided."

"But I haven't—"

"You may not know it yet," Merlin said, standing, "but you have. Oh, who's this?"

Pin had stood and moved to place his paws on Merlin's leg.

"Ah, Pin," Ahnri said. "He's been following me since I got here."

Merlin picked up the cat, poking at him.

Pin hissed, batting at Merlin's hand.

"Interesting. He's got some magic in him."

Ahnri's head snapped up. "I knew it."

"Stability, I think," Merlin said. "It's hard to tell."

"Is that why you're so smart?" Ahnri asked Pin.

"Mrrow!"

Ahnri turned to Merlin. "What did he say?"

"How should I know?" Merlin said. "I told you I speak Hawk, not Cat." He let Pin hop to the floor, then patted Ahnri's shoulder. "I'm staying up in the highest level. Let me know if you need anything. I'll be around. Oh, and Ahnri?"

"Yes?"

Merlin hesitated a moment, then said, "Don't tell Carina you saw me, all right? It might hurt her, and that's the last thing I want."

Ahnri understood. He nodded.

Merlin made his way out of the bar. Only now did Ahnri realize he'd been picking at the rough table surface, tiny pieces of wood now piled like the start of a campfire. Nerves were getting to him.

He loved his work—spying and investigating—that's where his skills lie. Then the fact that Remi didn't believe him made it all far more difficult; he couldn't tell-all to the prince whose mother was the enemy. Had the time apart caused this rift? Did Ahnri need to spend more time with him, rebuild the trust between them?

There wasn't time for time.

"I can't..." he started. "I have to follow my orders. Remi will...hopefully he'll understand in the end."

"*Mrrow?*" Pin said from the chair beside him.

"Yeah," Ahnri said. "I'll be all right."

Next steps. He had to get more information, find a way into that room, stop whatever was happening there.

And pray that Remi would forgive him when this was all over.

Interlude

–

Percy

Percy followed Ahnri back to his rooms, making sure he wasn't going to jump off the tower again—that had been a shock. He didn't know humans knew how to do that.

When they got back, Percy made sure to snuggle up beside Ahnri to help him fall asleep. He knew humans did scary things when they were hurt or sad, but Percy found that often, snuggling up to something warm and soft seemed to help them.

And—bonus—Percy got scritches out of it.

Once Ahnri had fallen asleep however, Percy got up and went to make sure he knew where that other man was staying—whatever his name was, with the grey eyes. He'd promised to help Ahnri, and so Percy wanted to make sure he had the right smell.

So he could find him again. If he needed to.

PART TWO

BREAK

IO

NATALIA

Natalia applied Mama's medicines and made sure she was asleep before closing the door to her room as softly as possible. Even a simple breakfast of rice and dried fruit was enough to exhaust her.

A knock sounded at the door then. Nat frowned. They hadn't been expecting anyone… She went to answer—

—and came face to face with Queen Elya.

"Ah, Miss Natalia."

Nat dropped to one knee in the doorway. "Your Majesty," she said.

A soft chuckle rose from the queen. "We came to have a word with you, in private."

Nat took a breath, forcing herself to stay calm. The *queen* was visiting her apartment? Blinking, she took in the rest of the details: the queen herself wore far more casual clothing than

Natalia had ever seen her, including a cloak with a wide hood that covered her face almost entirely. Behind her stood her personal adviser, and six guards holding spears.

"Of course," Nat said. She stepped aside to allow the queen to enter, and the adviser followed.

"Stay outside," the queen ordered her guards.

The guards took up positions surrounding the door, and down the hallway in each direction. Nat closed it, turning to face her monarch. She looked from the queen to the adviser and back, confused. "Have I done something wrong, Your Majesty?"

"No no, child," the queen said. "We simply have a few questions for you." Her gaze fell on the small table and two chairs nearby. "Shall we sit?"

Nat did so, across from the queen. The adviser stood near the door. Confusion tangled her thoughts. Why would the queen herself come to their apartment, and not summon Natalia to the throne room or something?

"We've seen your dedication lately; your work has been nothing but precise," the queen said, clasping her hands in her lap. "I'm extremely pleased. For someone so young, I hadn't anticipated such care."

Nat bowed her head. "Thank you, Your Majesty. I only want to help my mother keep up with her duties."

"A worthy cause," the queen said. "Now, Miss Natalia. My adviser and I are engaging in a very important work. One that we hope will strengthen Fugera for years to come. However, we find ourselves in need of more minds. And Brielle suggested you."

Nat blinked, glancing at the adviser. "I'm sorry…me?"

"Yes, you," the queen said. She leaned forward slightly, an excited glimmer in her eyes as she met Nat's gaze. "We know what you can do, Natalia."

Fear snaked up Nat's back at these words and she stood, knocking the chair over in her haste. She reached toward the darkness behind her, drew in the shadows, and moved to block the door to Mama's bedroom.

"No, no," Brielle said, stepping forward, extending a hand. "It's all right. Please."

Nat's eyes were wide, her mouth had gone dry. "How did you know?"

"Every Vessel born is recorded by the priests," Brielle said. "Despite you not using your abilities much, your name has been listed since you were born."

Nat gritted her teeth, trying not to let frustration overtake her. She'd heard that there were ways to tell when an infant would have Vessel abilities, but she'd never researched it. She should ask Mama what that meant. For now, she refocused on the two women before her.

"And what do you want with me?"

"We only want to talk," Brielle said. "Please."

Nat's hands trembled, but as her eyes darted from one woman to the other, she saw nothing but caution and calm. Nat did not want to kill. She did not want to hurt them. Slowly, she safely released the magic she'd drawn in and lowered her hands to her side—instinctively folding her skirt to form another bit of shadow.

"I can listen," she said.

The two exchanged a quick glance Nat couldn't read. Then the queen said, "We would like to ask for your assistance. We need someone like you."

Nat eyed them both. "Why me?"

Queen Elya gestured to Brielle.

"We're conducting some experiments," Brielle said, "surrounding the Powers granted by the gods. We've concluded some amazing things in regard to the other three, but we couldn't find a Virus to help with the final one."

"So, we went to the priests, asked for their records," the queen said, "and saw your name. Someone sitting on the royal council, who we already have a great deal of trust for."

Nat said nothing, but let the words sink in. The *queen* trusted her? Needed her help? Her abilities, the ones she'd feared using her whole life, that she'd only really practiced so she could earn more of a living for herself and Mama...the queen needed that?

"I'll understand if you're hesitant," Queen Elya said. "But we need a Virus we can trust to be discreet and dedicated. The future of Fugera depends on these experiments."

Nat's stomach twisted. She wasn't sure what they meant by all this. "What kind of experiments?"

"The basis," Brielle said, "is simple use of your abilities. How long the Power can remain in a given material, and what the effects are when imbued."

"I won't have to...hurt anyone?"

"Oh, no, that is not the aim," Brielle said. "Death magic is of course dangerous, but we will take every precaution we can to avoid any accidents."

Nat swallowed her nerves. That was reassuring to hear. "And if I'm not comfortable doing these…can I retract my agreement?"

"At any point," the queen said. "We only want you to feel capable. We believe in you."

Her solid confidence made Nat's fears ease slightly. She'd lived in Fugera her whole life, and she'd been the one who appeared to fit in. Tomaz had been born with their father's darker skin and blue hair color—a lighter blue than Father's, but nowhere near as pale as Nat's—and though he was three years younger, she knew he'd always felt like an outsider here. She assumed that's why he'd left for Calidar to search for their father.

The thought of him sent a shock through her. She glanced to a shelf nearby, where an awkward clay sculpture of a camel— though it looked more like a tortoise—sat in a place of honor. Tomaz had always been quick witted and intelligent, making him seem older than he was. He'd only been thirteen when he left with a group of nomads. His birthday passed a few months back. And, while they'd received letters and he sounded safe and whole, Nat couldn't help missing him.

Nat, despite looking like she fit in—with the exception of her curls—had felt like an outsider because of what she could *do.* She'd feared hurting people, and so she'd never truly used these abilities, except to kill pests.

Now, here she stood with the queen herself, possibly finding a *place* in Isille.

"Oh, and," Queen Elya said, "as I mentioned before, I will be taking care of you and your mother. You said she is not improving, correct?"

Nat's heart lightened. "Yes, Your Majesty."

"I've arranged for you both to be moved to an exterior apartment. Windows in each room, and a lovely view of the sunset."

Nat's heart seemed to swell inside her chest. "Truly?"

"Of course," the queen said. "Consider this initial kindness, a gift. The new apartment is not dependent upon your cooperation; you'll be moved regardless. However," she leaned closer. "You will also be compensated for your work with us. Ten gold per day, each time we meet. That payment *will* be dependent upon your continued cooperation."

Ten gold per day? Nat couldn't respond. Her voice caught in her throat. The stipend Mama received as a council member was only one hundred gold per *month*. Ten gold per day could get them enough to travel if they wanted…maybe go find Tomaz…

"The research we're doing will benefit Fugerans for generations," the queen said. "And *you* will be aiding in that effort. It's the least we can do to make you comfortable while that happens."

"Will I still have time to attend the council meetings and see to my mother's responsibilities?"

"We will make sure of it," Brielle said. "And, if you'd like any Cures or doctors to see to your mother—"

"No!" Nat said, holding up her hands. Then quickly lowering them, calming herself. "No, thank you. I…we've had them all visit before, and we know what to do."

"Very well," Queen Elya said. "Do we have your agreement, then? Or would you like more time to consider it?"

Nat drew in a deep breath. She really should speak to Mama before making such a decision, but if they were being truthful—and she had no reason to doubt they were—she was certain Mama would want her to help.

"You have my agreement," she said, nerves and hesitant excitement bubbling inside. "I'll do what I can."

II

AHNRI

Ahnri settled into the shadows behind a decorative sculpture of a coiled snake at the upper edge of an exterior archway. Glowing lumenite crystals made up the eyes and fangs of the serpent, and—having been exposed to the sun all day—shone brightly away from Ahnri's hiding place, down onto a private exterior balcony below.

About half an hour ago, he'd caused a small disaster in the royal dining room—with a few desert rodents and Pin's help—in hopes that the meal would be moved here instead. He made sure to get himself comfortable. He'd be here a while.

In most areas of the palace, he had to either glimpse through windows—and risk being seen—or get inside to observe. The latter of which he'd done twice now, and wanted to wait a while before trying again. On this balcony though, he wouldn't have to strain to stay hidden. All he had to do was hold still, beneath his cloak.

Merlin's words rang in his mind—*stay true to yourself, and accept that not everyone will see the same truth you do.*

He'd tried to tell Remi what he could, but Ahnri had screwed up their meeting terribly, and they might not get another chance to talk for a while. And even if they did, for security of information, there were things Ahnri couldn't be specific about. And being vague was akin to being confusing.

He closed his eyes, subconsciously scratching at Pin's ears—the cat lay curled up beside Ahnri, having just finished off a scrap of meat he'd stolen from somewhere. Pin knew to be silent and still, Ahnri wasn't worried about that.

He *was* worried about how much longer he'd have to wait though. The sun had set over an hour ago, and he knew the queen preferred to eat late, but—

A soft clattering of dishes came from the corridor beneath him.

Finally.

A servant entered the space, pushing a wooden cart that held multiple shining metal platters. Another servant followed with a long torch to light the lamps encircling the balcony. Ahnri stayed still as the stone around him, his hood pulled over his face while they worked. A moment later, Elya's voice floated up out of the hallway.

"—understand what you do when you leave the palace," she said. "There's no reason a prince should be gallivanting around the city unaccompanied."

"But I am *always* accompanied, Mother," Remi said, a reassuring tone to his voice. "As you've so firmly ordered. I never go anywhere alone, I promise."

Ahnri's chest ached at the sight of the prince. Not for the first time, he wished their last encounter had gone differently.

Elya sighed as she sat at the head of the long dining table. "As is appropriate to your station. But leaving the palace unannounced is nearly as dangerous. If you refuse to tell me where you're going, I cannot guarantee your safety."

Remi sat in his chair to Elya's right, and Ahnri said a silent prayer of thanks to the gods that both of them were facing away from him. They'd be slightly harder to hear, but at least he wouldn't be seen.

"You've been overly cautious lately, Mother," Remi finally said, swirling the wine in his goblet. "Is everything all right? The increase of your personal guard, your sudden attention on my safety…it worries me."

Fine dishes and cutlery were brought and laid before them, while a servant ladled steaming soup from a pot nearby.

"Your worry is comforting," Elya said. "Has this been tested?"

The servant bowed. "Yes, Your Majesty."

The queen nodded, turning back to her son. "As royalty, our lives are in constant danger, are they not? I'm increasing in years; I simply want to be sure I live to see the great things our kingdom will accomplish."

"You've survived many years already," Remi said as the soup was placed before him. "Why the sudden added precautions now?"

"Are you questioning my judgement, child?" Elya said.

"Of course not," Remi said quickly. "I'm simply curious."

Ahnri could hear the caution in his voice. One always had to take care when speaking to the queen, to avoid setting her off. Ahnri had noticed in the last few days of watching her that she'd become extremely skilled at keeping up her kind, gentle persona with most people. But around only her guards or adviser, and occasionally Remi, she tended to be less careful.

Elya leaned forward, taking a sip of her soup. "Because I deserve it. I should've been doing it for years. Your father discouraged it."

Ahnri watched Remi's profile. He seemed unconvinced, but didn't press the matter.

They continued eating and the discussion moved on to city council issues, the quality of the meal, and more mundane topics. Ahnri let his mind wander, half-listening in case something important came up. The queen had secrets. She'd always had secrets, ever since Ahnri and Remi were kids. And Ahnri had a knack for knowing when she was lying.

Perhaps that's why she'd never liked him much.

He continued watching and listening through three courses of food. Remi did not broach the subject of Elya's plans, and Ahnri wondered whether the prince remembered saying he would. Their emotions had been rather…compromised, at the time.

Then, when their dessert plates were whisked off, Remi did something Ahnri would never have predicted.

"Away," Remi called to those around them. "Leave us."

The queen did not counter the command, though she did appear nervous, and Ahnri spotted her taking her dinner knife and tucking it into her lap.

Stars…did she suspect her own son would attack her? Or would *she* attack *Remi?*

One by one, the servants and guards made their way back into the main structure of the tower. Ahnri sat unmoving, and beside him Pin stood still as a statue, ears perked. Something about the moment made the hairs raise on Ahnri's arms. He slowly slid the small dagger from his boot.

Elya eyed her son for a moment, and Ahnri sensed she was measuring something in him.

"Mother," Remi said, keeping his voice low, "I've heard rumors. Servants gossiping, that you're planning something dangerous."

"Child." Elya smiled, a patronizing gaze. "I'm always planning something dangerous."

"Mother, please," Remi said, tossing his napkin to the table. "First you double your guard, then I hear you've offered a one hundred gold bonus to anyone who joins the army, *and* you're raising weekly pay to all soldiers by *ten percent?* And I'm not supposed to notice?"

Ahnri raised a brow, impressed.

"We can't afford to spend that much on the army," Remi continued. "We're not in a war, and the city budget is tight as it is. Why would we need—"

"Because," Elya said, her voice almost a growl, "there are dangers you do not see."

Remi flinched away at these words, and Ahnri's heart broke at the sight. It reminded him too much of when they were children.

He leaned forward, squinting to see…Elya's free hand had formed a fist on the table, and from this distance appeared to be trembling. He imagined the other holding tightly to the knife she'd hidden as well.

Remi seemed to sense the same danger, and held up his hands in a motion of surrender. "Surely, you know more than I do. I'm certain there is wisdom in your actions."

Slowly, Elya's tension eased. As soon as it did, Remi spoke again.

"Do you ever worry…you're being lied to?"

Elya took a deep breath. "Of course."

"How do you verify sources?"

"Our intelligence organization is extremely thorough," Elya said. "Captain Lind has copies of every kingdom's royal seals to compare against, as well as handwriting samples. There are three dozen agents gathering intel, moving in and out of each kingdom on a regular basis."

Remi sat forward, clasping his hands before him.

The queen watched him. "Are you questioning our own people?"

"No," Remi said. "I believe you. You have me oversee the city and all its moving parts, while you handle the army, intelligence, and inter-kingdom relations. I know that."

"Then why do you appear so…melancholy?"

Her tone dripped with disdain and disapproval. Ahnri adjusted his grip on the dagger, wishing for a good excuse to throw it toward her sneering face.

"I'd like to propose a deal," Remi said.

What? Ahnri thought.

Elya paused, eyeing her son. "I'm listening."

"I would hope you've noticed," Remi said, "in the past months, that I have a knack for working with people. If you'd like, I would offer my help in whatever it is you're planning. I know you've never liked to be the face of royal things to the citizens of Isille. I can be that for you."

She eyed him carefully, critically. "And if I accept your help," she said, "bring you in and use your skills…what do you ask in return?"

"No more secrets," Remi said. "That's all. You've reminded me many times recently that I am your heir. This city—this kingdom—will be mine to rule one day—"

Elya flinched at those words.

"—and I feel a responsibility to make certain I'm well-educated in every aspect."

Elya straightened her expression quickly; Ahnri wasn't sure whether Remi noticed.

"I am…hesitant," she said, "to have you directly involved. It's quite dangerous."

"Could I earn your full trust?"

Elya considered. "Perhaps. We can discuss."

Remi's focus did not waver. "I would like that."

"And I expect complete and total silence on the subject. You will not speak of it to anyone. Am I understood?"

"Yes, Mother."

Elya took a sip of her wine, settling back. "What I'm working on will protect us. Anyone who comes near the city with a threat of force will regret it."

Ahnri immediately reminded himself to write to Carina. He had a small report written already, but hadn't sent it yet. He'd have to include this warning.

Remi frowned. "So, you're strengthening our army?"

"And providing protection to the city," Elya said. "Fugera will be the might of the Unbroken Lands for years to come. I won't say more here, but I will share with you what we know."

Bumps rose on Ahnri's skin.

"Thank you, Mother," Remi said. "I look forward to hearing more."

Elya sent Remi to call back the servants, and Ahnri watched as they took dishes away and cleared things, and before long the queen and the prince made their way back inside the tower. Ahnri continued to wait while the table was cleared and cleaned, the lanterns doused, and the doors latched behind the final servants.

He let himself relax, and beside him, Pin moved as well, stretching his legs out in front of him, arching his back.

"Well," Ahnri said, "Remi is definitely closer to his mother now than ever. At least he did ask her about her plans. Who knows what she'll show him though. And there's no way for him to know those letters are fake if the whole of Fugeran Intelligence thought they were real."

"*Mrrrow?*"

Ahnri grunted, leaning back against the tower behind them. "It worries me more. This isn't going to be easy."

Pin placed a paw on Ahnri's knee.

Ahnri let out a breath. "Thank you, friend."

Together, they made their way across the outside of the tower, to the nearest entrance, and back to Ahnri's small rooms.

12

AHNRI

Ahnri stayed up late making sure his letter to Carina was thorough, coded, and as informative as possible, sending Kahr off in the middle of the night. The copies he'd made in Elya's office weren't perfect, but he'd remembered enough to correct some things and solidify others with heavier strokes of his pencil.

According to the notes he'd found, Elya believed that Medelios—and other kingdoms—were dangers to Isille, threatening them. There hadn't been outright actions mentioned, but the implication was clear. Ahnri still didn't know if those letters had been created by the queen herself, or someone else. And if it had been someone else, his first guess would be someone in Fugeran Intelligence. Ahnri had only been involved with them for a short time before Damond's death, and he didn't remember anyone by name.

He knew Elya wanted more soldiers, which meant anyone who joined the army was at risk. He knew Viruses were involved, but he had no idea what for.

He went to bed with his head spinning, Pin having fallen asleep hours before. The next morning dawned cold, as though wintEr was fighting to hold on in those early hours before the sun rose high. Ahnri tried not to associate the chill with what he needed to do today—get into a room he'd never seen, nor had any knowledge of except a roughly copied sketch of a dig plan.

He dressed quickly. Five days in the city, and he'd learned just enough to have even *more* questions than before. But it was enough that he'd felt confident sending Kahn back. Maybe Carina could even help him work out some answers.

He rubbed at his eyes, then glanced around the room. Where had he taken off his boots? He'd been exhausted…probably he'd taken them off near the bed? He turned toward his cot and knelt to check underneath, where he could indeed see the sole of one of his boots.

He reached for it, but paused. As his eyes adjusted to the shadows beneath the bed, he realized Pin was curled up, lying on top of both tall boots, purring like a rumbling distant thunderstorm.

"Mucking cat," Ahnri muttered. "Might as well wear them yourself."

Ahnri didn't have the heart to wake him, so he stood and scavenged his pack for food. All he found was a few pieces of jerky and some stale bread—good enough, for now. He'd have to get something else for Pin. He took a moment to go through the rest of his supplies and make a mental list of what he needed to replenish. His poisons were well-stocked, notebook and pencils were good, and his water skin was mostly full, but he definitely needed more rations.

By the time he'd choked down the bread with the help of some water, Pin had slunk out from under the bed and was sniffing at the dried meat.

"Uh-uh," Ahnri said, pulling it away from the cat. "It's too salty for you, you'll get sick."

"Mrrow!"

"We're getting food when we get down to the market," he said, scratching Pin's ears. "I won't make it on this either."

After a street-food breakfast of warm bread stuffed with bean and gravy filling—and some grilled meats for Pin—Ahnri braced himself. He had a room to find. The queen wouldn't be there yet, it was too early in the day, but he had to hurry.

So, he and Pin made their way down to the ground level of the palace. According to his rough sketch of the map, the room was below, with the military training caverns. He'd need to look the part of someone with the clearance to be there...

First he had to get into the palace, once again. Pin's charismatic cuddling wasn't needed today, as a crowd of workers milled around the laundry area, moving crates and barrels in and out. Ahnri had Pin climb into his satchel, then made himself useful for a few minutes and got past them without issue.

It never failed to surprise him how far he could get by simply acting as though he belonged.

Near the center of the palace complex on level one, separated from the kitchen and laundry and servants' quarters, stood a ten-foot-wide archway that opened to a single spiral staircase leading down. Ahnri had used it before; it led to the military caverns where he'd received training with Fugeran Intelligence. He and Damond had gone each day to practice swordplay, running, and climbing. Memories flashed through his mind of learning different sword styles from visiting guards or soldiers…he hadn't had much time to use those skills recently.

There were two guards at the entrance, but many men and women going in and out without any need for identification, so Ahnri simply made his way through.

The staircase was wide enough that the people going down stayed on the outer portion, and those coming up stayed on the inner. Ahnri reached the base of the staircase, and stepped to one side to allow those behind him to go their way, and no one looked twice at him.

The hallway here led both left and right, curving slightly in either direction. His memory told him that the military training caverns were to the left, along with the mess hall and weapon storage. He'd seen and been in all of those places before. Checking to the right, he saw a handful of closed doors…he'd always assumed these were offices, but he'd never asked. He checked his map again. The lab room would be to the right. Ahnri made his way, counting the doors carefully, finally stopping before a blank stretch of wall.

"*Mrrow!*"

Pin popped out of his bag, landing gracefully on the floor. "What is it?"

The cat went straight for the wall, leaping up to tap his paw on a spot of the stone that looked darker than the rest. Unfortunately, that didn't do anything.

"Do I press it?" Ahnri asked.

"Mrrow!"

"How do you know that?"

The cat just stared at him.

Ahnri's eyes narrowed. "Have you been *in* here before?"

Pin *nodded.*

Ahnri knelt. "Why didn't you tell me?"

Pin glared. *"Mrrow!"* He leaped up to the spot on the wall again.

Ahnri sighed. "One of these days, I'm going to get answers out of you."

He stared at the seemingly empty wall and shook his head. Two secret doors in two days felt like a lot. He glanced up and down the corridor to make sure they were alone, then put his hand on the spot, and pressed.

A low *click* sounded, much quieter than he would've expected. Soft lantern light flowed out as the door opened, but Ahnri had hardly caught a glance of the inside—where he saw two long tables and some cages—before someone flew toward him, shoving him away.

His back hit the wall on the other side of the hallway, and a knife point met his chest.

"Who are you? And what are you doing here?"

A short woman with dark red hair had him pinned, and by the fury on her face, she was not one to cross.

Brielle. The queen's adviser.

"I-I'm sorry, Miss," Ahnri said, attempting to make himself sound younger. "I was delivering a message and got lost finding my way back. I don't know what I did, I swear it!"

The woman's eyes narrowed, but she didn't back away. "What's your name?"

"Davin, Miss," he said.

"And where do you live, Davin?"

"Um, level four, near the Dusty Dragon."

"Do you have family?"

"Y-yes, my mum and sister."

"That's a shame."

She moved to press the knife into him, and managed a scrape before Ahnri's defenses kicked in. Both arms swung upward, shoving her knife hand up and away, leaving a gash in his jaw.

Ahnri didn't stay to fight. He ran.

Gathering his cloak, he pressed it to the cut on his face to avoid leaving a blood trail, and instead of going up the spiral staircase, he went past it, heading for the military training caverns. He ducked through a door he'd known to be a storage room before, pulling the door mostly closed behind him, leaving a small slit to be able to see through. A strange scent he could only identify as *heat* filled the room behind him, but he ignored it for the moment.

Awkwardly, still holding his cloak to the cut Brielle had given him, he pulled the dagger from his boot, set his foot against the base of the door, and watched the hallway.

He spared a thought for Pin, who he assumed—hoped—had run back up the staircase at the first sign of Brielle's aggression. Ahnri had seen no sign of the cat since before he'd pressed the latch to open that door.

The more time passed, the more Ahnri worried about Brielle. The cut she'd given him stung, and he'd prefer to find a Cure to heal it rather than let it fester for too long. He'd expected her to follow immediately, to shout for someone to stop him, but no signs of it came. He waited still. Ten minutes passed before he saw her. She calmly made her way through the corridor, passing his hiding spot.

Ahnri stayed put. Another few minutes passed before she came by again, this time with the general.

"—nondescript, pale hair and tanned skin," she said. "But he tried to get into the records room. Would have if I hadn't scared him off."

"That description won't help much," the general said. "It matches two thirds of the men of the city. But I'll let my guards know to keep an eye."

"Good," Brielle said. "Are the new recruits ready yet?"

"Not quite, but within a day or two. They're eager, though. That pay rise helped a great deal, Your Grace."

"Good. We're getting close. I want reports of the strongest soldiers and most loyal. They'll be the first we meet with."

"I'll see to it."

They exchanged farewells and Brielle made her way back toward the hidden room, while the general went the opposite direction, toward the training caverns.

So, whatever they were doing in that hidden room…they needed the *existing* army for? Ahnri frowned at that. He knew the queen was encouraging new recruits, but was that the same or separate from this *elite force* she needed the Viruses for?

Ahnri waited another five minutes before letting himself relax. Many soldiers and workers had passed by him by that point, hopefully he could blend in again. When he opened the door to leave, light filled the space, and confusion filled his mind.

The room that had once held spare swords and spears and armor now appeared to be some kind of smithy, though on a smaller scale. Toward the back of the room were a small hearth and bellows and a chimney cut into the ceiling. Beside it, a work table lined the wall where dozens of small ingots lay, of a deep black metal he didn't recognize, as well as multiple molds of cast iron.

Footsteps sounded from down the hallway.

Ahnri quickly snatched one of the ingots, pocketing it, and left the room.

Maybe a blacksmith could tell him more.

As he walked, he arranged his cloak to cover the cut on his jaw, which had—thankfully—stopped bleeding for the time being. He made his way straight back to the spiral staircase, and up and out past the guards there, and a moment later, Pin was beside him.

"Glad you got out unseen," Ahnri said.

"*Mrrow.*"

He still didn't know the purpose of that lab, but whatever it was, the queen and her adviser didn't want anyone knowing about it. Which meant all the more that Ahnri needed to try again.

13

NATALIA

Miss Natalia,

Thank you again for your willingness to work with us. Shortly after this note arrives, movers will come to transport you, your mother, and your possessions to your new apartment. Please instruct them where to place things, and they will do so. You are excused from this morning's council meeting to see to this, but will be expected to attend the afternoon meeting.

When that adjourns, please meet Brielle at the north entrance to the palace. She will direct you to where we will be working.

—Elya Caselle, Queen of Fugera

"My heart?" Mama called. "What is it?"

"A letter," Nat said, going to her bed. She sat beside Mama and took her hands. "I wanted to speak with you about it first, but…Queen Elya has heard about your condition, and she's insisted on moving us to a different apartment. One with windows, Mama." Nat reached forward, running a hand over Mama's hair. "You'll get to see the sun again soon."

"The…the queen?" Mama said, her voice breathy. Then tears welled in her eyes. "That sounds wonderful, my heart."

Nat hugged her. "They'll be here soon, though. I'll pack what I can, you stay there."

"Where else would I go, my love?" Mama said, laughing softly to herself.

Nat quickly gathered Mama's medicines, as well as their most precious and fragile trinkets: clay sculptures she and Tomaz had made as children, a few drawings, a drawer of letters from Tomaz and older ones from their father. By the time she'd finished arranging these in a spare crate, a knock came at the door.

Within hours, all of their possessions—few though they were—had been moved by complete strangers to a new space. Four guards had been assigned specifically to carry Mama on a litter. Nat watched nervously at first, but the men showed incredible care with her, making sure not to jostle or jolt as they went.

The entire process took less than three hours, and by the time everyone had gone Nat stood in the new space with a lump in her throat. It was only a little larger than their previous rooms, but it felt like a significant change, so much that Nat had to give herself a few minutes to take it all in.

This apartment had a main living area with double doors to a small balcony facing southwest, and two bedrooms, each one with its own window. The walls here were more polished than their previous home, with a beautiful border carved along the top. And the queen had provided more comfortable beds and other furniture, as well as new linens, blankets, and pillows.

The curtains had remained closed while everything was moved in, but once everyone had gone and the doors were closed, Nat sat on the edge of Mama's bed, taking her hand.

"Would you like me to open the curtains?"

"In a moment, my heart," Mama said. She squeezed Nat's hands, as though no time had passed from their conversation earlier, before the moving had taken place. "You know I'm proud of you, right?"

A lump rising in her throat, Nat couldn't speak, so she nodded.

"If the queen has spoken to you," Mama said, "that is a good thing."

Nat took a breath, remembering the rest of what the note had said. "Mama...there's something else I need to tell you."

"Yes?"

"The queen said this gift is freely given," Nat said. "She assured me she only wants to help us. But...she's also asked for me to help her as well."

Mama's brows came together. "Help...the queen?"

"She and her adviser are doing some research, some experiments, and they asked for my help."

"What kind of research?"

"It...has to do with my powers."

"I see," Mama said slowly. "So, they know?"

"I tried to keep it a secret, Mama, but they found my name on a list from when I was born and I couldn't deny it, I—"

"It's all right, my heart," Mama said. "You're safe, and it seems your abilities have blessed us."

Nat let out a slow breath. "They also said they'd pay me handsomely for my help."

Mama patted her hand. "Be cautious, my heart. I'm grateful the queen seems to appreciate your talent, but there are those who fear it. Be wary of them. Protect yourself."

"Yes, Mama."

"Now," Mama said, "open those curtains. I haven't seen the sky in too long."

Nat beamed, her heart soaring as though above the clouds as she went to the window. She parted the heavy curtains, tucking them behind two hooks on either side of the window. The sun shone down from above them, turning the sky a bright, sharp blue, marked with a few puffy white clouds.

Beyond, closer to the mountains, the ground seemed like a folded blanket dotted with shadows, the land smooth and soft. Nat stepped aside and stared for a moment, taking in the beauty. A sight she got to see regularly, but was different every time.

She heard a sigh, and turned to see tears on Mama's cheeks.

"The sun is a thing of beauty," Mama said, "but it brings me more joy than I can say to see that light on your cheeks, my heart."

Nat smiled. "Thank you, Mama." She went to her and took a cloth to dry her tears. "I feel the same about you. I've wished to take you out of that room for weeks, but I couldn't do it alone."

"And now you have friends to help."

"Well," Nat shrugged. "Acquaintances."

Mama smiled. "I'm grateful nonetheless."

"So am I." She squeezed Mama's hand. "I have to get to the council meetings. I'll try to be back before sunset, but they've asked me to meet for the first session of research tonight, so I may be late."

"Thank you, my heart. Good luck today."

Natalia got through her meeting and stopped to purchase some dinner on her way to the north palace entrance. When she arrived, Brielle was there, going through a handful of papers, seemingly searching for something. She looked up as Nat approached.

"Ah, perfect timing. Follow me."

She turned into the palace, and Nat followed.

Through her meetings, Nat had wondered what she might be doing this evening. And, while part of her still feared her abilities, afraid of possibly hurting someone, there was also a measure of excitement. They *needed* her. The queen had sought her out, specifically. Surely that meant she had a place here.

The wide corridor was brightly lit, with sconces on either wall every ten feet or so. Like most spaces in the palace she could recognize the natural stone of the mountain in which they lived, but this space had been much more intentionally shaped, with sharp corners and designs carved in. Parts of the wall were left the natural tan brown, and others had been painted white, or tiled with murals.

One such wall she passed depicted the four gods in a row, their likenesses holding their Power in their hands. Nat faltered when she got to Fina, the goddess of Death. It seemed as though the purple glow in her hands should've lit up the space beneath her hood, but the shadows there remained. Nat shuddered, then continued on.

Brielle eventually led her to an archway in the center of the palace complex, and down a wide spiraling staircase. Natalia tried to keep herself oriented, but after so many revolutions she lost track of which direction she was facing. On the way down, the dull pain inside her gave a sting, and she stumbled, catching herself on the banister.

"Are you all right?" Brielle asked.

"Fine," Nat said. "Slipped a bit."

Brielle turned, continuing down. Nat followed, grateful that the pain hadn't lingered, and it seemed the adviser hadn't noticed.

She *would* stay strong, for Mama.

Finally, they stepped through another archway at the base of the staircase, then went to the right down a long thin hallway, before Brielle stopped at a blank stretch of wall. She pressed on a section Nat couldn't have identified if she'd tried, and a door appeared. Shifting open to reveal a brightly lit room

Her eyes widened at the sight of long thin tables set with lab equipment. Vials, and bottles, and small fire pits, along with notebooks, pencils, ink and quills. And along the wall were cages of many sizes that held animals—rabbits, rats, and other rodents, even some snakes and—in one glass box—a scorpion. At the far end of the room was a more open space with a circular metal table in the center, and there stood the queen, organizing some things on the table before her.

"Wonderful," Queen Elya said. "Thank you for coming, Natalia."

"This way, please," Brielle said.

Nat followed her toward the circular table where she could now see small trinkets laid out in groups. One group of a few daggers and knives of different metals, one a necklace with a huge red gem alongside rings with stones of blue, green, and clear, and another section held wooden utensils, spoons, and a mallet. There was even a block of ice, and a lovely glasswork ball that held a sphere of shadow in its center.

"Brielle," the queen said, "please explain what we're doing tonight."

"Right. What we'd like you to do, Natalia, is imbue some items with Power. I don't know if you've ever done it before, but from what we've seen with most human Vessels, it comes fairly naturally. We'll start with this larger piece, to give you a nice solid target."

She followed Brielle's gesture to see a circular column shape of a pure black metal she didn't recognize, perhaps four feet tall and two feet wide. It sat in a carrier made of wood, with handles designed to allow individuals to carry it by their shoulders.

Brielle gestured to it. "This metal is called Elyum. A new mineral, named for our lovely queen. Our prospectors discovered a deposit at the base of the Arontas mountains a few months ago, and we've been experimenting with it since. It's far stronger than steel, particularly when refined and purified like this."

Nat nodded along. She didn't know anything about metals or how to refine them, but it sounded interesting. "And…what will this be used for?"

"This large one will only be for practice," Brielle said. "A sort of warm up for you, each time you visit us here, as well as a vessel into which to pour any large amounts of excess Power you're holding. Releasing it into the air is fine when the amount is small, but in greater volume…well, we've had accidents. So this is a safety precaution. Then these," she gestured to the smaller items, "because of the nature of a carriable vessel—being that if it is touched at all, the magic releases immediately—we can't do much with them. What we're hoping to observe is how long the different materials will hold their charge."

"Right," Nat said, interlocking her fingers nervously. "Um…what do you mean by their charge?"

"The charge is what we call it when something is holding the Power," Brielle explained. "Priests and scribes from ages past have recorded that different materials can carry the magic for different lengths of time, but we've not found any record to tell us which, or why. And if not used, the energy eventually fades from all of them anyway. How long they can hold their charge, however, seems to vary Power to Power and material to material."

Nat tightened then loosened her grip on her own hands. "So, you need me to put Death magic into each of these, and you'll watch and see which one holds it the longest?"

"Precisely."

"How can you tell if it still has a charge?"

"They usually glow for a short time, particularly if they're very full," Brielle said, "but we'll also be testing them every so often on small things like bugs or rodents. Hence why we need multiple of each. Once small things like these are used, their charge is gone."

Nat understood. It seemed simple enough.

"That said," Brielle continued, "we'll begin with the column here to give you a large target area, particularly while you're starting out."

Nat did as instructed, standing before the column of Elyum metal. It's surface was polished and reflective, and in it she saw herself—a nervous line between her brows.

Forcing herself to relax, she searched around for a bit of shadow to draw in—but found none. Charged lumenite on nearby tables, and lanterns on the walls filled the space with too much light. "Could we put out some of the lanterns?"

"Oh, of course!" Brielle said, moving quickly. "Can't believe I forgot about that. Every Vessel needs their fuel."

In moments, Brielle had put out all of the lanterns on the walls around them, and even threw dark cloth over the lumenite, plunging the room into near darkness. Nat took a deep breath.

I can do this.

Carefully, she raised her hand in a patch of darkness and drew from the shadows. For a moment, a patch of *light* appeared where her hand had been. Then she took that same hand and placed it on the column, doing her best to slowly push the magic *into* the material.

She'd never done this before, however. As she tried, her habit of releasing the energy quickly in order to kill rodents sent the Power out with a quick flash of purple light, and she was fairly certain none of it made it into the Elyum.

"That's all right," Brielle said, standing back a few feet. "Try again."

Nat took a breath to refocus. That patch of shadow she'd drawn from had already repaired itself, so she drew from it again—it did constantly amaze her how nature was so infinite. It healed itself no matter how many times humans drew Power from it to fuel their abilities. She had no idea what would happen if she drew in a larger amount…she'd always been afraid to try.

A second time, she attempted to release Power into the metal. It still flashed, and nothing made it in, but Nat thought the flash had been *almost* more like a glow. She didn't wait for Brielle to speak this time, she simply tried again. And again. By the fifth attempt, the purple light of Death magic glowed solid, and when she pulled her hand away the smooth Elyum held its own aura for a few seconds before fading away.

"I did it!"

"Excellent!" Brielle said. "Well done."

"Once more," the queen said from behind them.

Nat gave a small bow in acquiescence, took a deep breath, and this time pulled in *more* magic than before.

Surprisingly, taking in more initially made it easier to imbue it. It flowed like a steady stream from her hand into the column.

"Well done, Miss Natalia," Brielle said. "I think—"

"Now the gems," the queen said.

Brielle hesitated. "Respectfully, Your Majesty, I don't want to risk burning her out on her first night."

"I'm all right," Nat said. "I can try a few more if you want."

Brielle nodded then, leading them back over to the table. Nat spent the next half hour imbuing various materials with erratic success. The larger pieces were indeed easier, and the stones and metal items took in the Power more smoothly than the wood, or the glass, or the ice.

"I think that's probably enough for today," the queen finally said. "Quite the accomplishments. If you have the time to practice this tonight, Miss Natalia, we can fill the rest of these items tomorrow afternoon."

Nat hesitated a moment, then said, "Could I try one more thing, Your Majesty?"

Nat caught an eager expression on Brielle's face as the queen considered. "Very well," Queen Elya said.

Nat moved back over to the column and focused her attention on the shadows again. Nerves flowed through her, but she was determined to try.

This time, she pulled in more magic than she'd ever held at one time. An amount of Power that felt like carrying a boulder on her back. It thrummed inside her like a second heartbeat, reverberating all the way from her fingertips to her toes, and left a large patch of light in the air of the room where there should've been shadow. Carefully, she placed her hands to the column, and, holding herself firmly in control, slowly released.

Now that she'd learned the process, she noticed that this new metal, Elyum, seemed to almost *pull* on the Power she held, as though it *wanted* it. For the first time, as her Power moved it shone like a lamp, without flickering. She imagined it like pouring water from a pitcher into a vase, slowly and deliberately. It was a steady glow, with perhaps a small pulse every few seconds. For a full minute, Natalia stood, her hands trembling as she deposited Power into the column. When the last drops had left her, she slumped, nearly collapsing to the floor. Brielle came forward to help support her.

"Natalia," Brielle said. "Look."

Before her, the Elyum glowed a deep, but bright, purple. And this time, the aura it held stayed strong for a solid minute before fading. Pride bloomed in her chest.

"Make sure no one touches that," the queen said. "I worry it's dangerous even getting close."

"Of course, ma'am," Brielle said, directing Nat away and still supporting her.

"I didn't realize that would make me so tired," Nat muttered.

"It's not something most Vessels have to worry about," Brielle said. "The average Cure or Shifter only need draw very little to do what they need to do. But Miss Natalia?"

Nat met her eyes.

"That was *incredible*."

"Thank you," Nat said. A wave of satisfaction washed over her. She'd rarely done anything in her life to merit that kind of praise. She had to admit—it felt nice.

"*Now*, we are done," the queen said. "Brielle is right, you've accomplished a great deal in only a couple of hours, particularly for one who has never attempted this before. Plan on coming again tomorrow afternoon, and we will work on the rest."

"Yes, Your Majesty."

The queen leaned forward to get Nat to meet her eye. "We are more grateful for your help than you realize, child. I would remind you, please do not speak of this to anyone. What we do here could frighten the average citizen, but we will accomplish great things. Oh, and I nearly forgot."

From a pocket of her robes, the queen took out a small pouch and handed it to Nat.

"Your payment."

"Thank you, Your Majesty."

"You're very welcome." The queen said. "Enjoy your evening."

Nat bowed, and was led out by Brielle. The adviser showed her back the way they'd come, down the hallway to the winding staircase.

"You truly did well today, Natalia."

"Thank you," Nat said. "It didn't seem like much."

"I know being a Virus can seem like a curse, but your cooperation in this will do so much good. Fugera is in danger, and we're working to protect it."

"In danger?"

Brielle hesitated. "Yes. Keep this quiet, but…we suspect an attack on the city is coming, though we don't have proof yet. We're doing everything we can to protect our people, and the work you're doing will help."

"Of course," Nat said. She would gladly lend her abilities if it meant protecting Mama.

When they reached the top of the staircase Brielle said, "Can you find your way from here?"

"Yes, thank you."

"You're welcome," Brielle said. "We'll see you again tomorrow."

14

REMI

Remi stood with squared shoulders watching activity in the military training cavern, and the special unit his mother finally revealed to him. A sense of pride brought warmth to his chest. She was finally opening up to him, and he *would* live up to it.

Before him, soldiers were paired off and fighting each other in hand-to-hand martial combat, their only weapon a long staff. The weapons looked like wood from a distance, but Remi had seen up close that they were some kind of metal, with the middle wrapped in leather for a handle.

Remi flinched as one soldier took a hit to the temple and went down. And, Remi quickly realized, not only *down*, but *out*. The man did not move, and blood poured freely from his head wound. Cures quickly ran in, water at the ready to provide healing. Within moments the man was on his feet preparing to fight once more.

"Isn't it amazing," his mother said softly at his side, "how much good the Powers can do?"

"It is," Remi said. He continued watching the man who had fallen. His efforts seemed to have doubled. "It's enough to make one feel invincible."

"Indeed." The queen said firmly. "As they should."

"Is it…wise to train them to feel that way?"

Mother turned to him. "I deem it so. Do you disagree?"

Remi hesitated. He'd struggled most of his life to be honest with his mother. Past experience told him he would be dismissed, ignored. However, his very presence here was a sign of that changing, wasn't it? "I question the wisdom," he finally said, choosing his words carefully. "Simply because it seems unlikely that there will be Cures readily available in field combat scenarios. If a soldier is *too* reckless, they may die because they're not protecting themselves. If a Cure isn't able to heal them quickly, that's one less soldier to fight for us."

The queen considered this for a time—long enough that Remi began to wonder whether she would answer at all. When she did speak, it was a single sentence.

"I understand your concern."

Remi waited for more, but she did not continue. That wasn't a dismissal, necessarily, and it seemed to validate his concerns, at least on the surface. But it said nothing about whether she agreed or would make changes based on his words.

His stomach twisted uncomfortably. His father had always taught him that soldiers were not simply numbers, they were people. Individuals with homes and families, lovers and children. Their lives mattered as much as his did. To hear his mother speak of them like this, as though they were expendable, made him worry. He should push the issue.

"Mother, I—"

"I said I understand," she snapped. "I will not make rash, impulsive decisions, son. And *you* would do well to exercise patience."

His mouth clamped shut, and he faced forward again. Of course she wasn't going to decide right here and now—that made sense, didn't it? Changes to military training required significant consideration, he knew that. He could bring the subject up again later, maybe ask what she'd decided. Either way, she was the queen. And it wasn't his place to tell her how to do her job.

"Let me show you something," she said, turning away from the sparring soldiers and toward a door in the side of the large cavern.

They entered an office space, with bookshelves and a desk and a single dim lamp. Mother turned the light brighter and shuffled through a stack of papers, then handed them to Remi.

"Read through these," she said. "Then if you have questions, I'll answer them while we're here."

Curious, Remi began to read. The pages were a series of reports from Fugeran Intelligence detailing locations of enemy troops, Medelian military training, and predicted movements. Reports were being brought in every three to five days, and each newer one confirmed elements of the last. The recommendation was preparation for war with Medelios, in no uncertain terms.

Surely Ahnri did not know about this…if he did, wouldn't he agree that they should do whatever it took to protect Fugera?

Remi swallowed, examining each page more closely. Signatures matched, information seemed clear and concise. Part of him wondered if maybe Ahnri was right; maybe Remi didn't know what to look for here. But to his eyes, it all appeared accurate, and nothing seemed altered.

"And these are the original reports?" Remi asked.

"Exactly what I see when they bring them in. There are others, of course, but these are the relevant ones to this cause."

Remi frowned, thinking of Ahnri's insistence. "And…does anyone else handle them before they reach you?"

"Only one person," she said. "They are delivered completely sealed to Captain Lind when they arrive, and he reviews them before re-sealing them and sending them to me in the hands of a messenger."

"The same messenger?"

"No," Mother said. "A different one each time, to avoid anyone seeing a pattern in our work."

Ah. Remi looked back down at the papers. That didn't sit right with him…if he were receiving reports, he'd want them handed to him directly, no one in the middle.

Maybe he could check in on Captain Lind and try to streamline that process.

"Remi," Mother said, drawing his attention. "I am placing a great deal of trust in you by even showing you this. You understand that, don't you?"

He set the papers down. "Of course, Mother."

"Good. Do you see now why I am pushing our troops so hard?"

"I do."

She placed a hand on his arm. "I know you care for our people. You get your heart from your father—"

Remi's heart ached at those words.

"—but our soldiers know what they're signing up for," she continued. "We must protect our city, and we cannot show any weakness."

He straightened his back. "I understand."

She lowered her hand. "There will be more to see and discuss, but for now I have a few more things to do here, and then I would like to retire for the evening."

"Of course," Remi said. "Is there anything I can help with?"

"Not tonight," she said. "Goodnight, son."

An abrupt dismissal, but that wasn't uncommon from her. Remi bowed to her, then turned toward the exit.

"And Remi?"

"Yes, Mother?"

She looked him over, as though measuring him. "Thank you for joining me. I value your support."

Warmth bloomed inside him at her words. He beamed, bowing to her once more, before making his way out of the basement caverns and back to his rooms.

The palace column was an incredible structure, and Remi did love living there. But the *walking*. So many stairs and ramps, and only a few lifts. At least he knew his legs would always be in the best shape possible.

He made his way up through the palace, hardly glancing at the servants and staff as they bowed to him, his mind repeating the things he'd learned. Finally, he made it to his rooms, turned, and locked the doors behind him. He had of course been followed by two guards the entire time, though he barely registered them anymore. They remained outside.

His head ached, thinking about the coming threat, his mother's plans. On impulse, he poured himself a glass of wine and leaned back against the desk, his mind still working. If an attack was coming, strengthening the Fugeran army and working to make each individual soldier more effective *was* the best course of action.

Ahnri had said Mother was being lied to. Remi trusted him…but it wasn't about trust when certainly the agents working for his mother knew and saw more than Ahnri, was it? Remi read the reports himself, many of them. If Ahnri knew what he did, he would certainly agree that preparing for defense was necessary. But would telling Ahnri that information be a breach of Mother's newfound trust?

He thought back to that look she'd given him—one of approval, of trust. He'd wanted his whole life for her to be proud of him, and it finally seemed to be happening. She wanted his help; she saw and validated his work and abilities. It was everything he'd worked toward for years. He couldn't lose that…couldn't risk it.

But perhaps he could shift Ahnri's perspective…

Remi downed the rest of his wine and set the goblet down, going to his bookshelf. Between the pages of an old journal, as though a bookmark, lay a thin purple ribbon that hadn't been used in months. A flutter of nerves rose in his stomach at the sight of it.

Would he come?

Particularly after their last meeting…

Remi took the ribbon to his window, tied it to a notch on the window frame, and waited. It had been nearly a week since he'd seen Ahnri last, and as he changed into his nightclothes—thin linen pants and shirt—and laid down to rest, he reminded himself that Ahnri was a mover, a watcher. He hardly stayed in one spot for more than a few minutes. But Remi knew he'd often come by that window, and hopefully he would tonight.

It took a few hours before Remi woke to the sound of soft movement coming from his office. He stood from his bed and turned up the lamp beside him to see Ahnri's silhouette climbing down from the window.

Remi's heart leaped at the familiar sight, before he remembered everything that had happened between them. For a moment, he wished he could pretend this was a dream, and that nothing was wrong…

Remi went toward him, setting the lamp on his desk and closing the doors to the office space to further avoid being heard by the guards.

Ahnri stood unmoving, one hand on the window, as though he might leap from it.

Remi clasped his hands, not knowing what to do with them. "Ahnri…thank you for coming."

Remi watched his face in the flickering light, and thought he saw sadness.

"Thank you for inviting me," Ahnri said.

His voice…Remi had dreamed of that voice for so long…

"I wanted—" they both said together.

Remi laughed softly, and so did Ahnri.

"I…" Remi said, "I wanted to talk to you about what you said. About my mother."

"Well, before you do that," Ahnri said, "I want to apologize."

Remi felt a flutter rise in his stomach.

"I got carried away," Ahnri said. "Kissing you, I mean. Not that I didn't *want* to kiss you, I did very much, but I had also wanted to *talk* to you, and I should've done it in a different order, or…differently. I didn't mean to hurt you."

"Thank you. And…I'm sorry I shouted. I was overwhelmed, and hurt, yes, but I shouldn't have lashed out."

Ahnri gave a hesitant half-smile.

And Remi thought his heart might explode.

"You said," Ahnri started, "you wanted to talk about your mother?"

"Yes!" Remi stepped forward eagerly. "I spoke to her, and she's allowing me into her confidence."

Ahnri's smile shifted. "Is she? That's wonderful."

"It is," Remi said. "I've seen what she's planning, and her reasons why. I've seen the reports from Fugeran Intelligence, and…well I probably can't share more than that, I've promised silence, but I wanted to reassure you that everything is all right.

I believe she's doing what's right for Fugera, to protect us and our city."

As Remi spoke, he kept an eye on Ahnri's face. Those eyes he loved to stare into gradually narrowed, becoming a polite, yet somehow ingenuine gaze.

"I see."

Remi frowned. "You seem upset."

"Do I?"

"Yes." Remi drew nearer, placing a hand on Ahnri's arm. "Shouldn't you be happy? You told me something bad was happening, I've checked into it, and I promise you your fears are unfounded. Everything is fine."

Ahnri laughed softly, shaking his head.

"Ahnri?" Remi said. "Everything is fine, right?"

"I'm glad you are comforted," Ahnri said, turning away.

"Wait."

Ahnri paused.

Remi stared at Ahnri, his strong silhouette, the flowing cloak he always wore, and the profile of him half-turned back. All Remi wanted was to hold him, to be held by him.

"Ahnri…" Remi began, not sure what to say to make this better. "I…never mind. I've said what I needed to, and you'll do what you will. Can we just…*be* together? For a while?"

Ahnri's eyes grew sad, of a kind Remi had never seen before.

"Please?"

Ahnri's hand dropped from the window, and he reached up to remove his heavy cloak, laying it over Remi's desk.

Beneath it was the familiar shape of Ahnri's shoulders, his torso, hips, and hands.

Remi's heartbeat stuttered as Ahnri drew closer, putting his hand to Remi's cheek.

"Your eyes are still sad," Remi said.

"I know." Ahnri ran his thumb along Remi's jaw, leaning forward until their lips were inches apart. "But that's never stopped me before, has it?"

They kissed, softer and slower than the last time. Far more intentional, the warmth of it reaching deeper into Remi's heart than before.

This. He'd missed this. The middle of the night meetings, the connection without having to say a word. The stress of the day evaporated. Worries crumbled into dust on the wind as Ahnri kissed away Remi's fears.

I love you…

Remi pulled away slightly, meaning to say it between kisses, but the words wouldn't come. They'd said it as friends for years, but ever since their first kiss—hidden in a kitchen pantry only a year or so ago—neither of them had spoken those words out loud.

Remi wanted to…he wanted to say them, and he wanted to hear them. His heart ached for them. Without warning, tears began to burn behind his eyes. Emotion swelled in his chest. His breathing grew shallow, and before he knew it, his head was buried against Ahnri's chest, tears falling onto his tunic, their arms wrapped around each other.

Ahnri stroked Remi's hair, holding him tightly. And yet, worry tugged at him. Remi held tighter, hoping that whatever was pulling them apart might be fixed if they simply held on.

"You should rest," Ahnri whispered against Remi's hair.

Remi laughed through his tears. "Probably."

Then Ahnri leaned down and scooped Remi's knees up and held him. Remi closed his eyes, grateful for the closeness as Ahnri took him into the bedchamber. Exhaustion and tears had made his eyes heavy, and he'd nearly fallen asleep already by the time he'd been laid down.

"Ahnri?"

"Yes?"

Remi closed his eyes as a heavy blanket was pulled over him. "Wait for me?"

A beat of silence. Remi settled into the soft, sweet-smelling fabrics, drifting into sleep, hoping he would dream of Ahnri.

"I will…my prince."

15

AHNRI

Nothing has changed…nothing has changed.

Ahnri repeated this to himself over and over as he made his way around Isille the following day. He hadn't slept much the night before. Between getting in to see Remi and the brief conversation they'd had—including Remi's desperation for them to be on the same side of things—Ahnri's worries were at an all-time high.

He'd already decided to work against the queen's efforts. And while it frustrated him to no end that whoever fooled the queen had now also fooled Remi, it didn't change the fact that Ahnri had to stop them.

He didn't fault Remi for believing the lies—the forgery Ahnri found had been quite convincing. If he hadn't seen Carina's personal seal and handwriting himself, he would have probably believed the fake was real. It hurt that Remi didn't take Ahnri at his word, but nor could Ahnri take Remi at his.

A mucking impasse, is what it was.

After his fitful sleep, Ahnri made his way to the lower levels, stopping at a food cart for breakfast—enough for himself and Pin, who bounded along behind.

As they walked through interior corridors, taking stairways and ramps today instead of the exterior of the tower, Ahnri filled in the cat on his conversation with Remi the night before.

"He fully believes her," Ahnri said, tossing a bit of chicken to Pin. "I couldn't...I couldn't bring myself to argue with him again."

"Mrrow..."

Ahnri didn't reply, his mind wasn't in a state to try to guess what Pin meant. But as he continued on, Pin leaped from the satchel and ran ahead.

"What are you—"

Pin paused at a section of the corridor they were in, and began scratching at the floor.

Ahnri knelt, trying to block the cat from view of anyone who might be passing by. And a moment later, Pin stepped back to reveal words etched into the stone.

I go Rem

Ahnri felt a lump rise in his throat. "You want to go visit Remi?"

Pin nodded.

Ahnri closed his eyes, a kind of sadness mixed with relief-
-if *he* couldn't comfort Remi, perhaps Pin could. "I think he'd like that. It's pretty early, he might even still be in his rooms."

Pin stood on his hind legs, and reached up to pat Ahnri's face with his paws. Ahnri closed his eyes, feeling both comforted by his friend, and amused that a cat had so quickly bEcome so trusted by him. For a moment, it felt as though his mind cleared and he was able to think better.

He felt Pin lean away, and opened his eyes.

"I'll meet you back in my rooms tonight, then," Ahnri said. "You can feed yourself for one day, right?"

Pin gave one more nod, then turned away, heading in the opposite direction.

With a deep breath, Ahnri stood and continued down. Today was for sabotage, which may be no more than creating chaos for the sake of it, but he had to hope it would be enough to impede Elya's efforts.

He would start with the new recruits being trained. The army caverns were below the city, and Brielle was asking for their strongest soldiers…maybe they were using the Viruses they'd gathered as captains? Did the army in general know about the queen's plans to use Viruses? He had to find out what he could. And maybe he could try again to get into that hidden room.

Ahnri made it a point to never use the same way into the palace twice in a row, so as not to be recognized, but there were only so many entrances. Last time he'd used the laundry. Today it would be the kitchens again. He watched and waited for an opportunity, then hefted a sack of flour and joined a line of workers entering the palace pantry. He set his down, made sure no one was watching, and turned opposite of the others, making his way deeper into the palace.

Away from the kitchens, he turned into an alcove and opened his bag, removing a deep purple tunic—the uniform of a palace servant he'd snagged from the laundry the night before. He took time to pull the upper half of his hair back and arranged his expression to give himself a distinctly different shape from his normal appearance. Then, as unassumingly as possible, Ahnri began making his way back to the underground cavern entrance.

It was once again watched by two guards, as people in uniforms made their way in and out freely. Ahnri hid himself among them.

Most people—even guards on duty—didn't really look closely at passers-by. Nor would they remember features or details, particularly the nondescript ones. And so, when Ahnri made himself appear like a servant—hands in front, and a quick nod to the guards with a flat expression—he made it past without issue.

At the base of the staircase he checked left and right, part of him wishing he had Pin to make sure the way was clear. The hidden room was to the right, but he didn't want to chance that until he'd done what he knew he could do first.

He made his way left.

He passed a few doors, but as none of them were guarded he didn't pay them any mind. Farther down, past the room where he'd hidden the other day—which he still wanted to investigate more thoroughly—he came to a large arched opening where three uniformed soldiers stood, though they were facing into the room, away from his approach. He stayed back a little, but crept close enough to hear what these three were saying.

"—says we'll be divided into companies soon," one said. "They think an attack is coming."

"I hadn't heard that," a second man said—this one had stripes on his uniform that indicated higher rank. "I'll speak with the general to make sure. I don't want anyone seeing combat without their training completed."

"Sir," the third man said, holding out a stack of papers, "Her Majesty raised the pay *again* to garner more recruits."

The higher ranked man grunted. "I'm unsure whether the influx should be encouraging or a cause for concern…I'll bring it up at the meeting this afternoon."

Ahnri took a step backward, intending to leave the way he'd come, but hesitated. His vision shifted, and he glanced beyond the three men standing there into the large space before them. Hundreds of soldiers were paired off, fencing with wooden practice swords. At first glance, some were good, but most were barely decent by his estimation.

The more he watched however, the more he noticed how…how angry they seemed. The soldiers fought with scowls and gritted teeth, striking each other without mercy, and occasionally someone was even knocked unconscious, causing

Cures to come from the edges of the room to heal and get them back on their feet.

He had never seen fight training quite like this. And that, more than anything else thus far, sent a chill through him. None of these soldiers—men or women or neither—seemed to have any kind of style to their motions. They were aggressive, yes, but not at all strategic. It was as though they were relying solely on getting a single hit in order to win.

Something was not right.

"Who are you?"

Ahnri blinked. He'd been spotted.

He straightened. "Apologies, sirs," he said, bowing. "I was sent to find the queen's adviser but I think I've lost my way and…well I admit I got mesmerized."

The high-ranking officer chuckled. "As you should be, son. But these training grounds aren't for public viewing. The offices are back the other side. Three doors past the stairwell."

"Thank you, sir," Ahnri said, bowing. "Again, my apologies."

The three men dismissed him, turning back to their observation of the training soldiers. Ahnri watched for another moment, and in that split second, he spotted something else: doors. Multiple wide double doors on the far end of that huge cavern.

So *that's* where they'd exit the entire army at once.

Ahnri forced himself to turn back toward the stairwell. A knot twisted uncomfortably in his stomach at what he'd seen and heard. He tried to memorize the face of that officer, probably a captain. He may be a good resource to attempt to sabotage if Ahnri wanted to go that route. But for now, he needed something simpler…something a little easier…

Ahead of him, a pair of double doors swung open on his right and a crowd of more soldiers flooded into the hallway. Jovial and joking, they made their way toward the stairwell without glancing back toward Ahnri. As they did, he peeked in toward the room they'd exited to see long tables and benches— the mess hall—and on the far side, wide fireplaces and ovens and counters.

A kitchen.

An idea planted itself in his mind then. Ahnri waited for the soldiers to exit. As soon as they'd left, he shrugged off the servant's tunic and set his things in a small corner out of sight, making his way into the kitchen area. It was bustling, busy, with many people in the middle of many tasks. All he had to do was approach and—

"Sari send you?" a tall, thin woman asked. "Good. Go help Nathan with the soup. Our next service starts in thirty minutes and that should've been going already."

"Right away," Ahnri said. He made his way toward a large cauldron where a savory broth boiled over hot coals.

Nathan looked slightly younger than Ahnri, and stood out with hair of a pale icy blue—as though he'd had one Fugeran parent and one Callidian. Ahnri had never seen that color before, and for a moment he stared.

Until Nathan shoved a sack of vegetables into his arms.

"Get these washed and chopped and in the pot," Nathan said. "And fast."

Ahnri followed orders exactly, while keeping his ears open to the talk surrounding him.

"—more soldiers everywhere," a kitchen worker said.

"Right," his neighbor replied. "Can't decide if I should feel safer or worried."

"Worried?"

"That's how it works in the stories, ain't it? More soldiers, then the evils come?"

"You read too much. It's getting to your head."

"How can you be sure?"

"Remember King Alain's motto? Always for the people. Whatever the queen's doing, I'm sure it's for our benefit."

Ahnri's brow furrowed at that as he dumped one batch of chopped roots into the pot beside him, wiping his brow in the heat. He refocused, listening in to a pair of soldiers sitting nearby.

"—queen's promises?"

"I did. Sounds like a lot."

"You believe it?"

"Not sure I can afford not to."

"Yeah…"

Those soldiers quietly stood then as a large group began to enter, and the kitchen staff moved to start serving.

So there were members of the kitchen staff and the army who weren't so sure about Elya's movement to recruit so quickly…and others who seemed to have complete faith in her.

Ahnri had tried to spend time listening in to conversations throughout the city as well, and thus far hadn't heard a single regular citizen discuss the rise in soldiers and guards, or anything about Elya's plans. In fact, he'd only heard anyone mention the queen once, and that was in praise of her and how lovely a young man the crown prince had grown into.

When Nathan stepped away, Ahnri continued stirring the soup. And it was at that moment his hand *slipped*, pouring a small vial of scorpion venom into the cauldron. Diluted enough, it should simply make them sick, and wouldn't severely harm anyone.

Ahnri helped serve the food, his internal clock growing confused. It couldn't be later than midday outside, but down here they were treating it as the end of a day. The cooks were gathering supplies to be cleaned, tidying up and preparing to return to their homes. A group of servants entered and began to wash dishes as the soldiers finished their meals—not a thank you to be heard, which was mildly annoying to Ahnri.

As the cooks began to make their way out, Nathan waved to Ahnri. "Come on, we're done. What was your name, anyway?"

"Pin," Ahnri said. "But I'm all right, I think I'll stay and help for a bit."

"Suit yourself," Nathan said. "We could use you again tomorrow though."

Ahnri split the difference between Nathan's exit and the other servants cleaning, and sneaked his way out with some of the final soldiers. He took up his things from the corner, following the crowd toward the exit. And in that hallway, he began to hear the results of his tampering.

"Muck, I'm not feeling well," one soldier said, exiting the stairwell.

"Me either," another said, his hand going to his stomach. "I might have to call out…"

"Can't do that," a third said. "We're spread too thin; they won't have a replacement."

"It's either that or I'll be vomiting all over the palace," the second said.

Ahnri stayed toward the back of the group, letting them get ahead. He regretted making the soldiers suffer, but if it would delay Elya at all—if a day or two of illness would end up saving these soldiers' lives—it would be worth it.

If his calculations were correct, that entire group of soldiers would be out of commission for at least a few days. And depending on how well they cleaned that pot, the next batch to eat from it might suffer too.

As soon as he was alone in the hallway, he hurried toward the storage room door where he'd hidden the other day. He first pressed an ear to it and listened. Hearing nothing, he tried the door and found it unlocked once more.

The space was, again, completely dark. Ahnri kept the door open slightly long enough to find a lantern, and flint to light it. With that, he closed the door and locked it behind him.

By the light of the lantern, Ahnri observed the space. The hearth and bellows were small for a smithy, but it made sense given the size of the room.

There was definitely a chimney shaft leading up and out, though he imagined it would get very warm in here when working. He pulled the ingot he'd taken from his pocket. He'd visited three blacksmiths and none had been able to identify the metal. It was new, undiscovered, they said. They'd each offered him a significant amount of gold in exchange for it, but he'd declined.

"What are they making…" he muttered to himself. He could see where the metal would be melted down, and the tools used to pour it into molds. One of these, he opened.

Circular shapes were embedded in the mold, slightly larger than the average coin. Ahnri stared at the two halves of the mold, trying to identify the cast. One side was flat and blank, the other…

"Fina?" he whispered.

He'd never seen it inverted like this, but it was certainly an image of the goddess of Death herself, hooded, with wisps of shadow rising from where her face should be.

He set the mold down, unsettled. He did a scan of the rest of the space, but found nothing else of interest, so he quickly put out the lantern, and left the way he'd come.

At the base of the staircase he glanced in the direction of the lab room. Could he risk trying again right now? He tapped his fingers together, nerves beginning to get the better of him.

No. This was enough for now…he'd come again later.

His instincts told him to get out quickly, and he listened.

16

NATALIA

Nat finished filling the items with Power, a surge of pride blooming in her chest. By her fourth session, an hour or two each day, she'd grown far more skilled at this. Finally, it felt like she was using her abilities for something worthwhile.

"Excellent," Brielle said, scribbling something in her notebook. "You're doing such great work, Natalia."

"Thank you," Nat said, slumping slightly. "The tiredness is still there, but seems to be coming slower than last time. Is that normal?"

"It is," Queen Elya said from the opposite side of the room. "We've seen it with every Vessel so far. The process of imbuing items seems to take more energy from the Vessel than using the Power does. But like any muscle, with practice and training, you can strengthen the ability."

Brielle added, "We're aware it's a struggle, so if you begin to feel faint, please let us know."

"I feel fine at the moment," Nat said. "A little tired perhaps, but not faint."

"And are you certain these are full?" Brielle asked, glancing over each one.

"I think so," Nat said. "At a certain point it becomes more difficult to push the magic into the material, so I stop."

"Excellent," Brielle said, glancing up from her notes. "That matches what our notes say should be happening. This is wonderful work, Miss Natalia."

A small flame of pride began to flicker in Nat's heart. Maybe she could belong here…maybe this kind of work was what she could contribute.

"If you're willing, I think we have time to attempt one more thing this evening?"

"Of course," Nat said.

Brielle grinned excitedly, turning toward one of the long thin tables in the main portion of the room. Nat followed. A space had been cleared away, leaving in its center a rectangular bar of Elyum, polished and pure as the column she started with each day.

"What I'd like you to do," Brielle said, "is imbue this small ingot with as much magic as you can. When you think it's full, try to keep pushing, understand?"

"All right…do we know what will happen if I keep going?"

"From our other experiments, it should reach a point where you physically cannot push anymore. When it slows, you can continue pushing, until it won't allow intake any longer. We haven't seen any other effects."

"All right," Nat said. "I'll try again."

"Wonderful," Brielle said, taking a step back. "Give it a go."

Nat placed a hand on the bar. Closing her eyes, she reached out to the darkness, channeling it through herself and into the metal. Like the larger column made from the same material, this bar seemed to suck her magic in eagerly. It had been a struggle to get things like wood and cloth to hold the magic; they seemed too fragile. Brielle had reported those materials withered away a matter of hours after being imbued. But stone, metal, gems and minerals—especially when purified—these held the magic of Death with apparent ease.

Nat kept her eyes closed, channeling the magic as fast as the metal would accept it—and it accepted more than any other item she'd tried to imbue. Time passed, an uncomfortable amount, and Nat nearly opened her eyes to ask how long it had been.

Finally, she began to meet resistance. Focusing, she continued channeling, letting the magic flow through her. It wasn't long before she felt a sudden jolt, as though running into a wall. Tentatively, she tried again to put more Power into the bar, but it would not accept it.

Opening her eyes, Nat instinctively turned to the column and released into it what Power she still held. They'd been doing this with any excess Nat had every day. The amount of magic in that column was growing, and at first that had made Nat nervous. But Brielle assured her it was simply backup, so that they could have a supply if they needed to work in the light—which had happened a handful of times when the queen wanted to see the process more closely. After their sessions, the column would be locked in a box, to keep it safe from anyone accidentally touching it.

Before her, the ingot Brielle had given her lay on the table. It glowed brightly purple for a few seconds before dimming, but didn't fade entirely.

"Excellent," Brielle muttered from across the table. "Perfect, perfect. Now, Miss Natalia, if you would take two steps back please?"

Nat did as instructed. The adviser went to the far wall and took down a small cage. Inside was a rabbit, grey and brown with tall ears and a white puff of a tail. Brielle pulled down the entire cage, and set it on the table.

Nat's excitement at her success shifted to confusion. "What are you—"

"Shhh," the queen said. "Let us observe."

Heart torn between obedience and worry for the poor creature, Nat fell silent.

Brielle took up a wooden beam now, longer than she was tall, and began to push the rabbit's cage closer to the metal bar. Two feet away, one foot away, six inches, then three, then one…

A flash of light.

The rabbit collapsed.

Nat's heart dropped. Beside her the queen let out a mirthful laugh, and began to applaud.

"Well done!" Queen Elya sang. "Exactly as we'd hoped, yes?"

"Yes, Your Majesty," Brielle said excitedly. She took out her notebook again. "In every scripture and sermon it's been said that magic can only be transferred via touch. But it's clear from this that if the concentration of Power is high enough, it *can* affect things at a distance."

"Wonderful," Queen Elya said. She turned to Nat. "You have been instrumental in these discoveries, child. We cannot thank you enough." Then the queen pulled a small pouch from her pockets, and handed it to Nat. "Here is your payment, as well as an extra token of my appreciation."

Nat hefted the coin purse. "Thank you, Your Majesty." She glanced sideways at the rabbit. It wasn't so different from a rat, she supposed...and if it meant success and enough coin to continue to care for Mama, it was worth the cost, right?

"Are we done, Brielle?" the queen asked.

"With one exception," Brielle said, approaching from where she'd gone to record her findings. "Miss Natalia, obviously leaving this metal out in the open is dangerous. Before we go, would you mind transferring that Power into the column?"

Nat lowered the coin purse, still slightly shaken. "Um...of course, yes."

"We don't want anyone getting hurt," Brielle said.

Nat felt drained, but forced a smile. Placing one hand on the small bar on the tabletop, and the other on the column, she didn't force it. She was simply the conduit. The concentration in that small piece nearly *jumped* out at her when she called to it. As though it were eager to be free from the cramped space.

This transfer didn't take as long as the initial imbuing, and soon Nat opened her eyes and let out a deep sigh.

"Very well done, my dear," the queen said.

"Thank you, Your Majesty."

"Enjoy your evening, get plenty of rest, and we'll see you again tomorrow."

Brielle went to the exit and pulled a lever to open the hidden doorway. As Nat passed, she whispered, "You were amazing today."

Nat felt a warmth in her chest at those words, though something about it unnerved her. She made her way out on her own. Hardly paying attention, she hurried down the hallway, up the spiral stairs, and out into the palace, then the ground level of the city. She quickly found a familiar alcove and ducked inside to open the pouch she'd been given.

Inside were *twenty* gold coins, as well as three silver rings. Nothing noteworthy about them, plain bands with vine-like etching. Still, she tried one on, switching fingers until it fit on one comfortably. Perhaps Mama would like one too. The rest she could either trade, or hold on to for later use.

But the gold would be extremely useful. With this, she now had sixty gold pieces from five days of work. Far more than she'd ever earned killing rats.

By light coming in from down the tunnel, she could tell that the sun had nearly set, so she hurried toward the Callidian medic shop next. As soon as she entered, the shopkeeper's young daughter, Kaya, set down her book.

"Natalia! We weren't expecting you for another week." Her dark blue curls swayed like waves of the ocean as she moved. And it wasn't the first time Nat felt a twinge of envy that she hadn't inherited the blue Callidian hair of her father.

"I know," Nat said. "But I got some extra work, so…do you have enough to do double my normal order?"

"Of course!" Kaya went behind the counter and began pulling sacks off of shelves there, along with containers a size larger than what Nat normally bought. She hoped they'd fit beneath her hiding box, but if they didn't, she'd think of something else.

"Have you heard from Tomaz lately?" Kaya asked.

Nat raised a brow. "The last letter was nearly a month ago now…why?"

"Just curious." Kaya shrugged one shoulder, then gave a sly smile. "I've always kind of liked him, that's all."

Nat leaned forward, elbows on the counter. "You have *feelings* for my little brother?"

"Maybe?" Kaya said. "I just think he's cute, is all."

Nat grinned. She liked Kaya, maybe Tomaz could be convinced to come back here and court her in a few years—he was only fourteen at the moment, that seemed a little young to Nat. "You lived in Calidar as a child, right?"

"I did," Kaya said. "It's a lovely place. Forests, and meadows, and rolling hills…I miss it."

"Why don't you go back?"

Kaya sighed, corking the blue bottle. "My mother was outlawed, unfortunately. So, she can't return without getting arrested. At least here, we can live and practice in peace."

"Would they arrest *you* though, if you went alone, or without your mother?"

"I don't know, honestly," Kaya said. "The council only put an order out for her capture, not mine. But if they recognize me…who knows." She tied off the pouch of powder, then put that, the jar of paste, and bottle of syrup into a larger sack. "Here you are. That's forty gold for the double order, but I'll knock off five, since you're a regular—don't tell my mother."

"Thank you so much," Nat said. "I'm just grateful you're in the city. Having to get these medicines all the way from Calidar would cost so much more."

They stood in silence for a moment while Nat counted coins, then slid them across the counter.

Then Kaya spoke again. "Honestly, Nat…how *is* your mother doing?"

"She's…the same." Nat said. "She's not getting better, but she's not getting worse. I'm hoping, maybe if I can afford more medicine, if I apply it more often, it might make more of a difference?"

"It's worth a try. Sometimes it helps, sometimes it doesn't."

"Right," Nat said. "We're getting by. I have to keep hoping."

"We're all hoping with you," Kaya said. She reached across the counter and took Nat's hand, squeezing it gently.

"Thank you, Kaya."

"See you soon," Kaya said.

Nat bid her farewell, then hefted the sack over her shoulder as she wound through the crowds, hurrying to make her way home.

17

AHNRI

Ahnri kept a close eye on the queen whenever he could, though even with his abilities he couldn't keep track of her every minute of every day. It was about an hour before sunset when he spotted her calling the general into her office, and Ahnri grinned at the prospect of using the hidden entryway he'd found to eavesdrop.

It took him five minutes to get from his spot watching her to the tunnel entrance, taking as many shortcuts as he knew, Pir following behind. Ahnri made sure to take a lantern this time. The conversation was already underway, but hopefully he hadn't missed too much.

"—mobilizing, Your Majesty," a male voice said. Ahnri closed his eyes…that had to be the general. "The capital, Reinos, is fortifying, and soldiers are being trained to the north of the city."

"They lack even the decency to hide their intentions anymore," Elya said with a sneer in her voice. "Very well. And our recruits?"

"They're doing extremely well," the man said. "Training is nearly completed for the companies we have now."

"Excellent," Elya said. "As soon as those are ready, put them into the guard rotation in the city. Do not take any away, onLy add. I want extra protection as quickly as we can make it.

"Of course, Your Majesty."

"And I want your best soldiers added to my personal guard. I need to see them myself before we move forward."

"To…your personal guard, ma'am?" the general said. "You already have three dozen of our best in your rotation. If I may recommend—"

"You may not, General," Elya said. "I want an additional dozen before the week is out. I need six with me at all times, in shifts so that none get too tired to be unaware. Am I understood?"

A tense silence followed, and Ahnri wished he could see their faces.

"Very well, Your Majesty."

"You are dismissed."

One set of footsteps exited the room, closing the door behind him.

"Do you trust him?" a female voice said—Ahnri now recognized that as Brielle.

"I used to," the queen said, "but I'm beginning to doubt."

"General Saunier has served our family his entire life," Remi said. "He's never been anything but true."

Ahnri winced. He hadn't realized Remi was here…the sound of the prince's voice sent an ache to Ahnri's heart. He truly was working against the prince now.

"Yes," Elya said. "But time changes us all, boy."

Silence, then Brielle spoke again. "I've seen the reports he speaks of. I believe he is underestimating the strength and possible swiftness of Somnuria and Medelios attacking us—potentially at the same time. Strengthening the city guard and the army is of the utmost importance right now."

Ahnri frowned. He was still waiting on a reply from Carina but he was certain she wouldn't be marching her troops to the border.

"I appreciate your concern," Elya said. "I'll look over them tonight and decide for myself."

A knock sounded at the door.

"Enter," Elya called.

The door opened, and footsteps approached. "Apologies, Your Majesty. But I've given the general a report and he asked me to also inform you of the situation. He's gone down to the training caverns to inspect for himself."

"What has happened?" Elya's voice was tense now, Ahnri heard the rustle of paper.

Silence. Then the queen swore. "Return to the general and let him know I'll be there as soon as I can."

A shuffle, then the messenger retreated and the door closed again.

A beat of uncomfortable silence passed before Remi spoke again. "I really should prepare for the council meeting, Mother. Shall I meet you below later?"

"Yes, of course." Elya said, sounding distracted.

An exchange was made, and Remi's footsteps also left the room.

"Your son is eager," Brielle said.

"He is naive," Elya snapped. "I only hope I can guide him. But come, we have work to do, and I need to see what this illness is about."

"I'll head straight for the lab then, shall I?"

"Yes," Elya said. "Prepare for tonight's session. I'll meet you there."

The final two sets of footsteps made their way out.

"Lab? Session?" he whispered.

It had to be the hidden room.

Brielle had been there last time he'd tried to get in, because he'd tracked the queen's movements, not the advisor's. He needed *both* of them to be elsewhere for him to get in unseen.

Ahnri and Pin made their way out of the tunnel to the main corridors of the city, Ahnri's thoughts running all the way.

"I want to find out how they're receiving their intelligence reports," Ahnri muttered. "It's got to be a secret entrance; maybe if I find that I can alter the information...and I still need to get into that room. The lab. Where they're headed right now."

"*Mrrow?*"

Ahnri had no idea what the cat was asking, but he filled in the communication with his own questions. "I could watch for them to leave… It would be tricky though. That stairwell is always guarded these days."

He continued to talk to Pin as they walked the city. Habitually, he found himself wandering through a busy market, to the central spiral road that curved around the palace column, and around to the south side. They passed by the main palace entrance at the southern point, and then the kitchen and servant entrances on the west side, all of which he was intimately familiar with.

It wasn't until he glanced up from his feet and found he'd rounded back to the north side—a section Ahnri would consider the back of the palace—that memories began to rise in his mind. He'd only come this way a few times, but he should remember what was here…

Carts made their way down from markets toward the base of the palace column, breaking up Ahnri's view and forcing him to one side of the road.

"*Mrrow,*" Pin said, patting Ahnri's leg.

"What is it?"

Pin turned, stepping forward and seeming to point with his nose. Ahnri followed the gaze. An archway had been erected here across the road, through which traffic could pass, perhaps thirty to forty feet across, and the space above it that would normally be open to the ceiling had been closed off. As Ahnri watched, he spotted glints of torchlight from slits in the stone above.

"There's a bridge there…"

As he spoke it, the memories clicked into place. To the north of the palace complex, connected by this bridge, were the prisons. Cells built of a separate stone—granite quarried from miles away, brought in to prevent prisoners from digging their way out.

Memories rose in his mind, like embers from a fire being rekindled. His eyes closed and he was there...following a soldier, crossing that bridge, entering a prison cell, and the *clang* of it being shut behind him.

"You're to be interrogated."

Interrogated. Elya had said she'd heard a rumor about him, but Ahnri knew better. He was Damond's son, and the queen had wanted to know if Ahnri knew anything too.

He had lied well that day. Elya had concluded that he didn't know anything, and since he'd already begun to be trained by Fugeran Intelligence, decided he could be useful. A private mission for her, to Medelios. To prove his loyalty.

Ahnri forced his eyes open. That bridge, those cells...it hadn't even been that long ago, and yet he'd nearly forgotten about them...blocked them from memory. Until being faced with them once more.

"Mrrow?"

"Sorry," Ahnri said, shaking his head. "Remembering..."

Pin looked from Ahnri to the bridge, then took a step forward as though to say, *"Should we go?"*

"No," Ahnri said. "I don't think I can go in there yet...not unless I have a mucking good reason to."

"Mrrow."

"Yes, well. Figure out how to tell me what it is and I'll think about it."

Pin gave what Ahnri could only describe as a flat stare.

"Come on," Ahnri said. "Let's see if we can't keep an eye on that stairwell."

18

REMI

"Can we get that approved, Highness?"

Remi blinked out of his thoughts, refocusing on the council meeting. They had half an hour left but his mind was elsewhere.

"Apologies," he said. "I missed part of that. Approval for what?"

"More members of the city guard to patrol the nomadic areas of the outer city," Councilor Lita said. "We have the manpower, especially with the queen bringing in more soldiers to be trained."

Remi cleared his throat. "Right...we're going to need to hold off on that unfortunately. Could you mark it down to discuss again in three days? There are some details I need to check on before—"

The doors of the council chamber opened without warning, and a messenger hurried inside, going directly to Remi.

"Pardon, Your Highness," the girl said, her face pale. "But your presence is needed, urgently. It's the queen."

Mother...

"My apologies, council," Remi said, standing, keeping the worry from his voice as much as possible. "I've been summoned by Her Majesty the Queen. Please pause all considerations and we will resume discussions tomorrow. Thank you for your understanding."

He nodded to them collectively, catching Natalia's worried eyes as he turned, then made his way out of the room. He followed the messenger, and his guards followed him, ever present, though he ignored them.

"Can you tell me anything else?" Remi asked the messenger girl.

"Her Majesty is...angry, sir," she said haltingly. "I've nEver seen her like this, though I've heard others say it happens sometimes. It's only...the staff grew worried, and asked for you to come."

Remi frowned as they increased their speed. She led them through the palace, down to the subterranean army grounds and training caverns.

Unfortunately, when he arrived he found his mother in a tirade.

She stood in the mess hall, screaming at all around her. Her usually calm demeanor was nowhere to be found, her hair disheveled, her face flushed with anger.

Remi had seen his mother in this state many times before, but it had been years. The sharpness of her gaze, the fervor in her voice, it pricked something inside him like a freshly sharpened needle. He took two steps backward, running into the door frame behind him. He gripped it for support. Flashes of his childhood revived in his mind, like some strange stage play reminding him of what his mother had done to him.

Shouts while he hid beneath his bed.

Standing still as a statue before the throne while Mother berated him.

Locked in his room because he hadn't said, "Majesty."

Moment after moment rang like explosions in his mind, and Mother continued screaming at the cooks and cleaners of these underground kitchens. Remi put a hand to his chest and forced himself to take a deep, slow breath.

Somehow, a different memory appeared then: Ahnri. And Natalia. The palace's balcony gardens, when they were perhaps only eight or nine years old. Natalia's joyful laughter when the roses had finally bloomed, and how Remi's heart ached to tell Ahnri how much he cared for him…

That memory soothed the tremors in his body and mind, centering him amid the noise. Finally, he opened his eyes to see the mess hall where chaos reigned. He made his way slowly toward the center of the storm where Mother pointed her finger at the head cook.

"—obviously planted!" she screamed. "Four companies down? *Four hundred* troops? This is unacceptable!"

"My greatest apologies, Your Majesty," the cook said, on her knees, head bowed. "My usual staff are meticulous, but we've been so busy lately we've taken any extra hands we could get."

The queen's voice finally lowered—quiet, but not at all calm. "Those extra hands have *poisoned my army*. You have until nightfall to find me some evidence of who is behind this, or you will lose your job—and be grateful it's not your life."

The woman kept her eyes down—probably for the best. Remi scoured his mind for *something* to say. Some way to stand up for this woman who was only doing the best she could…

Mother finally noticed Remi there, and came toward him, shaking her head. "Come with me," she said.

He followed her out into the corridor and out of earshot of the mess hall before she stopped.

"Have you heard the reports?"

"No," he said, trying to think through the tangle of thoughts and emotions inside him. "You said…poison?"

"The last company to train yesterday has come down with a messy illness of the bowels. All one-hundred-some of them." She met Ahnri's gaze. "And the first that trained this morning have two-thirds of their soldiers down, the two following that are experiencing the same symptoms to a milder degree."

"Four whole companies?"

"Four companies affected," Mother said. "That cannot possibly be an accident."

"Well," Remi frowned. "Illnesses like that do tend to be very contagious though. Are we certain it's all of them?"

"Yes," she snapped. "And a few have nearly died from dehydration already. It's taking more resources to keep them alive than it would to simply let them die."

Remi's response caught in his throat. Surely his mother wasn't *that* heartless…but that wasn't the point…was it? He refocused himself. "If it's a simple case of upset stomachs, I'm sure they'll be fine in a few days. We'll monitor them and—"

"We don't *have* a few days!" she hissed. "Those other kingdoms could be on our doorstep at any moment and I *will not* have Isille unprotected. We *need* those soldiers."

Right. Build up the city. Protect Fugera. "I'll speak to the generals, Mother. I'm certain there's a way around this."

Her demeanor shifted then, calming slightly at his words. "Thank you, my son."

"You should get some rest." He turned, waving to her personal guards who had stayed back.

"Unfortunately, I can't yet," Mother said. "I have work to do with Brielle. But I will try to…go easy on myself while there."

Remi turned to his mother's guards. "Please escort the queen to her research chambers, and arrange for dinner and wine to be brought to her there—from the palace kitchens, not this one."

"At once, Your Highness."

"I'll speak with these kitchen staff, Mother," he said. "I'm sure we won't have to fire them. We can bring our best investigators down here and we'll figure it out."

The queen placed a hand on Remi's arm, her grip surprisingly strong. "You will protect me, won't you?"

He squeezed her hand, feeling her desperation. "Of course," he said. "You're my mother."

Her eyes closed, then fluttered back open in a relieved sigh. "Handle it, then. I trust you."

She turned away. He watched her go until she rounded the corner to the stairway up, then he let out a breath.

She's my mother, he told himself. *She trusts me.*

Straightening his back once more, he made his way again into the mess hall to find the head cook. After an hour of calm interviews with the entire kitchen staff, Remi learned that there had been at least five new workers helping the day before. Two were female, and three male, all with pale blond hair and dark Fugeran skin, and four of the five had worn standard palace servant attire.

So, essentially, he'd not narrowed it down at all.

He ordered them to be gathered when seen again, and hoped they'd have something by the end of the day. He managed to assure the head cook that his mother wouldn't actually fire her—though he wasn't sure he could stop her if she did—and then made his way back up to his rooms. When he arrived, he found a stack of requests for royal approval from the council on his desk.

With a sigh, he slumped into his chair and began to read. Unfortunately, his mind would not focus. He forced himself to get through the first page, before tossing it back onto the desk and rubbing his eyes. When he opened them, he caught sight of the purple ribbon again, and an idea came to him.

For the second time in a week, he tied the ribbon to his window, and the mere action of it gave him a sense of relief. Things between he and Ahnri weren't perfect—he knew Ahnri didn't agree with Mother's plans—but surely they could spend more than a few minutes together without fighting?

Remi wanted that…so much it hurt.

And, he reminded himself, Ahnri was technically a member of Fugeran Intelligence, maybe he could investigate the issues with the kitchen downstairs. Remi would trust him more than any of the other agents.

He glanced at the purple ribbon once more, before pulling the curtains closed, then ordered for dinner to be sent to him, and he waited.

19

NATALIA

Natalia tried to take notes throughout the council meeting, but her eyelids were so heavy she could hardly keep them open. Between these meetings, the lab work with Brielle and the queen, and taking care of Mama, even with a full night's sleep the tiredness had sunk into her bones. She was only half listening until she realized Prince Remi had stood to speak.

"—pause all considerations and we will resume discussions tomorrow. Thank you for your understanding."

He gave the room a nod—she caught his eyes for a moment and saw worry there—then made his way out. When the doors closed there was a heartbeat of silence. Then Councilor Erre grunted, heaving himself to his feet, and others began to move as well.

Nat was glad of the early end to that meeting. She would be working in the lab again tonight, as she had been for nearly a week now, and this might give her enough time to take a short rest before then.

She quickly gathered her things and wove her way through the others to escape the council room. As she started down the corridor, she spotted a familiar grey cat farther along, and a smile grew on her face as she made her way toward it.

"Miss Natalia?"

Nat spun to see Brielle approaching from behind her.

"I saw the prince leaving and guessed the meeting ended early," Brielle said. "If we begin now, we can be done earlier as well." She smiled, then turned and began walking away.

Nat blinked. It took a moment to process what the adviser had said. She glanced back to where Pin had been, but he was gone.

"Miss Natalia?" Brielle called.

"Coming."

In minutes they were down below. In the hallway Nat thought she heard shouting in the opposite direction from the lab, but couldn't make out any words.

"What's down that way?" she asked.

"That's the military training caverns," Brielle said. "They're always rather noisy, I wouldn't pay it any mind."

Once they reached the lab, Brielle went straight for one table and began to gather papers as Nat glanced around. The queen was not there yet. The space felt odd without her steady presence, but most of the work had been directed by Brielle anyway, with the queen only observing. Nat took a breath, and tried to shake off the feeling of unease.

"All right," Brielle said, "Time for stage two." She turned back to their work table holding two notebooks Nat hadn't seen before. Stepping closer, she could see that the handwriting in them was not Brielle's, nor did Nat recognize it.

"Stage two?"

"Correct," Brielle said. "Stage one was practicing the imbuing, gradually increasing the amount of magic until the piece can't hold any more. The goal of stage one was to imbue an item with enough Power that it could affect a being without touch."

"Which we succeeded at, right?" Nat asked.

"Also correct."

"All right…so what is stage two?"

"Well, similar to the first, we have a few steps to it. To begin, we'll use this." She pulled out a small medallion, made of the same black metal from before. Except this was stamped with the symbol of Fina, the hooded skull of shadow. She held it out.

Nat took it, wonder overcoming her. Fina had always been frightening to her, but this…it was a beautiful depiction.

"I'd like you to try," Brielle said, "to draw Power out of a source that already contains it, then back *through* it, and into this medallion."

Nat frowned. "Through it? I'm not sure what you mean…"

"It's difficult to explain and easier to attempt," Brielle said, making her way around the room to turn down the lanterns. "Here."

She brought out the rectangular bar that Natalia had filled and then emptied the day before, but this time she placed it in a sort of stand that held it suspended six inches or so above the table.

"First, put as much magic into this as you can again," Brielle said. "Then we'll try the next step."

Nat rolled her shoulders, taking a deep breath. All her life, she'd only learned to draw in the shadows and then release it into the world, affecting things in such harmful ways. But with the help of these people, she was finally learning how to *control* it. She'd become familiar with the specific sensation, the feel of the transfer, and had confidence in her abilities. Her ability—while it still frightened her—had become a tool now, not a weapon.

Closing her eyes, she drew in Power from the darkness around her. Then, slowly, she slid her fingers over the metal, and *channeled*.

Like before, the Elyum metal seemed to *drink* in the Power as Nat offered it. She took shadow from all around her, moving her hand through the dark room and leaving light in her wake, then going back over the spaces she'd already used as the shadows healed themselves.

Between breaths, a stab of pain shot through her from the spot in her lower back. Nat held her breath, hands suddenly shaking, but managed to hold herself upright. Only her shoulders curled in slightly.

"Miss Natalia," Brielle said. "Is everything all right?"

Don't… fold… she told herself. "F-fine," she said, holding her magic for a moment and focusing to send it to that spot, fighting back the thing inside her—a terrible time for it to attack. In a moment the pain was gone, though nausea had replaced it.

"Are you sure?"

"I'm *fine,*" Nat snapped. "I mean… I'm sorry. I'm fine. All is well."

Refocusing, she continued pressing her Power into the ingot—the bar taking in an incredible amount. Nat pushed herself until the material wouldn't take more.

When done, she opened her eyes and stepped back, tired. The piece before her shone brightly with that purple light which faded slightly, but—especially in the darkness with the lamps out—remained steady. Indicating it held an incredibly large amount of Power.

"Excellent," Brielle said. "Now this is the tricky part. I need you to take the medallion and place it on the table below that ingot."

Nat did so. The magic in the Elyum reached out to her, but took no effect. This did not make her immortal, it simply meant she couldn't be killed by that magic.

"Good, good," Brielle said. "Next you're going to draw that Power back into you, then focus it *through* the ingot, and *into* the medallion."

Nat stared. "You mean…without touching the medallion?"

"Correct," Brielle said.

Nat paused; she wasn't sure she understood how, but she thought she could picture it. Still, she imagined the magic flowing like a river, into her, out of her, and through the metal bar like a waterfall, to meet the medallion.

With a deep breath, she placed both hands on the ingot and tried.

The magic once again *wanted* to come out. That wasn't the difficult part. Allowing it into her, Nat imagined it coming up her hand and arm to circle inside her chest, then make its way back out her opposite arm. On reentering the ingot, it seemed as though there were no resistance at all to encourage it *through*, as though the metal were so focused on releasing to Nat's left hand that it ignored her right forcing the Power through it like a filter.

Except, when she felt the Power reach the medallion, the momentum slowed. Nat braced herself, and tried pushing it in, but it was difficult having to do it from a distance.

"It's…not going any farther…" Nat said.

"That's all right," Brielle said. "You can slowly draw away now."

Nat did so, opening her eyes and glancing to the medallion. A second later and she'd have missed it, but there was a trail of purple light flowing from the ingot down to the medallion.

"How…" she breathed. "What did that do?"

"Not much, yet," Brielle said, already turned away. "That was only the first step. Next, we'll need this." She went to the back of the room, and pulled out a suit of heavy leather, which she held up in front of Natalia.

"What is this?" Nat asked.

"For protection," Brielle said. "This next part is one we've seen the Powers resist, to the point that it can be unstable and lash out. In case that happens, I'd like you to wear this. We don't want anything happening to you."

Nat hesitated. They'd acknowledged danger being a possibility, and promised they would take precautions, and Nat had agreed. This was simply one of those precautions. She stepped forward, and Brielle helped her into the suit. Almost like a backward cloak, it slid on her arms from the front and attached with hooks in the back. It weighed her down a bit, but not uncomfortably so. Nat moved around in it for a moment, testing her range of motion.

"How does it feel?" Brielle asked.

"Fine," Nat said. "I'm glad to have it."

"Excellent," Brielle said. "Next, we'll try this." She came back to the table carrying a heavy board, on which an animal was strapped down with thin leather strips. A small rat.

"I'm sorry…what?"

"We'll now place the medallion onto the rat," Brielle said, doing so with gloved hands, "with the Elyum ingot suspended over it. And you'll perform the same exercise you just did."

"You want me to—"

"Do *exactly* what you just did," Brielle repeated, holding a finger up to Natalia. "*Exactly*. Remember, this is an experiment. We've done this with the other Powers but never with Death magic, so while I have some guesses of what will happen, there are no hard facts yet. You're helping us gather those, filling in those blanks."

Nat's stomach twisted uncomfortably. She'd been killing rats as pests for years, but something about the sight of this creature being held down felt…wrong. "I…do I have to?"

"Miss Natalia," Brielle said. She placed a hand on Nat's arm, comforting, encouraging. "You *do* want to continue this work, don't you? The queen always rewards those who *serve* Fugera."

Nat remembered the light in Mama's eyes when she'd finally seen the sky again after weeks of being bedridden. She couldn't back out now. And if this was what the queen required…

She nodded.

"Very good," Brielle said, stepping back. "Give it your best try. Don't force anything, work slowly, and if you start to feel worried, you can rest at any point."

Nat's heart raced in her chest faster than a spinning top. Swallowing to fight her nerves, she reached forward, resting her hand on the fur. It was brown, with dark patches on the hindquarters and ears. It let out a squeak as she touched it.

"Ah ah no, don't touch it," Brielle said. "Hand on the ingot. Treat the Power there as *part* of the thing to be imbued."

Nat adjusted hastily. Right. Placing both hands on the small bar of Elyum, she closed her eyes and drew in the Power. She had to do this well. *Had* to get it right.

The Power flowed into her like water, only warm like a fire. Carefully, she visualized that energy flowing up her left arm, through her chest, and down her right, like before. Through the metal once more, and then *out* the other side…

Once again, the initial pass through the Elyum was simple, and the Power drew almost magnetically to the coin-like medallion on the rat's chest, which helped directionally, but it once again resisted going further. It did not want to pass into the medallion.

Nat had never felt the sensation before, as though the Death magic had an opinion of its own, opposed to hers. Gently, she pushed it.

Please, I need you to do this…

In her mind's eye, she imagined herself standing before an enormous black wall, both hands flat against it and pushing fruitlessly. It seemed entirely immovable. Until at once, she felt a slight shift. Her mind latched on to it quickly and she instinctually shoved hard at the magic she held, trying to take advantage of the weakness she found, and then—

A boom of sound. A flash of light. The Power she'd been sending into the medallion released like a thunderclap, throwing Natalia to the floor. In a moment, Brielle was there, helping her stand. Asking…something. Nat could hardly hear her. She held her head, her hearing slowly returning as the reality of what had happened sunk in. She looked to the rat.

It was dead. Burned all over.

"Well," Brielle said, "that was a possibility, unfortunately."

Nat stared. A rush of anger flooded her. "With all due respect, Lady Brielle, if there is more information about possible failures or danger to me, I would appreciate knowing the details. Since I am the one performing these experiments."

Brielle eyed her for a moment. "Of course, my apologies. I sent you in unprepared, I will not do so again."

Relief. "Thank you."

Brielle glanced around the lab, and Nat followed her gaze. Smoke drifted from the round table where they always performed, and the smell of burning flesh and fur now filled the space. Papers and notes on that table were singed, but otherwise the damage seemed to be relatively contained.

At that moment the door to the lab shifted, and Nat and Brielle both stood as Queen Elya entered, her face immediately scrunching up at the smell.

"I take it," the queen said, "we've had an unfortunate result?"

"Indeed, Your Majesty," Brielle said, gesturing to the dead rat. "But failure is still progress. I was about to send Miss Natalia home; the session seems to have shaken her quite a bit."

Queen Elya's eyes fell on Nat then, and for a moment it seemed the queen was angry before her expression shifted to one of understanding. "Very well. I myself should retire as well. It's been quite an eventful evening."

Queen Elya turned and exited as swiftly as she'd arrived, though Brielle signaled for the guards to leave the door open.

Brielle walked Nat to the door. "I will allow you a few minutes to scan these notebooks next time before we begin. But again, please keep this information to yourself. Nothing spoken outside this room."

"I understand," Nat said.

"Excellent. Oh, and of course, here is your payment."

Nat accepted another coin purse, easily the ten gold she was promised.

"Goodnight, Miss Natalia," Brielle said, pulling the latch to close the door.

Natalia left, letting her feet take the path straight to her new home. The whole way there, she weighed coins in her hand, and implications in her mind.

20

AHNRI

Ahnri grinned at the sight of the purple ribbon. It never failed to amuse him when he and Remi had the same thought at the same time. He wanted to see the prince, but he'd need to do it early so he'd still have time to sneak into the lab tonight. Unless…unless he could get some information out of Remi.

He hated that he had that thought at all. And he hated more that he knew he would have to try it. He was breaking Remi's trust, but he'd tried to warn him. Despite their closeness, he couldn't tell the truth yet about working for Medelios, or how against the queen he actually was. Not until he knew that Remi would not go running to Elya with the information.

Either way, the thought of spending some significant time with Remi was too tempting to pass up, so he had Pin climb into the satchel, and Ahnri waited for a break in the guard rotation on the street below, before he climbed quickly over the road and into the prince's office window once more.

Stepping inside, he saw that the lanterns had been dimmed, and two glasses of wine were already poured on Remi's desk. A moment later, Remi rounded the corner, dressed in his nightclothes, and relief washed over his face.

"Thank you for coming," he said, rising onto his toes to kiss Ahnri.

Stars, he loved this boy.

"You weren't seen?" Remi asked.

"Not that I noticed," Ahnri said. "How much time do we have?"

"As much as we want," Remi said. "I do need to sleep though; today has been…well, I have a lot on my shoulders."

Ahnri paused. "Is there any way I can help?"

"With royal stuff?" Remi laughed. "You never want to help with that. It is, as I believe you've said, 'boring beyond belief,' right?"

"Well…" Ahnri shrugged. "Maybe it's time I learned more about the responsibilities you carry."

Remi looked twice, as though needing to be certain he'd heard correctly. "You…you'd really help?"

"If I can," Ahnri said. "I don't know much about 'royal stuff,' but I'm a fairly quick learner…if you're willing to teach me."

Remi turned away, seeming more timid than he usually did. "Not right now, I think," he said. "But the fact that you're offering means a great deal to me. Tonight, I'm very tired and don't really want to talk about anything important."

"Fair enough," Ahnri said, taking Remi by the hand. "Then maybe I can help in a different way for now." He pulled Remi over to a sofa and set him on the floor, then Ahnri went to Remi's bookshelf and took down a bottle of distilled oils. After applying a little to his hands, he sat on the sofa behind the prince and began to massage his shoulders. At the first touch, the prince's body slumped as the strain slipped away. His muscles were tight, even when relaxed. "You weren't joking."

Remi only laughed. "You know, we have a royal masseuse for things like this."

"Yes, but you like it better when I do it."

"That is true." He sighed. "This does help. Thank you."

"Of course," Ahnri said, leaning forward to kiss his cheek. He continued massaging, working out the knots in Remi's back and shoulders for a while. Soon, Pin bounded through the doorway to the offices and curled up in Remi's lap.

"Oh, kitten cuddles too?" he said. "I am a lucky man."

Ahnri laughed. He waited a moment, considering how to bring up a topic Remi didn't necessarily want to discuss. "I know you don't want to talk about important things," he finally said, "but is there anything you'd like to complain about?"

"Hmm," Remi said.

Pin purred from the prince's lap.

"I find a good complaining session to be helpful every now and then," Ahnri said.

"Well," Remi said. "I've been tasked with an investigation that feels like a dead end…something has made a large number of the troops sick and we're not sure what."

Ahnri closed his eyes, careful to not falter in his movements despite knowing the answers. "That's odd…what kind of illness?"

"An 'issue of the bowels,' Mother said." Remi looked up at the ceiling. "Nearly three hundred soldiers affected, and we have no idea what caused it."

Ahnri chose his words carefully. "Sounds like a random illness."

"Perhaps," Remi sighed. "Mother is convinced it's not, she's thinking poison. And I'm supposed to find out who did it."

I did…I'm sorry, Ahnri thought. "Do you have any leads?"

"Unfortunately, no. But I did want to ask you," Remi said, turning around, "would *you* be willing to check into it for me? You're still technically a member of Fugeran Intelligence. I could even get you a badge and you could investigate."

"I…" Ahnri hesitated. An official badge could get him into a lot of places, though he doubted he'd use it, considering he *didn't* want to be noticed. Still, it couldn't hurt to have… He hated himself for this, but said, "I…suppose I could try."

Remi sighed, pulling Ahnri down for another kiss. "Thank you. I'll see about getting you a badge first thing tomorrow." He turned to face forward again. "Having one less thing to worry about will be helpful. Mother is busy and stressed, and that means I have to pick up what she can't handle."

"I'm sorry," Ahnri said. Without thinking, he began to run his fingers through Remi's hair. After a moment of silence, he added, "You know…just because you're the prince doesn't mean you should have to do everything."

Remi sighed. "I know that, logically…but if I *don't* do it, it won't get done. And so I must."

Ahnri shifted to scratching Remi's back. The prince hummed, and Ahnri found a great deal of satisfaction in that.

"Gods above—I wish I could stay with you all day…"

Ahnri chuckled. "We would never get anything done."

Remi turned to meet Ahnri's gaze with a raised brow. "I'm sure we could think of some things."

Ahnri's face and neck flushed with warmth as Remi turned away again. Remi had always been the more forward of the two of them. Ahnri wanted to be with him, but it had never quite felt like the right time. They had, however, spent many hours together over the years, simply talking, kissing, sharing secrets and stories…

It hurt to lie to him.

Remi would figure it out eventually, and Ahnri knew it would be worse. But he'd made his decision. He would follow through.

"Tell me about Medelios?" Remi asked after a time.

"It's lovely," Ahnri said. "A desert, like Fugera, but of a different make. More plant life, less sand. The capital city, Reinos, sits beside a wide river, and is organized in circles, divided mainly by class. The city is colorful nearly to the point of being garish, but once you're used to it, it's hard to imagine it any other way."

He spoke on for some time, telling Remi about the shops, the people, and some of the things he'd learned while there. Never going near the fact that he was friends with the new queen, or that he now worked for her, and communicated with her regularly.

"How are you feeling?"

"Hmm?" Remi said. "I think I may have missed the last thing you said."

Ahnri laughed. "Are you falling asleep on me?"

"I believe I am," Remi said, his words ever so slightly slurred. "What a shame, I think you'll have to carry me to my bed again."

Ahnri kept his laughter soft as he moved to pick up his prince. In a cradle carry, he brought him into the bedchamber— the blankets were already turned—and laid him down. Ahnri tried to pull away, but Remi held him there.

"Stay?" Remi said. "For a while?"

Ahnri hesitated, unsure for a moment. They weren't on the best of terms right now, but part of him desperately wanted to be *close* to Remi…just for a short time.

"All right," Ahnri said, lying down beside the prince and shifting so that his chest could serve as a pillow.

The prince and the spy lay there in the dim light, Remi's hand over Ahnri's heart. Ahnri stared down at the boy he loved, his heart breaking, hating what he had to do—what he was currently doing.

"Someday," Remi said softly, "we'll be able to fall asleep like this every night."

Ahnri sighed, closing his eyes to the problems around them. He rested his cheek against Remi's hair, running his fingers across the prince's back and shoulder.

Ahnri waited until Remi was fully asleep, snoring lightly, before untucking himself from the prince's arms. Asleep, Remi looked peaceful, his features smoothed and relaxed in spite of the stress of the day. Ahnri stood there, watching him for a moment, thinking about…everything.

He hated this. Hated what he had to do, hated Elya for causing the things that made him have to choose between his sworn loyalty to Carina and his love for Remi. The things Ahnri was doing in trying to stop a coming war were causing Remi stress and anxiety…but, he thought, if he were going to cause it, even by extension, then he would do his best to be here for his prince, to relieve at least some of it.

Pin hopped up onto the bed then. Ahnri met the cat's eyes. "Would you stay with him until morning?"

Pin turned, settling himself under Remi's arm.

"Thank you." Ahnri leaned over, placing one last kiss on Remi's forehead. "…I'm sorry."

The hour had grown late, so Ahnri carefully checked outside the office window to make sure he wouldn't be seen. He removed the purple ribbon before he crawled out, watched for guards, and climbed down to the street below.

Maybe in the cover of night he could get into that hidden room downstairs.

21

AHNRI

Even at this late hour, there were soldiers, cooks, and guards going in and out of the military caverns. Ahnri had noted it was really only late afternoon when the traffic slowed, and then it picked up again a few hours before midnight.

He made his way down in the back of a group of young recruits, listening as he went.

"Have you been given your sword yet?"

"Not yet," a second said. "We're supposed to start training with them tomorrow. They seem heavy though."

"They're a lot lighter than you'd think," a third replied. "We've been using them for a week. They're very specific though, you've got to keep your hands on the wrappings."

As they left sight of the guards, Ahnri let the group get ahead of him. What swords were they talking about? He hasn't seen any mention of special weapons yet anywhere, but he'd have to keep an eye out for it.

He reached the base of the staircase and immediately went right, the hallway curving around slightly until he reached the blank stretch of wall. As a precaution, he pulled out his dagger and held it at the ready before pressing the wall where Pin had shown him, and watched as the door opened itself.

The smell hit him first. Burned flesh and hair, and something metallic. It made his stomach turn, though he didn't let it deter him.

What he stepped into was absolutely what he'd define as a laboratory. Though the lamps were unlit, light from the hallway showed him long thin tables that created a path straight into the space, with work surfaces on both the sides closest to him and the opposite, and thin spindly shelves running down the center of each.

He took a moment to find the nearest lamp and light it, then searched for the door's closing mechanism and got that shut.

Now, to search.

He would make a first pass through the room without touching anything. Oddly, at least to his mind, there were no papers, notes, books, or anything resembling records, at least that he could see on a first pass. He swore under his breath. His first attempt at entry might've given them reason to carry all of that out every time they left. Annoying that that made sense.

One table held multiple pieces of the same dark metal he'd seen in the small smithy down the hallway. Rectangular ingots and strips of it were scattered across the tabletop, and in one spot lay a pile of large coins—he immediately recognized the Fina mold used here.

Behind the initial tables, the walls were lined with cages; most of which had one or more animals in them, all sickly and depressed.

Ahnri could understand why.

Stuck underground for who knew how long, at the whims of a queen who probably used them for experiments. A lump formed in his throat. If he could do it without the queen knowing, he would free every single one of them this very night—unfortunately, that wasn't an option without them knowing someone had been here.

He knelt near a beautiful Ignatian wolfhound, his heart breaking to see it chained by its neck and feet. Its white fur was thin and yellowed from being away from the cleansing snow for too long.

"Hello friend," Ahnri said. "You hungry?" He took a piece of old grilled meat from his pack and offering it through the bars.

In a flash, the animal lunged forward. Ahnri pulled his hand away in time for the hound's teeth to graze his skin, but the barking rang in the silence like alarm bells.

Ahnri shuffled backward, running into the table behind him and knocking some things over. He swore, but couldn't take his eyes off the hound. It took up the meat and began to gnaw as though it hadn't been taught how to eat like a wolfhound should. Ahnri stared, confusion rising in his mind.

One moment its eyes had been closed, the next they were wide and full of rage. And now, almost as fast as it had leaped up, the creature settled. As though all its energy had been spent on that single effort.

"Stars above," Ahnri muttered. "What have they done to you?"

Hands and breath still shaking, he forced himself to stand. He did not interact with any of the other animals.

At the back of the space, he finally located the source of the burning scent—a small piece of burned wood lay on a circular table, framed by a very odd contraption. Four rods and wires held one of those dark ingots above the plank. But something even more out of the ordinary caught his eye. He took a moment to lower the brightness of the lantern, to examine it more closely.

The ingot, the one suspended over the scorched wood, was *glowing*.

A subtle light, and one he wouldn't have noticed if the room had been properly lit, but in the darkness it was definitely there.

He frowned, staring at it. Every time he'd seen magic used, the Vessel—whether human or inorganic—would glow during the time the magic was being used or transferred, and each branch of magic had a different color. Blue for Life, green for Growth, red for Stability, and purple for Death. He'd seen Merlin do it with each type—an oddity in itself, as users of more than one branch were extremely rare—and watched Cures with the injured plenty of times in his life. The magic always gave off a soft glow of light when it was used, but as soon as the movement of Power ended, the glow would fade.

This was not fading.

Ahnri took a step closer, crouching to get on eye level with the ingot. "So…they're filling metal with Death magic?" he muttered. "And…killing animals with it?"

It didn't make sense.

Were they creating some kind of weapon that used this ingot as a power source? Was this evidence of a failed experiment, or a successful one? Without notes, he had no way to know.

He took a moment to open his own notebook and sketch out the unusual contraption on the table, as well as the designs of the coins, which he should've done earlier.

He did not touch *any* of these, however. Knowing that single ingot was imbued with Death magic made him hesitant to touch anything in the room at all, but especially the things made of that same black metal.

Snapping his book closed, he stood in the center of the lab and glanced around once more, thinking about everything he'd seen thus far.

This black metal…Viruses…an unusually high amount of Death magic…soldiers promised new weapons…anger driving their attacks…he had no idea what was actually being done with this magic, but between this lab, and how eager Elya was to recruit new soldiers, Ahnri had to assume they were connected.

Either the troops were going to be used in this experiment, or they were a cover up for what was being done here. With Death magic involved, Ahnri wouldn't want to be among them.

Sighing, disappointed at the lack of information here, Ahnri moved to go—when his eye caught on a patch of something white toward the back of the room, near a pile of crates. The crates seemed to only contain more scraps of this dark metal, but the white he'd spotted was a crumpled-up paper tucked between two crates.

Ahnri pulled it out. Setting the lamp down, he used both hands to flatten the page against the floor.

His stomach dropped.

Research by Tavin DuPont
with credit and dedication to the memories of
Louis Moreau and Chloe Chapelle-Moreau

Ahnri had no idea who Tavin DuPont was, but Louis and Chloe…he knew those names.

They were his birth parents.

Why would his birth parents' names be on a paper in a lab like *this?*

Muttering swears under his breath, he replaced the lantern—and everything he could find that he'd accidentally knocked over or moved. And with one final glance, a single page in his pocket, he left the laboratory.

22

NATALIA

The next afternoon, Natalia entered the lab with shaking hands. Her last session ending in an explosion—even if it hadn't harmed her—had been more stressful than she'd expected, but she came back. Mama deserved the best, and if Nat could provide it, she would.

"We have some time before the queen arrives," Brielle said after closing the door behind them. She gestured to the circular table where a chair had been placed before the two tattered notebooks. "I'm going to share with you more information than we'd initially planned to, but you've proved yourself trustworthy thus far...I believe you can hold your silence?"

"I can," Nat said, straightening. "And I will."

"Good. Anything you read in these books will not be spoken of outside this room, is that understood?"

"Understood."

"And you acknowledge that if you do speak of it, you are committing treason against the Fugeran crown?"

Bumps rose on Natalia's arms. "Yes."

"Very well," Brielle said, relaxing slightly. "Within these notebooks are research notes from a group of brilliant scientists who are no longer with us. They spent their lives researching the Powers and their limits. Doctor Tavin DuPont, and his associates. They discovered...incredible things." Brielle gazed bright-eyed at the notebook she held. "Our research here is an attempt to continue where they left off."

"And, where did they leave off?" Nat asked.

"Well, it's complicated," Brielle said. "But there are notes about an effort to transfer not only magic, but *ability* as well. According to this, Tavin did manage it with an animal, and we wanted to make sure that works—"

Nat thought back to the rat she'd scorched, confused. Brielle's voice carried on in the back of her mind as Nat stared at the smoldering remains of the poor animal, trying to understand...

"—incredibly vague. There are so many holes to fill. Fascinating, isn't it?"

"Wait," Nat said, her mind still reeling. "You mean, that was an attempt to give my *ability* to the *rat*?"

"Yes," Brielle said. "It wouldn't take it away from you, there's no need to worry about that. And—according to Tavin's notes—the transfer doesn't run out or fade at all. Think of it as simply...sharing your gifts."

Nat frowned, confusion twisting her thoughts. "Giving Death magic to a rat seems like a terrible idea to me…"

Brielle let out a sweet-sounding laugh, and Nat gave a reluctant smile.

"Of course, of course," Brielle said. "We'd never let it run free. After some research we will dispose of it properly. No waste, of course."

That seemed…economical.

"Now, I need to get us set up," Brielle said. "But you can read through that until the queen arrives. Let me know if you have any questions."

"Thank you." Nat said, her nerves easing. If they trusted her enough to hand her the notes they were working from, she could stay informed and hopefully feel more comfortable continuing this.

The page Brielle left open was labeled at the top with the words, *Vessel Transfer*. This scientist, Tavin DuPont, had wanted to find a way to share his abilities with another person. Not simply share the Power by channeling it to them, or putting it in an inanimate vessel for them to utilize, but share the *innate ability* to draw upon the Four Powers.

And, it seemed he'd been successful.

There were mentions of many failed experiments—and mentions of accidents that caused him to take a break from the work as a result. Nat stopped to look closer at these, but the notes seemed to jump ahead…she flipped through the pages before noticing some had been torn out.

"Lady Brielle?"

The adviser stepped away from her preparations.

"There are pages missing," Nat said, pointing out at least three she'd found where information skipped, and there was remnants of a torn page between.

Brielle sighed. "I know. I don't know who removed them, but it's unfortunate. We found these notebooks in Doctor DuPont's things when he left, and the pages had already been removed."

Nat frowned as Brielle went back to her work. The adviser had mentioned holes in the research, perhaps those missing pages was what they needed Nat to help fill in.

"And you said," Nat asked, "you've worked with other Vessels before me?"

"Of the other branches of Power, yes," Brielle said. "We did have some Viruses who worked with us for a short time, but unfortunately they couldn't continue for a variety of reasons. The same held true for Vessels of the other branches. It's difficult to find help who cAn commit as fully as we need them to. The time commitment alone is a great deal to ask."

"How far had those Vessels gotten in your research?"

"About as far as we are now," Brielle said. "Some had the experience you did last time and were frightened away, others left because of work or family reasons. We've only had a couple attempt this next stage, and this is really the most important step."

Nat turned back to the notes. She read that DuPont always come back to it despite the failures and risks, until finally, he'd discovered the strategy Brielle had been trying to execute—and which Nat had failed at so spectacularly the day before.

This scientist had been a Clarity, so he'd worked with raw stone and the Power of Stability—that seemed far less risky than her Death magic. And yet, accidents had happened anyway. She found descriptions of explosions similar to the one she'd had the day before.

At that moment, the lab door opened and Queen Elya entered. She left her guards outside, as usual, and Nat and Brielle bowed at her approach.

"Well, we made progress yesterday," the queen said. "Let us see how much more we can accomplish tonight."

"Of course, Your Majesty," Brielle said, going to the back of the room to get the leather suit for Nat to wear.

Nat stood, moving the chair back to a corner of the room, out of their way. She and Brielle got her into the suit, and Brielle brought out another rat, strapped down to a board. Its tiny chest rose and fell quickly, and its black eyes were wide and darting around.

Nat took a deep breath. She knew the concept, Doctor DuPont's notes made sense, she just had to figure out how to focus her Power…

Brielle retrieved the small stand, and placed it directly over the rat in the center of the table. She then put on thick gloves and used a long-handled clamp to move the bar of Elyum they'd used yesterday and placed it on the stand, suspended above the rat. Then she reached into her pocket and offered Nat the Elyum medallion, with Fina's likeness embossed into it.

Nat reminded herself of Mama, lying in bed in their apartment above. With a deep breath, she swallowed her nerves and placed the medallion on the rat's chest while Brielle lowered the lights, and the queen sat in her usual seat at the side of the room, watching.

Deep breath. Calm. Focus.

Nat extended her hands, placing the tips of her fingers against the Elyum ingot. Closing her eyes, she took a moment to extend her senses, feeling where the Power sat, the fuel for her abilities. She could also feel the rat's nervous energy, wanting to move.

Don't think about that…she told herself. *Focus.*

Slowly releasing her breath, she drew in Power from the ingot. And then, willing the Power to follow her guidance, gave it momentum to go back through the ingot, and toward the medallion, and the rat.

This time, when she came to the wall of resistance, she expected it, and waited, focusing. In her mind, she could again see the endless black wall, and a cloud of purple magic gathering behind her. She focused, pushing, but not forcing. In her heart, she sent a prayer to Fina for strength.

After a few minutes of constant, low pressure, Nat felt something give. She gave a sharp intake of breath, reminding herself not to reach for it too quickly. Keeping herself steady, she brought her efforts to that area.

An almost physical *crack* came to her senses as she pushed against the very nature of the Power. She focused on that, that small break in its defenses, expecting to be thrown back as she'd been yesterday, and gently pushed again.

This time, like a dam crashing down, the barrier vanished before her. Her magic released like a flood, channeling through the Elyum ingot and toward the medallion, and the rat.

Nat instinctively slowed the flow of energy, so as to not overwhelm the tiny body. A strange level of connection grew then, and she could feel the rat's amazement, and fear.

"Gods above," Brielle whispered. "It's beautiful."

Tentatively, letting the Power follow the flow she'd set, Nat opened her eyes.

In the darkness of the lab, her Power glowed bright. A stream of deep purple light flowed from the ingot into her left hand, then a second from her right hand back to the ingot and a third, of a slightly darker, more dense coloration, from the ingot to the rat.

It really was beautiful.

After a few moments, Nat cut off the flow. The light of her magic faded—most of it slipping back into the ingot—and Brielle hurried to turn the lanterns up once more.

Nat stared at the rat. It was still moving, breathing quickly, twitching its little claws.

"How do we tell if it worked?" the queen asked.

"Well, it's not dead," Brielle said. "I'd call that an excellent sign. But now, we give it an opportunity to use its abilities." She donned her thick gloves again and went to the rat, removing it from the restraints. Then she put it in an empty glass cage, and went to another to choose a small beetle, bringing that to the rat's cage and letting it loose inside.

Nat watched as, for a moment, the rat only attempted to catch the beetle by using its claws and teeth. Then, as if on instinct, the rat did what Nat always did—drew in Power, leaving a small section of light where there should've been shadow, and leaped onto the beetle, releasing the magic in a flash of dark light.

The beetle stopped moving, and the rat enjoyed his meal.

"It worked?" Brielle breathed.

"It worked," Queen Elya said.

"It worked." Nat shuddered.

An hour after leaving the lab, Natalia knelt beside Mama's bed, her voice hoarse from having told her everything.

"It started so simple," Nat said, as she finished describing the most recent experiment. "But now...I'm afraid, Mama."

Mama pushed Nat's curls out of her eyes, and Nat reached up to take her hand.

"My heart," Mama said. "If you're not comfortable doing it anymore, then stop. Tell them. They seem to have been understanding so far, haven't they?"

"They...they have."

"Then it shouldn't be an issue." Mama patted her hand.

Nat let her head fall to the mattress. "What if they take away the apartment?" she said, her voice muffled in the blankets.

"Then we move back to our old one," Mama said. "It won't be so bad."

"But you deserve to see the sky."

"I deserve no such thing," Mama said. "I have *you*, my heart. And that is all I need. Everything else? Well. It's nothing but sugar dust, right?"

A weight settled in Nat's chest. "But…" She looked Mama over. With the added applications of medicine recently, Mama was doing much better. Tears burned behind Nat's eyes. "If I don't keep working for them, we won't have the extra money for more medicine."

Mama's eyes grew sad. "My heart. I know you want to keep me, but—"

"Please don't, Mama," Nat said, letting her head fall back down. "I can't think of that."

"I'm proud of you, my Natalia," Mama said, stroking Nat's hair. "You're growing up, and part of growing up means protecting the peace in your heart. No matter the cost."

Nat's knees were beginning to ache.

"Speak what it is you want." Mama said. "Do not think of me or anyone else. Listen to *your* heart."

Nat lifted her head, sniffing, and braced herself. "I want to be done," she said softly. "I don't want to help the queen any longer." She put her face in her hands. "I'm breaking their confidence by even telling you all this."

Mama put a hand on Nat's head. "It's all right." She put her hand to Nat's cheek. "Who am I going to tell, my heart?"

Nat wiped her eyes with her sleeve.

"You can do this," Mama said.

"Could you…help me think of what to say?" Nat asked.

"I will," Mama said, "But it's late. We should hurry before I fall asleep halfway through a sentence. Get your notes out, let's get started."

23

AHNRI

Ahnri received a response from Carina the next morning. She reassured him the letters in Elya's possession were fake, that she—Carina—was *not* sending troops toward Fugera, nor, to her knowledge, was the Somnurian monarch. Both were mobilizing, and fortifying their cities, but only because Elya had done the same already.

Ahnri rubbed at tired eyes as he finished reading it, before hurriedly taking a page from his notebook and scribbling down in code everything he'd learned since his last communication. The lab, the small underground smithy and the black metal, the references to Fina, Elya's numerous increases to her personal guard, the investigation into the sabotages—caused by himself—and finally, the crumpled paper with his birth parents' names on it.

He felt for the hawk. Kahn usually rested a day before making the flight back to Carina, but after seeing his parents' names in the lab the night before, desperation had begun to grow in him. He needed help, and maybe Carina would be able to make sense of it all before Elya did anything rash.

Today, Ahnri entered the underground training area in the guise of a messenger boy, following Captain Lind—the man in charge of receiving Fugeran Intelligence reports. Ahnri had learned this more than a week ago, and now kicked himself for not investigating this Captain Lind earlier.

Ahnri stayed a few steps behind as they passed multiple doors leading to rooms he'd managed to scout out over the past week and a half: the mess hall, a meeting room, the intelligence network center.

Throughout this hallway were notices asking for anyone who had seen a young man with Ahnri's features listed, and to report it to the head cook immediately. Ahnri was skilled enough at adjusting his features that so far, he hadn't been recognized. But he worried it may only be a matter of time.

He'd thought more than once that it was a good thing his arrest five months ago and subsequent mission had been kept quiet, the queen not wanting to shout about her secret dealings. If the whole city had known, Ahnri would've assuredly been recognized by now.

They passed right by the hidden room, which he fully ignored. In his mind he boxed up his irritation. The fact that he'd managed to get in and found his birth parents' names on a piece of paper and not a connection to anything else was eating at him. He'd surely missed something.

He'd even shown the paper to Pin, and the cat had seemed excited. He'd led Ahnri out of their room and through the tunnels of the city, back to that same spot where they'd seen the bridge—the one leading to the prisons.

Yes, Pin wanted him to go in there...but Ahnri couldn't make himself go yet.

"Soon," he'd told the cat. *"I promise."*

Pin had seemed disappointed. Ahnri assumed there was something important there, but he would attempt every other avenue he could before resorting to reliving those memories.

Unfortunately, it seemed the cat had taken that rejection personally, because Ahnri hadn't seen him since. Perhaps Pin simply had other business...but Ahnri couldn't help feeling like every relationship he had was breaking one mistake at a time.

For now, there was only one room in this subterranean hallway that Ahnri hadn't been able to sneak into without suspicion, and only because one couldn't casually pass by it. Luckily, the captain was leading him there now. The very last door, where only high-level leaders and intelligence officers ever went in or out. But now, he would get a glimpse.

The captain he followed was tall and thin, but had darker hair than most Fugerans: a deep golden brown. Almost Reganian in tone. Ahnri wondered for a moment whether the man was part Reganian. The spectacles perched on his nose framed keen eyes—eyes Ahnri tried not to meet.

They arrived at the last room, and Captain Lind pulled out a key. Unlocking the latch, he tucked it back in his pocket quickly, and opened the door.

Ahnri caught sight of a small space with a single circular wooden table covered in burns and cuts, but on the opposite side he saw a staircase leading upward. To the city, perhaps? Near the stairs stood a pale woman with blue hair covered in a kerchief, dressed in brown cloth that wrapped around her body like sand in the wind—excellent camouflage.

"You remain here," he said firmly to Ahnri, and closed the door behind him.

Ahnri swore under his breath, but leaned as close to the doorframe as he could, and closed his eyes to listen.

"Report?" the captain said.

"As requested," the woman replied. Ahnri heard some movement, something being set on the table perhaps, followed by the shuffling of papers. "Movements of the Medelian troops recorded by Vitan in the Tiero range." A momentary pause, and more shuffling. "Here, see? They're approaching Vei Lake and the valley between the Arontas and Tiero mountains, though it's uncertain whether they're setting up to stay there."

"Excellent," the captain said. "Her Majesty will be pleased."

A muffled sound—a coin pouch probably—then papers again, and footsteps.

Ahnri stepped away from the door, across the hallway to give him another glance inside. As the captain exited—holding a waterproof tube slung over one shoulder—Ahnri caught a glimpse of the blue-haired girl, who turned away as the captain exited.

But what troop movements was she reporting on? Were they fake reports? And if so, who had made them? Were the agents being paid off? How high up did this go?

The captain led Ahnri to the spiral stairs without speaking, then handed him the tube as well as a sealed letter. "Take these *directly* to the queen. She'll be in her quarters by now, and she'll want to see these as soon as possible."

"Yes, sir," Ahnri said, bowing. He took the tube and left immediately.

Up the stairs and through the palace, Ahnri took a slight detour to a wing where he knew there were empty rooms where he ducked into one set, closing and locking the doors behind him.

He didn't have much time…

Ahnri opened the tube and began rolling the papers out. Before him lay a map of the border between Fugera and Medelios. The Arontas mountains to the west, the Tiero range to the south, and below the mountains a mark and a note, *Medelian troops camp.*

"That is an outright *lie…*" he muttered under his breath. "Who is doing this…and *why?*"

He'd spent the past *twelve days* trying to stop or stall the queen's efforts in every way he could think of. First poisoning the troops, then he'd managed to reroute a food supply delivery which had caused the queen to pull from the local merchants causing a shortage in the city that had upset the citizens—he hadn't intended that, but it was an unfortunate side effect, and it meant more pressure on Elya regardless. Then he'd sent a fake letter to the queen from one of the council members, threatening to pull support for the new recruitments if she didn't approve their proposals—that hadn't worked well, because Remi gave those approvals not Elya.

And now, he had in his hands a report meant to go directly to the queen. And that captain had already seen it…if Ahnri altered or damaged it in any way, he would be suspect. And while that captain didn't know Ahnri from any other messenger boy, he was certain there would be a search for him. Well, *another* search for him. He couldn't afford to be caught. If the queen discovered he was here, or anyone began truly watching for *him*, it would make his job much more difficult.

Not impossible, but more difficult.

He straightened, wishing Pin were there to talk to. Instead, he spoke out loud to himself. "I can't give this to the queen…she's already doubled the city's border guard. Not that a secure city is a bad thing, but I still don't mucking know what she's planning to *do* with all of these soldiers."

He scanned the other papers, notes from this supposed intelligence officer, a full-page summary of what her informants had "seen." It noted that the Medelian camp seemed temporary, but they were unsure whether that meant they intended to march farther north, or return to the capital…a perfect cover if nothing ever happened. First that letter with the false seal, now this?

In the moment, he felt he had two options. One: he tried his best to disguise himself and went into Elya's office, then attempted to trip and throw the papers into the fire *right in front of her*. He didn't think she'd recognize him, but if he succeeded he would be apprehended by the guards and possibly executed. He could maybe get away…unless she ordered him killed right then.

He stretched his neck, trying not to imagine that.

Or…he could simply *not* deliver the report.

Captain Lind would be able to give a very good description of him, certainly…better than the kitchen staff had. Was this report worth that risk? The last thing he needed was Elya marching toward Medelios…

No…he couldn't risk her not getting a report she expected. He hadn't disguised himself well enough to Captain Lind to avoid that. He'd have to risk the first option.

He checked the room's fireplace, and luckily this one hadn't been fully cleaned after its last tenant. Taking the darkest ashes, he rubbed them into his light hair and brushed them out repeatedly until it wasn't splotchy, to leave a gray-black color. It wouldn't blend in as well here as Medelios, but at least it would be a different description than himself. Then he used the ash to give himself deep circles under his eyes as well, and to darken his brows.

He used his water skin to wash the ash from his hands, then returned all the papers to the tube, closing it up, and steeled himself.

Into the wildcat's den.

Queen Elya's private quarters were on the same floor as Remi's, only a couple of hallways away. On the way, Ahnri rearranged his hair to hang across his face, adjusted his expression, and slumped forward a little, drawing his cloak tight to appear to take up less space. Then, he carefully loosened the lid to the protective tube, trying to make it appear as though it were closed, while keeping it unsecured.

Finally, he reached the queen's doors—guarded by a half dozen soldiers.

"Who approaches?" one of the guards asked, hand tightening on his spear.

"Messenger, here for the queen," Ahnri replied, raising his voice slightly. "Got a package from Captain Lind."

The guard relaxed, extending a hand to take the package.

Ahnri held it close. "Apologies, sir, I've been instructed to pass this off to Her Majesty directly."

The man sighed, exchanging an eye roll with his fellows. But they turned and made way, unlocking the huge double doors—painted blue and inlaid with gold. The first guard stepped inside. "A message from Captain Lind, Your Majesty."

Ahnri followed, keeping his head bowed, letting his hair fall across his eyes.

Elya sat at her desk in that high-backed chair of dark wood and velvet. The thick, beautiful rug filled the floor around her, and—thankfully—flames lit the fireplace between the two curtain-framed windows. She set a cup of tea on her desk and stood, waving for Ahnri to approach.

He did so, keeping his posture curled inward.

Here goes...

He tripped on the edge of the carpet, crying out, and loosening his grip on the tube. The momentum did as he'd hoped, flinging off the cap and launching the contents toward the fireplace.

The queen screamed, guards converged, and Ahnri immediately went to the fireplace. "Sorry! I'm so sorry, Your Majesty!" With as much stealth and speed as he could, he saved certain pages, and allowed others to burn.

As many notes as he could, he let singe before pulling them free and patting the fire from them, leaving scorch marks in her rug in the process. He let the map sit for a moment longer, though the queen herself reached in and grabbed it before Ahnri would've liked. At that moment, guards came forward and pulled him up by his arms.

Two more guards began pulling as much from the fireplace as they could, but Ahnri was fully satisfied that the information—false though it had been—was now broken.

"You *imbecile!*" the queen shrieked. "How *dare* you be so careless!"

She slapped him across his face.

He only just saw it coming, and tried to turn his head to lessen the blow, but it still made his head ring.

"I will not have this kind of thoughtless, inept, asinine behavior in anyone working in the palace," she said, her voice shrill. A fire in her eyes. "Take him to the dungeons immediately, and arrange his execution—I do not care to attend.

See that he loses his head *tonight*, and inform his employer that he will not be returning!"

With bows and compliance, the guards dragged him out of the room. Ahnri cried out, begging forgiveness, as a normal person would. He half-heard her call for them to summon Remi, though Ahnri's own cries drowned much of that out.

Most of the guards stayed at the queen's doors, while two carried Ahnri away. As he got farther from the queen, he was simply grateful to have gotten out of there unrecognized.

Now, he had to get away. Elya had grown more and more paranoid, yes. She'd tripled her personal guard, and was doing the same with the city guard. There were experiments with a Virus, most likely in that hidden lab downstairs, but he had no idea how all these things were connected.

He still had work to do.

He kept up the pathetic sounds of crying as they led him up a ramp, but the guards taking him didn't seem to care. Then, he suddenly remembered where he was going—

Across the bridge.

Sharp fear rose in his chest, his heart thumping harder with each step they took. He'd been there before. He could go again…and he could get himself out this time—maybe? Anxiety and memories swirled in his mind, making him dizzy. He could see the bridge, the entrance. His vision grew blurry.

"Hey," one of the guards said. "He's fading."

Ahnri didn't know if he actually fainted, or if he'd simply faked it well enough that his body went along with it. But in a heartbeat, he found himself lying on the ground, the two guards standing over him.

"Feel bad for the kid," one said. "It was definitely an accident."

"Yeah," the other agreed. "I've tripped on that mucking rug more times than I can count."

Silence. "Seems cruel to kill a messenger…"

"We can't just *not* take him…she'll know."

Ahnri blinked, shaking his head.

"Come on now, son," one said, and they began to try lifting him. "Up we go."

A sharp *hiss* sounded nearby. Ahnri was dropped again as one guard shouted out in pain. The other swore, and Ahnri heard a grunt, and a high-pitched feline cry.

"Ow! Mucking cat!"

Ahnri opened his eyes in time to see Pin climb up the leg of one guard and scratch at his face a half dozen times before the man managed to throw Pin off him. And as soon as Pin's feet hit the ground, he leapt at the other guard and clawed across his neck and ears.

Ahnri didn't wait for any more of a signal. He turned away from the source of his fear, forced himself to stand, and ran.

He was halfway down the corridor when Pin caught up to him and let out a "*Mrrow!*"

Ahnri turned.

"*Mrrow!*" the cat said again, gesturing *toward* the prison cells.

"Are you joking?" Ahnri said. "I'm not going in there; they'll lock me up! And Elya ordered me *executed*."

Pin growled low.

"Not now," Ahnri said. "Later."

As they continued on, Ahnri had a feeling Pin would hold him to that promise.

24

REMI

Remi followed the guards to his mother's chambers. He'd been in the middle of dinner when the call had come, and despite not having eaten all day he stood so fast he'd knocked his chair to the floor. He didn't care about the chair at this point. The weight Mother carried had grown heavier lately, and it seemed things kept going wrong.

If it wasn't the supply chain, it was sick soldiers. If it wasn't that, it was the council badgering her over things that were Remi's responsibility. He still didn't understand that one…had they been trying to go over his head? As the higher power, Mother technically could have given approval, yes, but she'd placed him in charge and the council respected that…or he thought they had.

He had managed to avert that disaster, thankfully. But his patience had grown nearly as thin as hers. Running a kingdom was a constant game of putting out the worst fire at the moment, but the past few days seemed to have far more heat than normal.

The double doors opened for him, and he made his way directly to Mother's desk. Papers were laid out as though a perfect puzzle. And each had some level of burn to them. The largest, what appeared to be a map of the Fugeran-Medelian border, lay spread in three different pieces with multiple holes burned right through.

Mother stood there, hands clasped before her, an unreadable expression on her face.

Keeping his voice quiet, Remi asked, "What happened?"

"The messenger *tripped*," she said, a heavy annoyance to her tone. "The cylinder opened, and the papers in this *extremely important report* from our spies on the border, were launched into the fire."

Remi frowned. "These reports are securely contained," he said. "If this happened, it's likely to have been tampered with, yes?"

"That is my conclusion as well," the queen said, "The boy quickly began trying to save the papers. I would like to think it truly an accident, but…it's either that, or Captain Lind did something to the container before he handed it off to the messenger, as he reads through them before sending them to me."

Captain Lind? "Isn't he the one who's been receiving the reports for months?"

"He is," Mother said. "But that doesn't exclude him from suspicion. There is barely enough information remaining to infer what was intended here. As such, I've ordered for the agents to be brought to me personally."

Silently, Remi hoped she would go easy on them.

"The Medelian army is camped near the border, though I can't tell exactly where. These reports," she picked up a smoldering piece of parchment, "indicate the position is likely temporary, which tells me they're likely to continue their approach and we're running out of time. Still, I cannot tell for certain. Perhaps you could take a look."

A swell of pride filled his chest at her words. She trusted him. *She trusted him.*

He read through the remaining notes and letters, trying to see what she saw. Trying to find anything she may have missed. She turned away as he did so, and a moment later she set a cup of tea on the desk beside him.

He finished his examination before taking up the tea. It was strong, and lacked any sugar or lemon the way he preferred. But she probably didn't know his tea preference, and she had prepared it for him, so he wouldn't complain.

"It seems to me," he said finally, "as though they're lying in wait, perhaps for us to make a move?"

Mother considered this. She sighed, setting her own tea on the table and moving toward the fireplace. Remi watched her. Her pale blonde hair had gone fully white at the temples—a subtle difference, but one he noticed because he'd known her all his life. The corners of her eyes were slightly more crinkled than he remembered.

Stars, when had he last truly *looked* at her? She wasn't so old, but no longer the young mother he pictured when he thought of her. He'd tried for so many years to get her to see him, and yet, had he ever truly seen *her*?

She stood in silence for a time, the crackling fire the only sound around them.

He felt helpless. She was the queen; he was only the prince. He had some power, yes, but all at the behest of her. In her name, and by her command. Finally, she spoke.

"Someone is working against us."

Remi frowned. "What makes you think this?"

"These plans have been in motion for months," she whispered. "In all that time, there's been hardly a minor inconvenience. Yet in the past week, everything has begun to unravel."

The final words were spoken in what Remi could only describe as a snarl. He blinked, watching and listening.

"Whoever they are, they won't stop us. They *can't*. We have power on our side they can hardly dream of, and it will only increase."

"Mother?"

She turned, meeting his eyes. And he saw hers, alight with something manic. "We'll show them," she said. "*I'll* show them."

"Show who?" Remi said. "Mother, what's—"

She moved back to the desk, picking up a burned note. "They don't know who they're dealing with. We'll catch them." She slammed the paper down with a fist, then turned to Remi. "Triple the guard underground."

"Mother, we can't keep tripling—"

"Tell them to watch for anyone getting in anywhere they shouldn't. If they don't have an armed escort, they shouldn't be there. And if they're caught, they're to be executed immediately."

"That seems rather—"

"*Immediately!*"

Remi flinched away. She meant this.

"Yes, Mother," he said. "Of course."

She spun away, muttering to herself. Remi held back, closed his eyes, forced himself to breathe. How he wished he had Ahnri…

…Ahnri.

Remi paused. "Mother…how long did you say things had been going wrong?"

"I suspect about a week ago…" she said softly. "That poisoning of the troops was the first large scale attempt, but I believe there were earlier ones we brushed off as coincidence."

Ahnri's voice filled Remi's mind.

"It's about your mother, she's being lied to."

Surely, not…

Ahnri was loyal to Fugera. Remi was certain of it.

"…forged documents…do you have any idea what she's actually doing?"

Or at least, he *had* been certain…

He clasped his hands together to keep them from shaking "Mother…what did this messenger boy look like?"

She waved a hand. "Rather tall, tan skin, grey-ish hair…you can see for yourself, I sent him to be locked in prison and executed."

Executed?

Remi suddenly hoped more than ever that his conclusions were incorrect.

"I'll see to the added guard, then," he said, going to the door. "Don't worry, Mother. We'll figure this out."

She said nothing, letting him leave.

His guards struggled to keep up with him this time. Remi gave them orders to send to the general, but otherwise went straight to his rooms. He gave the guards no special instructions, hoping that might help Ahnri in getting in. Because Remi definitely needed to speak with Ahnri.

He hurried to his bookcase, pulled out the purple ribbon, and tied it to the window. He hated the waiting part, but it was necessary.

Nerves flooded him. He opened his doors again and ordered wine and more food to be brought. He wouldn't be able to do this sober, let alone on an empty stomach.

He knew Ahnri would come, though. Ahnri always did.

Remi just wasn't certain he'd want him to come again after this.

25

AHNRI

Ahnri had been so focused on getting back to his rooms on level six that he'd nearly missed the ribbon. Rather than attempt more disguises—especially given his recent escape—he once again waited for an opening in the guard rotation outside the palace, and climbed in through Remi's window.

His hair still messy with ash, he dropped in to find Remi pacing on the opposite side of his desk. The prince didn't acknowledge Ahnri right away, but something was definitely wrong. Remi wore flowing silk pants and tunic, and seemed to be muttering under his breath. He turned.

Their eyes met as Ahnri took a step forward. Remi's eyes shifted from Ahnri's face, to his hair, to his clothing.

"Remi?"

The prince turned, going to the doors and flipping two extra locks Ahnri wasn't even aware he had. Something about the decisiveness of Remi's motions sent a chill over Ahnri.

Remi returned, going straight to his desk that stood between them. Fresh fruit covered one platter, sael bread and honey on another, and two varieties of wine to one side. Remi poured himself a heavy serving of deep red wine, ignoring the rules of letting it breathe, and simply downed half the glass in a single breath.

Ahnri's brows shot up. "Rem, what's wrong?"

Remi let out a sigh as he finished his drink. "You know this vintage is one of the rarest we own?"

Ahnri frowned.

"Regania is practically overgrown with grapes of dozens of varieties," Remi said, setting the glass down. "Their wine is delicious, but quite easy to come by. Perdonian wine, on the other hand…it comes from much farther away, and they make far less of it, so of course it's much more rare. All the more special to savor. It's almost like a secret, you know? Something to be shared only with those you deeply care about."

"Remi, what's—"

"Why are you doing this?" Remi said. His eyes latched onto Ahnri's, a desperation deeper than Ahnri had ever seen.

Sorrow bloomed in Ahnri's chest.

Remi knew.

"When you told me," Remi said, "that you thought my mother was planning things, that she was being manipulated, I didn't think that meant you were going to *ruin* everything she's worked for."

Ahnri swallowed his fears, and closed his eyes. He'd made his choice, and he still believed it to be the right one.

This was going to hurt.

"Remi…"

"I'm listening."

Ahnri met the prince's eyes, wishing he could tell him everything.

"I…I still don't know if your mother is the one being tricked, or if she's the one *doing* the tricking."

Remi turned, running a hand through his hair.

"Until I know for sure," Ahnri said, moving around the desk, "I have to assume she's complicit."

"And make my life a mucking mess?" Remi snapped.

Ahnri's shoulders slumped. "I didn't want—"

"But you did it anyway," Remi said. Tears were forming in his eyes, his voice rising with each accusation. "You've sabotaged so many efforts, caused so much stress for Mother *and* me. I *told* you everything was fine!"

"And you were *wrong*," Ahnri snapped back. "Your trust in her is based in lies, and your mother is about to hurt more people than she'd protect."

"Of course," Remi said. "Ahnri The Spy knows all."

"Oh, don't be patronizing." Ahnri couldn't help sneering.

"Tell me, Ahnri The Spy, what exactly do you know that I don't?"

"There is *no* invasion force," Ahnri said. "Fugera is not in danger from anyone except itself."

"You haven't seen the reports I have," Remi said, shaking his head. "The letters, the threats, there is danger coming. We *must* be prepared."

"You've been fooled as well," Ahnri said. "Those reports are complete fabrications. Whatever she's planning, this threat of war is an illusion to cover up something bigger. She is working with *Viruses.*"

Remi actually laughed. "Viruses? Of all the things you could've lied about, you chose *Viruses?*"

"Remi, please…"

"My mother promised me no more secrets," Remi said. "She *promised.* I think I would know if she was working with Death magic."

Ahnri took a step back, as he did, he bumped Remi's desk, sending the glass goblet to the floor.

Shattered.

Staring at the mess, he realized his hands were shaking. Here he stood, while the boy he cared for more than anyone laughed in his face…he couldn't do it anymore.

"All right." He moved toward the window.

"That's it?" Remi said. "You're just leaving?"

"Do you *want* me to stay?" Ahnri asked, holding out his arms, as though welcoming Remi's glare. "Nothing I say is going to convince you to believe me."

"I want you to *stop* sabotaging my mother," Remi said. "Say you'll stop, and we can move on."

Ahnri braced himself, and held Remi's gaze. "I truly regret that my actions are hurting you. I wish things could be different. But I won't stop, because I *know* that what I'm doing is right." He put a hand on the window. "And I hope someday you'll understand why I made the choices I did."

"I thought I knew you," Remi scoffed. "It seems you've changed far more than your hair in the time you've been away."

Ahnri stood frozen for a heartbeat as Remi turned toward his bed chamber. Then, in desperation, the confession rose to his lips before he could stop it.

"I love you."

Remi stilled.

Ahnri watched him, saw how the words caused Remi's shoulders to stiffen, then relax. Ahnri had never said it out loud, nor had the prince. And though now seemed like the absolute worst time…it had to be said.

"I love you, Remi. You are the only person in the world I trust with my heart, and if I could, I would trust you with everything else. But the safety of thousands of people is at stake—maybe more—I can't ignore that."

Remi turned back, and Ahnri met those eyes. Those perfect crystalline eyes. Eyes that brought joy to Ahnri's heart every time he saw them. Eyes that—at this moment—shone with tears.

It took every sand grain of strength Ahnri had to turn away from those eyes. But he did. Knowing—hoping—that he could still save Remi, even if it meant breaking his heart. With a tightness in his throat, Ahnri hopped up onto the window ledge.

Remi didn't stop him.

26

REMI

Remi took a step forward as Ahnri hopped out the window, escaping in plain sight of the main thoroughfare and market. Luckily it was late, and there wouldn't be many people out, but—

He let out a growl of frustration, whirling away with teeth clenched. He shouldn't be worried about Ahnri's safety right now.

Dizziness overtook his head. A wave of uncertainty and confusion. He sat at the table, facing trays covered in food, the neat displays a stark contrast to the anger inside him. Remi put his head in his hands.

What was he supposed to do now?

Part of him wanted to throw these trays to the floor. Shatter every glass he could reach. Tear pages out of his books— the journals where he'd confessed his feelings time and again—

and throw them into the fireplace. The *anger* inside him wanted that. A roaring flame of fury encircling heartbreak at its center.

But destroying his own possessions wasn't going to hurt Ahnri…it would only sadden Remi later.

He shoved away from the table and stalked toward his bedroom. Surely there was *some* way he could let off steam…

A soft patter behind him made him turn. It was that cat, the grey striped one Ahnri always had with him. Pin, was it? The cat had stayed with Remi overnight once, and even come visit him once during the day. Remi liked him, but…

The cat stood, one leg raised mid-step, watching back.

"I thought you'd take his side," Remi finally said out loud.

The cat blinked, but didn't move.

"Stupid…" Remi muttered, turning away. The cat couldn't understand him, it made no sense to talk out loud.

And yet…

"Why won't he listen?" he said, spinning back to face the cat. "I told him *everything* I could, and he throws back ridiculous things like *Viruses?*"

At that, the cat tilted his head in such a way, he almost seemed sad.

"It's not fair," Remi said, pacing back into the office.

He glanced at the food on the table again: berries and citrus, sael bread and sweet honey. His stomach suddenly ached—had he eaten anything since that morning? He picked up a section of an orange and popped it into his mouth, hoping the acidic juices would straighten his mind out. But it tasted bland to his tongue.

It seemed nothing could cool the fire in his blood.

He paced from the table to his bedroom entry and back, every part of his body still wanting to rage. It was more than a feeling, it was visceral, a heat in his skin as though the sun were on him. The more he contemplated his circumstances, the more he realized that nothing in his life had ever made him feel as betrayed as Ahnri's actions had this night. Remi had finally gained his mother's approval and support and trust, and Ahnri's sabotage threatened to undo it all.

Movement caught his eye as something fell from the windowsill—the purple ribbon. Ahnri must have untied it and dropped it in on his way out. Remi went to it. Picked it up. Ran the satin fabric between his fingers.

"How did it come to this..."

"*Mrrow?*"

Remi glanced at the cat, and frowned. "Why are you still here? Shouldn't you be helping him?"

With a sigh, he went to the bookshelf and opened the book where he kept the ribbon. He placed it, then flipped through the pages. Between them were notes from Ahnri, asking to meet him, telling him he was special, beautiful...then there were pressed flowers, tiny trinkets, gifts from a boy Remi would've given everything for.

Sometimes he wished things could be the way they were then. Simpler. Happier. Quieter.

Not always quieter...

He winced at the thought. It was true, Mother had dealt with anger all Remi's life. He hadn't believed he'd take after her in that, but this moment seemed to suggest otherwise. When Father had been alive, he'd been like a shield to Remi. He'd taken care, protected, eased punishments. Mother had always been the strict one, the livid one. And, now that Remi was older—now that he had these emotions roiling through him— he understood why.

When things went wrong, it felt like *this*.

He slammed the book shut, shoving it onto the shelf with such force, he knocked two others down. He left them, turning away and pacing once more.

How could this person, the boy Remi thought he would spend the rest of his days with, do this to him? How could Ahnri *love* him, and still do this?

It seemed obvious, now he thought about it. Ahnri didn't truly love Remi.

Ahnri didn't trust Remi.

But Mother does.

Mother had, finally, come to trust him. With running the city, with top secret plans, with resolving issues she didn't have time for. She relied on him. She told him everything, showed him all the plans and reports. And if she trusted him, then he could trust her.

Remi took up a robe and tied it around himself, then turned to the doors.

"Ow!"

He'd walked right into the path of the shattered glass, and a shard cut into the side of his bare foot.

Limping, he made his way to a chair and took a moment to breathe. The blood on his foot dripped, falling to the floor, sparking a memory…

His father.

"Never make important decisions when you're compromised, son." His pale curls were loose that night, as he knelt before a twelve-year-old Remi who had a cut on his hand—the result of a stray piece of stone in a dig zone at the edge of the tower. Young Remi had demanded the workers be punished, but Father was far more patient.

"These people are doing the job they've been set, and we were careless in their space," Father said, wrapping the cut. *"If you calm yourself, you'll agree it wasn't their fault. Tired, hurt, or hungry, that puts your emotion in control. A strong ruler will do their best to lead with a clear head."*

Remi remembered the cool night air on his skin, and the scent of rain on the wind. *"But how can you tell,"* he'd asked. *"Sometimes I feel strongly about things…is that emotion controlling me?"*

His father had met his eyes with raised brows. *"That is a very insightful question, son. I would say…be wary of rushing into things. Time can bring clarity to a decision."*

"Clarity, like magic?"

"No, no, a different kind of clarity. Or rather, a similar kind, but one that comes from within you."

Remi blinked, shaking his head as the memory faded from his mind and a wave of lucidity washed over him, the heat in his chest dimming like a lantern turned low. He had been ready to run straight to Mother, to tell her everything…

But he could do that in the morning as easily, and he would feel better about it then, too.

He stood, limping to unlatch his extra locks and open the doors. His two guards made their way in hurriedly, spears at the ready—perhaps they'd heard the argument, but none of them mentioned it if they had.

"All is well," Remi said. He pointed to the broken shards of glass on the floor. "Find someone to clean that up, and call for a Cure."

"Right away, sire."

A clean cloth was pressed to his cut to control the bleeding, and within minutes a royal Cure entered and Remi's wound had been fully healed. Not half an hour had passed before his rooms were back to their pristine state, fresh food brought—along with a sleeping draught—and the doors locked once more for the night.

Remi still sat in the armchair near the window, his mind reeling. He sipped the sleeping draught, unwilling yet to fully commit to rest.

"Mrrow?"

Snapping out of his contemplation, Remi spotted the cat again.

"You certainly are persistent," he said.

The cat gave a motion that, if Remi didn't know better, he would've called a shrug.

"Well, get over here."

The cat bounded up, and Remi welcomed him, offering ear-scratches as the cat curled up.

He considered once more going to his mother...she needed to know. But, he reasoned, she would be angry if he woke her at this time of night. Besides, there was little Ahnri could do between now and morning to make things worse than they already were.

"No," he said softly. "It can wait until tomorrow."

He downed the rest of the draught, and carefully lifted the cat, placing him back on the cushioned seat of the armchair.

The drowsiness already kicking in, Remi curled up beneath his silken covers. And there, as he finally let himself relax, the hurt set in, and tears began to fall.

27

AHNRI

Ahnri's hands shook as he ducked in through the window of his tiny rented room, lit only by a still-glowing lumenite crystal. Immediately, he began to pace. Tapping his legs with his fingers, creating a steady beat that he hoped would sooth the nerves and fear flowing through him.

The movement of traveling from Remi's rooms up to this higher level of the city *should* have calmed him. He hadn't taken the stairs, of course. Despite it being the middle of the night, he'd climbed the outside of the tower, needing to feel the stone beneath his hands, force his muscles to their limits. It hadn't worked. Sweat dripped from his hairline, and he swiped it away with a sleeve.

He closed his eyes, digging his fingers into his hair and tugging. Most of the time he could put problems in boxes in his mind, things to be observed and dealt with but never interacted with directly. He did the same with intense feelings, but sometimes, without Ahnri's permission, the box opened itself. And the feeling demanded to be felt.

He'd spent the entire climb up to his room replaying the conversation in his mind. The things he shouldn't have said. What if he'd moved differently, kept his tone level. How he should've responded. What else he *could* have told Remi to soothe the situation…nothing helped the feelings go away.

The pressure of tugging at his hair began to center him, bring him back to himself. Slowly, he lowered to his knees in the center of the room, and the tears formed.

His hands slid from his head, falling to his lap as dark spots began to appear on his tunic. His chest shuddered, his breathing ragged. Thoughts continued to bounce around his mind like popping corn. He couldn't seem to slow them, and before long—between the thoughts, the tears, and the hurt in his heart—his head began to ache.

He stayed like that for some time. Part of him feared that if he moved, he would make things worse. The thought wasn't rational, perhaps, but the feeling behind it was very real. He loved Remi. He didn't want to lose him…but he may have already, with what he'd done. And what he knew he still needed to do.

Hours passed in which Ahnri lay in his bed, a prisoner in his own mind, overcome by the emotions he wished he didn't have to feel…until finally, a warmth settled against his side.

Pin.

The cat tucked his nose beneath Ahnri's hand and rested his chin on Ahnri's other arm. Ahnri sniffed, scratching absentmindedly at the cat's ears.

"It hurts, you know?"

"*Mrrow.*"

"It hurts knowing that I'm protecting him, but he can't know how, or why." Ahnri sighed. "The damage might be done regardless. He knows I'm working against them, he'll likely tell Elya, and I don't know how easy it'll be to move around the city anymore."

Pin straightened.

"If she's using Viruses as weapons of war, people will die. Children will lose their parents to this effort, I can't—"

At that thought, a memory came to him—Damond, his eyes crinkled in amusement, throwing his game of sticks to the ground while he showed Ahnri how to play. He appeared young in this memory, no gray in his hair yet…that was early on, shortly after Ahnri's parents had died. It was one of the earliest things he could remember.

No. No one should have to lose their family to the whims of a monarch. If he could do something to prevent that, he would.

He rolled onto his back and put his face in his hands. He'd already decided this. He had. And he'd known Remi wouldn't like it. What he'd predicted had happened, exactly. So why did it bother him so much?

"*Mrrow?*" Pin placed a paw on Ahnri's chest.

"Yeah," Ahnri said, petting the cat again, his mind growing a little less cloudy. "I was thinking about Damond."

Pin tilted his head to one side.

"Have I told you about Damond?"

Pin shook his head in a very clear *"No."*

"He was my Da. Well, adopted father, but he's the only Da I remember." He sat up and turned, leaning against the wall, and stretched a bit. "My birth parents died when I was three years old. I hardly remember them. I know they both had Fugeran features—dark skin, pale hair, blue eyes—and both of a lithe build. I'm told my Mama was very beautiful, sought after by a dozen suitors despite being of lower class. 'Chloe Chapelle, the belle of the ball'—they never went to any balls, though. Weren't high class enough. And my father was even lower class than her—more of a pariah, according to Damond. He said it lovingly, you know, they were good friends."

He sighed, remembering Damond's excitement when Ahnri finally asked about his parents. Pin leaned beside him, head on Ahnri's leg. Without glancing to him, Ahnri put a hand to the cat's head and began to scratch his ears, before staring out the window, choosing now to let himself be pulled into the past.

"My birth father was a researcher," he continued. "A scientist. Louis Moreau—remember those names on that paper from the lab? That's them. Damond always said he never really grasped what they were researching, but it had to do with the Powers and how they could benefit daily life, especially for people who didn't have easy access to them."

Pin frowned a bit, but seemed eager to learn more.

"I guess everyone was shocked when my mom pursued my da, because he was such an unexpected choice. A bookish guy, no one ever thought a beautiful girl would go for him. But she did. Damond always said that sometimes opposites can work well together."

And that thought sent him thinking about Remi again. They were really so different. Remi would never truly understand what it was like to live on the streets, and Ahnri would never fully comprehend the weight carried by a born royal. But love bloomed anyway…now, he hoped it wouldn't wither entirely before he had a chance to re-nurture it.

He forced those thoughts away, refocusing. "Anyway, they grew close, and eventually married, and I think Mom's family disowned her for it. Damond never really said that, but I got the impression her family didn't want anything to do with Dad."

Pin lifted his head slightly, and Ahnri thought he understood the question.

"No," he said. "I've never sought them out. I have no desire to know people who would push their own family away over who they choose to love."

Pin settled back down, seeming satisfied.

"They got married, and I was born about a year later. Damond was around the whole time, climbing the ranks in the royal guard. He babysat me a lot when my parents needed to work. Then, right after I turned three, there was an accident where they worked, and…they were gone. I was with Damond that day, and after he heard the news, he just…kept me."

Betraying tears were forming again, sliding down his cheeks and jaw. He tried to ignore them.

"He was the best parent I could've asked for," Ahnri said. "He taught me how to fight, how to duel, how to climb, how to read…I wouldn't be who I am without him."

"*Mrrow…*"

Ahnri scratched at Pin's neck, then picked him up and laid back down, setting the cat on his chest. He didn't say anything else, but closed his eyes and let his mind wander.

Damond would've been in his life regardless, but how could he have been different if his parents had been there too? He was sure he'd still be himself, but maybe he would've gotten into the science of magic, or had more time to read books. And for a brief moment, he wondered what it would feel like to receive a hug from his mother. He knew she'd loved him. She'd held him close for the first three years of his life…he wished he could remember any of that.

He took a deep breath, letting his body settle into the cot. It was late. And much had happened this day. Likely, he would face repercussions tomorrow, but for now, he needed to sleep.

Interlude
–
Percy

Once Ahnri's breathing had settled into a steady, slow rhythm, Percy carefully slid himself from beneath the young man's arm, and hopped from the cot.

Information. So much information. He liked Ahnri a great deal, but the boy didn't talk much. Except tonight. Tonight he talked a *lot*. And the prince had talked too. Lots of talking. And all of it good. Very good.

He needed to get to Tavin. Tavin should know.

Louis…Louis Moreau…Percy knew that name. Something in his *before* memory…he couldn't quite grasp it.

Tavin. Tavin would know. And maybe that Merlin person…Percy should find him too.

Ahnri would need all the help he could get.

Percy checked on Ahnri again, making sure he really was asleep, then slipped out of the room and made his way down to the royal dungeons.

28

AHNRI

Ahnri rubbed at his burning eyes. He didn't remember crying the night before, but with everything he'd felt, it wouldn't have been unexpected. He kept his hood up to cover his face and hair as he made his way down the central ramp road of the city, passing apartment entrances, side streets, markets…he hadn't seen Pin anywhere yet, which was odd. The cat was normally asleep under Ahnri's cot first thing most mornings. Today, the second day in a row, he was nowhere to be found.

Still, Ahnri had a job to do. A job he'd been successful at thus far, and he intended to continue to be so. Whether he could would depend on Remi, and what he'd done last night after Ahnri left him.

You left him…

Ahnri put a hand to his head, rubbing at his temple. He hated the thought of leaving Remi hurt, but that's exactly what he'd done. And he couldn't take it back now.

Ahnri's instincts told him that Elya's plans would cause pain to this city. But so far, all he'd managed to find in his investigation was some false reports and letters, and a lab full of abused animals and Death-infused metal.

All of which he'd sent to Carina—poor Kahn was going to need a break soon.

A desperation was growing inside Ahnri. He'd tried sabotage, he'd tried gathering intel, but now he needed something more solid. He *needed* to know. Needed proof of actual plans. He needed the truth.

Because if he didn't have that, he worried, maybe there was a chance he was wrong, and he'd hurt Remi for no reason.

He couldn't live with himself if that were the case.

Taking deep breaths, he made his way down to the palace levels. It was mid-morning by the time he woke, but there still wasn't much movement in the city, so he could get by with his hood on and keeping his eyes down. All he wanted was to spot either Elya or her adviser. He'd tried everything he knew how to do with caution, now it was time to take chances.

Before reaching the kitchen loading area, he swapped his hood for a palace servant's uniform, and immediately bEgan to help the kitchen staff, carrying crates of fruit and rolling barrels of ale. When the others were occupied, he ducked into the palace proper and made his way farther in.

He didn't want to go toward the subterranean area yet, but he suspected he'd end up there. First, he would check the adviser's rooms, and possibly the queen's—assuming they were both headed down as they did most days.

He took as many servant's passages as he could, avoiding the main corridors. The adviser's rooms, he knew, were down the hall and around the corner from the queen's. When he reached them, there were no guards.

Empty. Good.

He tried the door, and to his surprise, it wasn't locked. With a single step, he went in.

The adviser Brielle's space was sparsely decorated, though the colors were brighter and more vivid than he most palace rooms, decorated with shades of red and floral patterns. He went left and straight to the study, where a thin-legged desk stood with only a single book on its surface.

It seemed more like a journal than anything, but when he thumbed through it…nothing but blank pages, though there were places where pages were torn out. Frowning, he carried it to a lamp to check for signs of invisible ink, but the remaining pages were truly blank.

He did a pass through the room, and found nothing else.

Cursing, he recalled the lack of papers in the lab when he'd finally gotten inside it. Brielle had been the only one to see him attempt to get in, and it seemed she was keeping her notes on her person, instead of either in her rooms *or* the lab.

Well, he'd have to try again.

Rather than enter the queen's rooms through the main doors, Ahnri made his way up one floor and took the secret tunnel, climbing down the dark shaft to the pocket of space behind the queen's bookshelves.

When he arrived, his feet quietly hitting the dusty floor, there were two voices on the other side. Precisely the ones he hoped to hear.

"—don't see what could possibly be causing all this," Elya snapped. "Months of work, the goal is so close, and everything starts falling apart *now?*"

"It could be coincidence, ma'am," the adviser's voice said.

"It's *not coincidence!*"

Silence.

"Someone is after me," Elya said, her volume lower now. "Someone knows what we're trying to do, and they want the advancements for *themselves.*"

"They won't get it, Your Majesty."

Ahnri frowned. He was missing something here…

"Go," the queen said. "I'll meet with that soldier, then join you."

"Yes, Your Majesty."

Footsteps retreated, and doors closed. Ahnri waited a moment to be sure they'd both gone, before pressing the button to open the shelves.

The door shifted, allowing him entrance, and he quickly wiped up the line of dust that had fallen as a result, then went over everything in the space as he had before. He checked the hidden drawer bottom, every file, the desktop, but found nothing new.

Going back into the hidden tunnel, he closed the shelves behind him and hurried up and out. He could move faster than either of them, but whether he could get to the ground floor before they entered the spiral staircase was going to be close.

Servant's passages, ramps, short-cut staircases, and Ahnri was out of breath when he finally got a glimpse of the guarded archway to the underground space.

He paused to check around the last corner. The entrance was now encircled by six guards. He backed away from the corner, putting his back against the wall. He had no specific plan here, but if the adviser hadn't already gone down, he knew he needed to intercept her before she did. He wasn't certain he could risk facing Elya so close again, but the adviser…he might get away with that.

He thought through the palace layout. He'd come from a side staircase, but the adviser would likely come at this space from the opposite direction, so maybe he could—

"—do understand this is imperative, correct?"

That voice. That was the adviser, wasn't it?

Ahnri turned the corner on instinct, slumping his posture, pulling his brows together, and digging in his satchel to appear preoccupied as he passed the half dozen guards at the staircase entrance. He didn't know how observant the adviser was, or if she'd see through his hasty disguise—he preferred to take more time to prepare for circumstances like this. When she'd caught him attempting to enter the lab she had gotten a much closer look at him than he'd have liked.

He forced himself to take slow breaths. He faced away from her, eyes on his satchel. He watched from the corner of his eye as Brielle, the queen's most trusted adviser, flanked by two guards, drew closer and closer.

At the opportune moment, Ahnri slipped.

He knocked into one of the guards, who fell sideways into the adviser, who shrieked. The stack of books she held scattered to the floor.

"I'm terribly sorry, ma'am," Ahnri said, keeping his voice gravelly while he made a show of helping gather the pages, while pocketing a few. "I'm so sorry, I should've—"

"It's *fine*," Brielle said. "Hurry. I have an appointment."

"Of course, ma'am," Ahnri said, handing over a stack of loose pages.

She snatched them from him, not even meeting his eyes, and some from her guards as well, muttering about how she'd have to take time to put them back in order.

Ahnri stood, and bowed to let her move on. When she was beyond the guards at the staircase entrance, Ahnri turned and continued on...

No one stopped him.

His heart raced. Did that actually work? He cracked a smile, looking back to be sure no one had followed him. Patting his pockets, he checked where he'd stashed the papers he'd managed to steal—

"—certain we are not disturbed. Give the council—"

Ahnri's stomach dropped. Elya's voice carried down the ramp. He needed to hide.

Panick rising, doing his best to keep his expression calm, he turned to go back the way he'd come. A servant's station stood near the underground entrance. He walked immediately toward it and began to loudly shuffle the various dishes and cleaning supplies, while still listening to the queen.

"—likely be busy all morning, but it will depend how long this takes. Ah, Cheval, there you are. You're ready, I presume?"

"I am, Your Majesty."

Ahnri glanced sideways to see a stocky soldier bow to the queen, determination in his eyes.

"Excellent," Elya said. "Follow me."

The group made their way down. Despite his curiosity, Ahnri turned away, heart racing. He'd already risked revealing himself, and had nearly come face-to-face with the queen again. He wasn't quite ready to risk more yet. He headed up into the next level of the palace, savoring the crinkle sound from his pockets where he'd tucked the stolen pages.

Ahnri rushed—as fast as he could without drawing attention—through the palace hallways, searching for an empty room. Most of the doors led to private apartments or storage spaces, but he knew of a few that were meant for small private meetings between staff. Searching for a few minutes, he found one.

Inside stood a small circular table made of stone with a single lantern on its surface, and two spindly chairs of a light-colored wood. Ahnri lit the single lantern, locked the door behind him, and pulled the papers out from his pockets.

He'd managed three pages, and took a moment to lay them out flat on the table. Among neat, loopy handwriting were drawn multiple diagrams and sketches.

The first page held a drawing of a large funnel-like device, and below it a sketch of the various depictions of Fina he'd seen etched into metal in the lab. Text in the margins read:

Proposed means of amplification. Reach all soldiers at once. It is assumed Vessel will not survive transfer. Each soldier must wear a medallion, or the process will likely kill them. With it in place, they can receive properly.

"Amplification…are they amplifying Death magic?"

More information. Keep reading. This page, he folded and put in his right front trouser pocket.

The second page held a rough sketch of a thick hand, holding a piece of paper with some kind of grass being rolled into it, as though to be smoked. He recognized the process; he'd seen people do it…but this page lacked any writing. He frowned, examining it closer, holding it to the light just in case. It seemed a simple piece of art, unrelated in style or subject to the other two. But perhaps there were simply missing links. This, he tucked into the right inside pocket of his cloak.

Ahnri's heart races as he examined the final page. This one was *covered* in handwriting. Dated at the top—as though it were a journal entry—for only the day before.

We are so tantalizingly close. The girl has the abilities we've been seeking, and despite her inexperience—or perhaps because of it—she's been easily trained. She doesn't know what her limits are and so she presses beyond them. It is fascinating.

Every other Virus we've worked with has had much more experience, and I believe this is to their downfall. Because they think they already know what to do, they do it wrong. Every one of them has died or deserted us at various points in the process. This time though, we have someone we can mold, who will obey, and who has succeeded without losing her own life in the process. A good sign. Perhaps she may even survive the mass transfer if she's lucky.

We have the amount we need stored, though I don't think she knows she's done it. And she certainly doesn't seem to know what the end goal is. Unless she's a much better actress than I am—ludicrous, I'm sure you'll agree.

She successfully transferred her abilities to the rat; I fully believe she can give it to the man. Tomorrow, we'll bring in the first test soldier. He, at least, will be informed of the risk. I do want to test it on another uninformed, however. I am suspicious of awareness being a factor, and I'd hate to lose volunteers by giving them too much information.

Once we have a handful of successful tests—myself included— we will run it on the entire army. With luck, they'll only need to wear the tokens. I am confident that by tomorrow we will have two Viruses at our disposal, and if my guesses are correct, we'll have a thousand more within the week.

Ahnri frowned. "Transfer...abilities?"

He reread the passage again. And again.

Viruses.

Transfer of…abilities. Not Power—*abilities.*

A chill ran through him.

Elya wasn't gathering Viruses to lead her army. Nor using them to imbue weapons—though certainly that would happen too.

She was *creating* them?

Ahnri scoured his brain for everything he'd learned about human Vessels. Months ago, Merlin had explained the process to him. Most Vessels—humans who could manipulate the Four Powers—were *born*, not made. It had something to do with their time growing inside their mothers, and midwives could tell based on the circumstances of a birth whether or not abilities would present.

But *making* a Vessel, *becoming* one, Merlin had said the process could take years—decades sometimes. It required immense amounts of study and dedication, as well as a final act to prove oneself worthy of the Power one sought.

And Elya was managing it in a matter of *days?*

Ahnri slumped into a chair. Silence surrounded him, but his mind buzzed.

How?

How was she doing this? And the bigger question: *why?*

He folded this last sheet and tucked it into a different pocket still. Finally, he had *proof*, he had *answers*. He leaned forward, head in his hands, forcing his mind to think.

Five months ago, Elya had spoken of gathering Viruses to create an *elite force*, and Damond had overheard.

Knowing that information was enough to have him killed.

Now, Ahnri knew that the elite force was not simply a handful of Viruses, but an *entire army*. An army being *created* by Queen Elya.

And she was doing it in that lab.

Ahnri blinked, straightening in the dim room.

Since he'd been back, he'd observed her behavior growing more and more erratic…she was wound tight, jumpy and suspicious.

She'd increased her guard, and ordered for the *best* soldiers to be at her side.

"She's terrified." Things he already knew clicked into place. "She's so afraid of losing control, of someone coming after her, that she's going to these extreme lengths to protect herself in the name of protecting the city. It makes sense, doesn't—"

He cut himself off. He'd spoken as though to Pin, but the cat hadn't been with him all morning.

He frowned, suddenly thrown off balance by the lack of the cat's presence, especially as he made these connections.

Still, it was gratifying to know he'd been right. That his work hadn't been for nothing. From Damond's original eavesdrop to the reason Ahnri had come back. Elya was building an entire *army* of Viruses. A force like that would indeed be deadly to Fugera's enemies, but—Ahnri was sure—there was no way it would remain under Elya's command for long.

If they could simply kill anyone who disagreed with them? They'd wreak havoc on the Unbroken Lands.

Did Elya truly not see that?

And, he shuddered, did Remi know *this* was happening?

Ahnri stood, then put out the lantern and left the room. Striding through the corridors, he considered his next course of action.

He'd seen the queen, adviser, and a random soldier head down to the lab moments ago. He suspected they were already beginning the process.

He had to stop them.

He cursed his choice to send Kahn off the day before, or he would've sent this to Carina as well—possibly even asked for that backup she'd offered. He hadn't known things would escalate this quickly, but it seemed an ill omen.

Carefully double checking the papers in separate pockets, he made his way straight back to the spiral staircase, pausing in a hallway to watch for a way to get down there unnoticed. He had to get into that lab.

29

NATALIA

Natalia forced herself to take slow breaths as she approached the laboratory. Shortly after lunch a messenger had knocked at her door and summoned her immediately—which made her all the more nervous. She hadn't slept well, her mind going over and over what to say to the queen and adviser, how exactly she would get herself out of this agreement.

The words she wanted to say stayed clear in her mind all the way down the spiral staircase, following the guard who recognized her and escorted her to the lab. But here, facing the hidden doorway, it seemed everything she'd practiced slipped away like so much soft Fugeran sand.

The door opened, and Nat entered to see Brielle bustling around, rearranging things. The table where they usually worked had been pushed back, a chair now in its place.

"Ah, Miss Natalia. Excellent timing," Brielle said. "The queen should be here any moment, and we'll have a guest with us today as well."

"A guest?"

"Indeed. Now, if you would be so kind as to make sure that," she pointed to the bar of Elyum they'd used the day before, "is fully filled, that would be wonderful. I'm nearly ready."

Nat opened her mouth to speak, but Brielle had already turned away. The Elyum bar lay on the long thin table to her right. She took a moment—not touching it—to try to sense how much Power remained inside it after yesterday.

What?

She pulled her hand back, and tried again. Surely not…it felt as though it had hardly been used. There was still plenty of Power within, enough to complete the experiment many *many* times over.

Not that she would do that. She was done.

The door behind Natalia opened once more, and the queen entered. Natalia and Brielle bowed as she approached.

She was followed by three men. Two were uniformed royal guard, but the third wore only a simple tunic and trousers, with an arm band marking him as a soldier in the Fugeran army. He was young, but strong. Tall, with broad shoulders and a firm jaw, he stood very relaxed. When his eyes met Nat's he raised a brow, looking over her with curiosity.

"Perfect," Brielle said, going to this young man. "And what is your name, soldier?"

"Rin," he said. "Rin Cheval."

Brielle led him to the chair in the center of their usual workspace and attached straps to his wrists and legs, as well as one around his hips and waist.

Natalia's heart dropped.

"No," she whispered.

The queen turned to her. "Did you say something, dear?"

"Yes," Nat blurted. She took a breath, calming herself. "Yes, Your Majesty. Um…could I have a word with you in private?"

"Of course." The queen gestured to a corner of the room. Nat glanced back to see Brielle frowning at her.

Heart racing, she gave a small bow to the queen.

"What is it, child?"

Nat flinched. The endearments that had once meant so much felt wrong now. "Your Majesty, I…I don't think I can do this."

The queen took both of Natalia's hands in hers, holding them tightly. "I understand."

Nat blinked. "You do?"

"Of course," the queen said. "Holding the ability you do, why it's quite similar to the influence of a ruler, I'd say. I could, at any moment, give or take the life of one of my subjects. It is quite a heavy weight to bear."

Natalia frowned at the comparison. She'd never considered it that way, but she wasn't sure they were the same. Still, the queen was trying to relate. "Thank you, Your Majesty. I—"

"And," the queen continued, "with that weight, of course, comes the responsibility to use it *properly*. I assure you, what we're doing here will be a benefit to Fugera for generations to come. People will remember *you* for the good we're doing here. You're going to be a *legend*, child."

Nat's heart sank at those words. "I don't want to be a legend."

"I'm sorry?"

"I don't want to do this anymore."

The queen's expression shifted. "Well…that is a different concern, isn't it?"

Nat swallowed. "Can…can I go? Please? My mother and I will happily move back to our smaller apartment, we don't really need all the space. I…I can't do this anymore."

The queen stared at their hands for a moment. "I am saddened that it must end like this. But, Miss Natalia. May I ask for one final test? And then you're free to go. And you can keep the apartment—no one was using it anyway."

Natalia hesitated. She wanted to say no. More than anything at the moment, she wanted to leave this room and never return to it. But…the queen had asked one final favor.

"I do this last experiment," Nat said, "and that's all?"

"That is all," the queen said.

Nat took a deep breath.

"All right," Nat said. "I'll do it."

Still holding Nat's hands, the queen led her back to the center of the laboratory. Nat stared at the setup—Brielle had been busy.

The young soldier, Rin, was seated and strapped in, and the stand that had held the Elyum ingot over the rat the previous day had been re-fashioned into a harness. It held the bar six inches in front of Rin's chest.

And around his neck, hanging from a cord, lay that same small coin bearing Fina's likeness, resting directly against his skin.

Nat's stomach sank. *One last experiment…then I can go.*

"Has he been informed of the risks?" Nat asked to Brielle. "The potential result if this fails?"

"He has," Brielle said.

"I'm right here," the young man said. "You could ask *me*."

Nat met his gaze—her head beginning to ache. "Are you aware that this could kill you?"

"Fully aware," he said.

Nat's voice came out, quieter then, "That doesn't scare you?"

"Maybe it does," he said. "Maybe it doesn't. I don't think it's your concern."

Nat nearly took a step back, feeling berated by this stranger. Taking a breath to steady her nerves, Nat looked to Brielle, who brought her the leather coat, helping her put it on. Then Brielle went through the room to turn down the lights, and made sure everyone else had moved back near the door. With everything in shadow, Nat didn't have to hide the shaking of her hands.

Same as yesterday, she told herself. *Then I'm done.*

Intentionally slowing her breathing, she raised her hands and placed her fingertips against the cool, dark metal.

Don't think…just do it.

She closed her eyes. Reaching out with the senses she'd worked so hard recently to hone, she reached into the ingot, full of Death magic. She could feel the life force of Rin, close behind it. With a deep breath, she drew the magic out of the ingot, in one arm, through her chest, and out the other. Through the metal bar, to seek the coin on Rin's chest. She found it, like a shield blocking her from reaching him.

This time, rather than expending her strength pushing against the wall of resistance, she took her time to search it…checking for weak spots, cracks that may already exist. And soon, she found one.

It wasn't an actual wall of course, but it helped her to visualize it that way. She mentally wedged her Power into the crack, and then, *pushed.*

The barrier broke far faster than it had the day before. The Power flowed freely. She remembered the notes specifying that it didn't take much to transfer the ability, so she tried to feel this time, how much Rin might need. He was of course larger than the rat, so she assumed more would be necessary…but would too much hurt him?

Slowly, she lessened the flow of Power…though it was more difficult to do this time. With the rat, the Power had been a small stream, but going into Rin it flowed more like a wide river. With the amount of momentum it had, Nat found it took all her strength to slowly reduce the flow to a trickle, until she could cut it off entirely. Finally, she let the excess she held return to the ingot between them.

When every inkling of magic had been safely stored away, she finally opened her eyes.

Before her, Rin sat clutching the arms of the chair, teeth gritted, face scrunched in a grimace…

But he was breathing.

He let out a grunt of pain, and released his hands, stretching his fingers, flexing the muscles of his arms.

"Light," the queen called.

Someone turned up a single lamp hear the door. Nat took three steps backward, and the queen caught her, hands clasped around Nat's upper arms.

"Did it work?" the queen whispered.

"I think so?" Nat said. "It felt the same, but—"

"Here," Brielle said. She quickly removed the straps holding Rin to the chair, then donned her heavy gloves and brought a rat out from a cage, holding it before Rin.

He frowned. His breathing was labored, as though he'd just run miles.

"How…how do I…"

Nat didn't want to explain. It was instinctual, something she'd learned how to do at a very young age. Snatching small snakes off the ground, or swatting bugs in the air…she'd taken care of pests. It was scary at first, and she still feared the Power itself and the danger it posed, but she'd quickly decided to use her powers to help people.

The lights were still low, providing plenty of shadow. Rin focused, and she *felt* it as he drew in the Power, leaving a patch of light in the middle of the air. His eyes widened, and hesitantly he reached toward the rat in Brielle's hands, and touched it.

With a flash of light, the animal went limp.

Rin flashed a grin, but straightened his expression quickly. "I'd like more to practice on."

Brielle gestured gladly toward the wall of animals and bugs. Rin was on his feet before Nat could object. Her spirits fell with each flash of purple light as Rin tested his new abilities.

Beside her, Queen Elya beamed brightly in the dim space. "Isn't it *wonderful?* Marvel at what you've accomplished, my dear." She squeezed Nat's shoulders, fingers digging into the skin.

Unable to speak, Nat could only think to herself, *gods above…what have I done?*

30

NATALIA

She'd done it.

Bile rose in her throat. Natalia had successfully transferred her ability to channel Death magic to another person. The potential of that success suddenly set in like a mountain resting on her chest.

What were the implications of this? What would this mean? Surely, if they could duplicate it with Cures it could mean more healing for everyone. Clarities could provide assistance to those struggling with their minds. Growth could potentially mean longer lives for the elderly…but Death?

Natalia could imagine nothing but destruction. She would freely admit that Death magic was helping her and Mama survive, but they were a couple of raindrops among a monsoon. Seeing the faces of the queen and adviser, Natalia was certain they had something very different in mind than fighting off illnesses like Mama's.

Out.

She wanted out of here.

Out of this room, out of this deal, maybe even out of this city. She couldn't be part of this any longer. If they were going to create more Viruses, she didn't care why, she couldn't be part of it.

"Wait," Brielle said. "Miss Natalia, can you still use it?"

Nat's stomach turned, but she held herself together. She didn't want to try. Didn't want to kill any more animals…but instinctively, she reached for the Power, and found it waiting. She did not pull it in, she didn't have to.

"I can," she said. Her voice was so small, it didn't even sound like her own.

"This," the queen said, releasing Nat's arms and moving toward Rin, "is *wonderful*. Do it again…"

Rin grinned, pulling in a stream of shadow behind him and reaching out to a nearby bird's cage. Natalia turned away. The rest of the room gave polite applause.

Bile rose in Nat's throat, sharp and acidic.

"Indeed," Brielle said. "Your Majesty, we have more volunteers waiting, could we call them in as well?"

"I don't think there's a need for that," the queen said. "We should move forward immediately."

Nat spun back. "There are *more?*"

"Your Majesty," Brielle said, making more notes, "it would be much safer if we perform one final test to ensure—"

"I don't want to wait," Queen Elya said, a manic spark in her eyes. "Brielle, we finally have *our own* successful trial. If we wait any longer, someone will steal our research. We *cannot* risk that happening before we are *fully* protected." She turned to the guards at the door. "Send word to General Saunier. We will hold a war meeting in the throne room in twenty minutes."

The guards saluted, and one ran to find a messenger. Nat put a hand on the nearby table as the room spun around her. Too fast…this was happening too fast.

"Brielle, what is the progress on the medallions? Do we have enough for every soldier?"

"We do, ma'am."

"Excellent. Get them distributed."

"Wait—" Nat began.

"Your Majesty," Brielle said again, "We really should attempt a slightly larger scale—"

"It *worked*, Brielle," Elya said. "Everything we've been building toward for months has *finally* come to fruition."

"Yes, Your Majesty," Brielle said, flipping a few pages of her book. "I'm as pleased as you are, truly, but—"

"We don't *need* any more tests," the queen snapped. "I want this done *tonight*. We've had a traitor sabotaging our efforts at every turn, and I don't want them finding out about *this*."

Brielle's eyes flicked toward Nat. "And the girl?"

The queen spun to face Nat once more. For the first time, Nat noticed the way the queen's eyes widened, a madness behind them that sent dread through Nat's body.

"I…" Nat stammered. "I don't want to do this anymore."

The queen and Brielle shared a glance. Then Queen Elya spoke firmly: "Bind the girl."

The guards' hands gripped Natalia's arms, pinning them against her sides.

"Wait, no." She struggled in vain against the guards. "Please, Your Majesty. I just want to go home, I—" They shoved a gag in her mouth. Ropes wound around her wrists and brought them together behind her back.

No, she thought, shaking her head. *Mama…* Mama needed her.

She instinctively drew in the shadows. She didn't want to, the thought pained her, but she couldn't risk them taking her. Especially not in the state Mama was in. She pictured her lying there, staring out at the sky, happier than she'd been in weeks, ever since the illness had crept up on her. And she'd finally begun to improve…

If Mama didn't have help, she would die.

Even as they shoved at her Natalia closed her eyes, focusing on the points where the guards' hands met her skin. In a flash, she released her Power into them.

Their grips went slack. Two bodies fell to the floor. Dead.

She didn't let herself think of it. Natalia spun to the exit, pulling the gag from her mouth.

"Stop her!"

She gripped the latch and pulled, the door began to shift, but a moment later thick hands held onto her once more. With a sickening twist in her stomach, she again released Death onto the people holding her. Grips released her—except for one.

Rin.

Nat turned to see him staring down at her with that same curious expression. "Seems a Virus can't hurt another Virus." He smirked. "Interesting."

She tried to yank her arm away, but his hold stayed firm. He spun her back around to face the rest of the room.

"Hold, child!" the queen said, squaring her shoulders. "Or your mother will be joining us."

Nat's entire body went slack. The breath left her lungs. "You…please, Your Majesty. Please leave her alone. I'll…" Nat swallowed, her voice becoming a whimper. "I'll do what you want."

"As you should." Queen Elya said. "Do not fight us, girl. I will have your mother collected to be certain you are as accommodating as possible."

Collected? "Your Majesty, please. Please don't move her, she's weak!"

With no other response, the queen made her way past Natalia and out of the lab, followed by her guards.

Nat slumped in Rin's grip.

Brielle sighed, and waved for Rin to bring Nat farther into the room.

Nat did not resist. She felt broken, like a wolfhound muzzled into submission. Her mind was a dust storm of fear and confusion and desperation.

She didn't even notice the shackles until they were on her, locked shut.

She pulled against the chain. They'd shackled her hands in the front, but that didn't give her any more freedom than if it had been behind. She recognized this spot…there had been an Ignatian wolfhound in a cage here only a few days ago. The lack of the animal and the fact that she was in its place made Nat feel ill.

Brielle knelt at a distance to meet Nat's eyes, an inevitability there, mixed with regret. "It didn't have to be like this, you know," she said.

Unable to make herself speak, Nat turned away.

Brielle stood, turning toward Rin. "Thank you for your help. We wouldn't have been able to contain her without you."

"Of course," Rin said. "Should I stay?"

"That won't be necessary." Brielle moved through the room, turning the lamps on higher, brighter. Removing as much shadow as possible. "I'll be in touch with you though, you'll likely be needed to move her. We'll have to get something for the actual transfer—"

Their voices faded into the distance, then the door closed with a finality that sent a chill through her.

Natalia pulled against the chains binding her until blood began to trickle from the rubbed-raw skin. Her dried tears left the fabric over her face feeling stiff and scratchy. And the floor where she'd been placed was nothing but stone, covered with a thin layer of matted straw and the wolfhound's shed fur.

The chain wasn't even long enough to allow her to stand, and before long she felt the gnaw of hunger in her stomach, reminding her she hadn't eaten before coming here. Soon, the fight left her. Her legs curled close, she lay on the straw that smelled of dog, and cried herself into a daze.

She'd killed.

The fact sunk into her, suffocating and oppressive—her breath came in gasps. How many lives? They'd carried the bodies out as they'd left, though she'd hardly noticed. How could she have been so heartless? Those guards had lives, families, dreams…and she'd snuffed them out as easily as a candle.

She had never killed a person. Had never wanted to. Wished she hadn't had to.

And yet, she hadn't even hesitated.

The queen was right…a heavy weight to bear.

It couldn't have been more than a few minutes since they'd left her, but it already felt like an eternity. In the back of her mind, she prayed to Fina—the only god she thought might listen—*Please…please keep Mama safe.*

31

REMI

Remi paced his office, unable to focus on the pile of council requests or the lunch on his desk. This whole morning had been riddled with visitors he didn't want to take—but had anyway—not to mention he'd hardly slept the night before.

The nightmares were no help.

A maze of stone and vines had plagued him. Anxiety reigned as he'd met dead end after dead end, and with every intersection he came to he saw Ahnri to one side, and his mother to the other. Even in dreams he was unsure who to believe. He knew Mother trusted him, and it seemed clear Ahnri did not. At every juncture he tried going to one of them, but in the midst of fear he couldn't make himself move. Instead, he'd been shunted back to the beginning of the maze to try again. As though his mind was punishing him. Ahnri and

Mother, both their faces pleading for him to help them, begging to be believed.

He'd been turned away every time.

But now, he had to make a choice. This was no nightmare; it was real life. And Ahnri was ruining Mother's plans. Remi knew what he needed to do…he only wished he didn't have to. He didn't *want* to.

A knock came at his door, then. Remi called for them to enter.

"Highness," a messenger boy said. "I have an urgent summons from the queen. She's ordered you to join her immediately."

Deep breath.

"Lead the way."

Remi followed the boy through the palace halls and down to the throne room, where his mother sat with Brielle close by. General Saunier was there as well, and all the captains of their army.

"Mother?" Remi asked. "What is this?"

"Ah, good," she said, standing. "Son, I am going to need you to take charge of the city. I'll be accompanying the army on an excursion."

An excursion? Remi stared around at the general and captains, confused. "I can certainly do that, but you are the *queen*, may I ask why you're going?"

Her head snapped up to meet his eyes. "That is none of your concern."

Words caught in his throat as she passed by him, her robes sweeping softly over thick purple carpet while the others followed in her wake. Finally, Remi found his voice.

"You said you trusted me."

The queen stopped. With a single gesture, ordered for the others to go on ahead, leaving her alone in the throne room with Remi.

His heart beat an unsteady pace. How he waNted her to trust him…she'd said she trusted him.

Perhaps…one final confession might solidify his place in her confidence?

He steeled himself as she turned to face him.

She narrowed her eyes, and under that gaze, desperate to hold on to her trust, he couldn't stop the confession that rose to his lips:

"I know who's behind the sabotages."

She froze. "How?"

Regret filled his heart as he spoke. "They practically confessed."

Mother straightened, smoothing her robes.

"Tell me *everything.*"

32

AHNRI

Ahnri turned away from the guards at the staircase, muttering apologies under his breath in a creaking voice.

As soon as he was out of sight, he straightened from the hunched old-man guise and swore. He kept walking, stuffing his cloak into his bag as he tried to appear as though he belonged in the palace.

His first attempt to get down the spiral staircase had been as a messenger, but apparently there was now a special seal he lacked. He'd then waited for the guard to change—which happened every four hours, and he'd been lucky the time had been close—and tried again as an old man, claiming a need to inspect the training caverns. He'd been turned away again.

It had been two hours since he saw the queen and adviser go downstairs, and while he hadn't seen them come back up, it was possible he missed them. He hoped they were still working down in the lab.

A large group of servants carrying laundry approached. Ahnri stepped aside to allow them to pass, then spun to follow close behind and slowly donned his cloak once more, pulling his hood low. They walked toward the spiral staircase entrance, though they would pass it. As they did Ahnri quickly ducked into a shadowed alcove across from the entrance, hiding behind a large vase.

From here, he watched.

Ideally, he needed a crowd to hide in if he wanted to get down. He'd suspected Elya would tighten security at some point, but he wasn't going to let it stop him.

He watched for twenty minutes, crouched in the shadows, as soldiers entered and exited in no more than pairs. Then, something shifted.

A group of messengers ran past his alcove, and one separated, going to the staircase. The boy stopped to hand a small paper to each of the six guards there, before he showed them a seal and made his way down, more papers in his grip.

The guards began to talk about the papers, but Ahnri was too far to make out what they were saying. He narrowed his eyes to try to read their lips, but he'd never practiced that as he should've. Then another messenger flew past at a run, also making their way downstairs, except this time one of the papers fluttered right outside Ahnri's alcove. He snatched it, pulling it back to read.

APREHEND IMMEDIATELY—DEAD OR ALIVE

A drawing, a description—both *very* detailed—of Ahnri. Well…that changed things.

Ahnri's heart sank. He closed his eyes. He'd known it was a possibility that Remi would turn him in. Ahnri had practically dared him to with the way they'd spoken…that didn't stop the hurt. And for a moment, he thought this was probably how Remi felt about Ahnri right now too.

Two sides of the same coin.

Ahnri opened his eyes, staring at the paper. Ahnri had tried…he thought he had, anyway. But it hadn't been enough.

A loud murmur of voices sounded from down the hallway. Ahnri shoved the paper in his bag and his emotions to the back of his mind, and watched as at least thirty soldiers moved past him toward the staircase.

He nearly hesitated. They were searching for him. That drawing looked *exactly* like him. But this might be his only chance.

He adjusted his expression to hopefully hide himself and hopped up at the back of the group to mingle between them, nodding seriously as they all held up their seals to the guards— Ahnri mimed the same—and collectively made their way down the staircase.

Ahnri let himself breathe. Once in the spiral corridor, he could relax a little. Getting in was always the hard part, now he had to—

"Captain says it's time," one soldier said in front of him. "Can you believe it?"

"I heard Medelios is planning to attack the city tomorrow," another said. "We're gonna show them."

"Tonight's the night, friends," a third said, throwing an arm around another. "We'll bring Fugera glory!"

Cheers and delighted chatter surrounded him, making him feel sick to his stomach. Who knew if any of those people would survive the night?

Ahnri fell back, letting the soldiers get ahead of him until they were far enough to be out of sight around the spiral. By the time he reached the base of the staircase and turned right instead of left, he wasn't noticed.

Deep breaths.

He swore at the sight of the unguarded hallway. He was too late.

He wished Pin were there to stand watch, though there wouldn't be an escape route regardless. If anyone came in, he'd have to hide and hope he wasn't seen.

He pressed the wall, shifting the hidden door open and revealing the lab lit so brightly he had to raise his hand over his eyes to adjust from the torchlit hallways. He quickly entered, closing the door behind him, and started to shuffle through the space. A chair sat where the circular table had been before, and the long lab tables were arranged the same as before. He noticed a good portion of the animals were now dead in their cages, and then his eye caught on a body curled in the corner on a pile of straw. A young woman—tall, curved body, and a pouf of ringleted blonde-white hair.

Ahnri's blood ran cold.

"Natalia?"

He hurried to kneel beside her as she lifted her eyes, tears streaking her face.

"Ahnri? How are you—"

"No time," he said, searching for a way to unlock the shackles on her wrists. "You're a *Virus?*"

"I'm an *idiot*, Ahnri," she said, tears filling her eyes. "I've hidden my abilities for years, but…they promised to take care of Mama and…"

Ahnri's heart broke. They'd *used* her. Manipulated this girl who had one of the purest hearts Ahnri had ever met. "Don't worry, I'll get you out of here."

He began to search the tables for keys, telling himself that if they didn't have Nat, they couldn't go through with their plan.

Not seeing any keys, he knelt and pulled tools from his satchel, and began to pick at the locks.

"Ahnri?"

"Yes?"

"Thank you."

Ahnri met her gaze. "I'm only sorry I didn't know sooner."

Eyes back down, he focused on the shackles. Notched up the first pin.

"I don't know where they're going," she whispered. "Or what they want me to do except…"

"Transfer your abilities," Ahnri said. Two pins.

"Yes," Nat said. "But it sounds bigger than that."

Ahnri gritted his teeth. "It is," he said. He switched hands for a better grip.

"I don't know if…if I try, if I'm even supposed to survive…"

The door to the lab began to shift once more.

Ahnri swore. He pulled his picks out and slipped away from Natalia, toward the back of the room where crates were stacked in darkness.

"All right, Miss Natalia," Brielle said, entering. "You can cooperate, or we can bring you by force. I promise you won't enjoy the latter, and please remember that we can gather your mother at a moment's notice should you misbehave."

Ahnri watched in horror as Nat stood on command and followed the adviser out of the lab.

The scent of metal and sweat mingled in the air, as Ahnri's head hung in the darkness.

33

AHNRI

Ahnri hurried to leave the lab, a chilly unease creeping through him. Watching Natalia be carried away left him feeling more helpless than ever. Whatever the Queen's next steps were, he had to stop them. They were moving *tonight*.

At the base of the staircase, he stopped.

The guards above had an exact description of him. As did, probably, a majority of the palace guards by this point.

He would need to be far more careful now…

Back to the lab. He got in and searched the cages for a dangerous animal, and chose a large black snake—a breed he knew to be non-venomous, but would hopefully frighten the average person. As he lifted the cage, the serpent snapped at him, its fangs latching onto the cage for a moment before it curled up, defeated. The poor thing probably hadn't had a decent meal in months.

Well. Perhaps Ahnri could help.

He carried the cage up the staircase, and when he came in sight of the guards he held it out away from him by the handle.

"What is that!" one guard shouted.

"Adviser's order's," Ahnri said. "Need to get through!"

"Make way!" another guard called, and servants and passers-by drew back, all eyes on the snake, and not Ahnri.

He carried the snake through to exit the palace, then covered the cage with his cloak and found a path to the exterior of the tower city itself. There, in the light of the afternoon sun, he made his way across the road that wound up and around, and opened the cage.

"Thank you, friend," Ahnri said. "You drew the attention well."

The snake didn't acknowledge him, slithering its way down the mountain toward the city below.

Glancing around, Ahnri realized he was close to the market on level three. A lump caught in his throat.

He shouldn't risk it…

Up the road, he could see the main wide corridor where he could go straight through to Remi's window. He felt pulled in that direction, toward the prince's rooms. He'd been there only last night. Remi was furious with him, but…he couldn't help the need to check.

To see if the purple ribbon was out.

He made his way through the market with his hood low, passing stall after stall, scents that made his stomach growl in hunger as he realized he hadn't eaten all day. Until finally he reached the archway that intersected the spiraling central road.

Ahnri checked Remi's window. No ribbon.

He stared for a moment, wishing…*willing* something to happen. Imagining Remi appearing at that moment, their desires intertwined…

Nothing.

He turned away, wandering into the market again, not knowing what to do now. Head to his rooms? Search for Pin? Merlin, maybe? Elya was about to march her army out of the city in a few short hours and attempt to turn them all into Viruses, Natalia as her prisoner…he had to *do something*…but what?

He'd seen those wide doors in the training caverns below…there had to be a place where those came out. He'd have to search the outer city, maybe the exterior wall. Yes, that's where he'd start. He wished once again that Pin were with him…wherever that cat was, he'd been busy all day. Longer than Ahnri had ever gone without seeing him.

To his right a merchant tripped, falling across Ahnri's path. He reached out to catch them on instinct, momentarily intrigued by the pale, scale-like patches of skin framing their face.

"Got you," he said, helping them stand.

"Thank you, sir," they said, scooping up a gold hair clip from the ground where it had fallen, and re-attaching it to their brown hair. "My feet get away from me sometimes."

"Enjoy your day." Part of him felt insincere saying it, knowing a portion of citizens were potentially marching to their deaths soon…

His hood had fallen back when he'd moved, so he pulled it back up over his head.

"You there," a voice called from behind. "In the name of the queen, halt!"

Ahnri froze, waiting to see if they meant someone else.

"What's your name?"

Ahnri lifted his arms slightly to show empty hands. "Are you asking me?"

"I am." The voice had drawn closer. "Show your face."

Ahnri didn't move.

Wait…

"I said—" The sound of a sword unsheathed, people around them backed away. "—show your face."

On instinct, Ahnri turned and ducked in past the sword's reach, landed a punch to the man's stomach, and ran.

Through the crowded market, he weaved between shoppers and spun past wares, back toward the wide exterior road. The guards drew close behind him, shouting as they went for people to clear the way. A moment later he found his path forward blocked by more guards, swords out. Civilians scattered, hiding behind market stalls and barrels.

Three guards leaped at Ahnri at once—to their detriment. He easily jumped sideways, letting two of them slam into each other. The third, he managed to duck a swipe of his sword, and knocked him out at his knees.

Something Damond had once said floated to the forefront of his mind…*even the most talented swordsmen can be overcome by numbers when surrounded. So—don't let yourself get surrounded.*

Obvious enough, harder in practice. He had to use the environment somehow. Two more guards approached, wary this time. One lunged forward with his sword, and Ahnri managed to sidestep the attack and step in, slamming his elbow to the man's wrist and causing him to drop his blade.

Ahnri took up the weapon in a familiar stance, eyeing his enemies. He had to get out of here. Another two guards came at him, and Ahnri let muscle memory guide him. A parry to one, a slash to the other. He turned, dodging both their attacks at once, and managed to slice the arm of one of them in passing.

A path out. To his right were fewer guards, that was his chance.

He threw the sword at one man and ducked to the side, winding between two stalls to follow the cavern wall behind them. He ran along that, passing shouting merchants, until he'd flown past the guards, then leaped into the open once more and had reached the exterior road.

"Stop him!"

He needed to get down the tower, to the outer city, where he could hide. He dashed across the road, dodging carts and pedestrians alike as the guards' shouts continued to ring. He had to get sliding down the exterior. They'd never catch him there. He reached the edge. One hand on the rail, he launched his body over—

A rope looped around his leg.

Time slowed as his body was pulled against his will, out from under him. First his leg, then hips, then torso. His hand slipped from the railing, and he tried to grab on with his other, but the shock of such unfamiliar motion threw off his grip.

His head slammed into the railing as he fell, and he landed face-first onto gravelly ground. A wave of dizziness overcame him as time resumed its normal pace. With a grunt, he got his elbows beneath him, prepared to haul himself up. Rivulets of warm blood were already running down his cheek.

"Hold, you."

Hands gripped him, lifting him to kneel and holding him there. Rocks dug into the skin of his knees through the fabric of his trousers. Ropes began to wrap around his wrists.

No…

He pulled away, throwing his body weight, trying to get to the railing again.

"Enough!"

A kick to his stomach made him curl in on himself. His satchel was yanked off over his head. In a moment, his hands were bound tightly.

"Take him straight to the cells," someone said. "Queen's orders."

Ahnri wrenched his arms a dozen times trying to get away, but to no avail. They led him like a dog through the corridors of the city and into the palace. At least a dozen guards surrounded him for an escort. Which meant that even if he could get free, he'd have nowhere to run.

A dark corner of his mind knew where they were taking him; he ignored it for as long as he could. Until the brown stone of the tower turned to granite. Until the scent of metal and mildew reached his senses. Until the snap of the guards' boots brought on memories that caused Ahnri's breath to catch in his throat.

Yes, he knew this place.

He'd been locked here after Damond's death. Elya had offered him his life in exchange for his service—a deal she thought binding, but Ahnri did not honor.

The guards led him across the bridge, from the palace proper to the reinforced prison created specifically to be far more difficult to dig ones way out of. For a moment he tried to pull away again. He knew the layout of this place; he could find his way…

"Enough of that." One of the guards punched him in his side, bringing bile to his throat, subduing him for the moment.

They tossed him unceremoniously into a cell. A granite block, with bars on the front, a single door in the center. Whether it was the exact spot he'd been last time or not, he couldn't tell. It didn't matter. It was all too familiar.

They locked his cell. And without any other communication, left him.

Suddenly, every muscle in his body ached. His head throbbed where he'd hit, the blood beginning to dry on his temple and cheek. His mind spun at the memories returning to him. The drip of water deep in these cells. The footsteps of Elya approaching to extend her offer. The shock of pain at losing

Damond. The certainty that Remi wouldn't know what happened to him.

It all came flooding back. Overwhelming his senses from the inside out.

"You are to be executed."

Elya's words. Her threat.

"If you choose to serve the crown, I will spare your life. In return, you will owe me yours."

In Fugeran culture, when a person saved your life, you then owed and dedicated your life to them in return. A blood debt. It was more than tradition; it was a *way*. A covenant. A contract. But, Ahnri's memories brought back the confusion he felt, even at the time.

No…a person doing the threatening could not then also be the person doing the saving—that made no sense. She was not saving his life; she was sparing it.

And those were not the same.

So, Ahnri did not dedicate his life to Elya. He pretended to, at first. But it wasn't long into his assignment in Medelios that he turned away from her.

Except now, here he was. Back where he started.

A failure.

34

MERLIN

Merlin sat across the street from the base of the central palace column, sketching. There was a beautiful archway here with an enclosed bridge going over the street, something he'd seen when arriving and had told himself he wanted to come back and draw.

His charcoal pencil scraped the paper gently, harsh lines becoming soft as he rubbed them to blend. Getting the lighting and shadows right in charcoal was a challenge, one he enjoyed. It left his fingers black and his hands stiff sometimes, but he looked forward to the feeling. That pleasant ache that meant he'd created something beautiful to put out into the world.

Glancing up at the bridge again, he spotted a grey striped cat slinking out of one of the thin windows, then hopping from one tiny stone outcropping to another until it reached the street level.

Merlin squinted at it.

To no surprise, the cat practically pranced across the road and padded up to where Merlin sat.

"You're that cat Ahnri had with him, aren't you?"

The cat sat, eyes narrowed at Merlin.

"Sorry, I don't speak your language, you're gonna have to spEak mine."

"*Mrroww,*" the cat said.

"Don't take that tone with me, I'm not your owner."

The cat rolled his eyes.

Merlin grinned. "You are a clever one, aren't you."

Then the cat stepped forward and placed his paw on Merlin's arm. And—to Merlin's great surprise—he felt *magic* move from the cat, to him.

"Well now," Merlin said. "That's very interesting. How can I be of service, friend?"

Part Three

Stand

35

AHNRI

Time blurred as, with every tiny reminder, Ahnri's mind relived the experiences he'd had in this place. The darkness was oppressive, his space lit only by a single pale lantern on the wall across from him, barely hanging on. He had to force himself to take in a breath, then exhale it out. In, and out. As the memories of that day, that week, slammed into him. Repeatedly.

Entering their home on level six after a day of training, Ahnri grinned so hard his cheeks were sore. His supervisor had praised him today, said he had great promise.

Had he smiled like that in the last five months?

The scent of polished leather met his senses; Damond must be home early, already cleaning his gear. Ahnri made his way into the kitchen to brag about having beaten the Somnurian dignitary's guards in a spar, but stopped short at the sight of three armored men he did not recognize.

"Ahnri Breona?" one of them said. "Son of Damond Breona of the palace guard?"

Ahnri's eyes narrowed. "Who are you?"

"Queen's guard, son," the second man said. "We need you to come with us."

"Where's Damond?" Ahnri took a step back. The memory of their talk the night before played through his mind. Damond's words, "They might come for me…for us. Be ready."

"We'll explain on the way. Follow—"

Ahnri turned, and ran.

"Get him!"

He hadn't expected it to be a pleasant experience, returning to this place again. But he'd hoped to at least prepare himself…

He didn't have the chance.

Pain, of a kind that was not physical, raked over him like claws leaving no marks.

He would've gotten away if he'd made it to an exterior window, but they caught him before he could reach one. Shackles cut into the skin of his wrists, and someone threw a sack over his head as they manhandled him down to the prison cells. The clank of the lock. The musty smell of the whole place. The cold metal bars. Straw on the floors that poked every inch of him when he attempted to sleep.

Ten days of waiting. Of agonizing over where Damond might be, whether he was alive, then learning from the guards that he'd "died in action," or "in service to the crown."

Ahnri had acknowledged it...but he didn't mourn. The pain turned to anger, then a numb acceptance of his circumstances.

Then, the queen visited.

Ahnri closed his eyes against the memories, trying to shake them off...

"You are hereby sentenced to death," Elya said. "For being an accomplice to treason. What do you have to say for yourself?"

"I did nothing," Ahnri said.

How he'd thought he stood a chance...so much had changed in so little time...

"Certainly," Elya said. "And yet, knowledge is sometimes worse than action. Did Damond tell you anything before he died?"

"No."

Elya paused, examining him as though searching into his soul without permission.

"Why should I believe you?"

"Because I'm telling the truth," he'd lied.

Elya put a finger to her lips in thought. "I will give you a choice."

The sickly sweetness of her voice brought bile to his throat. He'd heard that tone before, in the years he'd been Remi's friend...and he did not welcome it.

"I do hate to execute a perfectly good spy," she'd said. "You've shown talent; you've been trained by some of Fugera's best."

Damond *was* the best, *Ahnri thought.*

"If I save your life, you must serve me," she said. "That is the way of things, is it not?"

Ahnri pressed his teeth together to keep from speaking.

Blood dripped from his lip, the metallic tang of it hot on his tongue as the memories would not relent.

"You will join my personal spy network. In the morning, you will leave for Medelios to fill the role of a servant in the Matano house. The old childless king is choosing his heir by tournament, and I would like the Matanos to win. You will assist them, and report your findings directly to me with your lovely carrier hawk."

Ahnri hadn't spoken. That was not *the* way *of things…*

"We have an accord," Elya had said.

She left, and the next morning Ahnri had been shipped off to Medelios…

Days seemed to pass before his heart finally slowed, though it couldn't have been more than an hour or so as his mind replayed the same moments over and over, in order and mixed up and one after another.

When the memories finally subsided, Ahnri found himself kneeling on the floor of his cell, one hand gripping the bars before him so tightly his knuckles were pale. His other hand held against his chest for a sense of grounding. Blinking, he looked around again, trying to take in the space without letting his memories overwhelm again.

Too much. Exhaustion weighed him down.

One hand slipped from the bars, and the other from his chest. A crinkle of paper sounded from one of his pockets.

Footsteps sounded from down the corridor. Soon, a much brighter light appeared, and Ahnri blinked at its approach. A lantern held by someone, with another individual close by.

Sage…lavender…

Remi.

And *her.*

"Well," a feminine voice said behind the light. "Get on with it."

Muck. If it had been only Remi, Ahnri would've told him everything—not that he was convinced Remi would listen; he hadn't yet. But Ahnri had *some* proof now. He couldn't say everything, but he could try once more to convince Remi that Elya was lying to him.

Once more.

Ahnri curled up against the wall, stealthily drawing one of the pages from where he'd tucked it—the one with the adviser's notes—and hid it in the palm of his hand.

A heartbeat later, a familiar figure knelt at the bars beside Ahnri. For a moment, neither spoke.

"Ahnri," Remi said softly. "Please."

Ahnri stared at the floor. Feeling nothing. "What more do you want from me?"

A pained sound came from Remi's throat, and Ahnri hated it. He wanted to take his prince and disappear into a fairytale—but that was not their lot.

"Why, Ahnri? Why are you doing this?"

As quietly as he could manage, Ahnri whispered, "You know I can't speak with her near."

Remi stiffened. "If you don't trust my mother—"

With his full voice, "You know I don't."

"Ahnri, please," Remi whispered, begging. "Just apologize. Admit you were wrong. I can try to convince her you were under duress or threat, and we can—"

Frustration bubbled up inside him like molten rock. Ahnri met Remi's eyes, defiance forcing out the words. "What makes you think *I'm* wrong, and not *her?*"

"Ahnri—"

"Remi."

The prince hesitated.

"You will address him as 'Your Highness,'" Elya snapped.

Remi gave half a sideways glance, as though wishing she hadn't spoken.

At that moment, a guard came down the corridor, bowed to the queen and began speaking to her.

Remi's voice fell to barely a whisper. "You can't *both* be right…"

Ahnri leaned in. "You want the truth, *Your Highness?*" he breathed, taking a risk and speaking quickly. "Your mother is going to kill Natalia—yes, our friend, Natalia—and possibly your entire army. I have proof that the reports you're getting from Fugeran Intelligence are lies, but I tried to tell you that multiple times, and *you refused to listen to me.*"

Remi flinched at those final words.

"Son," Elya said. "We're out of time. Finish this."

Remi swallowed. His mouth opened and closed, but words didn't come.

"Listen to me now," Ahnri said. He kept his voice as low as possible, meeting Remi's striking eyes. Those eyes he loved.

"Your mother is going to hurt people. She is taking too great a risk. It will not be worth it."

"How can you—"

"And you, my prince," Ahnri said, bringing the folded piece of paper out from his hand, hiding it between them and out of Elya's sight, "would do well…to pay closer attention to details."

As Ahnri spoke, keeping Remi's eyes on his, he slid the page bearing the adviser's notes into the cuff of Remi's sleeve.

Remi followed the motion with confusion in his gaze, but did not move. He glanced subtly from the sleeve, to Ahnri, his head tilting slightly in an unspoken question.

Ahnri stared at the boy he loved, pleading for him to *listen*. To learn the truth.

Silence hung between them. Ahnri closed his eyes, bowing his head. He'd made his choice.

Remi let go, fingertips brushing Ahnri's knuckles as his hands slid from the bars.

"I want to understand."

Ahnri stayed quiet.

"Scum like him are impossible to understand," Elya said. "And we have better things to do than cater to them."

Footsteps retreating.

Ahnri rested his head in his hands.

And said a prayer to whatever gods were listening, that he'd done enough.

36

REMI

The sun had just touched the horizon as Remi and his mother reached the top of the outer city walls, large polished spheres of lumenite glowing brightly at intervals as the sun touched the horizon. Remi laid a hand on one, still warm from its day in the sunshine, then scanned the wall itself. Twenty feet tall and ten feet thick, these walls were built to withstand an assault, as any well-built city should. Despite the strength inherent in them, however, Remi only felt weak.

The walk from the prison to the wall had been enough time for him to replay his short conversation with Ahnri multiple times over, the folded paper scratching at his wrist. He hadn't had time to open it with Mother nearby…at least, he assumed he should read it in private. Ahnri had been very clear that he didn't trust Mother. But Remi had promised no more lies…should he show the note to her?

He couldn't shake the feeling that something was wrong. He'd placed the blame on Ahnri, that he'd changed so much as to upend Remi's life. Mother was the *queen*, it seemed obvious that she would have more accurate information, but the way Ahnri spoke—the way he'd spoken since returning to Isille— Remi only now realized…he really hadn't listened.

Mother sighed. "Isn't it beautiful?"

He followed her gaze, and for the first time realized what he was seeing.

An army of over a thousand stood in companies, prepared to march. Captains made their way through the ranks line by line, checking for cleanliness and perfection.

"And…" Remi said haltingly. "They're all headed for…?"

"You saw the report," Mother said. "We believe the Medelian army is lying in wait around the southern edge of the Arontas mountain range. That is where we are heading, to keep them from crossing into our kingdom, and show them that Fugera is not to be toyed with."

Remi thought through that. "But, that's at least two days' march away."

"And we're starting *now*."

"At night?"

"You believe we should give them another day to get closer?"

An uneasy feeling settled in the pit of Remi's stomach. But, that was war, wasn't it?

"Come," Mother said. "I wanted the view, but I do need to receive reports." She began to make her way down the wall, and Remi followed.

She's my mother, he thought to himself. *She's the queen. She has a plan…she knows what she's doing.*

And yet, Ahnri's words now rang in his mind, *"Your mother is going to hurt people… She is taking too great a risk…"*

How could defending their home possibly result in more hurt than if Medelios actually attacked? Ahnri's words didn't make sense…and yet…

The paper shifted against the skin of his wrist.

"Ah, General Saunier," Mother said. "Is everything in order?"

"It is indeed, Your Majesty," the general said. "Medallions have been distributed as ordered, and your carriage is ready. We are prepared to march on your order."

"Carriage?" Remi said. "Mother, you're not truly going *with* them…"

"Silence, boy," she said, following the general. "Of course I'm going."

Knots tightened in Remi's stomach tighten. "But Mother, a monarch should stay—"

She spun to face him, her eyes bright. "Your coward of a father taught you that, child," she snapped. "I am not him. And if you have any sense at all, you'll stay out of my way."

Remi said nothing, but followed as she made her way through the ranks of soldiers to the front of the company. The royal carriage waited there, polished dark wood and deep red curtains with gold trim. And attached to the back of the carriage was a smaller cart guarded by multiple men, one in particular who stood close, while the others stayed five feet back.

As he drew nearer, in the fading light of the sunset Remi saw what—or rather *who*—was in the cart.

"Natalia?" he said. He went toward her.

The guards stepped between them, but not before Remi noticed shackles around Natalia Aimar's wrists.

"Excuse me?" Remi snapped. "I am the prince and you will let me through."

"No, they will not," Mother said.

Remi spun to face her.

"She is under arrest."

"Under arrest?" Remi said. "Mother, what is she doing here? Why is she bound?"

"Never mind that," Mother said. "She is being kept safe."

"But she—"

"I *said*," she snarled. "She is *safe*. From herself and others."

Remi's eyes darted from his mother to his old friend. He'd seen her only yesterday, hadn't he? At one of the council meetings? She'd been fine, free, and not chained up. So why…

Your mother is going to kill Natalia…

Remi made his way toward her, ducking past the guards, who had relaxed when he'd backed off.

"Remi," Natalia whispered. "Please—"

"Nat, what is going on?"

"Silence her," Mother said.

"—please, my mo—"

The closest guard stepped forward, slapping Natalia across the face. She cried out, putting a hand to her cheek.

"Mother!" Remi said. "You can't treat people like this!"

"I am the *queen!*" she screamed. "I can and *will* do as I please!"

Remi's voice would not work. He wanted to scream back at her, tell her she was wrong, that *this* was wrong. It had been years since he'd spent significant time with Natalia, but recenTly he'd seen her nearly every day at the council meetings. And whether they were as close as they'd once been or not, she should *not* be chained up and slapped into silence.

Mother reached the carriage, pausing to speak to him. "I should be back within the week. You are to remain in the city."

Remi's throat had grown so tight he could hardly speak. "…yes, Mother."

A servant opened the carriage door, holding a hand to assist the queen. She turned, meeting Remi's eyes. "I am *protecting* Fugera," she said. "They are after us. But we will prevail."

"But—"

"Trust me, son." She entered the carriage, the door closing behind her.

Trust me… Remi could do nothing.

Nat stared at him from the cart. Her eyes seemed to beg, plead for his help, but then the carriage began to move, pulling her cart and jerking her off balance.

Remi's breathing grew thin as he watched the army begin their march all around him. He backed away, turned, and hurried back into the city proper, his own guards following close behind.

He needed somewhere to be alone.

37

Natalia

Natalia's cheek stung as she watched Remi go. Her heart grew cold inside her chest.

If the prince couldn't help her…

With the queen now in her carriage, the company began to march. Nat beheld the men and women, the soldiers who had agreed to offer their lives in service of Queen Elya's plans. They'd been told they were going toward a battle, something to do with Medelios and defending Fugera, but Nat suspected that was a lie. Either way, it didn't matter where they were going, she only wished *she* wasn't going too.

As her cart began to shudder and move, however, a grey cat with golden eyes hopped gracefully into the cart, tucking itself low into a corner beside her.

"Pin?" she whispered. "What are you—"

From his mouth, he dropped a small pouch onto the floor of the cart and tapped it toward her with his paw. "*Mrrrr.*"

Nat carefully took the pouch and curled up close to the cat to open it. It was awkward, with her wrists shackled before her, but not impossible. Inside the black pouch lay a small wooden token secured by a leather cord, long enough to be worn around the neck. When she touched the token, it began to glow a soft blue. She hurriedly pulled her finger away, the glow diminishing.

The token held Life magic.

"Pin," she whispered. "Did Ahnri send you with this? Can he help me?"

The cat reached forward and laid a paw on her arm. For a moment, she felt reassurance. That he couldn't explain everything, but help was coming.

"Is that cat supposed to be there?" one of the guards said.

"Hey!" another snapped. "Get out of there!" he banged his sword against the side of the cart, shaking them.

Pin hissed at him. Then he nuzzled his nose against Nat's shoulder, and hopped out to head back toward the city.

She hated seeing another friendly face leave her, but his appearance gave her hope. Natalia awkwardly laid down in the cart, putting the leather cord around her neck out of sight of the guards. She stayed there for a time, staring at the token, careful not to touch it.

She thought she'd felt, at the single touch, a large amount of magic here…maybe…it might be enough to save her, if she were to die trying this experiment. She tucked it between the layers of her dress, keeping it hidden, but not touching her skin.

Hope.

The army traveled as one, even as light faded from the sky. And when she spotted the moon, Nat's heart sank. It was there, but only a thin crescent. Very little light. Though the sky was clear of clouds and the stars were bright, she wished for more.

Inside the carriage beside her, the queen spoke. Natalia couldn't make out words, but as she strained, she could hear two voices…one obviously the queen's, and the other, Brielle.

Nat laid her head on the floor of the cart, tears threatening. She may never see Mama again. After the successful experiment that afternoon, she had only an inkling of what they wanted her to do, and the size of this force confused her. Did they want her to stay up all night performing that experiment with every soldier?

The cart lurched, hitting a deep rut in the road and throwing her to one side. As her back hit the wall of the cart, the thing inside her flared like a bolt of lightning.

She gritted her teeth, grunting through the pain while trying to stay as quiet as possible—she didn't want to draw any more attention to herself than necessary.

Eyes closed tightly, Natalia forced herself to take a slow breath, drew in the shadow, and sent it to the spot in her back. She managed to alleviate the pain slightly, until the cart shuddered once more, and she instinctively released the magic she held.

Deep breaths, the pain was a memory, but the soreness lingered…a reminder that it would come again. Tears threatened to rise behind her eyes.

She wanted to go home.

Soon, night fully encompassed the army. Nat made sure to tuck the Life token into her collar, kept safe. And when she finally looked around again, the carriage was pulling her cart at an angle, going up a hill, while the rest of the army continued on through a wide basin below. When they stopped, Brielle practically leaped out of the carriage and began giving orders to the guards around them.

"That stand, over here," she called. "And those crates, you three, bring those this way. Carefully now, don't touch that except where specified."

Nat watched as a setup began to take place before her eyes. The more she saw, the less she understood…until she spotted what Brielle held.

That journal, with the notes on how to transfer Power.

Natalia went motionless, examining more closely how the stands and elements were set up. The largest piece was some kind of funnel shape, supported by many bracers bolted into the stone by guards.

Queen Elya circled the setup, examining each part and asking Brielle questions. She seemed satisfied, content.

"Now, Your Majesty," Brielle said, "I want to make it clear to you that this is an *experiment*. There is absolutely a chance of failure." She glanced toward Natalia. "But I think, with some encouragement, we can make it work."

"It will work," the queen said. "It will work, and no one—no kingdom or army or force of any kind—will be able to harm us ever again. We must protect Fugera."

Brielle bowed, then turned away to continue her tasks. The queen noticed Nat watching, and came closer.

"Miss Natalia," the queen said. "I am going to speak, and you will listen. You can be a willing part of this, or you can be forced. I don't want to have to do the latter, but I will if necessary."

The queen turned, and gestured to a guard across the plateau who stood beside a second carriage. The guard opened the door so that Nat could see in. Her blood ran cold.

"*Mama?*"

Her mother sat inside, a man beside her holding a dagger to her throat. Mama's hands were tied, her mouth gagged, body slumped against the side of the carriage with her eyes closed. In an instant the chill in Natalia's blood turned to white hot rage. How *dare* they. Mama should *not* be moved, she needed her rest. She could be hurt if they—

The door closed, blocking Nat's view.

"So you see," the queen said. "We do expect *full* cooperation. Do you understand?"

The anger faded instantly. There were now *many* things she wanted to say, but she knew if she said them, these people would do something terrible to Mama.

She didn't want to be here. But she was.

And she would do what they asked.

38

AHNRI

As soon as the queen and Remi took their leave, Ahnri slumped with his back against the wall, elbows resting on his knees and head in his hands.

Waiting. Hoping.

There had been times in his life when he hadn't accomplished what he'd set out to do, or when circumstances were so against him that he'd been thwarted, but none of those had felt as much like *failure* as this did. Every time he'd come close before, there had been a way out. Something he could do, or someone he could trust to help him.

When he'd broken something in the palace, Remi covered for him. When he'd nearly died in that fire, Merlin had saved him. And when he'd been captured and tortured, ChaNia got him out. Every time, he'd had friends close by. Friends who knew he'd gone missing, who had come for him.

But now…Remi hated him. Who knew if he'd read thE paper Ahnri had passed to him, or if it would even make a difference at this point. Merlin…well, even with magic there was little he could do. And Pin…Ahnri hadn't seen him since the night before. He had no idea how long he sat in the darkness. Whatever Elya was doing, she would do it. He couldn't stop her, couldn't help Nat, couldn't tell Remi the truth…

"*Mrrow?*"

Ahnri sat up. "Pin?" he whispered. He moved to the front of the cell, looking through the bars. Sure enough, the cat was there. He sat on his haunches in front of the cell next to Ahnri's. When he saw Ahnri, he leaped up and came over, sliding between the bars and nuzzling against Ahnri's chest.

A warmth came over him, his mind clearing as he hugged the cat back.

"I am so glad to see you, my friend."

Pin pulled back slightly and stood up on his hind legs, putting his front paws onto Ahnri's chest, and seemed to be examining him. After a moment, he nodded, then turned away and went back through the bars. Ahnri watched as the cat went to where he'd stood before and gingerly picked up a small fruit in his mouth, carrying it back to Ahnri.

"Percy?"

Ahnri froze in the act of picking up the fruit. He didn't recognize that voice.

"*Mrrow,*" Pin said, going back to the other cell.

"What is it, then?" the voice said.

The cat spoke, moving between the two cells. Ahnri watched as Pin stepped into the other cell for a moment, and a soft red light glowed from the space, before vanishing.

"Ahnri?"

Ahnri started. "How do you know my name?"

"My name is Tavin DuPont," he said, reaching a hand through his bars and toward Ahnri's cell. "And you're the one my cat has been helping."

"I am," Ahnri said, taking the man's hand in greeting.

"Well. I would say it's nice to finally meet you, but of course, there's very little that's nice about this place."

Ahnri gave a short laugh. "You're not wrong about that. Has he…the cat, has he told you about me?"

"Oh, yes," Tavin said. "He tells me everything. Very talkative when he wants to be."

Ahnri glared at Pin. "You can *talk?*"

Pin shook his head.

"He prefers not to," Tavin said. "It takes much more energy than simply being his normal cat self, so he doesn't do it often…only when he feels it's important. And you, my boy, are important."

Ahnri sighed. He certainly didn't *feel* important at the moment.

"You had some very special visitors earlier," Tavin said.

"That's one way of putting it…"

"I would say you must've done something terrible, but in my experience the queen puts people in here for less and less these days. Isn't that right, Percy?"

The cat let out a low growl.

Ahnri frowned. "Percy?"

"Yes, my cat."

"Per…it was an E and an R?" he said, looking at the cat. "This whole time you've let me call you Pin, when your name is Percy?"

Pin—Percy—shrugged.

"He doesn't much care for names, so long as he knows what to answer to," Tavin said. "From what I can surmise, he thinks names are a silly human thing. He relies on smell."

Ahnri stared at the cat. "He's your owner, then? So…why have you been helping me?"

Percy walked forward and put his nose to Ahnri's hand, and sniffed. "*Mrrrow.*"

"Right," Tavin said. "Ahnri, he told me some things…we should probably have a talk."

Ahnri shifted, angling himself to be able to hear better. "About what?"

"Percy told me what you found in the queen's lab. And he says he saw them take your friend—Natalia, you said her name was?—out of there in chains. She's being carted off with the army."

Ahnri closed his eyes against the images that conjured in his mind. "Pin—Percy—you saw her? Is she all right?"

"He said she's not hurt," Tavin said, "and he managed to get her a Life token from another friend of yours, but he can't remember the man's name."

Ahnri felt a small weight lift from his chest. "Merlin, probably?"

"Mrrow!"

"Yes, that was it," Tavin said.

Ahnri looked to Percy. "You've been busy."

The cat approached, ducking his head under Ahnri's hand to be scratched.

"Thank you," Ahnri said.

"Also," Tavin said. "He told me about your parents. I…I worked with them."

Ahnri considered his words before he spoke. "Do you mean my birth parents? They're different from the father who raised me."

"Yes, your birth parents—though I knew Damond, but not as well. Your birth father—Louis—was a good friend of mine. A brilliant man."

Ahnri froze for a moment. Part of him thought he should be feeling pain at the mention of his birth parents, but more than that he was…curious.

"You…were you there?"

Tavin didn't speak for a moment. When he did, his voice was small. "Yes."

Ahnri took in a breath. Held it for a moment. "Damond told me there was an explosion."

"It was more of a backfire. The Power they tried to transfer seemed to imbue into your mother, but then…well, I can only surmise that the Power seemed to realize where it was going, and rejected it. The energy left your mother with such force that neither of them survived. We didn't really know enough to take precautions then, and well…accidents happen."

"I didn't know that's what they were working on. I never really knew them."

"I know, son. I'm sorry."

"But you knew Damond?"

"I did, though he was more of an acquaintance," Tavin said. "He was a good man. I was saddened to hear of his death."

At this, Ahnri's chest swelled with emotion—so many, tangled up in knots and fighting to be felt. He tried to keep it in the Damond box in his mind, long enough to get more answers.

"You said," he started, forcing himself to speak, to make the connections, "they were…trying to imbue the *ability* to channel the Powers?"

"Yes," Tavin said. "It was a theory we'd read of in old records, though it had never been successful. So, we were sort of guessing…making it up as we went. And that was the terrible cost, unfortunately. And it's only grown worse."

Ahnri's brows drew together. "Worse?"

Tavin sighed. "After your parents died, I didn't go back to that work for a long time. But, a couple of years ago, the queen herself sought me out. She'd found our research papers, and wanted me to continue. Find a way to make it work. She had me experiment on animals, over and over again, until…I managed it. And, well. You've witnessed the result of that."

In the pale light of the single lantern across from them, Percy gave a rather elegant bow, particularly for a cat.

Ahnri tapped the bars before him, thinking, staring at the cat. "You succeeded on Percy."

"Yes," Tavin said. "I am a Clarity—I channel the Power of Stability. I believe it is this—along with the simple fact of having an increased amount of magic within him—that gives him higher intelligence than most cats."

Before them, Pin laid down on the floor, rolling to scratch his back.

"And yet," Ahnri said, "he is still a cat."

"Very true," Tavin said, chuckling softly. "And I love that about him."

"So…why are you in here?"

"Well," Tavin said, "when I succeeded on Percy, the queen insisted I try it on a human. I wasn't ready to, and refused. She threw me in here."

"I'm surprised she didn't kill you," Ahnri said.

Tavin grunted. "It seems to me she's done just that with plenty of others after me…but I believe she thinks me too valuable to kill, as it's my research they're trying to work from."

Silence fell between them, Ahnri latched onto that last phrase…

"It's *your* research they're using," he finally said.

"Indeed," Tavin answered.

"Tavin…are you aware that they're going to try to give the Virus ability to the entire Fugeran Army?"

Silence.

"I was not," Tavin finally said.

"I believe that's where the army is headed right now. And Natalia is the Virus they're using to do it."

"Well," Tavin said with a sigh. "The queen's ambitions have certainly grown."

39

REMI

Remi stepped out onto the south balcony, staring over the outer city of Isille from a hundred feet above.

With the sun fully set, and no lanterns lit here, no one on the streets below would be able to see him. He'd told his guards to stay behind the curtains, remain unseen, and while Remi had stepped through the heavy cloth, he found it difficult to move away from the illusion of safety there. He'd ordered for wine to be brought. Something gripped at his heart, left him feeling…unmoored. Like a feather on the wind.

Finally alone here, he slipped the folded paper from the cuff of his robes. But hesitated. He looked up. Out. Could he still see the army in the distance? Probably his mind playing tricks on him. The darkness wouldn't allow him to see that far anymore. Still, part of him feared Mother would come through those curtains as he looked at this note, and he'd be discovered—a traitor.

He shook his head. Why would he think that? Mother had gone. She wasn't here. Then there were more questions…

Why had Natalia been there? And restrained? And what were they going to do? Mother said they were marching to engage with the Medelian troops before they could get closer…that made sense, didn't it? But why was she taking Natalia?

For so many promises of no more secrets, Remi was left with a mountain of unanswered questions.

"Highness?"

He tucked the paper into one hand, turning to see a servant bring out a bottle of wine and a goblet. He accepted the drink, then dismissed them. A gulp of wine, and he glanced at the paper again.

He felt torn in two directions. He'd fought so hard, for so long, to earn his mother's trust, and Ahnri had been gone. Remi had thought him dead until only a few weeks ago, and then he'd come sweeping back into Remi's life like the ghost of some beautiful memory.

He walked to the railing and set down his wine. He needed answers…and he hadn't gotten them from Mother before she'd left. Nor had she given him any kind of assurance that she would reveal them moving forward, only more commands to trust her. He closed his eyes, leaning elbows on the balcony railing. Then, with a slow breath of desert air and a feeling that he was betraying his mother, he unfolded the paper and began to read.

The girl has the abilities…

The girl…Natalia?

We have the amount we need…

…transferred her abilities…test soldier…

…run it on the entire army…

… two Viruses at our disposal…a thousand more within the week…

Remi's heart dropped farther with each line. What was this? It wasn't Mother's handwriting, but possibly Brielle's? He didn't recognize it. Then Ahnri's voice floated into his mind…

"And you, my prince, would do well…to pay closer attention to details."

He gasped.

This could be a trick. He had to be cautious. But…seeing Mother with the army, seeing Natalia chained up…

Maybe…

He'd reported Ahnri. Had him thrown into prison for treason.

And the whole time, Ahnri had tried to tell him…

Remi glanced out at the dark horizon, barely lit by the stars and a thin crescent moon.

Something wasn't right. *That* he knew.

Thinking back to their interactions…it was Remi who hadn't been ready to hear. He'd shoved Ahnri away, refused to listen every time he'd tried to warn of danger.

Remi spun, ducking through the curtains. Maybe…maybe this time he would listen to Ahnri.

Remi made straight for the prison. When he reached the entrance to Ahnri's corridor, he turned to his guards. "Stay here…please. I need a few minutes."

They appeared unsure—Mother's orders would be to not let him out of their sight—but they did as he asked.

As soon as he reached the right cell, Ahnri stood and came to the bars.

"Remi, I—"

"Wait…" Remi held up a hand. "I don't know what to believe anymore. But I *want* to believe *you*. I know you've tried to tell me things, and I didn't listen. I didn't want to hear it. I realize you didn't feel you could trust me, but now our entire army has left the city and *Natalia* is chained up in a cart being slapped into silence and I—" He put one hand to his chest, catching his breath. "My mother has left the city. And I swear to you on my father's memory I will not repeat to her what you tell me if you just tell me *everything*."

Ahnri smiled at him, and it was as though the sun itself had risen in this dark place.

Then, Ahnri began to speak.

And Remi listened.

From Damond's death—the real truth behind it—to why Ahnri had left. His time in Medelios, his loyalty to the mage who had saved his life when Mother thought he'd died, and now his work for the Medelian queen. Returning to Isille to find the truth, the regret he'd felt that he couldn't tell Remi everything from the start, everything he'd done—by the stars, everywhere he'd snuck into—and everything he'd learned down to information from the man in the cell beside him, Tavin, and the cat at Remi's feet.

"The cat can…talk?" Remi asked.

"In a way," Tavin said. "He takes a while to warm up to people."

Ahnri raised a brow at the cat. "He still hasn't talked to *me.*"

Remi's mind reeled, his emotions tugging in every direction. It was a torrent of information, and yet…the suspicion his mother had hammered into him brought fears.

"You're working for Medelios?" he asked.

"I am," Ahnri said softly.

"But…Mother said she was approaching a Medelian force set to attack the city."

"Those reports are fake," Ahnri said. "Check in my satchel there, I have correspondence with the Medelian queen stating she hasn't moved any troops anywhere near the border."

Remi turned, spotting the bag that Ahnri always carried tossed to the ground on the opposite side of the tunnel. He dug through it, finding small packs of food, a water skin, a bundle of glass vials labeled poison, multiple daggers, and a notebook.

The notebook he removed and began flipping through pages until a few small strips fell out. He could feel Ahnri's eyes on him, but Remi kept his back to the cell, nerves raking through him.

Sure enough, the correspondence held a seal of the Medelian crown. And, Remi noticed, it had a few distinct differences to the one he was familiar with, marking it as the new queen's, not the old monarch's. He suddenly felt like an idiot. And yet, it could still be faked, couldn't it?

As he went to put the papers back, Remi's eyes caught on a page of the notebook where his name was written. Hesitantly, he opened to the page, dated three months earlier, and read Ahnri's words…

Had a dream about Remi tonight. I don't usually remember dreams, and even now it's fading, but I wanted to write it down to remember as much as I can. We were on a barge on Vei Lake, in springtime when the orange poppies were blooming. There was a blanket and food and wine, and Remi was laughing at something I said.

I haven't heard his laugh in months. I wish I could go back, but I'm scared. Elya is up to something, and Remi is there by himself. He probably thinks I'm dead, but even contacting him would put him at risk. It hurts to not know if he's safe. I miss him so—

Remi closed the book, his heart hammering. He closed his eyes.

What was the truth?

When Remi finally opened his eyes and turned back around, he saw the old man—Tavin—watching him.

"Something wrong?" Remi asked.

"Nothing, Highness…" Tavin said. "It's just…you look very much like your father."

Remi's throat tightened. "I'm sorry?"

"The late King Alain?" Tavin said. "He had the same posture, those squared shoulders and the chin up. You look very much like him."

What would Father do?

Remi swallowed his fears, and turned to Ahnri. "Let's say I believe all this. What are you asking of me?"

His head hanging, Ahnri spoke, "I'm asking for your help."

The pain in his voice surprised Remi.

"I can't do this alone," Ahnri said. "I tried. I need you to help me stop your mother, before she hurts *more* people."

His father, Damond, Remi thought. *He said Mother had him killed…*

Ahnri lifted his head, and Remi's heart wrenched in his chest at the expression there.

Pain.

Loss.

Remi knew those feelings. He'd felt them when Ahnri first hadn't come the day they'd agreed on all those months ago. And when he'd read the report that said he'd died. And again when he'd gotten the first note, that first sign that he might still be alive.

"Please, Remi," Ahnri said. "I don't want to see anyone else lose their family, least of all you."

"You hate my mother," Remi said. "After all that? If anyone would want her head, it would be you."

"Yes," Ahnri said. "But I don't want *you* to lose her."

It hit him then. The striking difference between Mother and Ahnri. The way Mother's eyes glowed when she praised him—looking, he now realized, like a dog trainer offering treats. And the way Ahnri's eyes shone, a well of sincerity that seemed unending, that sent a wave of emotion over him that he could only describe as *safe*.

He'd grown so used to Mother's pittances toward him, it had become second nature. And now, now that he had something else to believe, he wondered if any of it had been real.

Remi's mind finally began to catch up with all the information he'd been given. Connections formed, lines from one point to another...

"I'm sorry," Ahnri said, "that I couldn't tell you everything from the start. I tried to tell you what I could, and it wasn't enough. But if ever I needed you to trust me, Remi, it would be now. *Please.*"

Trust me...

Mother had said those same words, and left Remi with a pit in his stomach.

When Ahnri said them, here, now, everything fit together. It was a puzzle he'd been trying to force for weeks that needed more pieces, and Ahnri had offered them all.

"I trust you." Remi turned and shouted back down the corridor. "Guards! Bring the jailer."

Three men in uniforms arrived quickly. "Is everything all right, Your Highness?"

"Yes," Remi said. "I need both these cells opened."

The jailer frowned, glancing from Ahnri to Tavin, and back to Remi. "Sir? The queen specified these two were to be kept contained…"

"I know what the queen ordered," Remi said. "But the queen is not here, she is not even in the city. She left me in command, and I am ordering them to come with me."

The man hesitated, but did as he was told, opening Ahnri's cell first.

As Ahnri stepped into the open, Remi approached him. More than anything, he wanted to throw his arms around Ahnri's neck and hold him, but with everything that had passed between them…he hesitated.

"Maybe," Ahnri said, "we take care of the mess first?"

"Yes. Mess first."

"Thank you," Ahnri said. "For listening."

Beside them, Tavin exited the second cell. The other three men stood waiting for orders.

"Pardon, Your Highness," Tavin said. "But I might have an idea, if you're open to hearing it?"

"I am," Remi said. "But let's walk as you tell me. Whatever we're going to do, we have to hurry."

40

AHNRI

Ahnri felt a physical weight lift from him with each step he took leaving that prison. The memories that had plagued him were left behind, leaving his mind clear of the fog he'd been dealing with in there.

He followed Remi and Tavin through the palace corridors as they made their way to the council room. Guards were sent to wake the entire council for an emergency meeting, called by the prince.

"It's risky to interrupt the process once it's begun," Tavin said, his breath shaky as they walked.

"How risky?" Ahnri asked.

"Risky enough that it was part of the mistake that led to your parents' deaths."

Ahnri's heart stuttered at those words.

"Is there equipment we could damage?" Remi asked. "To interrupt without hurting Nat?"

"Possibly," Tavin said. "It's been a year, I'm not sure what the queen has developed in that time."

"Is there anything we could do to help Nat be able to stop it herself?"

"The necessary factor is focus of the central Vessel. When your father attempted to share his Life ability with your mother—"

Ahnri started—this was new information…

"—his mistake was fearing he would do it wrong. I saw his resolve waver, and the Power escaped his control, killing them both."

"Life magic," Remi said. "Killed them?"

"All the Four Powers can be dangerous in high enough quantities, Highness," Tavin said.

Ahnri hadn't known his father had been a Cure. But there wasn't time to address it now. With a shake of his head, he filed it away to ask about later.

"Miss Natalia needs to *focus*," Tavin said. "Whether she's sending the magic out or bringing it back in. Anything that could help her accomplish that will be useful."

"I'm not sure what we can do," Remi said, "but we'll try."

"I wish I had my old notes," Tavin said, brows drawn together, "but a year in an empty cell is plenty of time to think, and talking with both of you has given me some ideas…can I get pencil and paper?"

"We'll see that done," Remi said. He flagged down a passing servant immediately and gave the order to bring some to the council chamber.

"I don't know how we'll reach them in time," Remi muttered. "My understanding is that they're marching through the night. And though they'll be a bigger force they're still a *moving* target."

"Horses could help," Ahnri said. "You're the prince, Rem. We don't need to defeat the army, we only need the council's order to usurp command from your mother."

"We'll need to be stealthy," Remi said, running a hand over his face. "She took the entire army, but there should be members of the palace guard left, some city law enforcers…we'll have to ask the council to call in their people, and—"

"Hey," Ahnri said, putting a hand on Remi's back. "It's going to be all right."

Remi took in a breath, letting it out in a rush. "I'm just worried."

"Me too," Ahnri said. "But we'll take care of this. Together."

Remi reached to interlock their hands as they walked.

Ahnri savored the feel of it. Finally, they were on the same side.

They soon arrived at the council chamber, empty save for two servants lighting the lamps. A moment later, Tavin's requested paper and pencil arrived.

"Excellent," Remi said. He pulled out the chair usually reserved for him, and had Tavin sit. As soon as the pencil was in his hand, he began to notate and sketch. Percy ducked under the table and out of sight.

Remi pulled Ahnri to one side, holding to Ahnri's arm. "I'm still trying to grasp the implications of all this," he said, pulling out the folded paper Ahnri had slipped him earlier. "My mother has a hidden lab underground where she's been experimenting with Natalia, and has succeeded in transferring the ability to channel from Nat to another person?"

"Natalia confirmed it to me," Ahnri said. "I was hidden in there when they dragged her out, threatening her mother if she didn't comply."

Remi's eyes widened. He turned to the doors, calling for a servant. "Send someone to check on Councilor Mari Aimar. She should be in her rooms, but I need to know for certain."

The nearest servant bowed in acknowledgement and hurried away.

Ahnri closed his eyes for a moment in fear. "I hadn't even thought of that."

"We'll know soon," Remi said. "I only hope she's safe."

One by one, the council members began to arrive—all in nightclothes and robes, and questioning the prince, but they came. And in Ahnri's estimation, that said a lot to how much respect they held for Remi.

He continued to hold off their questions, waiting for the rest of the council. Finally, the last member arrived—an older, heavy-set councilman, accompanied by a rather familiar-looking young man. Pale skin, black hair, and grey eyes—features that stood out like a scorpion sting here in Fugera.

Ahnri met Merlin's eyes, and nodded in thanks.

Merlin—who appeared to be perhaps only fifteen at the moment—simply grinned, and took out a board and paper to take notes for his current employer.

With the entire council present—excluding Nat or her mother—Remi stood at the head of the table beside Tavin, holding up his hands to quiet the low mutterings.

"Esteemed Council," Remi said. "First, I want to thank you all for coming here at such an odd hour."

"Your Highness," one older man interjected. "This is highly unusual, we—"

"Yes, you're right," Remi said, a level of force behind his words Ahnri hadn't heard him use before. "Highly unusual circumstances require highly unusual actions." He took a breath, glancing around at each person before he bowed his head, and Ahnri thought he saw a hint of sadness in his prince's eyes.

"I regret to inform you all," Remi said, "that my mother is taking actions that will endanger the people of Fugera. And if we do not stop her tonight, she will put our entire army at risk and potentially bring war to our city."

Stillness. Then everyone spoke at once.

"What do you—"

"Her Majesty would never—"

"It's asinine to think—"

"Silence!" Remi called.

They obeyed.

"I know it seems outlandish," he said, his voice leveled now. "All of you see her as Queen Elya, gracious, cunning, and intelligent. But we have proof. Multiple witnesses to my mother's intentions and actions. One, in particular, whose word I trust implicitly." He turned toward Ahnri.

Ahnri's eyes went wide. Was he…did Remi expect him to speak?

The whole room waited. So, Ahnri stepped forward, and took a breath.

"Esteemed…council," he began, clearing his throat. "My name is Ahnri. I am, by trade, a spy. Trained here in Isille. Over the last many months someone has been manipulating the information collected by the Fugeran spy network. I can prove that the queen has received false information on multiple occasions, leading her to suspect that Isille is being threatened by the surrounding kingdoms. And I know for a fact—based on proof given me from the new Medelian queen—that the fight Queen Elya is headed toward tonight is *not real.*"

Exchanged looks of uncertainty passed around the table, and a few murmurs of confusion.

"These nonexistent threats have led Queen Elya to grow paranoid," Ahnri continued, "seeing shadows at every turn and increasing her guard—I'm sure you've witnessed this. As a result, she is attempting to take drastic and dangerous measures. In secret, she has been experimenting with Death magic, and ways to utilize it. Not only imbued in weapons, but…she is creating Viruses. I believe tonight she will attempt to share this ability with her entire army force."

"Then where did this information come from?" a councilman snapped. "The Fugeran spy network is one of the best in the world, and yet you say they've been, what, duped?"

"I'm saying," Ahnri continued, "that whoever did this knows what they're doing, and they've fooled many people."

"Who, then?" a younger councilman asked. "Who is behind this?"

Ahnri exchanged a glance with Remi.

"We don't know," Remi said. "But we have no time to investigate if we are to save those who could be hurt."

"Why should we believe," one woman said, addressing Ahnri, "that you are loyal to Fugera? You could easily be a spy for Medelios and we have nothing but your word to go on."

"Actually," Ahnri said, checking with Remi, who nodded, "I *am* a spy for Medelios. While I was trained here, I recently gained a position of some importance there and came back to investigate this very situation."

"Then we have even less reason to trust you!" the older man beside Merlin shouted.

"Councilor Erre," Remi said. "Please think through this. If Medelios was trying to sneak up on us, why would their spy reveal himself willingly? And not only that, but share confidential documents proving his honesty—which I have seen with my own eyes?"

Erre crossed his arms. "It would make sense if Medelios is coming to attack our city that they would try to tell us it's not happening. I'm going to need more proof than this boy's word."

"In that case," Remi said, "allow me to introduce Tavin DuPont. He is a researcher of the Powers and worked with my mother on this project for a time. Until she tried to push him to do *exactly this,* and he refused, landing him a place in our dungeons."

The council's attention turned to Tavin.

"I implore you to listen to him," Remi said, gesturing for Tavin to speak.

As Tavin stood and began to explain his research and what he suspected Elya was up to, Ahnri felt a pressure against his leg, and looked down to see Percy there. He smiled at the cat, grateful for his presence.

"It isn't unreasonable to believe," Tavin said, "that she may be attempting to pass the ability to many, or all of the soldiers. If she fails, it could kill the entire force she's trying to elevate—which would be devastating. But if she *succeeds...*" he took a breath. "We could potentially have a thousand new, untrained Viruses coming back to our city—which is a problem of a very different kind."

Silence hung thick in the air. It seemed that Tavin's more scientific explanations had struck a nerve Ahnri hadn't been able to hit, as the council's faces had gone slack and horrified.

Bumps rose on Ahnri's arms at the thought of an entire army of Viruses, or, the more likely possibility, that the experiment would fail, and Fugera would lose not only its fighting force, but the husbands and wives, mothers and fathers, sons and daughters, of so many still in the city.

"We have to stop her."

Ahnri turned to see Remi step forward once more, and their eyes met. Those clear eyes, like crystals in the sun. A light he would always come back to. Then, in front of the entire council, Ahnri slipped his hand into Remi's, and held.

"I would call for a vote," Remi said. "I propose that the best plan we have at the moment is for myself and a small force to follow the army and attempt to usurp command from my mother before she can do what she's planning. I'll need at least three council members to come, to act as witnesses to this, and ratify my actions on behalf of the council as a whole."

The person to Remi's right, a younger woman with a thick braid falling down her back, stood and addressed the council. Before she spoke, Ahnri spotted young-Merlin lean forward and whisper into Councilor Erre's ear.

"All in favor," the braided woman said, "of supporting our prince in this effort, and attempting to stop the queen, please show by a raise of hands."

All but one hand went up. Councilor Erre, the large man who had questioned Ahnri, sat with arms crossed, eyeing him again.

"That is a majority," Remi said, his eyes tracking the exchange between Ahnri and the older gentleman.

Ahnri cleared his throat and addressed Erre directly. "Please. Fugera is my home. I don't want to see it fall to the paranoia of one ruler."

At these words, Erre nodded, satisfied. He raised his hand.

"It is settled then," Remi said. "I'll need volunteers to accompany us, though you will stay back, away from the danger."

"I would like to come, Your Highness," a councilwoman said. "I may not be a fighter, but I would like to witness with my own eyes what *exactly* the queen is attempting."

"I welcome your presence," Remi said.

"I agree," Councilor Erre said, standing. "These claims seem outlandish, and I want to trust our prince, but I'd like to see what we're talking about.

"I will come as well," the younger councilman said. "I have a handful of guards I can bring along, if that would help."

"It would, thank you," Remi said. "Thank you all for your support. Those of you staying in the city, please do not alarm the citizens, but be prepared for either possibility we've discussed here. Those of you joining us, meet at the south gate in fifteen minutes, and we will depart together. Dismissed."

With that, the council began to leave and Remi turned to Tavin, who still sat scribbling.

"Tavin," Remi said, "You said you had an idea?"

"I did. I think," Tavin said, holding up a diagram he'd drawn.

"Psst…"

Ahnri turned to see Merlin behind him.

"I'm coming," Merlin said quickly. "Hand these out. Don't die." He shoved a pouch into Ahnri's hands, and then followed Councilor Erre from the room.

Ahnri had learned not to question Merlin, frustrating though he could be at times. When the council had left, he opened the pouch.

Five small wooden tokens lay inside, wrapped in leather ties long enough to be worn around one's neck. Suspecting he knew what they were, Ahnri reached in and touched one.

Life. Healing.

"—will take some time to cover the entire army," Tavin was saying. "When I managed it with only Percy here, it took a solid five minutes. Even if they've managed to create some kind of amplifier in order to reach the entire force, it would still take time for the energy to travel if your friend is exerting control over it. I would assume they have an amplifier though, and if you can find that you'll find your friend."

"Find the amplifier," Ahnri said. "Destroy it?"

"No," Tavin said firmly. "Do not damage the amplifier. If she hasn't begun, simply get her away from it. But if she has, do not force her away. You'll have to make sure *she* is safe, and allow *her* to pull away from it gently. With the amount of Power they must have stored in order to try this, if she were to be interrupted and suffer the same fate as your parents, it could result in an explosion large enough to lay waste to that entire force."

Remi ran a hand over his face, worry clear in his motions. "I just want to see her safe, and the rest of those soldiers. Gods protect us…"

"I don't believe in the gods," Tavin said, shaking his head as he stood. "I believe in my Power, and the nature that fuels it.

This Natalia friend of yours has a gift, and it is being exploited. I don't know what they're using to encourage or threaten her into cooperation, but there must be something."

"Highness?" A young messenger boy hurried into the room, out of breath. "Prince Remi? I'm sorry sir, but we had to break the door. Councilor Mari, she's not there. Nor is Miss Natalia."

Remi thanked the boy, then turned to Ahnri and Tavin. "I think we found the threat."

"Locate the amplifier," Tavin said, "that will point you to your friend. Get her mother safe, then do what you can to help her back out of the process safely."

"Find the amplifier, find Nat, secure Councilor Mari, help Natalia disengage," Ahnri said.

"Thank you, Master Tavin," Remi said. "Do you want to join us?"

"Oh no, no. I'm no use in a fight. I'll sit this out."

"Mrrow?"

"Ah," Tavin added. "But Percy could maybe be of help."

Ahnri crouched to let the cat hop up to ride on his shoulders.

Remi removed a pin from the sash across his chest and offered it to the scientist. "When we leave here, make your way to my rooms. If anyone asks, show them this and tell them you're on orders from the prince to wait for me there. You're welcome to rest if you can, and ask the servants to bring you food."

"Thank you, Highness," Tavin said. "Stay safe."

"And you as well," Remi said. Then he took Ahnri by the hand as they left the room—Remi's guards following behind.

"Where are we going?" Ahnri asked.

"The armory," Remi said. "We both need better protection, and you need a sword."

When they arrived, Remi went all the way to the back of the space where his personal effects hung and began to buckle leather armor on right over his pristine royal tunic.

Ahnri buckled on a sword with a comfortable weight, then searched for a leather breastplate that would fit him, and began to don it.

"Ahnri? I can't get these last straps, would you mind?"

He turned to see Remi nearly done, with one strap remaining to be tightened at his waist. Ahnri went to him, placing a hand on his side and tugging the strap so it fit snugly, then moved to the other side, and did the second. As he moved to pull away, Remi caught hold of him.

They stood very close, and for a moment, Ahnri wondered if Remi hadn't actually needed help with his armor at all.

"Thank you," Remi said softly.

"For your armor?"

Remi laughed. "Yes, but…for standing your ground. I wish I'd actually listened earlier, but…I wasn't ready to hear it."

Ahnri pulled on the strap he'd helped tighten, bringing Remi closer. "I'm glad you were ready tonight."

Remi leaned forward and pressed a kiss to Ahnri's lips. For a split second, everything went away. The danger, the risk, the possibility that they might fail…it all faded like smoke into the night sky. In that moment, Ahnri felt they could accomplish anything, so long as they did it together.

Remi pulled away too soon. "More kissing after we save our city, yes?"

"Absolutely," Ahnri said with a grin.

41

AHNRI

The night air should've been cool, a relief against his skin, but worry and fear made it impossible to appreciate. Sweat beaded at Ahnri's temples, dripping and tickling. He kept glancing to the side where Remi rode with furrowed brows, focused on the path ahead of them.

At their back were six guards, armed with everything from throwing daggers and darts to battle axes and swords. And behind them, three council members—flanked by half a dozen more guards—keeping a short distance back but staying within sight.

And around their necks—Ahnri, Remi, and the three council members—hung the wooden tokens Merlin had handed him.

Ahnri hoped they wouldn't need them.

He took in a breath, refocusing on the horse beneath him, the dusty road ahead. Search for the amplifier. Secure Councilor Mari. Help Natalia get out.

Find the amplifier. Save the councilor. Help Natalia.

Amplifier.

Councilor.

Natalia.

The darkness seemed to go on forever, the desert landscape lit only by the stars and a pale moon. Ahnri checked his bag occasionally for Percy. The cat disliked traveling in the satchel, but it was the safest option while on horseback.

Options and possibilities were a whirlwind in his mind. Ideas and strategies, how he could use Percy, what skills Ahnri had, what Remi could do, what supplies they had, the abilities of the six guards at their disposal…it wasn't much, but perhaps enough.

"Hold," Remi said, raising a hand to bring their force to a stop. Then he pointed. "There. Do you see?"

In the dim starlight, Ahnri could make out a section of the land, a basin where the elevation lowered slightly, covered by a huge dark shape blotting the landscape.

"That's the army," Ahnri said. "Where is—"

And then they both saw it. A plateau of rock jutting out over the basin from the west, where lanterns were lit and being carried around. There were two carriages and multiple carts and crates, and figures moving like ants in the distance.

Ahnri squinted, eyeing the landscape. "If we backtrack a little and make our way around behind that outcropping, we might be able to flank it. Capture your mother, take control of the leadership, and the rest of the army will follow."

Silence.

"Rem?"

Ahnri turned, worried the prince had gone off on his own. Remi hadn't, he sat on his horse only a few feet away. But tears rolled down his cheeks, and his jaw clenched.

"Are you…sad?" Ahnri asked.

"Yes," Remi said softly. "And no. It's complicated."

Ahnri extended his hand. Remi took it, and squeezed in gratitude.

"We can do this," Ahnri said.

"We can do this," Remi said, his voice now firm. "Tell the guards your plan. Make sure they understand they are *not* to attack unless they see fighting happening, and even then, the goal is to *capture*, not kill."

Ahnri narrowed his eyes. "And what are *you* going to do?"

"I'm going to go talk to my mother."

"Then I'm coming with you."

Remi's eyes snapped to his. "No."

"Rem," Ahnri said. "With all due respect to your station, you can't stop me."

"And I cannot *lose you again.*" Remi snapped.

Ahnri started at the strength in Remi's voice.

"For once in your life," Remi said, "let *me* protect *you*. You didn't see her when I told her you were alive. She wants your head."

"As though that's new," Ahnri muttered.

"Ahnri."

Ahnri steadily met his gaze. "You need the appearance of guards. I'll accompany you until we get close, then hide. I'll get to Councilor Mari and signal you when she's safe."

Remi considered this. "You'll stay hidden?"

"I promise."

Remi's shoulders relaxed. "All right."

Ahnri spoke to the guards and set two of them to accompany him and Remi, while the other four separated to go around the back of the outcropping to split up and flank from behind—one of which he recognized to be Merlin, now appearing to be perhaps in his mid-thirties, and leading the others. With luck, they'd all arrive within minutes of each other.

Together Ahnri and Remi kicked their horses into motion, and the two guards assigned to stay with them followed. As they drew closer, a squad from the army made their way to intercept, and the two groups slowed as they came within shouting distance.

"Who approaches?" a soldier shouted.

Ahnri raised his voice before Remi could respond, "His Royal Highness Remi Caselle, Crown Prince of Fugera and Lord of the Stone City, with royal guards accompanying him." He waited a beat, then asked, "And who are you?"

A moment of confusion spread among the soldiers. Remi leaned toward Ahnri and whispered, "I think that's the first time in a decade someone has used my full title."

"It's a good title."

"I like when you say it."

Ahnri couldn't help a smile despite the direness of their circumstances.

Finally, a voice called from across the distance, "You may continue your approach."

"They still might not believe it's you," Ahnri said. "They didn't risk getting any closer."

"I'll deal with it," Remi said.

They passed the soldiers, and Ahnri waited until he and Remi moved under a natural stone archway before ducking his horse into the shadows off to one side, nodding to Remi as he went. Remi and the two guards continued up a ramp-like slope of stone toward the place where they could see the carriages and carts.

Ahnri took a moment to settle the horse, tying it to a gnarled tree branch and giving it some grain, then helped Percy out of the satchel.

"All right," Ahnri said. "Moment of truth. Remi's going up there to talk, we know this probably won't go well. You're sneakier than I am though, so if you see an opportunity to do something, do it. Got it?"

The cat nodded, not risking a sound.

Together they followed the path Remi had taken, keeping to the shadows. Halfway up the path, Ahnri began to hear voices. He quickened his pace until he could make out words.

"Begin, *now*." Elya…

"No!" Natalia.

"Mother, there's—" Remi.

A flash of purple light lit the night around them. Ahnri's heart dropped.

They were too late.

42

NATALIA

They brought Natalia to the point of the funnel-like device, and she noticed for the first time that it was made of the same dark metal they'd been using in their experiments. A discouraging sight. For a moment, she considered falling into one of the guards moving her, trying to get away…but no. These people were only following orders.

She didn't want to end any more lives.

She cast her eyes around. About fifteen feet away stood that carriage. Mama was propped up inside, and the single glance Nat had seen told her that she was not well. Nat closed her eyes. She had to focus. Had to make this work. Maybe if she did, they could go back home. Get away.

"Miss Natalia," the queen said. "Preparations are complete, and we are ready for you."

Nat glared at her. "Tell me what you want me to do, then let me go."

Queen Elya stood regal as ever, her hands clasped before her as she scowled down at Nat. "I pity you, my dear. So much Power at your fingertips, and no nerve to use it."

Nat turned away. She didn't want to listen to this.

"If I remove your restraints," the queen said, "will you try to run?"

The carriage caught Nat's eye. "No."

"Good. And you won't try to use your abilities on anyone here?"

"No."

"Excellent." She waved for the guards to move closer.

Rin stepped forward and unlocked the manacles from Nat's wrists—the removal throwing off her balance slightly. The other guards nearby flinched when she stumbled, like she was some wildcat ready to pounce…and maybe she was. But she'd been tamed.

No, she'd been broken.

"Brielle?"

"Yes, Majesty," Brielle said, approaching. "Miss Natalia, if you please, stand here. Then put your hands here, yes, like that."

Do as they ask. Then you can go home.

"Now, you'll remember," Brielle said, "how you drew the magic *out* of the metal, then sent it back through, and toward the medallion on Rin, yes?"

Nat swallowed. She hadn't wanted to believe they were doing this. But she answered, "Yes."

"This device," Brielle said, "holds a great deal of Death magic. All you need to do is draw from this, then push it back through, and seek out the medallions we've given to each of the soldiers below. The device itself should magnify your efforts to a great extent, making it easier to reach each of them. This will take some time, but we have plenty of magic at our fingertips. If the device runs out, we will take time to put more in and we'll go again."

Queen Elya locked eyes with Nat. "We have all night, young lady. The force we're meant to attack can wait, so long as we get *this* right. And if we don't get to everyone tonight, we will continue tomorrow night."

The entire army? "But..." she started to speak.

Mama...

"Yes, Your Majesty," Nat said, bowing her head.

"Good. Guards?"

Every armed man and woman around them came closer at her call.

With a breath, seeming to steel herself, the queen said, "All of you were given medallions, I order you to join the forces below, to gain the abilities we can offer you."

The guards exchanged confused glances.

"Your Majesty," one said. "Are you certain? You'll be left unprotected."

Nat watched as Elya hesitated on her order. And then Nat understood—her paranoia warred with her need to have as many Viruses as possible. And if Nat died in this attempt, they'd have to re-train someone to do what she'd done, which would take time…

Better to get them all at once.

The queen seemed to come to the same conclusion, as she said, "I am certain. You will go."

The guards—there were at least two dozen—bowed to her, and began to make their way down. Except Rin.

"I'm happy to stay for your protection, Your Majesty," he said.

"Excellent." The queen said, seeming relieved. "Then let us begin."

Nat watched as Brielle shouted to a messenger, and word began to pass through the ranks below. Every soldier should stand tall, and face their medallion toward where the queen's company had set up. Every soldier should make certain their medallion was visible, and flat against the skin on their chests.

Nat finally gave her attention to the device before her. This close to it, she could feel the thrum of magic within, centered mostly in the large column portion that formed the base. A piece she suddenly recognized.

Oh gods… Her stomach sank. The column they'd had her pouring her "excess" Power into…she'd helped them prepare for this.

"We're ready," Brielle called.

Nat couldn't see her anymore, but the adviser's voice carried from the opposite side of the device.

"Begin!" Brielle shouted.

Nat swallowed her nerves, took a breath—

"Excuse me, Mother!"

Nat spun. Prince Remi approached on horseback, followed by two guards. Nearby, the queen swore under her breath.

"Surely you have a moment," Remi called. "I came because we had a bit of an emergency in the city, and—"

"And you couldn't send a messenger, *son?*"

Remi flinched at the tone in her words, but dismounted along with the others. "It seemed too important to risk it being manipulated."

The queen turned to Natalia. "Begin, *now.*"

Nat hesitated.

Queen Elya's eyes snapped to the carriage. Immediately, a cry sounded from inside.

"No!" Nat screamed.

Heart thundering in her chest, Nat held her hands up to the device and began to pull.

Part of her heard Remi speaking, but the amount of Power that flowed into her at that moment was *staggering*. A low *hum* reverberated through her body, making her ears ring. She pushed away her initial shock and tried to exert more control over the process. She herself began to glow with deep purple light; it filled her whole being. She'd barely started but her hands trembled.

Mama…

Natalia closed her eyes.

Focus.

43

AHNRI

Ahnri held his breath.

"Mother," Remi said, his voice even and calm, "there's no need for haste. This is…truly a fascinating setup. Is this the secret you've been hiding from me?"

Ahnri held his breath.

"I'm surprised you're not screaming at me to stop," Elya said. "But yes, this has been quite a personal project. And, as you can see, it is now underway."

"And Miss Natalia," Remi said. "She is…"

"A Vessel," Elya said. "A Virus, to be precise. If you notice the base of the funnel—"

Ahnri crept the rest of the way up the ramp to the plateau. As soon as he had eyes on Remi—standing beside the queen with a single guard behind her—he felt a momentary relief, before he saw the glowing purple structure twenty feet from them, where Natalia stood—also glowing—and the funnel grew brighter with the light of Death magic.

Amplifier…

Councilor…

He'd heard Elya's command, and Nat's shout…Ahnri's eyes narrowed as he scanned the area. He recognized the queen's carriage, crates in which the equipment had been transported, and beyond that, a second, much plainer carriage.

"Stay close," he said to Percy.

Together they wound through the shadows, behind the unguarded crates. Finally, he reached the carriage, approaching the opposite side from the others. By the torches lit nearby he could make out two figures through the window. He'd have to be fast.

First, he tried the door slowly—not locked. In a flash, Ahnri threw it open and reached in for the first figure—a man in black leathers, holding a knife.

Ahnri pulled him out onto the ground, grateful for the low hum Natalia's magic gave off, which hid the muffled grunt the man made. Ahnri went to snatch the knife, but the man swiped at his chest—caught, luckily, by his armor.

He pulled back, and the man—who appeared more spy than guard—leaped for him again. This time, Ahnri dodged and pulled his own dagger from his belt, landing a slash on the man's shoulder.

He cried out, gripping the injury, and moved his dagger to his off hand.

Ahnri needed to stop this, and fast. The man to attacked again, and this time instead of slashing back, Ahnri ducked under the attack and rolled, coming up behind the man and locking an arm around his neck—

--and squeezed.

The man struggled, but couldn't make a sound. Ahnri counted the seconds in his mind until the man went unconscious, then quickly took the coil of thin rope he kept in his satchel and bound the man's wrists and ankles, securing them to the wheel of the carriage. He'd just blinked to consciousness when Ahnri swiped a sash from his waist and tied it around his mouth.

He took in his situation and glared at Ahnri.

"Not sorry," Ahnri said. Finally, he checked the carriage more closely and gasped.

Natalia's mother, Councilwoman Mari Aimar, sat slumped inside. Her hair had thinned, as had her body, and she seemed barely able to hold herself in a sitting position.

"Stars above." He leaned into the space and gently scooped her up into his arms. She weighed so little, his concern grew. He spoke in whispers as he took her from the carriage. "I'm a friend of Natalia's, I'll get you safe."

Crouching as low as possible, he carried Mari away from the carriage and around the south side of the mass of boulders behind them. He quickly found a small alcove where a patch of grass grew, and laid her down.

"Natalia?" she wheezed.

"She'll…" Ahnri paused, shaking his head. "We're trying to help her. I'll do all I can."

Mari nodded, letting her head rest back in the grass.

Ahnri moved to pull the wooden token from around his neck, to offer her some healing, but hesitated at the sound of footsteps behind him.

"There you are."

Ahnri turned to see Merlin approach. He appeared much older this time, his hair greyed but trim. He knelt beside Ahnri, put a hand on a section of the grass, and closed his eyes.

Pale green light shone from his hand, flowing over his body like wine spilled off a table. When the light faded, Ahnri recognized his friend.

"Can you take care of her, then?"

"Of course," Merlin said. "Save what's in that token. You get out there and help *them*. I'll follow when I've got her stabilized."

"Thank you."

He hurried back to the front of the rock structure, and swore at the sight that greeted him. The amplifier shone brighter now, a steady glow, and the light at the wide end of the funnel shape had begun to split into smaller threads of magic, trailing down to the soldiers below.

Across the plateau, Ahnri watched Remi continue asking questions of the queen, keeping her engaged. For a small moment, Remi looked back at Ahnri and gave a subtle nod.

Ahnri's throat tightened as his eyes darted from the prince to the device, and steeled himself. Moving quickly and quietly,

Ahnri moved to the carriage where Councilor Mari had been, to get a closer view of Natalia and the device.

His throat tightened in fear at the sight of her. Nat stood with both hands on the device, her head bowed and eyes scrunched tight, glowing as brightly as the Power she wielded. He had to find a way to tell her that her mother was safe…that she could pull away…

"Mrrow…" Percy stood by his side, also staring at Natalia, with a sadness in his eyes.

"You have an idea?" Ahnri asked.

Percy looked up at him, stood and put both paws to Ahnri's leg, and patted him a few times. Ahnri frowned, but knelt to be on the cat's level.

"What is it?"

Then Percy placed a paw on the skin of Ahnri's arm, and a soft red light began to glow where they touched.

44

REMI

Remi could hardly hear his mother's voice over the pounding in his own head. His guards stood back, occasionally making eye contact, trying to guess whether they should intervene. Remi held them off. He had to keep Mother and her single guard distracted for as long as possible.

Twenty feet away, Natalia's entire form *radiated* the light of Death magic, as did the large funnel-shaped device she touched. Mother kept speaking, extoling the virtues of it, and all Remi had to do was occasionally respond with a "You don't say?" or, "Truly?" and she would go on.

It said a great deal about their relationship that she was finally open with him, at the precise point at which he could not care any less.

Ahnri had been right all along. And now, as Remi heard all the details straight from his mother's lips, a well of shame opened up inside him. If only he had listened to Ahnri sooner…maybe he could've saved Natalia from being pressured into this. Maybe he could've had time to find out who created the false reports. Maybe he could've brought the truth to his mother and changed her mind…

"Wouldn't you agree?"

"Oh yes, of course," Remi said automatically.

Mother gazed at Natalia and the magic in wide-eyed wonder. "It is a marvel, isn't it? The Power she wields."

Remi took in the scene before him once more. The purple glow at the wide end of the funnel had split into threads, lines of dark light snaking out from the amplifier, streaming toward the soldiers below.

"And soon," Mother said, "our entire army will have this capability. Remarkable."

"Yes…remarkable. You've achieved something great, Mother."

She turned to him and smiled. The soft smile he'd yearned to see, that he'd have given everything to produce. The smile she'd given him when he'd turned in Ahnri.

Remi felt sick.

Mother turned back to admire the threads of light emanating from the amplifier. Remi glanced behind her and caught sight of Ahnri moving out from the rocks. Their eyes met. Remi gave a terse nod.

Even at this distance, Remi thought he could see Ahnri's regret as he nodded in return, and made his way to hide behind the carriage opposite them.

Ahnri would help Nat. Remi had to trust that he could do that, and keep Mother distracted to help.

Below, the lines of magic were meeting the soldiers. Shouts and screams rose up to meet Remi's ears, and he couldn't tell if they were in alarm or pain or something else. Natalia let out a scream, her body buckling under the weight of her task. But beside him, Mother did not react.

It took all of Remi's willpower to remain still. *Please let her survive…*

"Beautiful and terrible," Remi said softly.

"I admit," Mother said, "I did not want you here. But having someone to enjoy this with is not unpleasant."

Remi swallowed, forcing a smile despite the knots in his stomach. "I am glad to have come."

With the Power flowing inside her, Nat sought out the device and began to send the magic back—not *in* this time, but *through*. Like before, she felt as though she were traveling through the very essence of the metal itself, until she reached the other side. And as she did, the Power sought out another home, moving quickly.

Too quickly…

As though they were stars in the night sky, Natalia could sense the medallions. Over a thousand of them, waiting for the magic. The Power seemed naturally drawn to them below, and

Nat tried to exert her will to slow it slightly, ease it where it wanted to go…but it resisted.

Her hands trembled against the cool metal.

Control this…work with me, not against me…

The momentum was so much stronger than the first two times. Before, the medallions had been a wall of resistance, but this time she felt it as the Power crashed through them one by one. Each a *crack* in her mind as though from a whip. It began to sound to her like an avalanche of stones falling down the tower city's exterior. Rock after rock hitting the ground, and each other. *Crack, crack, crackcrack, crack.*

It took all her strength to keep it in check. As line after line met the medallions, more and more Power flowed into and out of her. She was the Vessel, channeling it. From the device and back through it, then out to the army.

Trying to keep her focus on the trails of Power reaching out to the soldiers, part of her began to feel sharp points all over her skin. The magic began to prick at her in a way she'd never felt before. She forced her eyes open to see pinpricks of pale purple beginning to shine out from her skin, like needles in the night. Each one stabbed like a thorn—the thick dragon-head ones that she'd stepped on while playing as a child.

And they kept coming, another, and another, and another, all over her body.

Until those pinpricks reached the worst area…that section of her back that constantly grew too much, that she had to kill off a little bit every week or so…the magic found it, and *stabbed.*

Nat screamed, the pain forcing her body to fold, but her hands remained where they were. She closed her eyes again, trying to ignore the pain, to focus on the magic, the medallions... Impossible. She couldn't tell when she'd given enough to each person the way she had with Rin...should she stop for the earlier ones yet? Would she even be able to?

Fina...help me...

In the chaos of her struggle, she didn't notice the soft pressure of a paw against the skin at her ankle where the skirts had folded as she fell. From the contact, a thread of something new trailed up her leg. She finally noticed it as it crept over her torso, her chest, her shoulders, up the base of her neck, and into the whirlwind of her mind and the struggle to keep her magic in check.

Her eyes closed, Nat could almost see the colors behind her eyes as red intertwined with purple, and though the flow of Death magic continued, and part of her mind remained focused on that task, another part of her felt suddenly...calm.

And then, in her mind, she heard a soft voice.

Natalia?

If she'd heard that voice five seconds earlier, she likely would've shrieked. But with the blanket of peace settled over her mind, it didn't faze her.

Who are you? she asked.

My name is Percival, the voice said. *I am a friend to your friends.*

In that calm part of her mind, she saw images of Ahnri and Remi. Tentative relief began to grow in her heart.

Can they get me away from here?

They've rescued your mother, Percival said. *And they will handle the queen. But I'm afraid you are the only one who can get yourself out of this rat hole.*

She swallowed. *I can't…it's too strong…* In the other side of her mind, she could feel the threads connected to the soldiers below, nearly half of the force already.

Miss Natalia, Percival said. *Do you fear your magic?*

A chill came over her that had nothing to do with the cool night air. She couldn't answer, but she thought he could sense it.

Power is only something to fear in the hands of those unfit to wield it, Percival said. *You are a good person. You have nothing to fear.*

The thought that came next, she tried to keep hidden, in the back of her mind, because she felt ashamed that she had it: *I'm not a good person…I hurt people.*

You defend yourself, he said. *And* that *is brave. Miss Natalia, the only way to control this much Power is to* become *it. The shadows are no danger to you. You must embrace them, allow them to be part of you. Do this, and they will not fight you, but* help *you.*

At these words, she felt, in the chaotic half of her mind, the Power she wielded pressing at her…as though it were trying to break through some barrier the way she'd had to force it through the medallions.

But the thought of embracing it, *welcoming* the thing she'd feared her entire life, this ability she'd only recently learned to truly use…she couldn't fathom it. And yet, it *had* always been a part of her, whether she liked it or not. Surely, a guest who feels unwelcome will be more of a burden than one that is brought in with open arms...

Yes, Percival said. *You see.*

Nat's fingers tightened on the metal pieces of equipment before her. *I...I don't know how... Percival, I'm scared.*

It's all right, Percival said. *I'll help. Can you trust me?*

She took a slow breath, leaning into the balance his magic offered.

Tell me what to do.

Remi listened to Mother, nodding along with her explanations and doing his best to urge her to continue speaking.

"And of course, once we have this force we can—" She cut off, her calm fading as she beheld the crowd of soldiers. "What is happening?"

Remi followed her gaze. The threads of purple light that had been connecting to the army were...thinning, somehow. And as he watched, they began to *retract*, a little at a time, pulling away from the army and back toward the device.

"It can't be done already!" Mother snapped. "She didn't even reach the entire force yet."

"Maybe," Remi said, "Natalia ran into a problem?"

"Impossible, we checked every—"

Again, Remi followed his mother's gaze and saw—at the same moment she did—a pale red glow coming from Natalia's opposite side.

"What is *this?*" The queen stalked toward it, and Remi followed. As they rounded Natalia's form Remi recognized the cat, Percy—the red glow emanated from *him.*

"Filthy scum!" Elya screeched. Before Remi could speak, she stepped forward and landed a kick to the cat.

Remi's heart caught in his throat, seeing Percy's form flail as he flew through the air, a yowl of shock and pain fading in the night. Remi hurried to the edge of the outcropping. A desert tree stood below, swaying in the light of the magic above it— had the cat possibly caught himself? Remi couldn't see Percy anywhere.

Beside them, Natalia withered, grunting as though under pressure of a boulder. Out in the basin, the threads of light grew suddenly brighter, stronger. More appeared, connecting to more soldiers. Nearly two thirds of the army now encompassed in a cage of light.

"Mother," Remi finally spoke. "*Please* stop this."

She turned to face him, her eyes bright with mirth. "There it is," she said. "Your true feelings."

"This cannot be good for our people," Remi pleaded. "You don't know how many of them will die in the process tonight, or if it will even work at this scale."

He caught the eye of the single guard his mother had kept with her; the young man's face had become a mixture of shock and indecision.

"It *doesn't matter*," she said. "At the very least we will have more Viruses in our army than before, and that alone will strengthen us."

"At what cost?" Remi said. "There are hundreds of soldiers out there willing to fight for Fugera. If we thin their ranks with this attempt and gain a handful of Viruses, is that truly worth the sacrifice? You're killing parents out there, siblings—their families back at the city will be heartbroken at their loss."

At these words, Remi watched the young soldier break. He bolted toward the ramp down, toward the basin and the rest of the soldiers there.

"Please, Mother. You can't—"

"I am queen!" she snapped. "And you are nothing but a selfish, stupid, spineless child. Just like your father. He never had the courage to do the hard things to make our kingdom stronger. But *I do.*"

"You're murdering them!"

"I am *elevating them!*"

Remi gritted his teeth, then caught a flash of movement to his right—Ahnri. They shared a look of resignation, and Remi made his choice.

He pushed past his mother, toward Natalia, shouting.

"Nat! You're safe, you can—"

A sharp pain burned in his side, and words failed him. His breath grew heavy in his chest, his muscles refused to work.

He turned as his mother withdrew the dagger she'd sunk into him, causing him to stagger backward, before he fell to his knees on the stone beneath them, hands covered in blood, trying fruitlessly to hold it in.

"You know," she said, "the old Medelian king might've had one good idea, to choose his own heir."

Remi tried to breathe…tried to speak. His hands quaked as he tried to take hold of the token Ahnri had given him, to heal himself…his hands were slippery with blood…

"You," his mother said, "are nothing but a burden. And I don't need you."

Embrace the shadows…

Natalia listened to Percival, hoping he could help her get out of this mess, and to her shock, it began to work. In the vastness of her own mind, she met her magic as though it were a being of darkness itself. Human-shaped, with flowing hair of shadow and eyes darker than the deepest caverns. And through the fear—she could not help but feel it—she reached out anyway, and took it by the hand.

As she did, it wasn't as though her control over it strengthened, but rather the Power became more willing to do as she asked. Together, they viewed the experiment as though from a distance, they two on the clearer side of her mind, and the soldiers and mechanism on the other. With Percival's help, she could—

The calming presence tore away in an instant. Percival's voice gone, and the protections in her mind shattered. The two sides became one, and the swirling storm of Power once again became all she knew.

Except…

She held on to her darkness.

45

REMI

Pain. It wasn't the dagger. It was the words, the betrayal. The failure.

That after all these years, and so much effort.

He still.

Hadn't.

Been.

Enough.

46

AHNRI

"NO!"

Ahnri *ran.*

Not again, he thought. *Please, not again...*

Elya stood over Remi like a predator. In that split second, everything in Ahnri's being tore between immediately going to Remi—the one person he loved more than his own life, to try to save him—or going toward Elya—the one person who had taken everything from him, to see that she never hurt anyone again.

Time slowed as he ran. Revenge and love warred within him.

He'd returned to Fugera with the intent to stop Elya's plans, and now it seemed he had failed. She'd managed to go through with everything and would be a threat to the rest of the continent.

But he'd also returned with hope that the boy he loved would have him back, after everything that had happened. After everything they'd been through, everything they'd lost.

Emotion caught in his throat, and he found it hard to breathe…his heartbeat pounded in his ears as he ran…

To Remi.

Ahnri slid across the stones and loose sand, shoving the queen herself aside and knocking her to the ground as he met the prince's eyes, searching the prince's neck for the token. Remi's guards surrounded him at the same time.

"Rem?" Ahnri whispered. "Remi, please. Talk to me."

Remi gripped Ahnri's clothing, but only a choked sound came from his throat.

"No. No, no, no, please."

There. Ahnri gripped the token and tore the collar of Remi's tunic aside.

"You!" Elya shrieked.

"Stay with me," Ahnri said, pressing the token against Remi's chest. It began to glow, a soft blue-white light.

He met the eyes of the guard across from him, who met his eyes, then glanced past him.

Ahnri could sense it coming. He spun, his forearm meeting hers to knock the dagger away.

Elya's eyes widened for a moment, then narrowed once more. "You are pathetic. He's as good as dead, and you," she said, sneering, "will have to watch him die."

Tears burned behind his eyes. Beside him, the boy he loved was near death—but healing, thank the gods. Before him, the woman who had been the cause of every terrible thing in his life taunted him.

Ahnri drew his sword.

47

NATALIA

Natalia felt the Power's rage, its desire to seek out a home and the sweet temptation of the soldiers' medallions below. The connections strengthened. Nat no longer held control. She was simply the Vessel, the vehicle through which the raw magic would do what it meant to.

It threatened to tear her apart. It flowed into her, and seemed to take something from her before going back out and through the device. The pain in her back flared, and her body arched against it, attempting to escape, but to no avail. Already on her knees, her body so weak, she couldn't have pulled away from the device if she'd tried.

She couldn't fight it, couldn't control it, could hardly survive it…and then the memory of Percival's words rang in her mind…

Embrace the shadows…

In the whirlwind of darkness, she tightened her grip on the being she'd imagined. She held on, began to pull it toward her—

—and felt something from it...*fear.*

Here, in the chaos of an experiment she herself was afraid of, she realized the shadows didn't *want* to be torn from their existence. Their desire for a home, a place to *be,* was as raw and instinctual as Natalia's love for Mama. And with that understanding, she knew what to do.

I am your home.

It was as though a thousand eyes shifted toward her. Nat took a breath, and opened her heart in welcome.

Outside of her, the Power hesitated. Lines of light stilling in the night air. And in that moment of stillness, Nat could sense the souls of those soldiers near the front, who had been connected the longest...somehow, she could feel their emotions through the connection...

One thought of her husband.

Another prayed for his daughter.

One begged for her brother.

All of them, in pain...dying.

She pulled the darkness closer and wrapped her arms around it.

Let me be your home...

Slowly, the Power shifted.

Lines of magic thinned once more, letting go of the soldiers below. Nat could feel again some of them whose lives had already been lost—so many lives—and yet, some who had miraculously survived. Some who, like her, now bore the mark of a Virus.

The Power pulled away from them all and drew into her. A flood of shadows, but she was immune to their danger. The magic flowed into her, and as she welcomed it, she sent it back into the device.

It wasn't as much as before—a great amount had been utilized—but with all the effort she could spare, Natalia brought back everything she could, and stored it safely away.

She thought she heard a scream. In the last of her lucid thoughts, Natalia reached for the Life token at her neck, and held on. Her body took in the magic as she slumped against the column, her strength spent.

48

AHNRI

Ahnri raised his sword, pressing the tip against the queen's chest.

Elya backed away, coming to a stop only when her back hit the carriage.

"How *dare* you threaten me!" Elya cried. "Guards!"

But no one came.

"You can't kill me, boy," Elya snarled. "You'd face years of imprisonment, or banishment. You'd never see your precious prince again!"

"I don't want to kill you," Ahnri said, voice steady. "But I will arrest you."

"*What?*"

"For betrayal of the Fugeran crown—"

"I *am* the Fugeran crown, you—"

"—and the *mass murder* of your own citizens."

Elya cut herself off. "You idiot." She waved out to the army, now to her right as they stood directly on the edge of the outcropping. "These soldiers aren't dead, they're *elevated*. Higher beings, and they'll protect Fugera better than—"

She cut off as they both realized the lines of magic were once again growing thinner. Ahnri frowned, but did not remove his blade from the queen's chest.

"You've risked the lives of your entire army," Ahnri said, turning back to her, "in a tenuous experiment that you have no proof is safe."

"A few lives lost," she sneered. "It is worth the cost to protect me! To protect Fugera!"

"Your Highness!"

Ahnri did not take his gaze off Elya, but watched her eyes and listened. Multiple horses, then footfalls approaching where Remi lay. A groan, and soft encouragement to sit up, then stand.

"How…" Elya's eyes grew feral. "How does he live!"

Ahnri's relief must've shown on his face then. Elya noticed, and with a growl used his momentary distraction to knock the sword aside and lunge at him with another dagger.

Ahnri caught her wrist. He shoved her backward, trying to get his sword back up between them. Elya got her footing back, and once more leaped at him, but Ahnri moved quicker this time and sidestepped.

Elya's momentum carried her too far. Her foot caught a patch of loose stone, and she slipped, falling, and hitting more gravel.

She let go of her dagger and tried to grip the rocks as she slid farther, over the edge. Ahnri—despite his hatred for her—dropped his sword and reached out to take her by the wrist, finding a handhold in the rocks as instinctually as if he were climbing the walls of Isille again.

Screams sounded from below.

"Guards!" Merlin shouted. "Get down there and get healing! Save as many as you can!"

A weight settled in the pit of Ahnri's stomach. There had to be over a thousand soldiers down there. Volunteers who had been told who knows what to get them to stand out there while darkness and shadow came for them, who had risked their lives without ever raising a blade to an enemy…how many were lost?

"Pull me up!" Elya screamed. "You said you wouldn't kill me, pull me up!"

Ahnri grunted, holding tight to her.

"You're going to prison," he said.

"I *will not!*" Elya shrieked. "If you're going to imprison me, why not let me die!"

He gritted his teeth through the pain. "You took my father from me. I refuse to take you from Remi."

Elya continued to scream, vacillating between begging to be saved and daring him to let her die, but in moments a handful of guards—Remi's, along with those of the council members— arrived and helped Ahnri bring her up. Bound and gagged, they left the queen sitting on the stone surrounded by the council members, Remi, Ahnri, and the handful of guards they'd brought with them.

"Elya Caselle," Councilman Erre said, his voice heavy with regret. "You are hereby under arrest by the Fugeran Royal Council. You will remain in prison until you are brought before the court, tried for your crimes, and sentenced. In the interim, your son will take control of the throne and all powers vested to it."

The group stood in silence for a moment. Then Councilor Erre ordered Elya to be put into the plainer of the two carriages.

Many things happened at once. Someone helped Natalia to her feet. She seemed weak, leaning against the guards as they helped her to the royal carriage, where Councilor Mari already waited.

Ahnri stood beside Remi, one arm around the prince's waist for support.

As word reached them of the soldiers below, it became clear that despite being sold a dream of bravery, courage, and protecting their homeland, none of those soldiers had known what was going to happen to them.

The pain on Remi's face at hearing this, along with the numbers and the devastation, brought an ache to Ahnri's chest.

"The captains," Merlin said, "the ones remaining, have agreed to follow you, Your Highness. They all recognize what happened, and that they were not adequately informed."

"Thank you," Remi said. Then, frowning, he glanced around. "Where is my mother's adviser?"

Ahnri did the same. He'd heard Brielle at some point earlier on, hadn't he?

"Find her," Remi said to a guard nearby. "I have a terrible suspicion she was behind this all along."

Ahnri thought back to that page of notes, like a letter Brielle had written to someone... "If she's gone..."

Remi nodded, understanding. If Brielle had escaped in the chaos, they may never know the extent of these schemes.

Then Remi closed his eyes, resting his head against Ahnri's shoulder.

"Let's go home."

Interlude

–

Percy

Humans were funny.

Percy appreciated the scritches of course, but it often seemed like they needed to give them far more than he needed to receive them.

Tavin's new quarters were quite comfortable. A vast improvement to the prison cell, and even to where they'd lived before Tavin had been thrown into that cell. This new chamber had a soft bed, cushioned chairs perfect for naps, and even windows Percy could go in and out of at will.

At the moment, he found himself on the sofa beside Tavin, who held a book with one hand and rubbed Percy's ears with another. Tavin wasn't the best at giving scritches, but he was Percy's oldest friend. It felt necessary to allow Tavin scritching opportunities whenever possible.

It had only been a single day since the events in the desert, though the city had already dubbed it the Violet Night. A good name, if a little on-the-nose. Humans tended to name things exactly what they were, which while logical, it also bothered Percy. Couldn't they be a little more creative?

It hadn't been a great night for Percy though, what with the queen having kicked him off of a very high ledge. Thankfully, there had been a verdant tree right below him, and he'd managed to catch himself in the branches. It hurt, certainly. But he'd survived all right.

A knock at the door had Tavin stand—and left Percy annoyed at the interruption. A moment later, Tavin turned back but left the door ajar.

"Well, Master Percival, I've been summoned to visit with the prince," Tavin said, slipping on a decorative robe over his casual tunic. "I assume you'd like to come too?"

Percy hopped up and stretched his back, shaking himself before following Tavin out the door.

They were led to Remi's rooms—Percy was already quite familiar with these. Remi sat at his desk in his office, and on the sofa opposite sat Ahnri and the girl, Natalia. The three of them stood as Tavin and Percy approached.

"My friend," Remi said, reaching to shake Tavin's hand. "Thank you for coming."

"The pleasure is mine, Highness," Tavin said.

Percy didn't wait for permission. He made straight for Ahnri and stood on hind legs until he was picked up. Ahnri smelled like that stupid bird again—the one he wouldn't let Percy eat—but he gave the best scritches, so Percy would tolerate it. He settled into Ahnri's arms, closed his eyes, and began to purr.

"Mother's trial is in two days," Remi said. "I'd like to have you testify, if you're comfortable."

Percy's ears perked up at this. He opened one eye.

Tavin took a breath. "Gladly."

"She'll be implicated properly," Remi said. "Then the whole kingdom will know what she's done. With luck and some carefully worded communications we can reestablish the alliances my mother has brushed aside for too long."

Tavin nodded. "I don't know much of the politics, but I am sorry you've had to go through so much pain in all this."

"I'll be all right," Remi said, glancing at Ahnri. "I've got a very strong support system."

Percy purred.

"And you, young lady," Tavin said, turning to Natalia. "Are you well?"

"I am, sir," she said with a curtsey. "It's an honor to meet you. Your notes were fascinating, though I was rather unnerved when I first read them."

"No one should ever be forced to work as a lab rat," Tavin said. "You were taken advantage of, child. However, based on what I've been told, you accomplished a great feat. Tragic though the results have been, you are the only Vessel besides me who has managed it and survived."

"Yes," Remi said, sounding distracted. "Brielle took very detailed notes on those experiments." He ran a hand over his face. "I cannot comprehend how heartless my mother was through all of this. The Vessels she forced to do the work mostly deserted her at the mention of transferring the channeling ability, but there were some who tried and died. Not to mention all the soldiers we lost in the experiment itself…so many lives."

Ahnri stopped scratching Percy to put a hand on Remi's shoulder. "That blood is not on your hands, Remi."

"I know," Remi said. "But I could've done more to stop it."

Sensing a need, Percy twisted in Ahnri's arms and reached himself toward Remi. The prince took him, and Percy wound himself over the well-adorned shoulder to snuggle his head into the crook of Remi's neck. He laughed, and hugged back. Percy purred, satisfied.

"Do we know…" Nat began. "I mean, how many…"

Remi sighed, Percy's body rising and falling. "Out of just over a thousand troops, your magic reached nearly three-quarters of them. Of those, six-hundred and thirty-two did not survive, but there are one-hundred and two who did. Of those hundred and two," he paused, "twenty-three have been confirmed Viruses."

Natalia gasped. "So few…"

"At the cost of many, yes," Tavin agreed. "At the risk of stating the obvious, my friends, it is not an experiment worth repeating."

Percy rolled his eyes.

"However," Tavin said, "I hope it is not too soon to acknowledge that to a small extent it *did* work. A fact with which I am, admittedly, impressed. I believe the scale is the biggest problem. While I do not wish to risk so many lives at once ever again, and certainly not lives that have been manipulated into cooperation as these were, this tragedy has definitely answered some important questions."

Remi turned to face Tavin. "You believe it's worth continuing the research?"

Tavin took a breath, letting it out in a sigh. "All science, all discoveries really, almost always have the potential for great good, or great evil. Usually, it depends very much on the will and moral compass of those doing the discovering. Do I agree with what the queen did? Absolutely not. But Highness—forgive me, Majesty—think of how much good can be done if we use this process to make more *Cures*. More healers means less death, and could potentially make up for the losses we've seen this week."

"Nothing can *make up for* the loss of those lives," Nat said firmly.

"No," Ahnri said. "No life saved will bring back the ones who died. But...I see what you mean."

"My mother," Remi said, "wanted a more powerful kingdom...but this could build a *healthier* one."

"Miss Natalia," Tavin said. "I know you are young yet, and you have much life ahead of you. But if you're interested in making that lab downstairs a happier place—" he smiled, "—I could use a new assistant who is familiar with the processes."

Percy, sensing a need once more, squirmed in Remi's arms to reach for Natalia this time. He wasn't channeling to them in this. He was being an honest cat, doing what cats do. He knew they needed it as much as he needed scritches.

Nat held onto him, tighter than either of the other two had. Her heartbeat pulsed against Percy's shoulder.

"Can I consider it?"

"Of course," Tavin said. "I am in no rush."

"Thank you, Master Tavin," Nat said. "I truly—" Her words cut off, she dropped Percy to the floor as her body doubled over. He landed on all fours, his ears perked on high alert.

"Nat!" Ahnri cried. "What's wrong?"

"I'm fine," she said through gritted teeth. "One moment..."

Natalia moved to a shadowed corner, and drew from the darkness. One hand went to her lower back, but otherwise Percy couldn't see where the magic had gone...then she straightened, breathing deeply as though she'd just run a long distance.

"I'm sorry," she said. "I—"

"What did you just do?" Tavin asked.

Percy wondered the same thing.

Nat hesitated. "I...I have a...particular illness..."

Tavin stepped forward. "Did you use your magic on yourself?"

"Not truly," Nat said. "I've been told the thing causing me pain isn't really *part* of me."

"The precision..." Tavin said, his eyes lighting up. "Miss Natalia, how long have you been doing this?"

"Over a year..."

"Oh, the possibilities," Tavin said. "When you're ready, Miss Natalia, I would *love* to speak with you more on this. It's possible that this ability was a large part of why you were able to succeed at the queen's experiments with so little practice."

Nat blinked in amazement. "You really think so?"

"It seems so," Tavin said. "And figuring out the reason behind your success could lead to new answers, and *that* sounds exciting to me."

Natalia seemed to consider this. "I...my mother could potentially benefit, as well. Could I bring her?"

"Of course," Tavin said. "And again, there's no hurry. But I believe you've accidentally made some incredible discoveries."

Behind them, Remi and Ahnri had stepped away to speak privately. Percy went to them, and hopped up into Ahnri's arms once more.

"—would like your help, if you'd be willing?" Remi said.

"Always. Now that your mother's not hovering everywhere, I can go anywhere I please."

Percy settled into Ahnri's arms, enjoying the scritches and the hum of conversation as he slowly fell asleep.

49

REMI

Ink. Sign. Pass.

Remi sat in his study with two servants and a stack of letters. Each one copied by scribes, each one needing to be signed by him.

Had the subject matter not been so tragic, he might've let his mind wander, or asked for Ahnri to keep him company while he kept these small consistent motions going. But part of him wanted to dwell on the grief here. He didn't care to be distracted by jokes or conversation. He would take a moment to read the names of each of the dead, of their family's name, and silently honor them before he signed away their life.

Six-hundred and thirty-two deaths. Six-hundred and thirty-two letters. Six-hundred and thirty-two signatures.

The families already knew, of course. The whole city knew what his mother had done. Few knew *how* it had happened, and rumors were rampant. But the pain had spread, and would continue. Purple drapes on windows to recognize the hand of Death. Pale blue flowers above doors as a reminder of Life. Candles lining the streets at night both in the tower and the outer city, each one representing a heartbroken family member who had lost someone. A sadness had fallen over his city.

Ink... sign... pass...

There were already threats to Remi's life as a result. He'd expected this, of course. It came with being royalty. And when royalty screwed up, people got angry. They wanted someone to blame, and he couldn't begrudge them choosing him.

He blamed himself as much or more.

The doors to his study opened softly, and he glanced up as he passed a letter to the servant on his right. Ahnri came in, carrying a tray of food and a bottle of wine.

"Time for a break, Your Majesty," he said.

Remi glanced at the timepiece on the wall. Nearly midnight...he'd been at this for two hours. Comparing the stacks on his left and right, he guessed he was a little more than halfway through. He set down his quill and immediately felt an ache in his wrist from so much of the same motion. In the midst of the signing, he hadn't noticed the ache. Though, he told himself, it was the least he could endure for the families who had lost loved ones.

"You may go," he said to the servants. "Be back in an hour and we can continue. I want to finish this before morning."

"No," Ahnri said. "Go home and rest. Be back in the morning. The king—and these servants—" he added pointedly, "all need rest."

The servants hesitated, looking to Remi for instruction.

He waved a hand wearily. "He's right. Ah…come back after the morning meal."

They bowed, and took their leave. Remi nodded to the guards outside the study, and the doors were closed and locked.

"Seems ironic," Ahnri said, taking two goblets from a shelf, "how insistent your mother was about your security, and now we're actually following through on it."

Remi gave a half-hearted smile. "Yes, well…at least there are enough guards left to *have* security…"

"Rem," Ahnri said, opening the wine bottle. "It's not your fault."

"It's one thing to know that, and another to feel it," Remi said. He sat on the sofa and stretched his wrist while Ahnri poured the wine.

"I know," Ahnri said. "I wish I could help you carry it."

Remi had to laugh, the sudden powerful emotion struck him, catching in his throat. "But you are."

"How so?"

"Making sure I eat," Remi said, gesturing to the tray of food. "Making sure I rest, helping me organize what forces we have left while also acknowledging the loss the remaining soldiers have experienced…it could've been them. We could've lost so many more, we—"

"Hey, hey," Ahnri said, putting a goblet into Remi's hands. "Stay here. We've been down that path, and we likely will again, but we don't need to face it right now."

Remi forced himself to take a breath. Stay here. Not go down the spiral that led to blame and pain.

"Wait for me…"

"I'm here."

Once his heart calmed, Remi took a sip of wine, and let Ahnri offer him food. He had no appetite whatsoever, but forced himself to eat.

"Has there been any word about Brielle?" Ahnri asked.

"None," Remi said. "And half the members of Fugeran Intelligence are nowhere to be found, which makes me wonder if she paid them off, or planted them to begin with."

Ahnri placed a hand on Remi's back, rubbing soothing circles.

"I hate that she did this," Remi said softly. He closed his eyes. "And I hate that we're not even certain it was her."

"Nothing we can do about it now," Ahnri said, "except take care of the city."

"A monumental task," Remi said, taking another bite of fruit.

"What's next, then," Ahnri asked. "After signing the letters?"

"I'll have to write to the other kingdoms," Remi said. "The council has given me recommended talking points and things to avoid, but I'll be writing them myself."

"You insisted?"

"I did."

"At least that's only five letters," Ahnri said. "Assuming you're writing to Perdonio as well?"

"I feel I should," Remi said. "They don't border us, but I worry word will spread there anyway. I'd rather head it off. But that makes six, not five."

"I already wrote to Carina," Ahnri said. "You don't have to worry about Medelios."

Remi gave a short laugh. "I'd like to write one to her anyway. I owe her thanks for letting me borrow her best spy."

"I think she'd appreciate that."

They sat in silence. Bread, cheese, fruit, wine…Remi's eyes began to feel heavy.

The tears came of their own accord, then. Grief held Remi's throat like a noose. The thought of all those lives lost, all those bodies they'd had to bring back unmoving, multiple trips with dozens of wagons, trying to be respectful to the dead while getting as many back as possible before the heat of day affected them. And the cemeteries were working overtime to provide space enough for proper burials in the next few days. He'd had to approve the breaking of new ground in the stone west of the city to make a new space for these dead.

He'd failed his people so deeply…

Ahnri's arms wound around him, pulling him close. Remi's body shuddered as he cried, the weight of everything pressing down on him, spreading him thin like a wisp of cloud that could blow away with a thought. For a moment he wished he could simply leave…run away and let the council figure it all out, let go of the responsibility and the pain and the blame…but he knew better.

After a moment, the tears eased a bit. Then a thought struck him. "Ahnri…when my father died, it broke my heart, but I had you and Natalia and an entire city to help me mourn and move forward. How did you handle losing your father? Your Damond?"

Ahnri turned away. He clasped his hands before him, as though he was about to reveal to Remi some great secret that would help him get through this.

"I didn't."

Remi blinked. "What?"

"I didn't, Rem. I didn't have time, I couldn't think about it. I blocked it out, the pain. Everything except the anger, the vengeance…" His brows were deeply furrowed. He shook his head. "I still haven't faced it. I threw myself into the next job, didn't think about anything else…"

Remi reached for Ahnri's hand.

Ahnri squeezed their hands, then stood, pulling Remi with him. "Come, my king. You need to rest."

"I'm not king yet."

"You're as good as."

Remi wanted to contend the point—his coronation wouldn't be until after the trial—but the thought of his bed sounded much nicer than arguing.

He let Ahnri lead him out of the office and past the guards into his bedchamber, where those doors were then closed and locked.

Ahnri helped him remove the trappings of royalty one item at a time, laying them carefully on a footstool. When the undershirt had been removed, and Remi felt cool air on his chest and back, his mind seemed to suddenly click into the present.

"I must be more exhausted than I thought," Remi said. "It took me until this moment to realize you're undressing me."

Ahnri's cheeks and neck darkened in a blush as he pulled a soft linen nightshirt over Remi's head. "Technically, I am now *dressing* you."

Remi leaned forward, putting his arms around Ahnri's neck and kissing him soundly. Ahnri's hands flattened against Remi's back, pressing their bodies closer.

Stars, how he wanted this…and yet, he was *so* tired…

"Wait," Remi said, dizziness overtaking him as he pulled away a little, their breath mingling and lips still close. "I…"

"We should sleep?"

"We should sleep."

Ahnri smirked. "Right this way, Your Majesty."

Remi rolled his eyes, smiling all the while. He didn't always like being referred to by title, but something about the way Ahnri said it made him feel…cherished.

Ahnri took Remi's hand, directing him to the soft cocoon of cool linens and plush pillows.

Remi was halfway to slumber when he felt Ahnri curl up behind him and wrap an arm around his chest, the warmth of his body like a balm to Remi's soul.

And for a heartbeat, he let every other thought float away, in favor of this moment.

50

AHNRI

Three days passed wherein Ahnri's only task was to keep Remi going. Make sure he ate and had plenty of water, make sure he got a proper amount of sleep each night, assist where he could to keep track of Remi's appointments and all the repercussions of Elya's actions.

Ahnri stood off to the side while Remi personally thanked members of the Fugeran court and council for their attendance at Elya's trial. She was declared guilty, and sentenced to life in prison, with the understanding that if she attempted an escape or coup of any kind, she would be sentenced to death. Ahnri knew Remi didn't want to kill his own mother, but they all knew now how dangerous and manipulative she was. She couldn't be allowed to influence the kingdom even in the smallest degree.

Now, Remi shook hands and nodded, exchanging pleasant smiles and looks of regret with each person who came by in a long line. Ahnri wished he could stand nearer for support, but Remi had asked him to stay back for now. He wanted to show them a strong prince, the young man who was, in all but formality, their king. And Ahnri respected that.

As soon as the final "Thank you for coming," was complete, Ahnri was there behind the prince with a hand on his back to steady him. Remi's posture loosened, and he let out a breath.

"Come on, sit," Ahnri said.

"No no," Remi said, "it's my turn. Come, this way."

Ahnri frowned, but followed. "How do you have the energy right now?"

"Because," Remi said, "I've been waiting all day for this."

"For what?"

Remi waved to his guards to follow and together they made their way out of the palace proper to where a carriage waited. Remi climbed inside, and Ahnri, with some insistence that the guards could handle protecting them without his help, joined him

The interior was cool and dark, and Remi took a seat beside Ahnri, curling under his arm to lay his head on Ahnri's shoulder. Ahnri chuckled. "Was cuddling in a carriage all you had planned?"

"No," Remi said. "But you wanted me to sit, so I'm sitting."

Ahnri let his arm settle around Remi, running a thumb over his shoulder. "Where are we going, then?"

"Shh, it's a surprise." Remi said. "Now let me rest. I need my rest, right?"

Ahnri did as he'd been told, and let Remi rest. He watched out the windows at the passing shops and corridors of the tower of Isille, until finally they exited into the open air, and down the tower's exterior road down to the outer city. Based on the buildings, he guessed the western side, but it was hard to tell through the imperfect glass. After some time, the carriage stopped and Ahnri nudged Remi awake.

"We seem to have arrived," he said.

Remi yawned and stretched, before knocking on the door to have the guards open it. When they stepped out, Remi took Ahnri by the hand and began to lead him through a stone archway.

Star Vine Cemetery

Something in Ahnri's chest seized up. He couldn't speak, but he thought he knew where they were going as they took a set of stairs down to an open-air walkway.

Remi seemed to notice a change, and pulled Ahnri's hand to his chest as they walked.

The cemetery had been carved out of the stone in twenty-foot-wide sections, with tombs lining either side. Ahnri felt as though he were walking through a chapel, the lines of stone as pews he passed one by one. Each section stood at least five tombs tall, and went for a hundred feet before it met another walkway, and another line of stone.

Sand scuffed the ground here, blown in from the surrounding desert—that would be swept up occasionally by workers. Ahnri tried to admire the coloring of the stone they passed, but he couldn't seem to focus on anything except the possibility of where Remi was leading him.

"You asked a while ago," Remi said. "if I knew where Damond was buried, or if he'd been given a funeral. At the time, I didn't know. But going through some records, I found it."

Ahnri's teeth clenched, his jaw tight. He clung to Remi's hand too hard, but Remi didn't complain. Finally, they turned into one of the aisles, and Remi waved for the guards to stay back a bit. They stopped before a column of tombs, and Remi pointed one out, second from the bottom. Ahnri knelt.

Damond Breona
Palace Guard, Died in Action

Waves of emotion rolled through him. First anger, fury, at the lie that had been placed here with Damond's name. That his cause of death had been reduced to the dangers of his job and nothing more. Shame followed, a tightness in his throat, that he hadn't been here to make sure Damond's family or friends were noted to have missed him or grieved at his loss. Then, finally, sorrow. A heartbreak so deep that his hands began to shake, and tears finally fell.

In his mind, he counted the time. Six months. It had now been six months since Damond's death, and Ahnri had never allowed these emotions to surface. He could now admit to himself that he had been scared to face them. That facing them meant acknowledging...

Damond was truly gone.

Ahnri pressed a hand to the plaque, and—finally—let his body feel what it needed to. Sobs shook him as Remi knelt and wrapped arms around him. Memories played through Ahnri's mind…time they spent in this city, interactions with visiting sword masters from across the continent and all he'd learned from them, all the places they'd visit, from the expensive restaurants near the palace to the dive bars on the outskirts of the city. Each one brought both joy and pain.

Ahnri couldn't say how long he stayed there. Not long enough. But after a time his body calmed, his breathing leveled, and the tears slowed enough for him to speak.

"Thank you," he said.

Remi had tears lining his cheeks as well. "Of course. I'm so sorry it happened. I wish I could've—"

"Don't go down that path," Ahnri said. "We both know who to blame for this."

Remi nodded, running a hand through Ahnri's hair.

Ahnri stared at the plaque again—eye level now that he knelt before it. "Can we have a new marker made?"

"Absolutely."

Ahnri sniffed, wiping his face with a sleeve. "This feels…good."

"Really?"

"Yes," he said, smiling despite the tears. "It hurts, but I needed it. This is closure, I think."

Remi leaned forward and they embraced, holding each other in the shadow of the cemetery around them.

51

AHNRI

Ahnri couldn't sleep.

It had been two weeks since the Violet Night, and Isille was—slowly—healing. The effects of Elya's rule were still showing themselves, and Remi had worked tirelessly to fix as much as he could in that time. Ahnri had helped where he could.

Remi's coronation would be tomorrow, and Ahnri would be there—tired or not. But now, at a little past midnight, he'd woken to a sound from the streets below and couldn't make himself lie down again.

He stood at the window of Remi's study, staring out at the city. The road leading past, and the market across the way. He sipped a cup of tea, remembering fondly the first time he'd sent Percy up here with a note…then, from his pocket, he took a different note. The paper had been rolled, flattened, folded, and tucked away, but he kept going back to it.

A-

I'm so sorry for Fugera's loss. You did all you could, and we'll handle what happens. Take your time wrapping things up, but know we're eager to have you back when you're ready.

-C

Ahnri read it through three more times. He knew that if he asked, Carina would release him from his position serving her. She would understand his desire to be near Remi. But something in him rebelled against that. He *loved* his job in Medelios. The two and a half months between Carina winning the tournament and Ahnri's mission to Fugera were some of the best he could remember, despite stuffing down the pain of losses he hadn't faced. He *wanted* to go back.

But he also wanted to stay here.

He put the note back, reached into another pocket, and took out a small, square box. The simple sight of it caused his heart to race and his hands to shake. He opened the box briefly—he kept doing that, checking on it, before closing it again.

He glanced toward the bedroom where Remi still slept, a weight in his heart. They were young, the two of them. But Ahnri couldn't imagine feeling this way about anyone else for the rest of his life…if Remi would have him, he'd do whatever it took to live up to it.

A shuffling movement sounded from the bedroom. Ahnri stuffed the box back into his pocket and refocused on the window. A moment later, Remi came through the doorway wearing linen pants and tying a robe around his waist.

"You're up late."

"Couldn't sleep."

"Any of that tea left?"

Ahnri went to the table and poured another cup, handing it to Remi.

"Thank you," Remi said. "You seem distracted. Is everything all right?"

"Fine," Ahnri said, sitting beside him on the sofa. The box was in a pocket between them. "Just…thinking about next steps."

Remi sipped his tea. "You mean how you'll be heading back to Medelios soon?"

Ahnri froze, a stab of guilt hitting him.

"I've seen how excited you get when you talk about that job," Remi said. "And Carina seems like a good person and a strong ruler. I know you'll go back."

"How can *you* know something I haven't even decided?"

"Because I know you." Remi set his cup on the low table before them. "And I know you won't be happy stuck in one city for the rest of your days, even if I am in it. You need to be moving, traveling, *spying*, as you do. And while I know you'll do training and organizing in Medelios, you'll also be sent on missions like this one. And you'll do well."

Ahnri glanced away, staring at his hands.

"Ahn." Remi gently directed Ahnri by the chin to face him. "I want you to be happy. If that means you live in Medelios most of the time, then so be it."

Ahnri breathed a soft, disbelieving laugh. "How are you so perfect?"

"I'm really not," Remi said, scooting closer. "Want to know why?"

"Why?"

"Because, even though I'm happy to let you go do the work I know you want to do...I am also extremely selfish." He reached into the pocket of his robe, and took out a small box. "You see, I thought I lost you once already, and I have no intention of losing you again."

He opened the box to reveal an engagement ring—two strands of stunning silver winding together, wrapping around a single amethyst stone at the top.

"So before you go, I'd really love to make you my husband."

Through his shock, Ahnri had to laugh even as gratitude swelled in his chest. Of course Remi would propose perfectly, far better than Ahnri ever could have. Still, he reached into his own pocket and took out the box there. And when he opened it to reveal another ring—this one a single smooth band of pale pink gold, cradling a clear white diamond in the shape of a square—it was Remi's turn to throw back his head and laugh.

"I'd planned to wait until things settled down," Ahnri said.

"That's unlikely to happen for a while." Remi took the silver ring, and placed it on Ahnri's finger, then Ahnri returned the favor with the gold. "Well, at least I know you already planned on sticking with me, wherever you go."

"For always," Ahnri said.

Remi leaned forward to kiss him, and Ahnri welcomed it. Remi's hand slid up into Ahnri's hair and tugged ever so gently, before Remi's lips moved to his jaw, then neck, then collarbone.

Ahnri sighed, holding on to his prince. His traitorous mind began to think back through the past weeks and all the pain and worry they'd both suffered…after all that, the ring on his finger and kisses on his skin felt like the final beautiful chapter to a tumultuous story.

Or perhaps, the first happy chapter of a new one.

Gently, he took Remi's chin in his hand and lifted it to face him. Ahnri placed a kiss against his prince's lips, then rested their foreheads together.

"You know I'm in love with you, right?"

Remi gave a sharp smile. "I do."

Ahnri laughed. "I thought we weren't supposed to say that until the wedding."

Remi leaned in and kissed him again. "I'll say it every day if I must. So that you know it's true."

Happier than he'd ever been, Ahnri stood, taking Remi by the hand and began leading him toward the bedroom. "Come. You have a long day tomorrow, Your Majesty. You should get back to sleep."

Remi followed, that sharp grin still on his face. "If I'm king, does that mean I can order you around?"

Ahnri raised a brow. "As though you hadn't before?"

"Well, of course. But now I have *authority.*"

Ahnri held open the door to the bedchamber, and bowed. "I am as always at your service, Your Majesty."

Remi laughed, taking Ahnri through hand in hand, the doors closing softly behind them.

Outside in the hallway, between two royal guards, Percy lay curled up on the floor where the double doors met.

And for a moment, the cat smiled.

Epilogue

–

Brielle

…can't keep…

You…let me go…

A gasp.

Darkness.

She blinked, clearing the fogginess from her eyes and mind. Where was she now?

The desert. Fugera. She remembered that.

Working with that queen…gods, that had taken so much patience. But where was…

Death. Dead bodies surrounded her.

The light…purple, dark…the experiment…

Had it failed?

In the distance, she heard movement. Voices calling. She squinted, sitting up slightly. Her hair was caked with sand and bits of plant life. From the east, the sun's light began to crest the horizon. In that dim light she saw motion. People scattering out toward the fallen soldiers, searching for signs of life.

"Lady Brielle?"

She shook herself. No. Whatever had happened, she couldn't go back there. Keeping up the "Brielle" persona had taken all her energy, and nearly cost her this chance. She'd done what she came to do, and either it worked or it hadn't. They could believe her dead, she didn't care anymore.

She had to get away.

She patted her clothing, searching for the medallion, but one hand already held something—a wooden trinket. Her Life token. Right, she'd pulled it out at the last second. A precaution.

Searching again, she found the Death medallion hanging around her neck. It was whole, so the process *should* have worked, right? But she'd died? Well, if she hadn't actually died, she'd come mucking close. The Life token had probably saved her.

If she'd died…all this work would've been for nothing.

She had to continue. Had to get him back.

Quietly, she forced herself to stand. The metal funnel still stood above on the ledge, but the queen and everyone else seemed to be gone. One step at a time, she made her way around to the back of the stone outcropping, out of sight of the people taking care of their dead.

So many dead. Still not enough.

She stared down at her hands. Hands that had only ever wielded a sword, never magic.

Please work… She reached for the shadows.

A purple light began to glow, drawing into her fingertips.

She smiled.

EPILOGUE

–

NATALIA

-Two years later-

"A table on the balcony, please?" Natalia said. "And I'm expecting someone."

Natalia followed the host to a circular table at the edge of the cafe's patio. The sun was halfway set behind the Arontas mountains, coloring the sky and clouds all manner of pinks and purples. She sat, arranging the folds of her new favorite gown and requesting two glasses of starflower wine.

A few minutes later, Mama sat down across from her. Nat greeted her with a hug, and—as she always did—looked over the color in Mama's skin, the plumpness of her cheeks and arms, and the way her smile beamed as though in competition with the sun itself. Three years ago, the result of an illness that had attacked quickly and ruthlessly, she'd been too thin, colorless, unable to even stand on her own or feed herself. Then, with the help of Tavin and a few other researchers they'd brought on, Mama had begun to look like herself again after only a year.

Now it had been three since the Violet Night, and both Mama and Nat had been able to get their cancers—as Tavin had dubbed them—eradicated completely. Some latent pain remained that would always be there, but it was far more manageable now than it had been. And Natalia couldn't think of anything to be more grateful for than that.

"How was your day, my heart?" Mama asked.

"The research is going well," Nat said. "We're much more confident about the medallions we've developed. We're not quite ready to try the transfers again, but Kaya's contributions are bringing so many new things to light, which has been fascinating. And you?"

Mama sighed. "The council is, as always, *unbroken.*" She smirked at the reference to their continent. "The only thing we can agree on is wanting what's best for Fugera. It's the *how* that has us arguing for hours on end."

Nat winced. "I do remember those meetings."

"It's nice to have an evening where we can relax after all that," Mama said, raising her glass.

Natalia followed suit, taking a drink as the server approached to take their orders.

When they'd gone, Mama leaned forward, elbows on the table. "Natalia?"

Nat immediately snapped to attention. "What is it? Is something wrong?"

She hesitated a moment, then turned to draw something from her satchel.

A sealed letter.

"This came to me today," Mama said, "because I'm head of our household. But it's your name on it, so I thought you should be the one to open it."

Natalia took the letter. The handwriting sent a jolt of surprise through her.

"Tomaz?"

"I think so," Mama said.

Nat hadn't received a letter from her brother since before Mama had gotten sick. Three years with no word, and she'd begun to worry she'd lost him, same as their father. With her heart pounding and tears beginning to burn behind her eyes, she carefully tore open the seal and began to read.

Nat,

This is letter forty-two. If you're reading this, one of my letters finally made it out. At least you'll know I'm still alive—hoPefully.

I found Da—he's been held in the Assassin's Guild fortress for the last eight years. I couldn't get to him. I offered to pay for his freedom, they refused, and captured me too. The good news is, we're both alive. But they've staRted training me to kill, and they're saying I'll be sent on a mission soon…

I'm scared. Please help.

-Tomaz

Nat finished the letter, then read it again. And again. With a weight in her chest, she handed it across to Mama.

Tomaz was in trouble. Stuck, because of the Guild. The Assassin's Guild that she'd grown up believing was the safety of Calidar. Trained killers who took care of the most dangerous people; those were the stories she'd grown up hearing. And now, her brother and father were part of it, unable to leave.

And they'd forced him to write that letter.

Tomaz's handwriting had always been messy, and though it had been two years since his last letter, Nat knew him well enough to spot which letters stood out. She believed Tomaz needed help; she also believed she'd be walking into a trap.

"He's alive?"

Nat glanced up to see tears at the corners of Mama's eyes.

"Kezen?" Mama said. "Your father—he's alive?"

Nat swallowed. "It seems he is."

Mama finished the letter, then handed it back. They sat in silence for a moment.

"I have to go," Nat said.

Mama nodded. "Can you take help?"

"I don't want to put anyone else in danger," Nat said. "I can protect myself, I'm not sure I can protect others."

Mama looked away, twisting her hands together.

"And you?" Nat asked. "Would you rather stay here, or come?"

Mama hesitated. "I thought I'd lost Kezen…I worried for Tomaz, and I don't want to lose you either. But," she took Nat's hand. "They need your help, my heart. You've trained with your magic now for so long, and become so skilled, I'm confident you can help them. I fear I would only get in the way."

Nat nodded, determined. "You stay here, then. Keep Fugera safe."

"And you," Mama said. "Will go save your brother and father."

"Right." Nat stared at the letter again, her mind spinning with dozens of possibilities.

Each less likely to succeed than the last.

Natalia will return in

DECEIT

Book Four of

THE UNBROKEN TALES

Book Club Discussion Questions

- Who was your favorite character, and what drew you to them?

- Are there any topics or issues presented in the story that you feel strongly about?

- Did you feel the characters' reactions to their conflicts were understandable?

- How did you feel about the main couple's chemistry and compatibility? Did you root for them or not?

- How did the main character(s) change or grow throughout the story?

- The city of Isille is built into a mountain—did you like or dislike it? Would you live there?

- What did this story teach you about yourself or others?

- How did the author use the setting and atmosphere of the book to enhance the mood of the story?

AUTHOR Q&A

What does your writing schedule look like?

Right now I write while my children are at school. It's normally three days a week from about 8AM to 2PM with a little time for lunch in the middle. I usually schedule appointments all on one day a week to make sure I can focus on the other days, and Fridays are half-days at our school, so that day I run errands. Then I usually get Monday and Thursday evenings when my husband takes care of the kids' bedtimes so that I can work. (But sometimes those nights are used for D&D or Writing Group.)

How do you know what to write?

Oof, I've always hated the answer to this question. Because the truth is: I don't. I start with what excites me, but so often writing feels like throwing spaghetti at the wall to see what sticks. And when something does, you run with it. So much of this process is trial and error, and it took me *literal years* to accept that. I always though surely the pros knew something I didn't, but no. We're all just out here flinging spaghetti. Good luck!

How long does it take you to write a book?

It really depends on the book. TARGET and SUMMON were fast-drafted in a matter of months, and then revised over years. While CLEVER was drafted over a period of two (plus) years, then revised in five months. I'm actually very interested to see what my process looks like *after* CLEVER, because I've learned a lot through this one and I'm hoping I'll be able to apply it to my work going forward.

What is the most difficult part of writing a book for you?

Probably that "trial and error" part mentioned above lol. Genuinely though, drafting is more work for me than revising. I have to keep chanting to myself, "you can't fix a blank page," in order to just get words down. Once the story is complete, it's much easier to see which spaghetti noodles stuck, and which ones didn't. (I like how this metaphor is going.)

What important advice would you give to a first-time author?

Fling that spaghetti, my friend. It's said that the best writing advice is "Just Write," and I believe that. People can give you all the advice they know, but they can't do it for you. How you find time will be different than them. How you make it work will not match anyone else. It's difficult, but the hard truth is: you won't know how to do it until you try doing it. Just like you can't fix a blank page, you won't know how to write a book until you've written one. Once again, good luck, my friend.

ACKNOWLEDGEMENTS

I know it's only been three books so far, but it still surprises me how difficult writing the acknowledgements is. And to be quite honest, this one feels even more difficult than the other two for a multitude of reasons.

When I first wrote Ahnri in Summon, I had no idea how much I—and my betas and critique partners—would come to fall in love with him. From the conception of the series, I hadn't really planned on writing a queer romantic relationship as one of the main couples, but it became clear during the writing of Summon that Ahnri was in love with his prince, and that was that. I owe that character my deepest thanks for showing me the way into his heart.

First, I'm gonna get a little personal.

I began writing Clever in fall of 2021. Then, in spring of 2022 I experienced a shift in my personal life that caused me go through a period of intense grieving. The experience forced me to take a deeper look at my life, particularly my self-care and support system, and I made the choice to invest in my mental and emotional health. I went to therapy for the first time, got an ADHD diagnosis—something we'd suspected for a long time—and started medication to treat it.

Getting that diagnosis was a trip in itself; I had to reframe my whole life and all my relationships through that lens, which took a huge amount of emotional energy. For the rest of 2022 and most of 2023 I struggled to write. It got to a point where I wondered if perhaps writing had simply been one very long hyperfocus, and maybe now that I'd published two books, my brain didn't want to do it anymore. My hands are shaking as I write this, remembering how difficult it was to face that possibility.

I'd been doing so much therapy and journaling and meditation, and I finally paused to ask myself—if I never wrote or published again, would I be able to let it go? Would I be satisfied with the two books I'd put out? I immediately cried at the thought of never writing another story. Despite the pain and grief I'd experienced, I knew I didn't want to let writing be taken from me. And so, I fought for it. I wrote through the pain. Though by fall of 2023 I'd barely managed fifty thousand words.

Then something shifted in November 2023, and things began to click. It was like someone had removed a curtain from my mind, and finally the words were coming again.

From December 2023 to March 2024, I finished the first draft of Clever. And what a relief it was to finally write "The End" once more. This book has so much of myself in it. Ahnri has my stubbornness, Remi has my heart, and Nat has my hope. I can only hope and pray that their experiences touch the lives of those who relate to them. That someone will read these books and feel seen.

So, first and foremost, I want to thank my stunning, handsome, supportive, sexy, beautiful husband Brandon Cole. I want him to know how much I love him, and how seen I feel by him. Without his support, his constant encouragement, his defense of my work time, his care of our kids, and so much more, none of these books would ever come to fruition. Thank you, my love. You are the most important person in my life, and I can't imagine ever doing this without you.

(To anyone who thinks the "Brandon" in my dedication of Target was Brandon Sanderson: no no, lol. It's my husband.)

Way back in 2021, Janci Patterson helped brainstorm and outline this story with me. I learned a lot from her, and I'll always be grateful for her help in that regard.

Next, almost immediately after the first draft was finished, came my single Alpha Reader on this book: the incomparable Gina Denny. She'd probably try to say she didn't do much on this one, but the mere act of telling me that my first draft wasn't terrible made all the difference to me. Not to mention her patience in me asking her questions about her feedback and begging for fixes and ideas lol. Thank you, Gina.

This book was my first attempt at using the Brandon Sanderson beta process that I've grown accustomed to over the last decade. I am so grateful for my little band of Betas and their dedication to the work of making this story better! To Becca Reppert, Emily Mosby, Heather Romito, Jaylee Kennedy, Jennifer Johnson, Karen Allen, Kendra Alexander, Mark Lindberg, Michael Cox, Rob West, Siena Buchanan, Verónica Pombo, and Will Henley, thank you, thank you, thank you!

A very special thanks goes to Kendra Alexander for also reading Natalia's chapters with an eye toward sensitivity and accuracy. Those who read my books know I try to show a wide variety of skin and hair colors and cultures. Natalia is my first main character who represents a race inspired by the African people of our world, and I wanted to get the balance right while being as respectful as possible. Kendra was a wonderful help and resource in this, and I really couldn't have done it without her.

Another very special thank you must go to Rob West for sensitivity reading Ahnri and Remi's romance, and to Shauntel Simper and Kristen Simper for sensitivity reading Ahnri for Asexual/Demisexual identities. While I feel more comfortable in these spaces, I truly appreciate the help in getting things right.

The last people to read this with an eye toward critique were Shauntel Simper and Megan Eccles—two of my closest and most trusted writing friends. Their feedback in these final stages was exactly what I needed to feel like I'd gotten the story to where it needed to be.

Then we have the even smaller but still amazing group of Gamma Readers, which include: Glen Vogelaar, Jennifer Johnson, and Will Henley. Your eye for detail was more helpful than you know. Thank you so much for putting the time into spotting those necessary fixes.

To wrap up, I want to also thank my kids. This book is dedicated to you four, and I am so proud of the people you're becoming. I hope you look back on these years and know that your mom did the best she could, and loved you through it all.

I am so grateful to my God in Heaven that I get to tell stories. That there are people out there who want to read them.

And so, my final thanks goes out to you, dear readers. Thank you for coming on this journey with me. I hope you'll be patient as I take a bit of a break before jumping into book four, but I promise I'm already excited to tell the next stage of Natalia's journey, and the next volume of the Unbroken Tales.

Follow Darci for Updates

DISCORD: Join the DarciVerse Discord channel to talk with other readers, ask the author questions, and have the opportunity to beta read future books.
Go to Linktree.com/DarciColeAuthor and click "Join the DarciVerse Discord"

SOCIAL MEDIA: @darcicoleauthor on Facebook, Threads, Instagram, and TikTok.

NEWSLETTER: Receive emails updating you on Darci's writing progress and process and be the first to know about awesome deals.
Visit www.DarciCole.com to sign up.

PATREON: For as little as $2/month you can receive access to the Patron-Only Discord channels as well as Patreon-exclusive updates and early looks at art, deleted scenes, and pre-release content. Higher tiers include Podcast episodes, conference classes, and more.
Go to Patreon.com/DarciColeAuthor

ABOUT THE AUTHOR

Darci Cole is author of the YA Fantasy series The Unbroken Tales. She has a passion for tackling deep topics and making them accessible to teens and young readers, and showing those who feel like outsiders that they are seen and worthy of love.

She loves tacos, oracle cards, and pretty dice with her TTRPGs. While she spends most of her time wrangling and chauffeuring her children, she also enjoys critiquing for her writer friends and has been on the Brandon Sanderson beta team since 2015. Darci lives in Arizona with her husband and four children.

Find her books, swag, and more at www.darcicole.com

9 781955 145091